FROM PARIS,

IN *Love*

ELODIE COLLIARD

First edition

Editing by Kate Angelella, Britt Tayler & Jennifer Herrington.
Book cover and design by Leni Kauffman

ISBN 9781778137914

IT'S ALWAYS BEEN YOU SERIES

The Last Encore (Book 1)

Available on all platforms (Amazon, Indigo, Barnes & Noble, Waterstones) and on Kindle Unlimited. Available on Audible.

TO LISTEN WHILE READING

1. Two Ghosts – Harry Styles
2. Tiff Song - Noah Reid
3. You're On Your Own, Kid – Taylor Swift
4. About Damn Time – Lizzo
5. Wonder Woman – Miley Cyrus
6. Girl Crush – Harry Styles
7. Rain - Ben Platt
8. Cinderella's Dead – Emeline
9. Hey Girl – Lady Gaga and Florence & The Machine
10. You – Miley Cyrus
11. Libre – Angèle
12. Figure it out – Anthony Ramos
13. Champagne Problems – Taylor Swift
14. I Can See You – Taylor Swift
15. New – Ben Platt
16. Invisible String – Taylor Swift
17. Rien à Dire – Christine & the Queens
18. She – Harry Styles
19. Ceilings – Lizzy McAlpine
20. La Déclaration d'Amour – Vanessa Paradis and M
21. Every Feeling – Ezra Furman
22. Conversations in the Dark – John Legend
23. Rub a Dub – Fauve
24. Dandelions – Ruth B
25. Wildest Dreams – Duomo
26. Love Me Like You Do – Vitamin String Quartet
27. If I Ain't Got You – Vitamin String Quartet
28. Bad Guy – Vitamin String Quartet
29. Grapejuice – Harry Styles
30. Onde Sensuelle – M

31. I Wanna Be Yours – Arctic Monkeys
32. Late Night Talking – Harry Styles
33. Flowers – Miley Cyrus
34. Rose Colored Lenses – Miley Cyrus
35. Dangerous Woman- Ariana Grande
36. Paris – New West
37. The Night We Met – Lord Huron
38. You Should See Me In a Crown – Billie Eilish
39. The Man – Taylor Swift
40. I Guess I'm in Love – Clinton Kan
41. Paris – Taylor Swift

TRIGGER WARNING

Domestic abuse, infertility

To Katie, the best friend I never thought I'd have in my wildest dreams.

For all our bad days and all our great nights,
Laughing, crying, talking, and loving each other so fucking much,
Hundreds of miles apart, but never far away in our hearts.

Summer

A year ago

Miles

*D*id I just make the biggest mistake of my life?

I don't think so, though it does feel like it.

Shit.

I pace my condo for the tenth time, my dog Happy following behind, tail wagging and tongue hanging out. My phone is on the kitchen counter, waiting for the inevitable call from my sister to tell me I fucked up. Big time.

I grab it and flop down in my leather chair.

Why did I just quit my dream job?

I don't even have a backup option. My savings are worth shit, and Toronto isn't cheap. I have a few months, at best, before I'm really screwed.

I open my phone to several panicked texts from my best friend, Tyler, and one from my sister.

Avery: Call me

I sigh, scrubbing my beard. Here we go—no point in delaying it. When I dial her number, she picks up right away.

"What do you mean you quit?" my sister shrieks in my ear.

"It's been a rough few years, Ave."

"But you can't just text me to tell me you quit, and that's it."

I pat my knee, and Happy lands on my lap. My hand goes straight between his ears to find that sweet spot that turns him into an airport runway.

"I didn't want to talk about it," I grumble.

"Like I care." She snorts. "What happened?"

"Just my boss being a total dickhead again. I can't work with someone like that." It's only a matter of time before the firm gets served with a lawsuit if the way people are fleeing the company like it just caught on fire is any indication.

My sister sighs at the other end of the line. "It's just... so unlike you to do something like this."

"I know."

"You always think everything through at least a dozen times."

"I know."

"Every decision you make is carefully calculated, the risks are weighed, and you never do anything unless you have a backup plan."

"I know," I say more forcefully. "But it was either I quit, or I stay working for an asshole who treats people like shit."

Happy groans on my lap at the sound of my voice rising before settling back with a sigh.

"It's not like I would have gone anywhere with the firm anyway," I add more gently. "Sean made it clear that to climb the ladder, I couldn't be afraid to play dirty."

My sister exhales. "Yeah, that doesn't sound like you."

I knew choosing to work in public relations would have its challenges; the business world is ruthless when it comes to egos and power. But I refuse to compromise my integrity for someone who doesn't have any.

"Does it have anything to do with…" Avery starts, leaving the name floating between us.

"It's not because of her, but I'm not gonna lie and say she didn't cross my mind either. I found her on the office bathroom floor last week after he yelled at her in front of everybody. She submitted her resignation a few days later, and from what I've heard, divorce papers too."

Fucking finally.

"No way!" Avery gasps. "How is your boss taking it? Sorry, *ex*-boss."

"Sean's been in rare form lately with the shit he's been pulling. A few weeks ago, he fired his secretary because she dressed 'like a slut'." Which, in Sean's language, probably means a knee-length skirt or a shirt with a bit of cleavage. I couldn't work there another minute and tolerate that behavior. What would it have said about me?

"Have you heard from her?"

Her. Still no name has been uttered because it is so painfully obvious who she's referring to. The only *her* I've been able to think about for the past three years.

Riley Fletcher.

My friend and now ex-coworker.

My sister and I both know I've had it bad for Riley since the day she set foot in our old office, well before I knew she was married to Sean, the firm's managing partner. I've never met a woman as confident, strong, and intelligent as her, charming every person who crosses her path with her dazzling smile and sharp brain. I never stood a chance.

Which is why it blew my mind to see her shrink into herself every time Sean belittled her publicly. She took the hits in silence, almost like he held an invisible leash around her delicate neck, tugging every time she adventured outside the boundaries he set for her. I'd wanted to intervene so many times—hell, I even considered punching his dumb, smug face. But it wasn't my place, and Riley didn't need me fighting her battles.

So I stayed in the shadows, gritting my teeth, hoping that one day, she'd wake up from under whatever spell she was under and realize she could do so much better—and deserved so much better.

"I haven't, no," I say. "I'm giving her space, I think she needs it."

Avery hums in approval. "I think that's wise, yeah. Seems like she's going through it."

"She knows I'm here if she needs anything."

"But who's there for you?" my sister asks, and it's like a punch in the gut.

I force a smile and look at Happy snoring softly on my thighs. "I've got the guys from rugby and Happy to keep me company. Don't worry about me."

"I'm not. But I know how much you loved your job and how you clam up sometimes when everything is too much to handle at once. I want to make sure you're moving forward and have people to be around."

I shrug. "I don't mind being alone for a while. I need to take a beat for a few weeks. I'm exhausted. Then we'll see. I have an old college friend who works for the competition. I don't know. Maybe I should explore other stuff."

"What do you mean other stuff?" I know Avery well enough to imagine the frown on her face right now.

"I've always been good at baking. Maybe I could look into that."

"You wouldn't last a week in a kitchen." She chuckles. "You'd get bored, Miles. You're a man who needs action, people around him. You'd be miserable."

She's annoying when she's right. "Still, I need a break. Maybe I'll come visit you in California. Enjoy the summer from the beach by your house." It would be a nice change of pace, and a much-needed balm on my heart after the last few years I've had.

"You know I'd love to have you here, Miles."

I smile. "Me too, Ave."

The fog in my mind is still thick when we hang up, my new reality slowly sinking in. So I grab my running shoes and Happy's leash and dash into the summer haze, trying hard to push the fact that I'm thirty-five and newly unemployed into the darkest corner of my mind.

Fall

Nine months ago

Riley

Now that the day is actually here, I'm wondering if he's going to show up. My fingers tap lightly on my mug to the rhythm of the music as I gaze around the coffee shop. The rain pattering against the windows drowns out the sound my nails make on the ceramic, leaving me instead with my own blaring thoughts.

Am I really doing this? Am I really going toe-to-toe with my husband? *Ex-husband*. Oof. It feels weird to say, but damn if I don't breathe easier every time.

He took everything from me, and I'm not letting him have my career either. And when I learned that Miles had resigned... The thought makes my heart thump faster, and I will myself to calm down. I don't know why he did it, but I need him to show up today and hear me out. That's all.

Just as I'm about to order a second latte, the door to the shop swings open, and a gulf of wind blows through, carrying a tall, broad man in with it. He's drenched, droplets of water fluttering off him as his fingers ruffle in his brown curls. He sheds his coat and hangs it on the rack next to the front door, rolling his shirt up his elbows, my eyes following every movement. When his gaze searches the room and land on me, a whisper of a smile stretches on his lips.

"What kind of weather is this, Fletcher?" he says when he comes up to my table, giving me a quick side hug. "Sorry, I look awful. I forgot my umbrella."

I wave him off. "You're fine." He is more than fine. "Don't you like days like these? I love a good rainy day. Makes me want to curl under the covers with a steaming coffee and a good book."

"That does sound tempting," Miles says, chuckling. "Walking outside while pouring, though? Not so much." He looks over his shoulder. "I'm gonna go order something. Do you need anything else?"

"All good," I say, raising my mug.

My gaze follows him toward the counter, where he leans against it, feet crossed at the ankles. I don't think I've ever seen him this relaxed, let alone in anything other than a suit. It's… distracting.

I whip my eyes down to my coffee when he turns around, and his gaze finds mine within a second, as if he knew I've been openly ogling him. He comes over, carrying a mug and a pot of tea.

"So," Miles says, settling in the chair. "How are you doing?"

Even though his question is nothing but ordinary, his tone conceals a hundred others.

"I've been better. I'm sure you've heard about the divorce."

"I did, yeah. I'm sorry."

"Oh no, please, don't be. I popped champagne when the signed papers came through in the mail."

His eyebrows shoot up. "You did? Good for you. I can't imagine how relieved you must have been." He looks at me like he's hoping I was, as if knowing that would bring him some kind of inner peace.

When I don't answer right away, he clears his throat and adds, "You don't have to talk about it, it's none of my business. I didn't mean to overstep."

"You didn't. I was just lost in thought." I pick up my mug and take a sip, the maple syrup giving my latte a caramelized edge. "It is a relief, you're right. But I'm also a bit scared of this next chapter in my life. It's like… imagine if you'd been denied…" I drum my fingers on the side of my cheek, trying to find an easy way to explain such a complex feeling. "Let's say, lactose. All your life. Because you were told that it's so bad for you. And then suddenly, you realize that you've been lied to, and you can do whatever you please. You can drink all the milk and eat all the yogurt you want. You find yourself in front of hundreds of thousands of different cheeses. Where do you start?"

Miles stares at me, a smirk forming at the corner of his mouth. "If I were told I couldn't have lactose and then found out it was a lie, I would definitely go for the cheese first."

I laugh. "I would have pinned you as more of a yogurt guy."

"Oh, I'm full of surprises," he says, almost too low for me to hear, the deep vibrations of his voice tickling goose bumps up my arms until they reach the base of my neck. "But if we stop talking about lactose for a second," he adds, "if I were suddenly free to be whomever I wanted to be, do whatever I dreamed of doing, I would close my eyes…"

Miles sets his tea down and closes his eyes. I wait for him to continue, but he doesn't. He cracks one eye open.

"Close your eyes, Riley."

I comply with his request, hearing that voice again, and my cheeks warm up at the intensity in his timbre.

"I would take three deep breaths…"

I sync my breathing with his as we inhale and exhale together. The sound of rain beating against the windows, the chattering around us, the music coming from the speakers— every outside noise disappears as my senses reduce my focus to the air filling my lungs and the sound of the man breathing with me.

"And then," Miles whispers, breaking the silence, "I would answer this question: what do I want to do right now?"

"I want to be my own boss."

I snap my eyes open. Miles is watching me intently, one eyebrow raised.

I hesitate. Oh, fuck it. "Since handing Sean my resignation, I've been craving to return to the PR ring. I miss it so much. But who's going to hire me without a reference? Sean might as well be the industry in this city."

"I'm sure his own reputation will soon precede him."

I shrug. "I don't want to work for somebody else anyway. I think I got what it takes to lead my own firm."

"You do," he says without missing a beat, and it's funny how two words can make me feel ready to conquer the world.

As if it's not just some dream in my head, stories I tell myself about being capable and succeeding. Miles sees it too.

"I want to know, though…" My nails are back to clinking against the ceramic. *Calm down. Start from the beginning.* "I can't do it alone, nor do I want to. Financially, after my divorce, I don't have the money to back myself completely. I know your work ethic. I know your professionalism." I muster all the determination for my next words, hoping they'll stick the landing. "I want to partner up with you and open a firm together and I truly believe this is a 'now or never' moment and you should say yes." I let out a long exhale.

Miles frowns. "Whoa, um… I don't know what to say." He brushes his beard and clasps his hands on his neck, stretching his shirt around his biceps. I lower my gaze to my nails tapping the mug.

"I don't expect you to give me an answer now, obviously," I say, offering him a little smile. "But I want you to know that I'm serious and there's nobody else I would rather do this with."

"Why?"

I look at him, confused. "Why what?"

"Why do you want to partner with me?"

I lean back in my chair, smirking. "Are you fetching for compliments, Clark?"

"Might be." He shrugs. "Wow me, Fletcher."

I snort-laugh, clapping a hand on my mouth at the embarrassing sound, which pulls a chuckle out of Miles.

"That was cute," he whispers to himself before clearing his throat and flicking his eyes up at me.

"All I can tell you," I say, pretending I didn't hear him slip and call me cute, "is that working with you over the years has shown me everything I need to know. I've had a lot of time to think it over this past summer. I know what you're capable of, and you and I make one hell of a team."

Miles nods. "We do. But starting a business is a whole different ballgame. I've never considered it."

"Consider it, then."

He tsks at me, amusement dancing in his eyes. "I will, but I need a bit more information. How much money are you looking for me to invest? What's your business plan? What are you expecting of me? How will this work? Can we even start our own business with the legal clauses in our old contracts?" Miles crosses his arms. "I've made enough reckless decisions to last me the next ten years. I am not saying no. I'm saying, show me what you've got."

Game on.

Winter

Six months ago

Miles

"*I* think now is a good time to take a break, what do you say?"

Riley looks up from her laptop, her hair piled on top of her head in a mass of thick blond strands, most escaping and fluttering wildly around her face.

"What time is it?"

I look at my phone. "Eight thirteen p.m." Her eyes round, making me chuckle. "We've been working since one. We should get something to eat."

My eyes glide across the length of her body. We're both sitting on the rug, our backs against the couch and laptops balancing on our crossed legs. I take in the straps of her tank top halfway down her shoulders—this is clearly a no-bra day—and her massive socks and Christmas sweatpants. "Maybe a shower too?"

She gapes at me, outraged. "I don't need a shower, *thankyouverymuch*. This is cozy fashion. Look it up." She looks back at her screen and pulls the nearby blanket around her tightly. "Ugh, this is bullshit. There's so much paperwork to do to start a business, I swear they want us to drown in forms."

I shut her laptop. "Hence why we need to take a break." So stubborn. "I'm sure everything will look clearer once we eat."

"I have a better idea," she says, a sparkle in her eyes. "Grab your ice skates."

"How do you know…"

She rolls her eyes. "Come on. It's the middle of December"—she starts ticking off her fingers—"you're a sports addict. Rugby is out for the season. It's simple math."

Okay, she's been paying way more attention than I've given her credit for. She's also so fucking hot when she's being bossy.

"Coming right back."

Shaking my head, I slide on my winter jacket, knitted hat, and boots, and open her front door to what has to be the coldest day in the history of December days. The weather's been unforgiving this year, constantly hitting sub-zero temperatures, freezing rain, and already a few blizzards piling snow on the sidewalks.

So, if it were up to me, we'd be under a blanket on the couch, enjoying a delicious, warm dinner prepared by yours truly. Not going outside… ice skating, apparently.

"Where do you plan on skating anyway?" I say when I come back. I look around Riley's living room, but she isn't there. Her kitchen's empty too. "Ry?"

"Changing!" she yells from her bedroom.

I sigh, sitting down on one of her lounge chairs. Working with Riley has been… interesting, to say the least. Not that we haven't worked together before, but everything feels different this time around. More intimate, familiar. Not so much colleagues, but partners, building something together, something that's our own.

It took me a while to give her my answer. It felt like I'd just quit my job when there she was, asking me to put all my savings into this project, to risk my career for the second time in the span of six months. And then, I had to consider the elephant in the room. Did I really want to get into business with the woman who colors my world in shades of rose? Yeah, I know. Big cheesy guy. That's who I become when I'm close to her. I'm sure there are hundreds of books and movies out there that tell you how bad of an idea it is to mix business and pleasure. But I was selfish and reckless and ignored them all.

Because it meant being with her. Helping her create something that she can be proud of. She smiled and cried when I finally gave her the green light, and damn if it didn't make me want to drop to my knees and beg her to share all her dreams with me so I could spend my entire life trying to make them come true just to see that happiness on her face again.

But then, on occasions like these, when Riley is emerging from her bedroom looking impossibly cute in yoga pants, fuzzy socks, and oversized wool sweater, I'm reminded that my self-control is as thin as a loose cotton thread and needs to be constantly sewn back into place.

"Ready?" she asks.

"Where are you taking me?" I grumble.

She pats my arm as she walks past me. "Don't worry, we're not going too far." Riley slides her bay windows open, flicks the terrasse lights on, and disappears into the backyard. I follow, discovering a rink that takes up almost the entirety of her yard.

"Didn't you used to have a pool here?" I ask, confused.

She sits down on the stairs leading to the rink and puts her skates on. "I do. It's underneath. Every year, I ask my neighbor to help me build it. He's a retired engineer and handles the logistics. I'm not sure how everything works and holds together, but it's safe, so come on, Clark, let's see those skills on the ice."

"That's pretty cool." I look at the rink before my eyes land on Riley, waiting for me with her arms crossed over her stomach. Sassy woman.

I plant my skates on the ice and take my first step, controlled and steady. Slowly, I pick up my pace—as much as the rink's size allows me. I glide in circles around Riley, the glacial wind whipping my face, and then I skate backward, alternating between gentle sweeps and longer strides, the crackling sound of ice under my blades echoing into the night.

"You're such a show-off," she says, laughing.

"Isn't it literally what you told me to do?" I shoot back.

She laughs again, the sound getting lost among the snowflakes starting to fall. And then she starts to move, and I can't look away. She has me trapped in the grace that carries each brush of her blades on the ice, almost like a light touch, before fluttering away to their next point of contact.

"Where did you learn to skate like that?" I say, a bit breathless.

"Like what?" she says, tucking her arms in and twirling on the spot.

"Are you serious? I'm sure you're aware of what you look like right now."

She floats toward me. "I taught myself." She shrugs. "I've always loved skating. There's something so free about it, like you can glide for miles and miles and feel like you're almost flying, nothing holding you back or down. I've been holding on to that feeling for years."

I detect the shift in her tone, almost melancholic, and store it away for another time. I want her moments with me to be filled with joy—something I've rarely seen on her face over the years. So if that means throwing every distraction in my arsenal at her to bring her back to her happy place, then that's what I'll do.

"Well, you might be a talented skater, but I think I'm faster."

That familiar competitive spark lights her gaze. There she is.

"Wanna bet?"

I nod. "I win, you let me pick our office space. You win, I'll cook for you anytime you want till opening day."

Riley snorts. "Deal. Ready?"

"One… Two… Three… Go!"

I take off at full speed, my skates sliding in big strokes, Riley keeping pace beside me. I glance at her, and she winks at me with a mischievous air as she doubles her speed. Except her rink isn't very long, and as I watch her cross the "finish line," I don't notice the fence approaching. I whip my head around and brake as hard as I can, but despite my best efforts, I drive in knee-first against the fence and crash to the ground, my feet taking Riley down with me.

I soften the fall for her as she lands on me, but the rock-hard ice on my back and her weight are unforgiving on my body, and I wince.

"Are you okay?" I ask, my arms holding her shoulders. Silence. "Ry? Are you okay?"

Riley starts laughing so loudly it almost makes me jump. She laughs uncontrollably, rolling on her back. "I can't... I can't believe... you... oh my god, Miles." She cracks up again.

"What?"

"You really gave it everything you had and... and... you lost. And then you fell," she says, her laughter battling with the need to breathe. "It's plain cruel."

I roll my eyes. "And here I was worried about you being hurt. Clearly, you're fine."

"Oh, don't be a sore loser, Miles. You were a worthy opponent, but I was better."

"Don't be an asshole winner," I retort but let a grin slip through.

We lie on the ice for a couple more minutes, staring at the cloudy dark sky, before the cold gets unbearable, and we decide to head back in.

After a quick and blissfully hot shower, I open her fridge.

"A bet is a bet. How do you feel about homemade lasagna?"

Spring

Three months ago

Riley

$\mathcal{I}$ don't think I will ever tire of watching Miles Clark cook for me. Has there ever been anything sexier than a man in the kitchen? So far, I'm leaning toward no. Not when I'm sitting on one of his kitchen stools, watching him beat eggs in a bowl with surprising intensity, a cute yellow-and-white apron neatly tied behind his back.

Big sigh.

We've been laying the groundwork for our firm for nearly eight months, and I can't ignore the fact that it's been distracting—at times challenging—being in such close proximity every hour of the day. And it's like I voluntarily agreed to make it more difficult for myself since I won the bet, and he's been cooking for me since December.

"What are you doing to those poor eggs?"

Miles gives me a cheeky grin over his shoulder, and I melt a little. "Your lack of cooking skills shocks me. How haven't you figured out what we're eating yet?"

"I prefer to see it as everybody has their own strengths and areas they excel in," I say, trying to understand how in the hell I'm supposed to know what we're eating for dinner when there's sausages, all kinds of berries, and what looks like... dough?

"Well," Miles starts. "Since we had two busy days of interviews, I thought we could have a little treat tonight. I don't know about you, but it's been a long time since I've had brinner."

I raise an eyebrow.

"Brinner? Breakfast and dinner...?" Miles stops beating his eggs. "Don't tell me you've never had breakfast for dinner."

"I've never had breakfast for dinner." I don't understand what the big deal is. From the look on his face, I might as well have just told him I've never seen snow in my life.

"I feel a tremendous amount of pressure now that I know I'm cooking you your very first brinner," he says, washing his hands and drying them with the towel on his shoulder.

"If it's anything like the rest of the meals you've made, I'm not worried one bit." The Ponzu roasted salmon is still living rent-free in my mind.

Miles chuckles and shakes his head, grabbing the flour and sprinkling some on the wooden table. "I hope you're hungry because we're having scrambled eggs, breakfast sausages and bacon, homemade brioche with strawberry jam, croissants, fruit salad, and freshly squeezed orange juice."

"You prepared all of this?"

"Sure did."

"I don't understand how."

He laughs and raises his hands up. "With these two. I just wanted us to have a nice, relaxing time tonight. We deserve it."

"I appreciate it," I say, my eyes softening. I can't remember the last time someone took care of me like this. It does a weird thing to my heart.

Miles places the brioche dough onto the surface and starts kneading it. My cheeks flame with heat as my eyes follow every movement of his hands, shaping and pressing into the dough, his wrists sinking deeper in the squishy mass, his forearms flexing from the exertion.

His focus is so intense that my mind goes straight to places I've forbidden myself to go. God, this should not be so arousing.

I look around, trying to take my mind off images of Miles kneading my body. Happy is lying down on his bed in the kitchen, eyes trained on us.

"Happy, come here," I say. I don't have to wait long before his head bumps my knees, demanding I give him all the love.

"What did you think about the candidates?" Miles asks me, sliding a tray into the oven.

"I liked Sydney. Thought she was very professional, put together. We need someone solid that we can rely on. I think she'd be great."

I think about the other applicants. God, I didn't think we'd have so many, but we must have interviewed at least twenty people. "What do you think about Katie?"

He rolls his eyes. "No."

I snort. "Why not?"

"You know why."

I put my elbows on the table and rest my chin on my hands. "Enlighten me."

Miles grunts my name. It shouldn't affect me, but it does. "I don't think she was all that interested in the job."

I laugh. "No, she was not."

"Adam texted me last week, by the way," he says. "He's getting tired of the politics at Myers and Associates. I said we could meet him for a coffee."

"That's an amazing idea. I always liked working with him." I fidget with the scrunchie around my wrist. "Rachel called me yesterday. Apparently, Sean is losing it."

Miles's gaze snaps to me. "Why?"

I sigh. "Yeah, he heard about our partnership. Doesn't sound like he's happy about it."

"Big fucking deal."

"I'm a bit stressed." I exhale. "I worry he'll do something to retaliate."

"I'd like to see him try," Miles says, looking at me. He reaches out and rests his hand on top of mine. "We're in this together now, and I'm not about to let him mess with something I've put my blood, sweat, and money in, nor with someone I care about."

I smile. "Thank you."

"I'm in your corner, Ry. There's no getting rid of me now."

The warmth of his words envelops me like a cozy blanket. "I'm in yours too."

Neither of us says anything else. We stay like this, in perfect silence, just content to be around one another. And that's a beautiful thing, isn't it? When you can sit with someone and be comfortable, their presence enough to fill the quietness of the room. I watch him as he continues putting our brinner together, exchanging soft smiles and long glances every now and then.

The timer on the oven cuts the moment short, but it's okay. That's what it should be anyway, just a moment. We're in the final stretch before our firm is up and running, and when it is, it'll be our primary focus. Just two friends who've gone into business together, doing everything they can to succeed.

Nothing else.

Summer

Today

ONE

Two Ghosts

Miles

"Ow, fuck!"

The blow came out of nowhere and knocked the wind out of me. I roll my back to soften the fall, but it does little against the hard, wet ground, and I hear the harsh sound of my shoulder cracking. Shit. I was so sure I could make the try. Still holding the ball tight against my chest, I wait for the inevitable heap of bodies to pile on top of me, trying as best as I can to cover my bruised shoulder. Freaking Ty. He could have spared me this. Could have tackled me at the waist to keep me from falling face-first in the grass, or even better, just let me run and score this one?

But no. "Gotta play the game, Miles." No regard for the fact that our Tuesday rugby nights are only supposed to help us blow off steam, not compete in the national league.

Under the weight of several six-foot-tall men, I wriggle the ball down between my legs and free it for my teammates. Scott shouts, "Got it!" and the weight suddenly lifts off me. I feel my lungs expand again, the air ruffling my damp hair.

"Feeling thirty-five yet?" Tyler looks down at me, a big grin on his face, hand extended in my direction.

"Fuck off." I get up on my own. "I may be older than you by a few years, but I'm not the one constantly complaining about my knees."

Tyler puts his hands up, a smile on his lips. "Wow. Low blow, Milesy. You know I've had a bad knee since my surgery."

I grunt. "Stop calling me that."

"What?" he taunts. "Milesy? But it's so cute!"

I roll my eyes. We both turn as victory screams erupt and Scott jogs back toward us, his bottom lip dripping blood. Hazards of the game.

"Looks like we beat your asses," I say to Tyler, flashing him my megawatt smile.

He snorts and pats me on the shoulder. "No thanks to you, old man. Come on, let's hit the bench for some water."

I signal that I'll join him in a minute and make my rounds, thanking the rest of my team before they all disappear into the locker room. It's already 8 p.m., most of them usually head home to their kids and wives right after practice. Not something either Tyler or I can relate to. My chest squeezes, but I push the thought away before it starts swirling in my head and I'm forced to do another forty minutes on the field to release the tension.

Ty is sitting on the bench, knees out wide and elbows lazily resting on the seat behind him. I head his way, taking in the pinks and oranges brushing the sky as the night finally sets in. The warmth is finally settling in Toronto, June's just around the corner, and the days are getting longer. Thank fuck. I don't think I can handle one more day where the sun disappears at 4 o'clock.

Tyler tosses me my water bottle. "Reflexes still sharp," he says when I catch it with one hand.

"Quit it." I sit beside him, the muscles of my thighs screaming from our hour of practice. I take a deep sip before dousing the rest in my hair, beard, and chest, the cold water blended with fresh air cooling my skin almost immediately.

"Too bad there's no audience today." Tyler chuckles. "We would have made some good money off *that* show." He nods to my drenched face, and I roll my eyes.

"So. Big day tomorrow, uh?"

I blow out a sigh, rubbing the back of my neck. "Yeah…yeah, big day."

"Ah, everything will go fine, man. You and Riley worked really hard."

We did. We really did. And tomorrow, we're starting a new chapter in our lives, one where I run my own fucking business.

"Haven't heard from Ry today," I say, the scent of fresh grass and sweat anchoring me to this moment. "I just hope she's doing okay."

"I'm sure she is. You know her, she's probably going over every last detail to make sure she didn't miss anything. She'll call if she needs you."

"I just feel so… useless around her sometimes."

Tyler claps his hand on my shoulder. "Look, man, don't dwell on it. From what you've told me, Riley has her own shit to work on. None of that's about you. Focus on what matters. You'll do great, everything will go smoothly, and it's the start of something exciting. Enjoy it. You built your motherfucking business, Miles!"

Fuck yeah. My own damn boss.

I look at Tyler. "Can't believe all those months butting heads and nitpicking over every detail are behind us." I shake my head. "It went by so fast." And they were some of the best days of my life.

"I wouldn't complain either if I got to spend every day with her." He bumps my shoulder with his, but the look I give him has his hands shooting up. "Hey, relax, I was just kidding! Man, you need to get laid already."

I grumble. "Fuck off."

"What? I'm not allowed to say Riley's hot as hell?"

I straighten, my finger an inch from his face. "Watch your mouth."

He gives me an eye roll for the books. "Your obsession with her is becoming a problem. You should really do something about it."

I scoff. "I'm not obsessed. I don't like you talking about her that way."

"I was just teasing," Tyler says, taking a big chug of water. "It's just mind-blowing to me that you're still sitting here, trailing behind her like a lost puppy, waiting for god knows what to fucking do something about it."

"It's not that easy, Ty, and you know it."

He sighs. "I know, I know. You're partners, you've banned yourself from crossing that line, yada yada. But honestly, dramatic much?"

"Look who's talking," I scoff. "You haven't had a serious relationship in what, two? Three years?"

"Four," he mumbles.

"Four years! You're thirty-four, man. Maybe it's time you stop dicking around and patch things up with Amy."

"Amy doesn't want to see me."

I get up, stretching my legs and arms. "Who's being dramatic now?"

Four years ago, he and Amy agreed it was time to put an end to their marriage. I never understood their reasoning, and Tyler's never shared anything other than the fact that it was a mutual decision.

But I don't know, none of it makes sense to me. Whatever happened must have been serious enough for him not to share it with me. I know he still thinks about her, and she was madly in love with him. If I looked up the definition of soulmates, their wedding photo would be right there with it.

I peer at my phone peeking out of my bag's front pocket. Still no text.

"All I'm saying is," Tyler starts. "Either do something with Riley or cut your losses and move in another direction. Get back on the apps."

"What? No way, nuh-uh."

"Go into it with an open mind and zero expectations."

"Have you forgotten how the first time turned out?"

I haven't. I joined as a naïve thirty-two-year-old who knew nothing about online dating. God, those apps are awful. Trying to carry a decent conversation with the women I matched with shaved years off my life. I discovered that starting a conversation with "Hi, how was your day?" was eight times out of ten enough reason for getting unmatched. And even then, when I got over my anxiety to actually meet in person, I would end up being disappointed.

Something about being unable to get those chocolate eyes out of my mind.

Or feel like I couldn't truly be myself around women who, most of the time, weren't interested in getting serious. More often than not, the conversation would end after I shared that I didn't want children but explaining why felt too intimate to share with a total stranger.

Whenever I caught myself getting ready to open up, I would find any excuse to get out of there. Because when I felt it becoming real, those damn eyes would come to the front of my mind again.

"Worth giving it another shot." Ty shrugs. "You never know, might surprise you."

"Maybe," I mumble. Probably not. I sigh, strapping my bag on my shoulder as I motion to get up.

"Thanks for the pep talk, Ty, appreciate it. Hey, do you want to come by the house this weekend? I'll cook us something."

Tyler smiles and dramatically places his hand over his heart. "For me, Milesy, really?"

I snort. "Fuck off. Keep this up, and I won't be held responsible for what you might find in your food."

"I'll be there. Just text the day and time. My weekend is wiiide open."

I nod and tell him goodnight, but as I'm halfway across the field, I hear him call out, "Hey, Miles!"

"What?" I shout.

"Maybe order a cab to get home. I wouldn't want you to get injured, you know, with your old age."

I flip him off and laugh as I leave behind the stadium's floodlights and head into the dark of the night.

TWO

Tiff Song

Miles

I don't typically run home after practice, but the air is warm tonight when I exit BMO Field, making me want to soak it in a little longer.

I plug my earphones in, hit play on my favorite workout playlist, and set up my pace. My feet hit the pavement as I skirt the edge of Lake Ontario, quiet and peaceful this time of day. This part of the city is usually bubbling with life, kids and parents feeding the seagulls, couples lazing in the grass while sports enthusiasts run, bike, or rollerblade with their dogs, the city's skyscrapers behind them, and the vastness of the lake ahead. I love it. This cohabitation of nature and city, feeling the crisp air whipping against my face as the buzzing of downtown surrounds my senses.

For the first twenty minutes, I focus on my breathing, on the music, on the positioning of my feet. But as my body switches to autopilot, I fall into a steady rhythm, and my thoughts turn to her.

And how monumental tomorrow is.

I think about how much is at stake for the both of us, how much we invested in this firm. She deserves this win. I need it. The pressure to succeed is at an all-time high.

No. Not now. I shake those thoughts out of my head. When I pass the halfway mark of the Rogers Centre and the CN Tower, I pick up my pace, refusing to let my exhaustion stop me. I push myself harder and harder, forcing my mind to zero its focus on keeping the speed that I've set and nothing else.

Just as I'm about to reach my apartment in Corktown, the industrial part of the city, my phone chimes in my ears. I slow down just enough to check the text.

Ry: Don't go to bed too late – big day tomorrow!

I smile as I tuck my phone back in my pocket. Finally.

I climb the stairs two at a time and open the door to my apartment, my goldendoodle Happy barreling toward me.

I crouch to welcome him. "Okay, boy, calm down." I chuckle as he jumps on me, licking the sweat off my face. I ruffle his head, pushing him away gently and standing up, making my way to the kitchen.

I open the fridge and grab the croissant dough I made yesterday.

Sunday nights aren't usually baking nights, but tomorrow is weighing on me like a heavy blanket, and I need to focus on something other than the possibility of my whole world imploding. Why not bring treats to the first meeting with our new employees in the morning?

I get my recipe notebook from the cupboard, opening it to Cyril Lignac's famous croissants. My favorite pastry to make. The man always sounds like he's singing when he speaks, his strong accent from the south of France shimmering like bells in the wind. I don't understand a word when I watch his YouTube channel, but luckily for me, his recipes are available in English.

I've learned everything I know from him, the details and preciseness of French baking, how a recipe with basic ingredients doesn't mean the techniques will in any way be easy to master. Most times, their success depends on how you mix the batter or prepare the dough.

Croissants seem like a simple recipe to make at first, only flour, high-fat butter, and water. But the difficulty lies in the folding technique required for the croissants to rise during baking, creating those airy, crispy French breakfast staples.

I set my phone on the counter, dialing my sister. She picks up after two rings.

"My favorite brother!" Avery's face fills my screen, and it's like sunshine bursts into my kitchen.

I snort. "Are you hiding another one I don't know about?"

"Mom didn't tell you? Shoot, I thought you knew." Her smile stretches widely.

I start to extend the dough on my floured counter, making sure the butter trapped inside doesn't escape.

"Ha-ha," I mock. "How are you, Ave? What time is it in LA right now?"

She slouches on a chair outside, the sun on her face.

I miss her so much.

"Busy, busy," she says, sliding her sunglasses on. "Just about six p.m. We went to the beach today; Josh is learning to surf."

I laugh. "Surf? Ha! How's that going?"

"I mean, it was the second time, so mostly drinking seawater and not much standing up." Her face gets closer to the screen. "What are you doing there?"

I move my phone so she can see the dough. "Your favorite."

"Jealous! Who are they for?"

I put the phone back down, folding the dough in three before turning it a quarter and stretching it again. "We're having a little kick-off meeting in the morning with everybody, so I thought I'd make some croissants we can all enjoy together."

"Always going above and beyond. I'm sure they'll love it."

"If any of them don't like croissants, I'm gonna question their future at the firm," I say. But I don't want to talk about the firm right now—it defeats the whole purpose of baking. I redirect my attention to something that occupies my mind just as much. "Any plans on coming back?"

Avery sighs. "Not in the near future. We're both so busy, I don't know how either of us could get the time off right now. Why don't you come back to spend a few weeks in LA? It's been almost a whole year since you last were here."

I cock an eyebrow.

"Right, right, your new business," she says. "I hate being separated from you this long."

We haven't seen each other since Christmas—the longest we've ever been apart—and truthfully, it feels like I'm missing a vital part of me. She's always been my rock, and I like to think I'm hers, even if she has her husband now.

"Me too, Ave," I say. "I'm going to see what I can do and try to make my way to you soon, okay?"

Avery smiles. "I'd love that."

We continue chatting while I finish cutting, rolling, and shaping the dough, coating the croissants with egg yolk before putting them in the oven.

It's late on this side of the globe, but I can't bring myself to end our conversation. Just like when we were younger, we would talk for hours, no matter if the sun was shining or the moon was out. Whenever we were alone at home, our dad working and our mom struggling with her depression, we would get Timbits and Canada Dry and settle on the window seat cushions at the top of the stairs, babbling until we didn't feel so lonely anymore.

As we got older and our lives became busier, we swore to always take the time to catch up and press pause to spend time together in whatever way we could. It's me and her, and nothing will ever change that.

After an hour, we hang up, and I finish the last batch. I tidy up the kitchen, putting everything back in its place. With

Happy snoring in his bed and the croissants cooling, I go to bed, tomorrow waiting for me on the other side of my dreams.

THREE

You're on Your Own, Kid

Riley

on't go to bed too late. I could honestly face-palm myself. Like Miles needs someone to tell him when he should hit the hay. You're not his mom, Ry, and stop imagining him on his pillow.

I grunt, flopping on my bed and dialing my emergency person. Charlee picks up almost straight away.

"Hey, Ry!" A static noise muffles my sister's voice.

"Hey, Char. Where are you? I can't hear you that well."

There's some commotion in the background and the sound of an engine starting. "Sorry, we're packing things up here, I'll call you back in fifteen when I have better reception."

The line goes dead. Getting my sister on the phone these days is ridiculously hard. She's always trotting around the globe, trying to discover all the world's wonders while raising awareness on climate change through her work as a journalist at *Wild Planet*. It's hard to keep track of her whereabouts, but if I'm not mistaken, she's currently somewhere in South America.

As I wait for her to call back, I go over tomorrow's schedule one last time:

- 8:30 — Meet Miles downstairs.
- 9 — Welcome new employees.
- 9:30 — First meeting with breakfast.
- Noon — Lunch with Steve (Microsoft).
- 2 — Meeting with Miles and Adam.

Not to mention all the things that will inevitably go wrong because, let's face it, there's no escaping malfunctions and meltdowns.

I set my phone down on my nightstand after trying Charlee again, without success.

She's going to make me lose my sanity.

I slide into my pajamas, feeling the heaviness of sleep slowly wash over me. Just as I'm about to close my eyes, my phone chimes, and my ex-husband's name pops up on my screen.

Sean: Thought I'd wish you good luck for tomorrow.

My stomach lurches in my throat. Before I can lock my phone and ignore his attempt to intimidate me once again, Sean sends another message.

Sean: And trust me, you and your boyfriend are going to need a lot of luck, Riley, because I'm coming for you. And when you think things can't get any worse, I'll be waiting, ready to prove you wrong.

When will this end? I thought that by signing the divorce papers, I would finally unshackle myself from his constant threats and cutting words. But here I am, a year later, making myself sick and feeling ashamed over a man who makes me feel beneath him, a man who reduces Miles's and my achievements and hard work with claims of an affair. I know I have nothing to feel ashamed about, but the feeling is there nonetheless.

But I have to tread carefully because, despite his behavior, Sean has built himself a solid reputation in the industry and has allies in every corner.

Riley: Always a pleasure, Sean.

Sean: Look who finally decided to be a big girl.

I ignore his jab, setting my phone down after turning the sleep mode on. I take three deep breaths through my nose, willing my heartbeat to quiet in my ears.

I anchor myself to my surroundings, the weight of my body against the mattress, my hands soft and relaxed on my warm stomach, my head sinking into my pillow, and slowly, I shift my focus from my past to my future.

MY ALARM RINGS AT 6:30, but my eyes are already wide open. Have been for the past two hours. In fact, I've been staring at my bedroom ceiling, thinking I should definitely call my paint guy because those two yellowish stains need to be removed. Immediately. I make a mental note to do so as soon as I have a spare second today, which frees some brain space to worry about what to wear for my first day at *my own freaking firm*. The understanding slowly creeps in.

This is real.

This is happening.

Today, I'm walking into my office, greeting my new employees, and getting shit done on my own terms—and Miles's, of course. Nothing—and no one—will take that away from me.

With the adrenaline kicking in and flowing through my veins, I get up and start rustling through my walk-in closet, tiptoeing around the dresses and sweaters lying on the floor.

You'd think I'd have an outfit prepared, but being so worried about everything going smoothly today, I didn't stop to think about what to wear.

Since it's starting to warm up, I settle on a sky-blue pencil skirt that falls just at the knee and tuck in a fitted black blouse.

I'm in the middle of brushing my teeth when my phone rings.

"Hey, Char," I say with my mouth full of toothpaste.

"Hey! Sorry about yesterday. We were still at Chapada dos Guimarães trying to get closer to a family of harpy eagles."

"Chapa-what? Where are you now?" It's way too early for me to comprehend another language.

Charlee laughs. "Chapada dos Guimarães. I'm in Brazil. Should be home in a week, though."

I sigh. "Okay, well… be careful, yeah?"

"Where's the fun in that, Ry?" The thrill in her voice sends goose bumps across my body.

Even when we were little, my sister was the adventurous one. Climbing trees in our backyard, diving headfirst into the ocean during our summer vacations, holding the steering wheel on our mom's lap. Me? I was the one gasping and shrieking on the sidelines each time she'd do something reckless, fearing that she'd put herself in harm's way for the last time.

It wasn't surprising that when Mom passed away, she found this job at *Wild Planet* and made it her career. It fits her like a glove. She's always looking for that adrenaline rush, thirsty for danger and adventure, toying with life like she's testing herself to see how far she can go before something irreversible happens. I always breathe the biggest sigh of relief when I see her name appear on my phone. And despite my constant state of worry when it comes to my sister, the last time I saw her this happy was when Mom was still here. So I'll take this over her shutting me out any day, even if it means I'll be growing white hair way before my time and will always be terrified for her. That's what big sisters are for, right?

I sigh. Mom would be proud of how far her daughters have come.

"You know you can enjoy what you do without putting yourself in danger, right?"

"I'm perfectly safe, Ry, relax. Plus, I'm with my amazing local guide Felipe who's taking great care of me, if you know what I mean." She clicks her tongue.

"Hard not to when you put it like that," I quip. God, to be this carefree.

"Why did you call me yesterday? Everything okay?"

I spit the rest of the toothpaste into the sink and rinse my mouth. "Yeah, I'm just a bit anxious about today, that's all." Turning off the tap, I start pacing in my bathroom, as I usually do when I'm on the phone.

"Oh yeah, today's the day, uh? Any news from Sean?"

At the mention of his name, my body tenses, and my shoulders hunch, as if muscle memory at his name makes me physically smaller.

"Yeah, he's been text-harassing me. Intimidating me, actually. About legal clauses in my old contract and… other stuff." I stop short, unsure how much of it I want my sister to know. How much I want to admit about Sean still doing everything in his power to control me.

"I think he's just threatened that we'll succeed and that his reputation will further take a hit," I add, shaking my head. "Doesn't look good when your ex-wife starts her own competing firm, I guess."

"The balls of this dude, I swear. And you will succeed, Ry. Today is just the start of it. Go kick ass. And knock him down while you're at it."

I laugh, feeling the warmth and strength of my sister through her words. "Thank you, Charlee. Please, be safe. I'll see you in a week."

"Fingers crossed!"

I groan and hang up, seeing the time on my phone. Fuck, I'm already late. I run to my bedroom, style my long wavy hair into a high ponytail, and finish the look with a dab of mascara and nude lipstick.

Outfit, check. Hair and make-up, check. Where is my notepad? Fuck. Can anything go right this morning? This little notepad contains everything about how today is supposed to go. I can't leave without it. I turn my entire house upside down, toss the decorative couch cushions onto the floor and check between the seats, open the cabinets in my kitchen, dig through my library. Nothing.

Ten minutes later, I finally spot it on my kitchen table under three books, a coffee mug, and a half-empty bag of chips.

Once the notebook is safely stored in my purse, I gulp down a cup of coffee and simultaneously grab my jacket before flying out the door. Only when my feet meet the hallway rug do I realize one crucial piece of clothing missing.

"Ugh, Riley, you dumbass!"

I turn back to my apartment, find my black pointed heels next to my running shoes and snow boots, and slide them on.

I am so late, I can already picture Miles's face when I arrive thirty minutes past the time we agreed on.

I make another mental note to get a cleaning crew in here as soon as possible, but right now, it's show time.

Miles

THE SUN IS BARELY UP WHEN I return to my condo after my usual morning run. I'm sweaty and hot, the morning air brushing softly against my damp skin. Happy is wagging his tail next to me, his tongue hanging out.

"Had enough with a 5K this morning, pal?" Happy barks before burying his nose in the palm of my hand. "Good boy," I say, ruffling his head. "Okay, come on."

After a cool shower that relaxed my strained muscles, I pour myself a cup of coffee, checking on my scrambled eggs so they don't overcook. Happy is already eating his breakfast. Or rather, inhaling it.

"Happy! Slow down, you'll throw it all up!" His ears perk up, but that doesn't stop him from gobbling down his meal like the little glutton he is.

I sit in my lounge chair with my eggs and coffee and open my iPad to today's *Globe and Mail* before reviewing the day's schedule. My adrenaline is running high. I was hoping my run this morning would have calmed me down, but I still feel the nerves sizzling under my skin. And the coffee isn't going to help, but oh well. Big day today.

I can't remember the last time I took such a big risk. Truth be told, I can't even remember the last time I felt this vulnerable.

I haven't always been like this. Hell no.

I used to challenge myself every day, I was the kind of guy who thrived under pressure and competition. I still do in sports, with my rugby team. But when it comes to my personal life, my goals, my ambitions—it's been hard, particularly since I got the call about my infertility. That took a huge hit on my mental health and self-worth. Especially because it also led to the end of my engagement with Kristina.

I take a deep breath, letting the feeling occupy the space it needs in my body, expanding, stretching a little. It's an exercise my therapist suggested: not to stifle what I'm feeling and to take the time to live every emotion, no matter how uncomfortable they can sometimes be. And right now, it's the apprehension that inhabits me—of trying again, awakening after several years of living in this bubble of numbness where everything has stood still and where I moved on autopilot. The fear of giving it my all and failing again.

I didn't need much convincing when Riley reached out last year. Especially after the stunt her then-husband pulled in front of all our old colleagues, humiliating her for something that wasn't even her fault. But what was new about that? Sean was a dick to her almost every single day, and I had to sit two feet away from her for four years, grinding my teeth to dust, watching and listening while he openly disrespected and belittled her.

That public humiliation was what finally tipped me over the edge. For her and for me. Riley left before me, and when Sean got served with the divorce paper at the office, it took all I had to hide the huge grin on my face when he lost his shit.

And so here we are now. It's been a crazy year in the making, meeting several times a week at her place and mine, sharing coffee breaks, dinners, and memories, planning the services we'd offer, interviewing our future staff, nailing our business plan, getting calls from old clients—all leading up to today.

Launch day.

I check my watch. Right on time. I finish clearing the kitchen, make sure my dog has enough water for the day, and give him a little pat.

"See you tonight, Happy!"

And off I go…

FOUR

About Damn Time

Riley

I'm parking my Audi in the underground garage when I spot Miles leaning against his own car, his legs crossed at the ankles, and two coffees in hands. I hide my smile in the lapel of my jacket. He knows me too well.

"Good morning, partner," I say as I reach him.

I have to look up to meet his twinkling brown eyes, and when I say up, I mean ouch-my-neck-hurts up. Miles is freakishly tall and probably made out of stone. He must be at least six-five and as large as the French doors leading to the pool in my backyard. Back when we worked together, I used to catch myself wondering where he got his suits tailored— the suits that hug him nicely *everywhere*.

He smiles, handing me a warm cup. "Morning, partner! Ready to start bossing people around?"

I groan and take the cup. His full beard has been neatly trimmed today, just above his Adam's apple, giving sharp edges to a jaw I suspect might already be able to cut glass on its own. No use denying it; Miles is hot.

I peek inside, giving the cup what I thought was a discreet sniff, but Miles snorts and shakes his head.

"You still think I don't know your coffee order?" I raise an eyebrow in challenge, and he smirks in response. "Medium vanilla latte, one pump, because two is too sweet, and you're super grumpy when you get too much sugar. Extra hot."

I gape at him, a slight blush creeping up my neck. "Grumpy is not part of my repertoire. I'm sorry, you must have me confused with Lynda from HR." I tap my chin with the tip of my finger as if pondering something. "I think what you meant was that I am committed and perseverant." I take a sip of my latte. Like a cloud of coziness in my mouth.

Miles's expression gets oddly serious when he mumbles something that sounds like "that you are." He clears his throat. "Ready, boss?"

Am I ready? No. Can anyone be ready to start what could very well be the biggest mistake of their life? What if I lead everybody down the wrong path, people who put their trust in me and are counting on me to succeed? Do I really know what I'm doing? What if I'm not—no. Not doing that. *This is not you talking; it's Sean. You know what you're capable of.*

I take a deep breath, Miles's intense gaze trained on me, and square my shoulders. "Ready."

WE RIDE THE ELEVATOR TOGETHER to the thirty-first floor of the Bay Adelaide Centre situated at the heart of Toronto's financial district. The glass doors are closed when we arrive, the lights turned off, and only the natural light from the early morning sun filters through the windows. It looks so peaceful like this, it's hard to imagine that in an hour or so, a dozen people will fill the space between these black-and-white walls with chatter, sounds of heels on the hardwood floor, and keyboards clicking. Anticipation floods my brain.

Miles holds his hand out, the keys dangling from his index finger. "Want to do the honors?"

I nod and slide the key into the lock. A soft click echoes, nothing but this sound filling the heavy silence that settled between us, as if we're both holding our breath, waiting to see what happens next. I feel it, and I know Miles does too, this fleeting "no turning back" moment vanishing as soon as the door opens.

The moment I'll step inside, I'll be saying goodbye to my old life, the one where I lived under the thumb of a man who didn't deserve me.

This is monumental.

Seeing my hesitancy, Miles puts his palm on my arm. "Do you need a minute?"

I smile and shake my head. "No, I'm good. I'm just trying to wrap my head around all of this." I gesture to the beautiful welcome area in front of us, off-white couches and rose gold decorative cushions.

Miles drops his hand to mine, squeezing it once like it's the simplest thing in the world to do—and it is— but it also makes my nerves quiet on the spot. And that's not an easy feat. I look at his hand covering mine, feeling like a child holding one of a grown-up. His palm engulfs mine in a reassuring warmth, and for the first time since this morning, my heart rate slows down just a little.

"It's a lot, I know," he says, squeezing again. "But we're a team, okay? I've got your back."

I exhale a shaky breath. "I know. I've got yours too."

We finally cross the threshold, and I flick the lights on, marveling at the open space before us, decorated in neutral shades and filled with couches and armchairs in different seating areas, tables, and chairs forming little workspace bubbles. Farther inside is a big white kitchen with all the equipment needed—especially the espresso machine.

Down the hall, glass offices occupy the right and left sides, leading to the conference room overlooking the financial district, with Lake Ontario in the distance.

When brainstorming ideas about what we wanted our office to look like, Miles and I agreed we needed to reflect on what our partnership was based on—mutual respect and trust. We envisioned a space where we could take on our clients' companies as if they were our own. We wanted someplace our employees could feel welcomed and thrive in a safe work environment and not drag their feet, counting down the minutes until it was time for them to head home. That's why we chose this building with a daycare on the tenth floor, a gym on the fifteenth, and a rooftop with a terrasse to enjoy the warm Canadian summers during lunch breaks.

We busy ourselves in the kitchen before our new employees arrive, making coffee, tea, setting the pastries and other sweets on plates for our breakfast meet and greet.

"I can't believe you did all of this," I say as I reach to grab a croissant, but Miles swats my hand away before I can snag one. "Hey!"

"Wait till everybody gets here, Grumpy."

Oh, is this how he wants to play it? All right. "I'm sorry, they just look so good, Milesy." I draw his nickname out for emphasis, and his reaction is a shot of serotonin to my heart.

"Wh-what? What did you—what?" Clearly caught off guard, he tries to act as if I didn't just call him by the cutest and most ridiculous nickname ever. Obviously, he fails.

"What? Croissants? Miles, you realize they're not a well-kept secret, right?" I hide my mouth under my hand, whispering, "Everybody knows about them."

He groans. "I *meant*, what did you just call me? Where did you hear that?"

I laugh and pat his arm. My fingers barely cover a fraction of his bicep. "I heard one of your buddies call you like that over the phone one time." I smile. "He was pretty loud. Don't worry, I'll keep your nickname a secret."

"I don't have a nickname. There's nothing to keep secret," he grumbles before heading out to the conference room with the sweets.

I stifle a laugh, following behind him. "Oh, is that your way of telling me I can call you that in front of everybody, then?"

Miles spins around. "Don't you dare."

"Well, you know, if this thing comes crashing down, at least you have a solid backup plan." I nod toward the tastefully decorated cupcakes.

His eyes shoot to me. "Don't say that."

"What?" His intensity takes me by surprise.

"This company will succeed. There's not a doubt in my mind," he says.

"How can you be so sure?" I breathe. It's not like I've ever done this before.

He shrugs, like the answer is the most evident truth in the world. "Because you're at the head of it. And I know you. You won't give up. You're committed and perseverant, remember?" He grins.

Just as I'm about to tell him that, sometimes, it's not enough, a voice calls out from the entry.

"I'm here, I'm here!"

Adam strolls toward us, his forehead gleaming under a thin coat of sweat. He braces his hands on his knees.

"I am so out of shape, ohmygod," he says between breaths. "Sorry, I'm late. What did I miss?"

"Way to kick off your first day as director, Kaplan." Miles chuckles and winks in my direction, making the blood in my veins flow a little bit faster. "Sweaty *and* late."

I swat Miles's chest with the back of my hand and hit a rock-hard wall of muscle. I massage my hand, and he smirks as if he knows exactly what happened. "Ignore him, he's just trying to act all bossy and authoritative, but we all know he's just a big teddy bear."

Miles's brows shoot up before his eyes bore into mine, a flicker of mischief flashing through them faster than lightning. A challenge. One I don't think I should rise to.

He clears his throat, sliding his attention back to Adam who looks like he didn't miss one bit of the silent exchange between us. "All right, now that the whole gang's here, let's finish this up before people start coming in."

I watch as both men walk toward the conference room, chatting about their dogs, and wonder how I got so lucky to have two of my favorite people agree to follow me into this wild idea. One that bloomed in my mind many moons ago while talking with my sister around a few bottles of wine.

If Miles is my rock in this partnership, the Clyde to my Bonnie, Adam is the smooth talker, the charmer. He was the one bringing all the new clients at our old firm, luring them in one dashing smile at a time. It was a no-brainer to bring him along.

Around nine, employees start trickling in, taking in their new surroundings. We welcome them, greet the new faces, hug the familiar ones. I glance at Miles, who's laughing with Laura, an old university friend, and a warm fuzzy feeling spreads over me, wrapping me in the confidence and calm he embodies. He catches my glance and winks, a knowing smile on his face.

And it's all I need.

I put my game face on and head for the conference room at a steady pace for the very first meeting of the day.

FIVE

Wonder Woman

Miles

*W*e did it. We actually did it. First day in the books. Almost everything went according to plan, except for a few minor issues here and there. Of course, we'd have a problem with the internet, feels almost like a rite of passage to struggle with technology on important days.

I scrub my beard absently, waiting for Riley at the St. George bar across our office street, exhaustion settling slowly in my bones.

I order myself a gin and tonic and start to loosen my tie when she walks through the door. And every fucking time, she takes my breath away. Every fucking time, I have to remind myself to school my features and to stop ogling her like I'm ready to lay her flat on the table and do unspeakable things to her, not stopping until she screams my name.

Her eyes search the room before they land on me, and a smile grows wide on her face, making my heart do a weird thump in my chest in response. I am so fucked.

Riley walks to our table, commanding the room with every step, swaying her hips, unaware of the attention drifting toward her. Not because of how beautiful she is, although it wouldn't be hard to believe it, but because she exudes power and confidence. With her back straight as an arrow, her chin held high, defiant, and her provoking brown eyes that have the ability to plunge into your soul and make you trust her with your life, she's a force. She's thirty-four, a year younger than me, and yet she has a hold on me that is too great to even articulate.

"Hey, partner," she says as she plops down in the oversized armchair in front of me, throwing her purse in the seat next to her. Her hair is messier than it was this morning, blond strands sticking out from her ponytail and falling around her face. I clench my fist on my lap, reining in the desire to reach out and tuck it behind her ear. Or wrap it around my finger to see how soft it'd be against my callused skin.

"Hey, boss," I say, clearing my throat and straightening in my seat. "You look like you could use a drink."

"Or ten, honestly." She sighs, taking her notebook out. "What. A. Day. Who knew running a company would be so stressful?" she deadpans.

I laugh. "I know, right? We did *not* think this through."

She waves at the waiter and orders herself a double whiskey, no ice, before settling her attention back on me. "Okay, but seriously. How do you think today went?"

"It was a great first day, Ry. You gave a very inspirational speech this morning, and I could tell from the looks on everyone's faces that they were drinking every word coming out of your mouth." She's a natural public speaker when given the chance to actually talk, which hasn't always been the case before.

"Ughh, I hope you're not saying that just to make me feel better."

"When have I ever lied to you?"

The straightforward tone of my voice startles her and, quite frankly, surprises me too. She looks up from the notes she scribbled down today, and something passes through her eyes. It's brief, but it was there. I don't have time to press her on it as the waiter brings us our drinks, leaving me with this lingering thought.

She closes her notepad and holds her palm up. "All right, all right, I get it. I'm too hard on myself. I just…" She sighs again. "This can't fail, Miles."

I know that. There are no secrets between us. I know she's testing herself, seeing if she can do it without her dickhead of an ex-husband. It's infuriating that she is even doubting herself. Of course, she can do it. I'll do anything to help her see her worth. I honestly don't know how subtle I've been these past years when it comes to my feelings for her. All I know is that I wasn't about to get in the middle of a marriage then—no matter how toxic I believed it to be. And now that we're partners… the line is just as blurry.

And still, knowing what she and I can never be, I reach out and lay my hand on hers.

"You won't. And if you fuck up, I'll be right there with you to tell you myself. That's what it means to be partners."

She flips her hand that's trapped under mine and draws small circles with her thumb along my skin. My eyes shoot to the slight pressure she applies there.

She cocks her eyebrow. "You'll tell me 'Ry, you fucked up' point blank?"

I nod, trying my best to get the words out. "Won't even hesitate."

She grins, and her shoulders drop instantly, tension visibly evaporating from her frame. She releases her hand from mine, the fog in my mind clearing immediately with it, and picks up her glass. "Okay. Well, cheers to a successful first day."

"Cheers." I smile back and clink my drink to hers.

We order some chips and guac while we dissect the day and plan for the rest of the month. Several clients from our previous firm heard about our move and have already contacted us to set up meetings. It's going to be a busy summer.

"So," Riley says, crunching on chips as she flips the pages of her planner. "We have Lise and Matthew coming tomorrow for their kickoff meeting, Charles is scheduled for… next month, and on Friday, I have lunch scheduled with Frank from Shopify."

I tap my pen against my lips. "Is everything ready for WestJet? It's a big account; I don't want us to miss a thing. Everything's been double-checked? Our old contracts?"

"I'll have Adam go over it. I'll take the lead on this one if you don't mind."

"Sure, works for me." I'm making a note when Riley's phone lights up on the table. I barely have time to see Sean's name before she rushes to flop it over.

"What does he want?"

Riley sighs, avoiding my eyes. "Nothing that matters."

"Ry."

She looks up, and what I see in her eyes makes me want to pay Sean a little visit. "He's been a bit... persistent lately. About old clients coming our way."

I scrub my jaw. I already know I'll need to run again tonight or stop by the rugby field to burn off this frustration coiling inside me. "How persistent?"

I hate it. I hate seeing him affect her.

"A few texts and calls every other day," she replies, dropping her attention to her nails.

"For fuck's sake," I mumble. "Why haven't you said anything? We could have put our lawyers on it."

Riley shrugs. "I'm capable of taking care of it myself."

"Of course you are. But if I can—"

"You can't," she interrupts. "He's just doing this to upset me, and I am trying really, *really* hard not to let it, Miles. The divorce has been a nightmare to go through as it is. He'll tire eventually, I just need to ignore him."

"I'm sorry. I didn't mean to overstep," I say. "He just… gets on my nerves, I guess."

"You guess?" She snorts. "Miles, you are the least chill person I know when it comes to Sean."

I run a hand in my hair. "I know, I'm working on it. I feel useless. I hate seeing you hurt because of him."

This time, Riley reaches out, hesitating slightly before placing her hand on mine. "I know," she whispers. "But you're wrong. He's not hurting me anymore. I am not giving him more than he's already taken. He doesn't get my hurt; he only gets my anger."

Her smile barely reaches her ears, which pales in comparison to the real deal. I trap her hand in mine, tugging her up. "Come on, let me drive you home."

"You sure? I didn't drink much."

"I know. I just want to celebrate a little bit longer."

"What about my car?"

I shrug. "I'll come pick you up tomorrow morning too." *And every day for the rest of my life if you asked me to.*

"Don't be a weirdo, you can just stay at my place, and we can carpool together tomorrow." The silence stretches between us. Did she—"I have a guest bedroom," she adds quickly, her cheeks coloring.

I know she said guest bedroom, but all my brain (and dick) registers is "bedroom," and suddenly, images of a naked and warm Riley arching under me invade my mind.

"Miles?"

"Yes, sorry."

"What do you say?" She arches an eyebrow, a smug smile tugging at the corner of her lips.

"Huh? About?"

She laughs openly, and the sound irradiates me inside like the Northern Lights dancing in the night sky. "I said, before I lost you,"—she swirls her finger in my face, and I kind of want to bite it—"my pool guy just got it up and running for the season. We could make an evening out of it! Order take-out, have some wine, and cool off with a swim to end our first successful day."

In the realm of bad ideas, "let's go enjoy a dip in the pool of the coworker you've been lusting after for years" must undoubtedly be in the top three. With a flashing sign saying, "especially bad idea for Miles!" in bold caps, red letters. And yet, all I can think of to say is, "Sure, why not!"

Although thinking about it, I have a little four-pawed friend who's counting on me at home, and there's no way I'm doing any sort of walk of shame tomorrow. I need fresh clothes and a clear head for the office.

Riley is already walking toward the door, so I scramble to gather my stuff and meet her outside on the sidewalk.

"Wait, Ry, I forgot. Wow, this is super complicated all of a sudden." I laugh. "I have to feed Happy and take him out, and I don't have a change of clothes for tomorrow." I scratch the back of my neck as I try to find a solution to the problem, because no matter how bad of an idea being around Riley in a swimsuit is, I can't seem to want to let it go. But as usual, Riley beats me to the punch.

"Tell you what. I'll drive myself home, you go to your place, grab Happy and whatever else you need, and meet me back at mine. I'm sure Happy'll be thrilled to splash in the pool with us."

I try to process this turn of events when she adds, "Please, Miles. I didn't think I needed it before inviting you, but turns out, I would really love some company tonight."

The protective side of me flares up at the vulnerability I detect in her voice. There's nothing I wouldn't do for her. But combine that with a "please" and a little begging? I'm a done man. "I'd love that," I say without an ounce of hesitancy, smiling warmly at her.

"Great." She clasps her hands together. "Let's say 7-ish?"

"I'll be there."

I head to my car parked just at the corner of the street, when she yells, "Oh, and Miles?"

"Yeah?"

"Pick up sushi on the way. And not the cheap kind!"

I DRIVE DOWN WOODLAWN AVENUE in the heart of Summerhill, a quaint neighborhood located in the center of Toronto, where Victorian-era houses and old maple trees line the streets. Happy's head is hanging out of the window in the backseat, tongue flapping in the wind. It's not hard to figure out where his name came from.

I park my car a few streets down, and we get out of the car, making our way to Riley's. I never got to enjoy her pool while at her place, which honestly might not have been the worst thing in the world because god knows I would have had nothing done.

Apprehension settles in as I wait in front of her gorgeous two-story walk-up, sushi in one hand and Happy's leash in the other. *It's just a casual get-together, Miles, don't get any ideas.* She doesn't need this right now. *Get it through that thick skull of yours.*

Riley opens the door, and a whoosh of her jasmine and sweet orange scent hits me straight in the face.

"Right on time." She beams at me before turning her attention to Happy. "Hello, little man," she says, kneeling down. "I missed you! Yes, I did! Did you miss me too?"

I chuckle, turning to take my shoes off and giving Ry some quality time with her "favorite dog." I'm still amused how, months later, she continues to talk to him like they're having their own private conversation. One only she and he can hear, apparently, judging by how I seem to disappear completely.

My laughter dies quickly in my throat, though, and I have to cough a few times not to choke to death when I turn back, and my eyes meet her plunging cleavage, Happy's head half buried in it.

Fuck.

From where I'm standing, I can see the edges of her lacy black bra under her T-shirt, hugging the curves of her chest and barely covering enough skin to leave any to my imagination.

"Are you okay?" Riley asks, still petting Happy. I shoot my eyes to the ceiling like a five-year-old who just got caught red-handed trying to steal candy. I probably look guilty as hell, but I'm grateful for my beard covering half of my now crimson face.

"Perfect," I say, but my voice is hoarse, and it sounds more like *Mmrfct*.

"Wanna see if I have something for you in the kitchen?" she asks my dog, and at that, Happy's ears perk up and his head tilts, charging onward and shoving Riley down to her ass.

"Ow!"

"Happy!" I yell, but Ry starts to laugh uncontrollably, slumping down on the floor as Happy sniffs her hair, causing my heart to detach from my body.

I have never seen her this carefree, and the sight knocks the wind from my chest. I want to lie down next to her and laugh with her. I want to grab her waist and pull her to me—bury my nose in the slope of her neck where the skin is so smooth and smells the most like her. I want to hold her tight and chase away the demons of her past, show her how a real man treats a woman. I want to kiss her so deeply she forgets her worries and gives me her tomorrows.

But I don't.

Instead, I hold out my hand to help her up, ignoring the familiar sensation coursing up my arm at the feel of her skin on mine.

Instead, once she's up on two feet, I take a step back, even though I can feel the tension between us like a rubber band stretched thin, wanting to pull me closer.

"Thank you," Riley says softly, straightening her clothes. And then she's off, strutting after Happy toward the kitchen, and—

"Fuck me," I mumble because those are very short shorts.

"Did you say something?" she calls.

I shake the bag in my hand as I make my way to her. "Your favorites."

Riley puts her hands on her heart and makes an "aww" sound before handing me a glass of white. "Your favorite." She winks. "It's from Winsome Winery. Remember, we had them as clients at the old firm. It's good, right?"

I nod and take a sip. "Very. I miss working with Peter. We accomplished so much for them."

"I know, me too. I don't want to jinx it, but he texted me earlier today and asked if I was free for lunch next week. 'Just to catch up.'" She makes air quotes, arranging the sushi onto a plate. "But enough shop talk. Tonight is for unwinding only."

"You're right." Happy and I follow her outside as she gets the table set up. I'm about to give her a hand when my phone vibrates in my pocket.

Avery: How was your first day? Did you nail it? How's Riley?

I tuck it away, smiling that my sister remembered.

"Wow, who's that smile for?" Riley asks, settling on the comfy outdoor couch.

"Why?" I shoot back.

She shrugs. "I don't know. You're usually a bit rough around the edges, I don't see you smile like that often." She picks a sashimi with her chopsticks and dips it into the soy sauce. "I like it."

I like you. I clear my throat. "I'm not rough. But it was Avery. She just wanted to know how today went."

"That's sweet," Riley says around a mouthful. "Is she still liking LA?"

"She loves it. She's such a hotshot there now with the company she works with. I'm so proud of her."

It wasn't always easy for her, she's come a long way between starting her own business, renewing her relationship with Josh, and despite everything, she's soldiered on, she never gave up. Headstrong, my sister? Only a little. But at least now she's reaping the benefit of all the sweat and tears she put into her own company. I'll admit I was skeptical of her move at first, that she was leaving with Josh on top of it, but I can admit now that I couldn't have asked for anything more for her. And to see her thriving like this, after what she's been through—well, there's no greater feeling. I'm a damn proud brother.

Riley's silent for a while before asking, "Do you miss her?"

I don't hesitate. "Yeah, I do. A lot. Last time I saw her was when I visited them for Christmas, and that was… yeah, I guess almost six months now." I sigh, scrubbing my beard.

"I'm happy for her. It's just… It's been the two of us for as long as I can remember."

When our mom was too sick to take care of us, or when Dad fucked the whole family over. When she needed a shoulder to cry on, or I needed to vent about what an asshole my boss was to the incredible woman in front of me right now. It was us, we were our own little family.

"She's still my little sister, and there will always be the overprotective and worried part of me that wishes she lived closer."

Riley pats Happy's head while she takes another piece of sushi. "I get it. My sister and I used to be really close, even though we're the polar opposite of each other." She chuckles. "But her work takes her all around the world, and she's rarely here."

I frown. "What do you mean by polar opposites?"

"She's the adventurous one, always looking for something that takes her out of her comfort zone. Sometimes I wonder if there's anything that scares her. I doubt there is. I think, if anything, she'd look the challenge dead in the eye with a big grin on her face."

She pauses to take a sip of her wine before continuing. "When we were kids, Charlee was always getting into trouble, missing school, forgetting family dinners. I was the one my parents counted on to be responsible, bring home good grades, and never raise my voice or disagree with a decision." She sighs, a forced smile on her face that tells me more than she'd like. "Charlee's the brave and fearless sister. I'm the boring one."

I shake my head. If only she could see what I see. "You're so far from boring, Ry. You're intelligent, daring, bold. You don't wait for things to come your way; you go after them. You're fearless too. Just not in the same way, and that's okay. Better than okay."

The way she's looking at me now, lips parted and eyes wide like I just revealed to her the secrets of the universe, makes me believe nobody has ever challenged her beliefs. All I did was give her the plain truth. Things everybody sees and knows when they get to know Ry. And if she can't see those things herself, Sean did a hell of a number on her.

Before I can say anything else, she turns her attention back to Happy. "Sometimes I wish she were here so we could have a girls' night in, and I could have someone to talk to."

"Does she know about—"

"Yes. She does. She was here through my divorce and stayed over for a bit before she had to fly to Saudi Arabia to cover a story on the Arabian reef."

"Well," I say, leaning my elbows on my thighs, "I know I'm not Charlee, and I'm not a woman, so technically speaking, I can't offer a girls' night in, but I'm here for you. I'm just a phone call away, Ry."

And maybe it was the tone of my voice, or maybe it's the way I'm looking at her, but the air grows a little thicker between us, time seems to slow as I wait for her to say something. Anything. Did I overstep? I don't think so, but again, I forget myself when I'm with her. She makes me lose my grasp on reality and boundaries. All I want is to wrap myself around her and never let go.

I don't have a chance to make it right before Happy's head swivels toward the pool, and he bolts, jumping straight in the water.

"Happy!" I yell, running toward the pool, only to find my dog splashing around, the canine version of a big cheesy grin on his face. "What the fuck, dude?" But the only answer I get to his sudden urge to frolic is a big bark. Yeah, go figure.

Ry joins us, laughing like she was in the doorway earlier, and my blood pumps faster. "Looks like someone wanted to get wet." She turns to me. "What do you say, Miles?"

I grin. "I say let's get in."

I remove my shirt, not missing the way her eyes trip on my chest and my tattooed skin before she quickly looks away. I hide my smile. I'm not stupid. I know I'm in great shape. Years of playing rugby have made my upper body bulky. And while I also work my abs and legs to sprint at every practice, it's the scrums that have built my broad frame.

I head inside to put on my swimming shorts, and when I return, I find myself face to face with Riley's ass, propped in the air as she discards her shorts. Her swimsuit is nothing more than a triangle-shaped scrap of gold that barely covers her cheeks and is tied by thin strings on either side of her hips. All I want to do is tug on the fabric and see how easy it'd be to make it fall down.

"Ready?" I ask, my voice strained.

She turns, and *goddamn*. I have to bite my tongue hard not to tell her how crazy she drives me.

All small golden triangles. Everywhere.

She tugs on the tie holding her hair, and golden strands cascade all around her face, down her shoulders, the tip of her hair brushing against her back and grazing her chest.

"Ready," she replies before diving headfirst and reappearing a moment later at the end of the pool. "Oh my god, this feels so good," she moans. "Come on in, Miles!"

I grunt. I swear she has decided to torture me tonight. I dive in and join her where she sits on the pool steps, Happy paddling in our direction.

"The temperature is perfect," I say, looking for a seat beside her. And the view isn't bad either. Her blond hair is slicked back, her heart-shaped face on full display, drops of water catching in her long lashes and making her maroon eyes pop.

"I've always wanted a pool," she says, looking at the last glimmers of daylight in the sky. "My dad wasn't around, and my mom worked two jobs so we could have a life the other kids our age had. We didn't have much growing up, to be honest, but I never truly realized it until I was a teenager and understood what money meant and how much our mom had sacrificed for us. And I remember one night, after I'd been to a pool party at my friend's house, telling my mom I'd have one of my own one day."

She smiles and closes her eyes, and I do the same. "When I did eventually get my house with a pool, the first thing I did was invite my mom over. We spent the whole day in the water, and when we got out, our skin was so pruny we looked like we were eighty years old."

I chuckle, imagining what she would've looked like, all wrinkled.

"I can still see my mom's face when she came here and saw it," Riley continues. "Because she knew what it meant, you know? She was so proud. This woman worked her ass off for us so we wouldn't lack a thing, and I watched her tire herself every day while my sister and I played with our brand-new Barbies. I'm so proud of the women Charlee and I are because of our mother. Proud that she managed to raise two daughters all on her own." She shakes her head. "No, I shouldn't say managed. She succeeded."

I nod, sinking my shoulders in the warm water. "She did. She sounds like she was an incredible woman."

Riley's eyes drop to her hands under the surface, resting on her thighs. When she speaks, her voice is laced with sadness and something resembling admiration. "She was. I wish she could've been around longer to enjoy all her hard work," she says, gesturing around her. "All of this is because of her. Thanks to her."

She keeps her gaze down, playing with ripples in the water. I can't help but reach out and place a finger under her chin, gently inviting her to look at me.

"She'd be so proud, Ry. I hope you know that." I say this with all the conviction I have within me and because, well, I know this feeling too. "My mom wasn't always around when Avery and I were kids. She was depressed, most of the time, but wasn't diagnosed until much later in our lives. It was really hard on Ave. It was hard for me too, but I was the older brother, and she needed someone to take care of her. So I stayed strong, hid how much not having my mom around affected me."

It's hard for me to say this out loud, like pronouncing the words makes me selfish, in a way.

I don't think I've ever said it to anyone, actually. Avery and I, for all the talking we do, haven't come close to talking about these deeper parts of our lives.

I comb my fingers through my wet hair. "Later on, when my mom got the help she needed to manage her episodes, we sat down one afternoon when it was just me and her at home. I must have been about thirty, I can't remember. She looked at me right in the eye and told me how grateful and proud she was of me. For taking care of my little sister and becoming the man I was."

I feel Riley's attention on me, and when I look at her, I'm overwhelmed by the tenderness in her eyes.

"I know it's not the same thing," I say, "because my mom is still here. But you and I both had to grow up a bit too fast and had way too many responsibilities resting on our shoulders for kids our age. If your mom could see you now, see what an incredibly fearless woman you are, I know she would tell you how proud she is of you."

Riley offers me a small smile, but her eyes, her beautiful chocolate eyes, hold so much more than what she could ever express with words.

"I'm sorry you had it rough when you were a kid," she whispers.

"Me too," I say back at her. "I'm glad your mom got to see the pool."

She waves me off. "I know it's silly. I shouldn't care about things like that. It's just... it was my dream as a kid, that's all."

"I don't think it's silly," I whisper.

"Sean said it was the most idiotic thing he'd ever heard. But he doesn't know what that would be like, growing up counting every dollar, seeing your mother run off her feet from working two jobs."

The tremors in her voice are unmistakable, and on instinct, I place my hand on her thigh, squeezing once. I have to take several breaths to calm the burning sensation in my throat.

"I'm sorry," I say, pulling my hand off her thigh, but she snags it back and laces her fingers around mine.

My eyes widen, slowly moving up to her face. I search her eyes for an answer, something that can explain why it suddenly feels impossible to breathe, why my heart is ready to leap out of my chest.

I grip her thigh tighter and her lips part, releasing a shallow breath. It tugs at something feral in me to see her react like this at my touch, and I lean in, splaying one hand on the curve of her neck, bringing her closer. She doesn't resist, her gaze fixed on my mouth, and mine on hers. Her choppy breath mixes with mine, fruity and spicy from our dinner.

My thumb strokes her cheek once. "Ry..."

A flurry of drops descends on us, snapping us out of our bubble. I jerk away, only to find Happy shaking himself outside the pool right next to her. Worst wingdog ever. When

I look back at Riley, the distance between us has grown, and not just physically.

"Ry, if I—"

"I can't, Miles," she cuts in, before continuing with more force, "I can't. My marriage almost destroyed me. I lost everything when I divorced Sean. He took everything from me. I was back to square one, with only my savings to my name. And you and I are colleagues. Partners. I can't jeopardize that. I can't. I can't. I—"

"Hey, hey, hey. Riley, listen to me." I want to wrap her in my arms so badly, but the contact of her nearly naked skin on mine would be too much to endure. So instead, I take her hands in mine. "It's okay. Don't worry, I understand. It was just a moment," I say, waving around us. "It doesn't mean anything. I wouldn't jeopardize what we've built together either."

I search her eyes, and when she finally looks back at me, I pour everything I can into my next words. "Do you trust me?"

Riley remains silent for a few seconds before nodding. "Yes."

"Good," I say, squeezing her fingers and ignoring the aching sensation in my chest at her hesitancy. "I won't jeopardize what we're building, Ry. You can trust me. This will never happen again."

SIX

Girl Crush

Miles

"*S*hit, shit, shit!" My apartment door slams behind me, and I throw my keys on the table next to it. Fucking shit, Miles.

I had one fucking job. One job. To never make Riley doubt that I have her back. Support her, and never act on my feelings, knowing how much it would fuck things up. And at the first glimpse of skin, at the first sign of vulnerability on her part, I went full horny teenager on her and threw everything out the window.

Now she'll probably never trust me again. In the back of her mind, she'll always wonder if I'm looking out for her best interest or if I'm being a selfish and greedy bastard.

And the look on her face afterward… damn it.

I don't want her looking at me like that ever again. Like she fears I'll try something again, like she can't *trust* me.

I sit on my couch, running my hands through my hair and pulling hard enough to sting, trying to numb the pain in my chest. Even if all the lights to Riley were flashing green, I still wouldn't go for it. She deserves so much more than I can offer her.

You're not enough for me, Miles.

The words echo loudly in my mind as if they've just been spoken out loud, and not three years ago. When the future that I could so distinctively see and almost touch evaporated at the tip of my fingers, as quickly as a mirage in the desert.

Sensing my mind spinning and spiraling, Happy jumps on the couch, wiggling his head between my arm and thigh. Smart little dude.

I grab my phone and check the time, taking a deep breath to try to steady my racing heart. It's still relatively early in the evening in LA when Avery picks up.

"Miles! I was starting to worry!" The sound of her voice soothes a few knots in my throat.

"Sorry, Riley and I got together after work to debrief the day."

"Ooooh." I don't like the interest in her voice. "Whatcha been talking about?"

"Work, Ave." Not the full truth. I sigh. "Okay, and then I might have driven to her house for dinner and a little pool party."

The silence stretches on the other end of the line as I wait for her to either press me on every little detail or make a joke about how it must have been hard to keep it in my pants. Which, honestly? Very hard.

"So when you say, 'pool party', do you mean you and a few other people from the office? Or was it an 'I want to make out with you so bad and this is my excuse to see you in a swimsuit' kind of pool party?"

"We almost kissed," I let out.

"I KNEW IT!" The screech reverberates in the whole apartment, and I have to move the phone away from my ear to prevent permanent damage.

"Are you okay?" a masculine voice asks in the background. Josh.

"Yes, I'm fine, J. More pressing matter. Miles kissed Riley."

"I didn't *kiss* her. We almost kissed."

She sighs through the phone. "Semantics. The point is, there is interest."

I shake my head. "No. Absolutely not. This will never happen again."

Avery scoffs, and I hear Josh speak. "What did he say?"

"He said this won't happen again," she repeats in what I can only assume is her best attempt to sound like me.

Josh snorts in turn. "That's sweet."

"I didn't know this was a three-person phone call," I say, annoyance seeping through my voice.

"You're such a baby, Miles. J, can you give us a minute? This is a sister/brother phone call only."

I hear muffled sounds on Avery's side of the line, followed by a playful "stoppp". I roll my eyes. They can't keep their hands off each other for a goddamn minute. After a few seconds, Avery picks up the phone again.

"There. It's just you and me. Please explain exactly what happened because I have a hard time understanding how my brother, who's been pining after the same girl for years, suddenly decided today was the day he would finally give it a go."

"That's the million-dollar question," I say, because where do I even start? "I guess it just finally caught up to me after all this time."

Why in the hell did I decide to give in to my primal urges when I was able to ignore them for so long? Pushing them down and burying them under piles of fear, self-preservation, and manners. I have been working so hard to get those impulses in check, spending more time than usual on the rugby field, running a few extra miles, cooking for the whole neighborhood.

But the way she looked tonight in the water...

She was so vulnerable, opening her heart and trusting me like I was deserving of soothing a few aches. It broke something in me, how similar we are, and then to hear her call herself silly. That the person who was supposed to love and cherish her had told her she was.

"Of course, it was going to happen," my sister says, certainty dripping from her tone. "What I'm more concerned about, though, is how you feel. I know you, Miles." I can almost see her pointed look through the phone, her brows knit together until I finally give in and tell her what's on my mind.

"I feel like the girl of my dreams will forever stay that way. An unattainable, silly dream"—I almost laugh at the irony of using Riley's words—"that I should give up on before I get any more ideas."

"You know, Riley's situation aside, she doesn't sound like the kind of woman who'd do something like Kristina... maybe you sh—"

"No," I cut in before she can finish her sentence. She doesn't know half of what happened with Kristina. As far as Avery's concerned, Kristina met somebody else and moved to Vancouver to be closer to him.

"But Miles—"

"Ave, fucking drop it already, okay? I made my decision, and I won't change my mind. I messed up tonight, that's all."

"Geez, take a chill pill," she says, annoyed. "I'm only trying to help."

I sigh, guilt welling up my throat. "I'm sorry. I'm just feeling a bit on edge right now." It's only when I let the words out that I feel how tense my whole body is, my muscles pulled tight, vibrating with emotions threatening to overflow at any second.

I suck in a shaky breath, getting barely enough air to my lungs to force the next words out. "Might go for a run. Talk later, okay?"

"Sure... okay," Avery says. "Call me if you need me. Please."

"I will. Don't worry about me."

I hang up, put on my running shoes, and fly out the door and into the night, running as fast as I can, lungs burning, legs screaming, heart racing, the wind drying the tears streaming down my cheeks almost instantly.

Miles: You up?

I stare at the screen, lip between my teeth, waiting for those three little dots to appear. It's almost one a.m., and the chances of Riley responding are low, but after running my feelings out, I knew I couldn't leave things as they were.

Riley: Yup. Can't sleep. Neighbors are having a party next door.

I groan. Fucking teenagers partying in the middle of the week.

Miles: That sucks.

And before I can think twice, my thumbs move on the screen and press send.

Miles: You should come here. The only sounds are from Happy snoring at my feet.

"You really went there, Miles." My heart is in my throat when I see she's typing again. I half expect her to tell me to go fuck myself and find another job because she can't work with someone who's text-harassing her.

Riley: Haha, perfect lullaby. What are you doing still awake then?

"Thank god," I sigh.

Miles: I want to apologize for what happened in the pool tonight. I'm sorry, Ry. It wasn't professional of me. And we're friends. I got lost in the moment.

Riley: It's okay, I told you. I was half responsible for it. It was a very stressful day, wine was involved. We're good.

My heart makes a little cheering thump when I read her last words, wrapping me in a sweet cloud of relief. We're good.

Miles: Thank you. No more of that, promise.

Riley: You're right, no more. We can't afford it.

Damn. I know it's the right thing to do, but fuck if it doesn't feel like a cold shower pouring down on me. Even if she's right, even if I know there are no viable options, it still stings like a motherfucker to have the confirmation in front of my eyes.

Miles: I know. You have my word.

The three little dots dance on my screen, but after a few seconds, they disappear. I raise an eyebrow when they show up again, the back-and-forth continuing for the next five minutes.

"What are you afraid of telling me, Ry?"

Finally, the grey bubble pops up.

Riley: There's something I haven't told you.

My heartbeat skyrockets. *That's it?* That's what took her five minutes to type?

Miles: You know you can tell me anything.

Riley: When we were at our old firm, and I was still married... do you remember how we used to hang out sometimes?

I snort.

Miles: Of course.

Riley: Sean wasn't pleased about that. He wasn't happy about me going out with anybody, but with men, even colleagues like you, he dialed it up to a whole other level.

Miles: We never crossed any boundaries.

Riley: I know that. You know that. Deep down, he knows that. But that hasn't stopped him from implying we did. We need to be careful, Miles. I can't have him spreading rumors and tarnishing all our hard work.

I grunt. That fucking asshole. Even a year later, he's still controlling her like the master puppeteer he is, and I am sick of it. I'm sick of seeing her tremble like a leaf when his name is uttered, having him make threats as often as he takes a breath. Sick of him getting in my way.

If my name leaves his mouth, if he even thinks about doing what Riley's insinuating… I can't promise I'll behave.

Miles: We won't let him, Ry. Nothing is standing in our way. Not even him.

Riley: Oh, to have the confidence of a man.

Miles: It's really nice, you should try it.

I smile at her failed attempt to steer my attention away. And I don't know if it's more for me or because she's the one who needs it, but I play along, and the effect on my ragged breathing, my wild heartbeat, is immediate. Maybe it wasn't a failed attempt after all…

Riley: Don't need it, Milesy. I'm already plenty enough for you to handle.

I roll my eyes, sending her the corresponding emoji accompanied by a cupcake, then set my phone down.

That she is.

But she could throw anything at me, and I would welcome it with arms wide open.

SEVEN

Rain

Miles

Noah Reid plays softly on my speaker as I whip the lemon curd that'll fill my macarons. Happy is sprawled against the kitchen island as I follow Pierre Hermé's step-by-step recipe on my iPad.

I know it by heart, but these little delicacies are some of the most complex desserts in French cuisine to master. I still haven't, after years of batches, different almond powders, cold or room-temperature egg whites, you name it. I've tried each technique, and never, from one batch to the other, have I gotten the same result. Most of the time, they turn out okay, but never quite perfect.

And that annoys the shit out of me.

But since Tyler is coming over later, I don't have time to be difficult. Plus, Ty will eat them half-baked if he could. Let's just say he loses his dignity when macarons are involved.

The curd ready, I let it cool on the counter before placing it in the fridge for the next hour and then get started on the shell batter. Carefully, I blend the powdered sugar with the almond powder before working on the Italian meringue that serves as the base. When the syrup reaches 118° Celsius, I add the whipped egg whites and continue to whisk the mixture until it reaches 35°. Too cold, and the shell won't rise correctly in the oven. Too hot, and it'll dry and crack during baking time.

Like everything else in life, patisserie is a delicate balance. And at least, while I'm focused on complicated recipes like this one, my mind doesn't wander to places I don't want it to go. It stays in the moment, on the movement of my hands, the taste of the different ingredients.

It brings me back to before Avery was born, and my mom and I would bake for hours in the afternoons, trying new recipes, and perfecting old ones, always ending with me cleaning the batter bowls with a spoon.

When her mental health deteriorated after Avery's birth, I taught myself what I didn't know and would bake for hours, coming up with elaborated cakes for my sister's birthdays, proudly showing my mom my creations. Like a thread still tethering me to her and those moments together.

And in baking, I found peace of mind. As if following a recipe's clear instructions gave me the clarity I needed to organize my thoughts.

I transfer the batter into a piping bag and carefully dress them in a round shape on the baking sheet. I let them sit for thirty minutes before I put them in the oven, crossing my fingers as hard as I can that they'll form the iconic feet that make the macaron shells perfect.

I snap a photo and hit send to Avery.

Miles: Look what you're missing on.

Avery: Are you trying to make me board a plane to Toronto? Because it's working.

I wouldn't mind having her here. In fact, I wish she were here right now. My sister gets more excited than anyone about my creations.

As I start cleaning, my phone vibrates on the counter, and Peter's name catches my attention. I set the bowl down, drying my hands with the towel sitting on my shoulder.

"Peter, what a surprise."

"Hey, Miles, it's good to hear you," he says. When Riley and I were still working at the old firm, Peter was one of our most esteemed clients. He owns a winery in Ontario that's currently dominating the market.

"How have you been?" I say, curious as to why he's calling me on a Sunday afternoon.

"Good. Business is booming. Demand is at an all-time high. We're dreaming big this year. I have a shitload of work, and I believe I've found the perfect firm to help me with it."

"What do you mean? Are you thinking about leaving Sean's?" I feign ignorance. Riley and Peter had lunch last month, a week after we opened the firm. I know he's considering a switch.

He chuckles on the other end of the line. "Yes, I am, though I'm sure you've heard. I called Riley yesterday to let her know I'd like to schedule a meeting with you, and thought it only fair to reach out to you as well."

"I appreciate it, Pete."

"I have a lot riding on the winery's success this year, so let's see what you guys have to offer."

"You know me, I won't let you down." And I won't, but damn if this doesn't raise the stakes.

"I know," he says. "I want to make it clear that I'm expecting a lot from this proposal. I know your work ethic, but it's also a risk for me to jump ship."

I nod. "Completely understandable. You won't be disappointed."

"Excellent," Peter says. "Talk soon!"

We hang up, a heavy feeling sitting on my chest. We can't screw this up.

EIGHT

Cinderella's Dead

Riley

*I*f I had to describe in a few words this past month, the ones that'd come to mind would be chaotic, exhilarating, intense, exhausting. I wouldn't say everything has gone smoothly, we've had to put a few fires out here and there, but overall, the firm's launch has been a massive success.

We've been drowning in requests from past clients who decided to follow us on this crazy new adventure, but also new businesses who've heard about us through word of mouth. Miles and I know this field like the back of our hand, and we know how to play and use it to our advantage when it matters. Let's just say I was able to call out a few favors on my end, and Miles's spotless reputation sealed the deal for many others.

It also helped that our company was featured in an article in *Hill's Time* on the top five new Canadian public relations firms to keep an eye on this year, and that Melany Lawrence, renown business journalist for the *Globe and Mail,* did a feature on women in business and was kind enough to include me.

That kind of spotlight is great, but it's also making me nervous. I haven't heard back from Sean yet, but I'm sure he's steaming right now, probably treating his employees like shit for letting clients get away when he's the only one to blame. It doesn't matter that he's a big name in PR, he lacks one crucial quality that I know our clients crave: empathetic understanding. Nobody wants to deal with an angry and agitated tiger in a cage. Sure, he goes after what he wants, but he doesn't give a shit about what he needs to do to get it, or who he hurts in the process.

I leave my office to find Miles in his. Since the pool incident, he and I haven't had time together one-on-one. It's both a blessing and a curse because, on the one hand, I don't have the mental capacity to deal with the ramifications of that day, but on the other, I've been replaying the moment nonstop, and my resolve is hanging by a thread. Nay, a fiber of a thread.

Especially when he's wearing that tailored dark teal suit over a white shirt like today, accentuating his brown hair and beard to perfection. I love that he's not too shy to wear bold colors like this. Yesterday, it was a crimson burgundy, and earlier this week, dark purple. And he was a total knockout every time.

I knock on the door, his gaze snapping to me. "Heya, do you have a minute?"

Heya? Really, Ry?

Miles smiles mockingly. "Can you greet me like this every day from now on, please?"

I roll my eyes. "Ha-ha, okay yeah, got it."

"No, no, no, better! Let's do 'howdy partner' tomorrow, okay? And maybe after that, we can try 'G'day mate!' What do you say?"

He's trying so hard to contain his laughter, but I can hear his snicker from the doorway. Oh, he thinks he's being real smart. "Works for me perfectly, Milesy."

His smile falls instantly. He clears his throat, looking behind my shoulder.

"What's wrong, Milesy?" I say a bit louder.

"Okay, okay, you win," he says, rushing to close the door behind me. He walks back to his chair, shaking his head. "Effective, I'll admit. Well done, Fletcher."

"You make it too easy," I shoot back, my eyes catching the stretch of his shirt around his biceps when he leans against the desk.

"You wanted to say something, Ry, or did you come here to mock me and to get a good look at how an office is supposed to look?"

He will never let this go.

"According to your standards," I say.

Everything in my chaos is where it should be. I wouldn't be able to function properly in this very neat and organized structure that he likes for himself. One day, I made the terrible mistake of stopping by his office, leaving a sticky note telling him I had a lunch meeting and not putting the pen back exactly where I'd found it. I heard about it for weeks. About all the "clutter" I left on his desk and how I "didn't care for his workspace."

"I did want to tell you something," I add.

Something big.

Potentially risky. Arguably scary. Definitely worth it.

High risk, high reward, right?

"I had a very interesting call with a former client of ours this weekend. Turns out they're not particularly pleased with how their account is being run over at Myers and Associates, and they're interested in coming over to us."

"Let me guess," Miles interjects. "Does it have anything to do with a certain Ontario winery with whom you had lunch last month?"

"Mm-hmm," I say, nodding.

"Peter called you back, didn't he?"

"He wants us to put a work proposal together for Winsome Winery."

"I know," he says and winks. "Peter called me yesterday to give me the heads up."

Of course. I should've figured. He and Peter used to work well together, and even though I was the one supervising the account, I barely did anything on it. "Well, it's good news for us. I think we have an excellent chance. Obviously, I want you to take the lead on this since you had the relationship with Peter before."

Miles nods once. "So what's the goal? They still want to expand in Canada?"

"Right now, they want to target the Quebec market," I say. "From what Peter told me, they're looking to do government outreach and try to better understand the legal province's obligations, but also get an idea of the demand and survey consumer interest in their product."

"I'm sure they'll have a solid consumer base over there." Miles chuckles. "What with all the French people immigrating from France to Quebec."

"Exactly."

Miles scribbles something on his notepad, or more accurately, he neatly writes the date, subject matter and starts a bullet point list of what he needs to do. The note looks like it's just been made in a design software. Even his handwriting is flawless. Sigh.

"All right, boss, I'll get right on it." He winks at me, again, and I melt a little bit more in my chair. It's so easy to give in to temptation when I'm around him. The night in the pool rushes through the forefront of my mind, how good it felt to feel desired by him, have his body close to mine. One more situation like that and I'll have no steer left in my stride.

It's dangerous for me to be around Miles Clark. But I will have to make it work, one way or another.

NINE
Hey Girl

Riley

F inally, after an hour stuck in traffic, I arrive home. As soon as I step into my house, I am greeted by a sight that is all too familiar—duffle bags and hiking shoes strewn across the floor, doubling the mess I had already created. I smile. I didn't know she was going to be back so soon.

"Char, you're here?" I walk toward my backyard to find my sister lounging in the late afternoon sun in a bikini. The book she was reading—*Daisy Jones and The Six*—is open and resting on her chest, while her beach hat covers most of her face.

"Char?" I get closer, but still no response. That's when I notice the AirPods in her ears.

Slowly, I bend down and take one out. "Hey," I whisper in her ear.

Charlee startles before shrieking loudly. "Ry, hiii!" She gets up and wraps me in her arms. She smells like summer and flowers, probably from her Monoi sunscreen. She also looks like she lost weight. I kiss her cheek, feeling how hollow they are.

"It's good to see you, Char," I say. I won't get straight into it; I know my sister better than that. She's like a wild cat. One sudden move, and she gets scared away. "I didn't know you were getting in today."

She tosses her hair up into a messy bun. "Yeah, we had a last-minute change in our schedule. There's a fire in Australia, so we had to come back from California a bit earlier to get organized. We're back out tomorrow."

"Oh wow, fire in Australia, huh? Why are they sending you there? Isn't it a bit too dangerous?"

"Because it's my job?"

"Oh yeah, duh," I joke, slapping my forehead. "Give me one minute to get in my bikini, and we'll have a little pool and rosé sesh."

I head back in, giddy and excited to have an impromptu night with my sister. God, I missed her. I never get to see her enough. I love to see her doing a job she's so passionate about, I just wish she would be home more so I could feel like I still have a family sometimes. But she wouldn't be happy being stuck here, working a nine-to-five job in an office… She's not meant to be trapped in place; she should roam free in the wild, where she thrives. That's Charlee.

The past few years have been even worse since Mom passed away. I think it really hit her that we didn't have any family left except each other, and to my surprise, she did the opposite of what I expected her to do; she ran farther away from me. She and Mom were inseparable. Two peas in a pod, more best friends than mother-and-daughter. When she got sick, Charlee became this stoic robot, fleeing every situation requiring her to be in the same room as Mom. I became the one to take care of her, bringing her to her doctors' appointments and watching her suffer through chemo. Mom was the glue that held our family together, but she was slowly slipping away, and the two pieces of the puzzle she created drifted apart.

When she passed, I didn't see Charlee for a whole year. I don't know if it was her way of coping with it because we've never talked about it. All I know is that my wild and lively sister became a stranger to me, and despite all my efforts to keep her in my life, she didn't want any part in it, and honestly, I couldn't blame her for it. We all grieve differently, and she dealt with it by closing in on herself and running away.

But I was the one left to deal with the funeral, my loneliness, and my grief. Counting on Sean wasn't even an option. He stayed an hour at the funeral before leaving to golf with a client. After that, he told me something along the lines of "everybody dies one day; you have to accept it and move on," and like the fool in love I was back then, I told myself that he was right, and that it was his way of supporting me.

Weirdly, my divorce brought my sister and me closer. And right now, all that matters is that Charlee is here, in my life again, being my sister again, and we are going to have a fantastic night, just the two of us if it's the last thing we do.

Once in my two-piece, I join my sister, who's waist-deep in the water, a bottle of wine in hand and a few slices of watermelon in a plate on the side.

I exhale when I enter the water. "It's been quite the day, I'm really glad you're here." I pour us two glasses and grab a slice. "Okay, so what's new with you? Tell me everything."

Charlee dips under the water, wetting her auburn hair. With the sun beating down on her face, her freckles are more prominent, giving her that "kid looking for trouble" expression. She looks so young like this, it makes me want to grab her by the shoulders, hold her against me, and never let her go. Protect her against fucked up men and a system that is all too often biased against women, but I know she doesn't need me for that. Our mother taught us to be strong and always stand up for ourselves—something I forgot to do for a long time.

"The crew and I have been in California for the past two weeks doing a feature on climate change and the challenges they're facing with recent droughts."

"Sounds interesting. Are you the one writing it?"

"Yeah, with another *Wild Planet* correspondent who's already in L.A. But with the fires in Australia, we didn't get to finish shooting what we needed." Charlee swims to the donut float and hoists herself onto it, plopping to face the warm June sun.

I dive underwater, and prop my elbows up when I come next to her. "So you'll have to go back?" I ask, splashing my feet gently.

Charlee shakes her head. "Nah. Boss said we're making it a bigger story, with all the weather-related disasters happening. It's going to be a lot of work, but looks like we're doing a full cover on climate change. And I'll be leading it."

"What?" I squeal. "That's amazing! So what's the plan now?"

"Basically, the Australia fires will be the starting point," Charlee says. "Then, we're going to travel to different places around the world and show the impacts of climate change, working with locals, experts, and *Wild Planet* journalists in different countries. It's going to be huge, Ry. Like, Netflix-huge."

I arch an eyebrow, taking a sip of my drink. "What do you mean?"

Char wiggles on her donut, making the plastic squeak underneath her. "Netflix is in talks with our execs about making a series on our travels and stories. I'll lead the assignments and write most of the articles, and they will use my work to build a TV show. They want a filming crew following us around everywhere. Can you imagine, Ry? A filming crew, following me!"

"Wait. Am I going to have a famous sister?"

Char laughs. "I mean, I don't know! Everything is still in the development stage right now."

"I can't believe it. You. On my TV. I'm so proud of you," I say with sincerity.

"Thanks," she says. "It's going to be a hectic year if it works out, but the payoff will be worth it."

"Well, make sure you're taking care of yourself, okay? Proper meals, lots of water," I say, gauging her reaction.

She turns her face away from the sun and looks at me, her sunglasses sliding down her nose. "Why do you say that?" she asks, her tone already on the defensive.

I shrug, eyes on the water gently rippling around me. "Oh, no reason. I know when you get into something, you tend to hyper-focus on it. I get it, I'm the same way. Just don't forget to take some breaks and get some food in you, that's all."

"I eat, Riley."

I put my hands up. "Okay, okay. I can't help but worry, that's all. The last time I saw you, you must have at least been ten pounds heavier. I just want you to take care of yourself in all this craziness."

"Riley," Charlee says slowly. "You don't have to be Mom anymore, okay? I'm old enough to know what I'm doing. I'm in the best shape of my life."

It's not like I'm fully reassured, but when it comes to my sister, I don't think there will ever be a time when I'll be perfectly at peace.

I nod, dropping the subject. "I'm so proud of you, Char," I say once more. "You want something, and you go for it."

She lays her hand on my forearm. "I had one hell of an example growing up."

"Thank you," I say, squeezing her hand in mine.

"I mean it. It feels so good to see you taking charge of your life again. You weren't yourself for so long."

"I know. I'm sorry. I'm still trying to adjust. Rediscover the things I love and all that."

I've been filling my free time with so many new things. Hiking, painting, crocheting, spinning class, yoga—you name it. Everything I did in the past ten years was usually with Sean. I used to spend hours at home just reading... It's hard to believe I used to go through hundreds of books in a year. It got to the point where I had to dedicate a whole room in my house to fit my bookshelves.

But having my own hobbies was always too tricky because of Sean's irrational paranoia. So I socialized with his friends, took part in his passions. I forgot the things that made me excited about the process. These days, kickboxing is what's keeping my head above water. I release more tension in my weekly hour-long class than I ever did golfing with Sean and his snobby friends on a Sunday afternoon.

"Don't apologize. Sometimes I wish I could go back in time and say or do something before things got as bad as they did."

"It's not on you, Char. It's not even on me. It's on Sean." Something I have to remind myself constantly. "Trust me, the past few months have put his character on perfect display."

My sister frowns as she slips off her donut, landing next to me. "What do you mean?"

"Remember how I told you he was texting me regularly?" I sigh. "He's been trying to steamroll me, threatening to spread rumors that I was having an affair with Miles while we were married. He's trying to get to my reputation."

"The nerve of this guy," Charlee grumbles. "Did you tell him to fuck off?"

"I'm trying to take the high road. I don't want to go toe-to-toe with him. And I already have to handle one overprotective alpha idiot, so I'm busy enough as it is."

"Overprotective alpha man," Charlee coos. "Tell me more, please."

We swim toward the pool stairs and grab our towels.

"Miles." I hide a smile. I know that my sister is secretly shipping us, and I'm sure she's going to have plenty to say about this new development.

"Ohh, Miles. I see." She wiggles her eyebrows, drying her hair. It looks like a burning fire with the sun's rays filtering through her strands. "He does give off alpha vibes, you're right."

I take a sip of my wine, warmth flowing inside me as images of Miles taking charge intrude my mind. Sweet Jesus.

"He does, yeah. But he's not what I need right now."

Charlee snorts. "I think he's exactly what you need. Someone who uplifts you any chance they get. Puts you in your place when you need it, because we both know you can get carried away. Loves you unconditionally the way you deserve. Gives you incredible, mind-blowing sex."

"Can you stop?" I say, my voice climbing higher. "I don't want to think about my colleague giving me incredible, mind-blowing sex." I shake my head. "You don't get it. I've worked so hard to be free of Sean and build something of my own. I'm not about to throw that all out the window for a man."

"Alpha man," Charlee corrects.

"Whatever." I roll my eyes. "Same difference. Order of importance goes: my well-being and yours, my firm, the environment, social injustice, and alllll the way down there"—I point to the ground—"men."

"One day," she says, wrapping her arms around my neck. It's like when we were little when she'd call, and I would pick her up from wherever she'd gotten herself into trouble. She'd put her tiny arms around me just like that before kissing me on my cheek, thanking me for always keeping her safe. Right now, though, it feels like the roles are reversed. "You'll realize that you can have it all, and that nothing, and no one, can dim your bright light."

Charlee pulls me against her, and for the first time since I can remember, I let my little sister comfort me, dropping my walls and the maternal role I've always played.

TEN
You

Miles

"*R*y!" I barge into her office. She's seated at her desk, her blond hair gathered into a tight high ponytail, long enough for the strands to brush the emerald-green suit she's wearing today. There are sticky notes ev-er-y-where. Piles of papers as high as the computer's screen. Books on books. Files opened and mixed together. And is that a salad stuck between her keyboard and mouse?

"Wow, hey! What's up?" she asks, her glasses perched on the bridge of her nose.

"Yeah, sorry 'bout that." I fall into the seat in front of her. "Your office is a mess."

She scoffs. "Was that the thing so urgent you couldn't wait to tell me?" She takes a bite of her salad. "And it's not. I know where everything is."

I raise an eyebrow.

"Try me."

I scan the room. "Your U of T mug."

She replies without breaking eye contact. "On my left, behind my laptop sleeve."

That was an easy one. "Okay, Fletcher. Your makeup bag?"

"Second shelf behind me, between my cactus and the citrus candle," she responds in a matter of seconds.

Okay, she's better at this than I'd have thought. "How do you do it? It looks like a tornado swept through the place."

Riley smirks. "I told you it's an organized mess." She shrugs. "It works for me."

"What about clients, huh? Where did you put the Winsome Winery file?"

This one gets her thinking for a second, but she pulls it from under the pile of books on her desk. "Right. Here."

"Well, keep it close."

"Why?"

"Peter got back to me. They want to meet with us this afternoon."

Riley jumps off her chair. "What, really? They do?"

"Damn right!"

"Oh my god!" Riley comes around her desk and pulls me into a hug.

I freeze for a moment before my arms come around her, reveling in her warmth. It's only a congratulatory gesture, but my mind is flooded with a thousand thoughts, none that include "friendly co-worker." I close my eyes and let myself imagine my hands traveling up her arms, massaging her shoulders, cupping her face while my lips meet hers.

"Sorry," she whispers, blushing as she steps back. "It's a good sign, right?"

I slip my hands in my pockets. "I think so, yeah. Peter seemed pretty excited about it on the phone this morning."

"That's an amazing catch for the firm, Miles. I can't believe we pulled it off."

"We were amazing at last week's pitch meeting. I'm not surprised."

Riley sits back in her chair and crosses her legs, her skirt riding up with the movement, drawing my focus from her eyes to her full thighs. "We make an amazing team."

I don't know how many times she's said that to me over the past few months, like she's just realizing how good we are together, or she's trying to convince herself of it.

"We do," I say, holding her gaze. There's a finality in my voice, a simple truth giving away way more than I intend to. I know she notices, but neither of us says anything, the seconds stretching between us as if time has suddenly lost all its meaning.

"So," I say, clearing my throat. "Peter and the team should be here in about an hour. I'll get the conference room ready. Let's run this home."

"MILES, RILEY, SO HAPPY TO SEE YOU both again," Peter says, shaking our hands.

I pat him on the back and lead him and Rachel, his PR director, into the conference room. Riley gives her a warm hug. The sheer amount of time we spent on their brand over the years has brought the two of them close.

"Glad you got back to us, Peter. Rachel, welcome. Please, take a seat."

We all find our seats around the oval table, Riley at the hem, me at her side. Sydney fills the glasses with fresh water while our guests settle in.

"So, Peter," Riley says. "What brings you here?"

"Well, as you know, we've been wanting to branch out of Ontario and, more broadly, Canada." Peter turns to his colleague. "Rachel, do you want to continue?"

"Of course," she says. She pushes two folders in front of Riley and me. "We love what you presented us with last week and your plan to help us expand our operations. Reaching out to stores across the country and working on our marketing tactics is exactly what we need. If you wouldn't mind opening the folder to the second page."

We do as she says, and I quickly glance at the page. Paris?

Rachel continues. "Our meeting last week sparked an intensive brainstorming session on our team, and since we loved your ideas to promote our brand, we want to sign with you and expand on the work we initially planned."

"We've been invited to the International Wine Festival in Paris," Peter says. "We want you to come with us and help get our products out on the French market. Ideally, we'd love an exclusivity contract with a winery in France, but we can discuss the details once we get the ball rolling. We would be there for two weeks: a full week of Festival and another to hopefully secure partnerships we will have built during the festival. So, what do you say? Anyone up for a Parisian summer?"

I glance at Riley, who seems as stunned as I am.

Peter folds his hands and straightens up. "It's really quite simple. You impressed us. This is a massive opportunity for Winsome Wines. We want you at the festival in Paris."

That was... not expected. But holy shit, what a huge opportunity for the firm.

Peter continues. "I know it adds a fair amount of work for you, and if you don't have the resources—"

"Oh, we have them, don't worry about that," Riley chimes in. "Sorry, we're a little caught off guard by your proposal. We weren't expecting this, but it's great news. We'll be more than happy to help you with this, right, Miles?"

"Absolutely. Peter, can you leave it with us for a few days? We'll have to figure out who'll go with you and revise the contract accordingly."

Peter shakes his head. "No, no. I want you both with me. This is a big move for our business, and I want the best people on the job. We don't get these types of opportunities often, so we'd like you to handle meetings with potential resellers and coordinate an impactful communication strategy that will award us a shit ton of contracts."

Riley and I exchange a look, and it's clear we both have our doubts about his offer. Fletcher and Clark is still new, and he's telling us he wants to pull us away for two weeks? What about our other clients? What if there's a crisis? Who's going to be responsible for managing the whole team, the clients' requests? Adam will be here, of course, and he has enough experience to keep the business afloat, but still. It's a lot of work, and it's a lot to ask.

"Look," Peter says. "I don't need an answer now. The festival isn't for another month. Take until the end of the week to get back to me with a yes." He winks at us. "As for our contract, I'll have my assistant contact you, but I have no objection to whatever amount you feel is appropriate. We'll arrange to pay for your travel to Paris and lodging, if that helps in your decision."

"Let us discuss it, and we'll get back to you by the end of the week," Riley says as she stands up.

Riley walks Peter and Rachel to the door. "Thanks for coming, we'll be in touch. Rachel, we're still on for five?"

Rachel squeezes Riley's arm. "Looking forward to catching up, lady."

"Think of all the delicious pastries," Peter yells as they walk out. The pastries, yeah, sure. But also a huge undertaking that I didn't see coming.

"OH. MY. GOD," RY SAYS as she walks back into the conference room. "That was… incredible!"

"Awful," I say at the same time.

We both laugh, but then Riley registers what I said. "What? Miles, did you hear what he wants? It's huge for us."

"I know, I know, but Ry…" I know I need to tread lightly. "We can't both leave the firm for two weeks. It's corporate suicide."

"Why not?" she asks, legitimately confused. "Adam can handle it. We'll have phones, we'll be able to check in regularly, we can even take meetings from there if needed. We're not going to disappear off the map for two weeks. France has internet, you know."

I know she's trying to lighten the mood because I'm sure she can read all over my face how stressed out I am about this. So many things can go wrong. We've been working on this proposal for months, making sure it's perfect, and now Peter expects us to develop a complete strategic communication and marketing plan to win over the French wine market and get his winery an exclusive contract, all in under a month? Might as well sign our firm's death certificate myself.

I think I may be spiraling here.

"We need to really think about this and carefully look at the pros and cons. Because this will mean our focus will be on Peter and Winsome Wines for two whole weeks. It's the future of our firm that we're putting on the line." I take a breath. This image is too daunting for me to let sink in. "I'm not saying we shouldn't say yes, I'm just saying let's give it a minute to see if it can even work. Let's brainstorm the shit out of this, Fletcher."

The conviction in my tone is lacking because inside, I'm terrified. And frankly, I'm a bit surprised Riley's so quick to give it the go-ahead. I'm aware of the warning pulling at my gut, despite how much it lights me up to see her excited.

Riley sits down, and a whiff of her jasmine perfume reaches me. I briefly close my eyes, enjoying the serenity it brings me. That's when I realize that two weeks in Paris means two weeks with Riley, nonstop. Two weeks in the most romantic city on earth, seeing her every minute of every day. Not that it would be a substantial difference to our days in Toronto, but it would mean late meetings, breakfast together, and I'm guessing a few networking events.

Ry lays her hand on mine. "Miles, hey." I raise my eyes to hers. "We're the dream team, you and I. You know that. Don't forget that we landed almost all the big clients at Myers and Associates. I know it's unexpected and a lot to process." She pauses. "But it's also exciting. Peter has one of the most renowned wineries in Canada. It would be the kick we need to be recognized among the top firms in Toronto. It would put our names out there. We're competitive overachievers, you and I. Remember when we were putting our business plan together? We set high goals for ourselves. We said, 'our first million before year one.' This is it, Miles. This is the client who will take us to that mil. So, like you said, let's brainstorm the shit out of this, Clark. What do you say?"

She's right. And her ambition, her drive, is all over her face. She is a force to be reckoned with, only in her element when she's faced with the biggest challenges. I smile because fuck does she have a lot of confidence. But that's my biggest turn on.

Some people might call her cocky; I call her brilliant. And the way she has with words, the way she makes your doubts evaporate in the snap of her fingers—neither one of us is surprised at what I say next. "Okay, let's do this."

And my reward is the bright smile those five little words put on her face.

ELEVEN

Libre

Riley

"*I*'m glad Peter reached out when he heard you'd started your own firm," Rachel says as we leave the crowded bar, having just ordered our drinks.

We find a sand-colored sofa on the rooftop of Baro, a trendy Mexican restaurant on King Street, and wait for our spicy margaritas under the ivy-covered bamboo roof.

I lean back, sinking deeper into the comfort of the cushions, and cross my legs. "Us too. We loved working with you, but I mostly miss getting drinks with you after work." I toss a playful grin her way.

Rachel bobs her head. "I second that. And I have to say, you owned the room back there. Peter was drinking in every word. It's nice to see that side of you."

"Which one?"

"The leader."

The waiter interrupts and sets our drinks down, handing me a little scrap of paper.

"From the man over there at the bar." He nods to a guy with perfect hair, perfect jaw, shirt rolled up to the elbows, highlighting perfectly toned forearms, resting on perfect muscular thighs. The man is a walking snack.

I look down at the piece of paper.

"Drinks on me. And if you ever want to drink them with me…"

His phone number follows. Bold move. And I won't lie, it's working a little bit. I smile, tucking the note in my pocket.

"Secret admirer?" Rachel coos.

"Apparently." I chuckle. "It's a nice feeling. I haven't dated since before my ex. So like…" I grimace. Okay, wow, that hurts. "Ten years?"

"Well, looks like you've still got it." She smirks.

I glance over my shoulder and find Perfect Guy raising his glass slightly, smiling his perfectly aligned teeth straight at me. Busted. I nod, flushed, raising mine before taking a refreshing sip, coating my lips with the salt from the rim.

It's nice to feel wanted. Desired. I remember when I thought being wanted meant Sean keeping a possessive hand on my lower back. I learned later that it wasn't because he was craving my touch but because he wanted to keep me in his line of sight. Wherever he went, I needed to be, right under his thumb. But back then, in the beginning, at least, I didn't see it that way.

Sean knew how to charm his way around every situation. And I fell for it.

Helplessly, desperately fell for it.

"*My boss is so fucking hot, Char, I've been staring at his ass all day.*" That's what I'd texted my sister after my first day at Myers and Associates. Did I know what a horrible idea it was to flirt and ogle the CEO of my new job? Of course, I knew. But my attraction wasn't one-sided, and even if the little voice in my head told me to pull hard on the brakes, my body was fully committed to getting its way.

And when Sean has his sight set on something, or someone… You better believe he'll go all in to get it. Every date he took me on was better than the last. We would hit the most popular restaurants, attend the most exclusive events, drink the best champagne.

At the time, I couldn't see the difference between his desire to impress me, to shower me with love, and his need to ensure my early dependence on him.

So I dated him, madly in love with the man he was pretending to be. Carefree, respectful, loved and looked up to by his peers, friends, and family.

The first years of my marriage were blissful. I should have known then that the other shoe would drop because life is rarely like a fairy tale.

It started with innocent comments about my appearance. "Are you really going to wear that dress tonight?" and "Why did you cut your hair? You looked better when it was longer."

I didn't pay much attention to it at the time. It hurt when he'd deliver the blow, but it would never last long before he went back to praising and adoring me.

But then, the little comments here and there morphed into daily criticism, blame, and accusations. "Are you sure you want dessert after the meal you just had?" or "I saw the way you flirted with that guy at the Christmas party, you made me look like a fool" and, as if to twist the knife, "If you had worked on this account better, maybe we would have signed the client." That last one did a number on my confidence professionally, and it took me years to recover from it. I'd never questioned my career abilities before Sean, and that stung.

Three years into our marriage, I was completely cut off from my friends, barely talked to Charlee, and my days were reduced to Sean and work. The changes happened so slowly it had barely been noticeable. And Sean would always act like he had my best intentions at heart, and I was so in love… I left my judgment at the door and gave him my unconditional trust.

When Miles came on board, he became the one person outside my marriage I could escape to. Sean couldn't prevent me from seeing him since we worked on many accounts together. I knew he didn't like me hanging out with Miles, he told me so enough times. But I held on. I refused to sacrifice what little reprieve I had found in Miles.

I hit my tipping point almost two years ago when Sean humiliated me in front of our colleagues for something that had been entirely out of my control. One of our clients—

whom we'd trained and prepared extensively for a press conference following a cyberattack—got up on stage in front of the media and politicians and went completely off-script after a journalist asked a provoking question.

The whole thing turned into a PR nightmare, and while I tried to save it as best I could, Sean wanted none of it. All he saw was incompetence, weakness, and failure.

When I came back to the firm later that afternoon, he called a meeting with the whole team and belittled me in front of my colleagues. He pinned the entire thing on me, openly blaming my incompetence in adequately preparing the client for probing journalists. He used me as an example on how not to handle run-of-the-mill situations like these.

And Miles, I still remember, had gone deathly still during that meeting.

When it ended, I ran to the bathroom and collapsed on the floor, crying like I never had before.

"Ry?" A soft knock on the bathroom door. "Ry, it's me, Miles," he said. "Are you all right?"

"I'm fine," I said between sniffles. "Thanks."

"Can I come in?"

I weighed my options, the chances of him leaving me alone. After a few seconds, I got up, splashed some water on my face, and told him to come in.

"Hey," he said, a frown on his face.

"Hi," I replied, leaning against the sink.

"That was rough back there. Are you okay?"

I shrugged. "Mm-hmm."

Miles took a hesitant step toward me. "Look, the day's over. Why don't we go get some drinks and talk, yeah?"

He squeezed both my arms, a simple gesture that softened the bruises on my heart.

We did go out for drinks then, and I remember how comfortable I felt spilling my guts out to him. With a simple question, a simple "so what's going on with you two?" he unlocked years of loneliness, isolation, and deprecation. I gave him the broad strokes, and as I was talking, I realized how much I'd been putting up with. The snarky and demeaning comments, the constant blame.

I couldn't believe what I was hearing, and yet, the words were coming from my own mouth. Such a strange sensation, I thought then, almost like who I was deep inside was finally waking up, and glanced at the shell of what was left of myself in shock.

When I got home that night, feeling more like myself than I had in the last few years, I was determined to face my husband and confront him about his behavior, Miles's words ringing in my head as clearly as if he were here, repeating them to me.

Be the strong woman I know you are, Ry.

But when I reached for the door handle and tried to open it, I was met with a locked door. I tried again, jiggling it more forcefully, but still nothing. I didn't have my keys on me, I'd left them at the office in my hurry to leave.

I pulled out my phone and called Sean. He picked up on the first ring.

"Hey, I'm outside. Can you open the door?"

"Where were you?" His voice was gruff, and I could tell he was pissed.

"I went out with some colleagues after work," I said flatly. "Can you open it, please?"

"Who?" The word had never sounded so cold.

"Open up, Sean, we can talk after."

A long sigh came through the phone. "Riley, I love you, you know that. But I won't open the door until you tell me which colleagues you went out with."

The realization that he was keeping me out of my own home dawned on me. I took a deep breath. I knew it wouldn't go over well. "Miles and I bumped into each other when I was heading out of the office. We got drinks. That's it."

The line went silent for a while, our breathing the only sound betraying that we were still both on the phone.

"Open the door now, Sean," I said, fear and nervousness growing inside me.

When he spoke, his tone was eerily calm. "I'm sorry, Ry, I don't recognize you anymore. My wife, the person I love most in the world, the person who I expect to be by my side, supporting me, would not have gone out with a colleague instead of coming home. Not to mention, one who openly flirts with her in front of everybody when he knows damn well she's happily married. I won't let a stranger into our home."

"What are you talking ab—" The line went dead.

I tried calling him back several times, my hands shaking from the cold and the unease creeping through me. What kind of game was he playing?

On the fifth try, he picked up. "Riley, please don't make this more difficult than it has to be."

"What do you mean, Sean?" I exclaimed, stunned. "Let me in!"

"You need to think about your choices, Riley, I'm sorry. I can't have you in the house tonight. We can re-evaluate in the morning."

On that, he hung up again.

I stared at my phone, the door to my house locked, tongue-tied. It was late, and there I was, locked out of my own house. I pounded on the door for several minutes, but Sean never answered.

After twenty minutes of yelling, crying, and kicking the door with everything in me, I decided to stop making a spectacle of myself. I got in my car and drove to a hotel downtown. I got myself a room—the most expensive they had—and put it on Sean's credit card. Once in the presidential suite, I cried until every drop of water in my body went dry. But then, I swore to myself that my piece-of-shit husband would get nothing more from me.

I pulled myself together and ordered the most extravagant late-night room service. I went to bed with the dreaded certainty that the life I had spent years building was crumbling all around me, but that, one day, I would be strong enough to rise from my own ashes.

The following morning, I filed for divorce.

"Are you going to stare at that gorgeous man all day?"

I startle, turning back to find Rachel smirking at me.

"Sorry." I shake my head and decide to play along for lack of a better explanation. "Got hypnotized there for a second."

"You didn't hear what I just said, then?" She chuckles in her drink.

"I'm the worst, I'm sorry."

Rachel waves me off. "No, no, I get it. I'd be lost in those forearms too."

We glance back, chuckling when we both let out a small sigh.

"I admire you," Rachel said. "That's what I said before I lost you."

I must be looking at her with a weird expression on my face because she laughs.

"What? I do! It takes courage to do what you did, quit and start all over again, and be successful at it. We work in a man's world. It's inspiring seeing women like you stand their ground in front of an army of dicks."

I nearly choke. Well, that's a side I didn't know Rachel had. And I gotta say, I love it.

"I don't know about 'standing my ground,' but I'm trying anyway. You're doing an amazing job yourself. You're what, twenty-six? And look at you, already Peter's right-hand woman."

"Ah, twenty-eight, but I appreciate you giving me back two years. You know," she says more hesitantly. "There are whispers about why you decided to leave Sean's firm and, well… get divorced too."

"Oh?"

I hold my breath for a few seconds. Did he actually go through with his threat?

"Don't worry," she rushes to add. "Nothing for you to worry about. More... him, actually. That's part of the reason why Peter decided to switch firms. That and the fact that we were being treated like second-tier clients."

I hate that people are speculating about my private life. Am I ever going to be freed of Sean's shadow? "What have you heard?"

Rachel looks sheepish for a second. "Just things in general about his... behavior. With you and other junior employees. Female ones. I have some friends over there that rant to me every now and then." She reaches out and pats the back of my hand softly. "Don't worry, this is staying between us. I would never betray a fellow woman's trust."

I smile sweetly. "Oh... well, yeah. Things got pretty bad toward the end. I don't know how I stayed asleep so long with him at the wheel."

Rachel crosses her arms on her chest. "I know the feeling," she murmurs.

"You do?"

"I was in a similar situation a few years ago. We weren't working together, thank god, but I sacrificed a lot for him. Gave him some of the best years of my life. I let it go too far." She sighs, fidgeting with her sunglasses. "I don't know exactly what you've been through, but I can relate."

"There's so much I could and want to say to you, Rachel," I say. "Maybe when work has dialed down a bit, we can have a girls' night."

She nods at that, and my heart swells. She's young. Too young to have gone through this. She reminds me of how I was, and I'd do anything to go back and help that young, easily impressed girl who didn't know better and got charmed by a man who had the power to make her dreams come true. If I can offer a dash of guidance to Rachel now... I'm going to jump at the chance.

"But you're wrong when you say that you gave away your best years. Twenties are overrated and awful, and honestly, depressing. I spent so long figuring out who I was during my twenties, getting to know myself as an adult. Your twenties are for making mistakes and learning from them." I chuckle. "Your thirties are where it's at, trust me."

Rachel makes a sour face. "I don't want to turn thirty."

"You do! Thirty is the new twenty, or whatever the fuck the saying is. I promise you, there's no better feeling than knowing who you are, what you want in life, and refusing to compromise on your goals."

"See? You're inspiring, Riley."

I wave her off. "Not more than you are. Look at what you've accomplished in such a short period. You're a strong woman, Rach." I pause.

"Thank you, friend. That means a lot."

Warmth fills my heart. She doesn't know how monumental this is for me, so I'm trying to play it cool and not scare her away.

I've felt alone for so long. Sean isolated me from my friends and family so he could be the only one I had to rely on. At first, my friends reached out, but as I kept blowing them off, they stopped, not before putting together a sort of intervention where they all expressed their worries for me and how toxic they thought my marriage had become.

I was so fucking pissed they'd do that to me. I remember leaving after a shouting match with my oldest friend. After that, I've never heard of them ever again. I can't really blame them.

Since my divorce, I've realized how completely disconnected and ostracized I had become. I was too ashamed to text our friends' group, didn't know where half of them were or what they were doing, whether they were still in touch with each other. How do you make friends as an adult? How do you meet new people? Nobody tells you how hard it is. I had my gym membership but never connected with anybody there. I kept in touch with some colleagues, but being completely open and vulnerable with people you work with daily is difficult.

It's been a pretty lonely decade, and in a society where social networking is highly valued, being alone all the time weighed heavily on my mental health.

I didn't realize how much Rachel and I had in common. I want to take her under my wing and help her continue to reach her full potential, love herself, and kick ass. And she just called me her friend. Big milestone over here being celebrated. Internally. I'm talking a whole cheerleading squad doing stunts on my heart and spelling out Rachel's name.

When we leave the restaurant, I retrieve the scrap of paper with Perfect Guy's number and drop it in the recycling bin outside. It's nice to feel wanted. And for today, that was all I needed.

TWELVE
Figure It Out

Miles

*"Y*ou look like shit."

"Thanks, man, appreciate it," I say as Tyler pulls up his grip socks and adjusts his laces.

"Are you feeling good enough for today? We can call Rick if your head isn't in it."

"What are you talking about, I'm fine," I mumble.

"Sure, Miles, okay," Tyler says. "Just focus on the game, okay? The guys worked their asses off to be ready to play Montreal. Don't let them down."

"I said I'm fine. Can you drop it?" I say more forcefully, and Tyler raises his hands in surrender.

Both teams are warming up on the field, and a small audience has gathered in the stands. Today is no ordinary game. Even though we play recreationally, we set one goal this year—to participate in the Canadian amateur rugby tournament. A win against the Eagles today will qualify us for the next round.

"All right, guys, bring it in." A circle forms around me. "We've been working hard these last few months, but I don't want us to forget that we're playing for fun, first and foremost. With that said, though, let's beat these motherfuckers."

"Yeah!" my teammates scream.

"On three! One, two, three!"

"Go, Bulldogs!"

We scatter on the field, taking our positions. I try to block every anxious thought from entering my brain. I need to focus, goddamn it. I can't let the stress of the week get in the way, but fuck, this is almost too much to handle at once. Tucking my feelings for Riley aside in the deepest corners of my soul, managing the firm, and now with the prospective trip to Europe—it's been weighing heavily.

I desperately need this win today.

It's in times like these I wish Avery wasn't so far away and I could just pop over to her place. We'd share a bottle of wine, make my lasagna from scratch. I would probably tease the shit out of her since it is our favorite pastime, but I know she'd give just as good as she got.

But she's not here, and my sister has enough of her own life and responsibilities. I need to learn to manage it myself. I shouldn't let my fears and insecurities squeeze my throat like they're doing right now, but no matter what breathing techniques I try, their grip is still firm around my neck.

"Miles!" Tyler shouts from the middle of the field, arms wide open. "Coming?"

I jog to where my teammates stand. I spent hours analyzing Montreal's plays. My speed will be to our advantage today, but they'll be tough competition with the sheer strength of their defense.

Tyler positions himself at my side. "Head in the game, Miles."

"I know."

My eyes catch a silhouette in the stands that makes me stop dead in my tracks. Riley, a smile warm like sunshine on her face, waving at me.

Fuck. I forgot I'd invited her.

"What's Riley doing here?" Tyler asks, following my gaze.

I groan. "I mentioned in passing that it was our first game today, but I didn't expect her to come."

"Well, shit."

"What?"

Ty shrugs. "It'd have been nice to win, that's all."

"You're an asshole."

I wave back to Riley before getting into position, letting everything but the field's dewy grass under my boots and the warble of the whistle fall away.

I kick the ball and set off running toward the Eagles' goal line. Their offense retrieves the ball, running back in our direction. I brace for impact as one of their players rushes forward with me in his line of sight. I run low, and when he's close enough, I squat and tackle him below the belt. The air leaves my lungs as I crash full force against him, his knee against my chest. We both fall hard on the grass, the player letting the ball slip. *Fuck yes, a loose carry.* I scramble to pick it up and pass it to Ron, who's right behind me to catch it.

The steal is awarded, clapping and cheering echoing from the stands, and I don't have to look to recognize Riley's voice. Goddamn, I love having her here just for me, yelling my name.

From the ground, I see Ron pass the ball behind him to another one of our guys. We're getting closer to the goal line, but as I straighten up, Tyler gets tackled above the waist, and the referee signals the foul.

"Asshole!"

I feel hands on my chest before I can register where they're coming from. I stumble back slightly, and when I raise my eyes to see which poor fucker is dumb enough to lay his hands on me, the guy I just tackled is coming back for a second hit.

I grit my teeth and clench my fist, ready to send it flying to his left cheek, but Ron appears in my periphery and palms my bicep, holding it back.

"Hey, hey, cool it, Miles."

The referee sprints to us, whistle stuck between his lips, while other Montreal players hold the dickhead back.

"He fucking high-tackled me!" he shouts.

"Fuck you! I did not," I shoot back. "Your teammate just did that to Tyler, not me."

"Miles!" Tyler puts his hand on my chest. "Look at me, man. Let it go, okay?"

I stare at him, willing my blood to stop roaring in my body.

"He's not worth it. Look at me, Miles," he says. "We're only twenty minutes into the first half, and all we've done is put them in a defensive position. We've been aggressive, just like we said we'd be. Montreal plays hard. Don't let them get the best of you." He clasps his hand on my shoulder. "Head in the game."

I turn and see Riley standing on the grass near the benches, watching me, a frown between her brows.

I let Tyler settle the matter with the referee, and jog toward her, my hair damp with sweat.

"What happened?" she asks, grabbing my shoulders.

"Oh, nothing. He thought I tackled him above the waist." When she doesn't say anything, I add. "It's an illegal move."

"Oh, okay." She's still holding on to me like she's afraid I'll disappear.

"Why are you down here? Do you need anything?"

"I just wanted to see if you were okay," she replies, blushing. "It looked pretty intense from up there."

I fight the urge to pull her closer. "I'm fine." I smile. "Just a rough sport."

The referee calls a scrum ten yards from the touchline.

"Hey," I shout as I turn on my heels to join my team. "Thank you for coming!"

Everybody gets in position, knees bent, arms around our teammates' shoulders, ready to go head-to-head with the ball. I stay behind, so as soon as the ball gets free, Tyler will slide it to me, and I'll make a run for the try line. Grunts and growls erupt everywhere as both teams struggle for the ball. Luckily, David moves his shoulder forward, blocking an attempt from Montreal which allows Ty to kick the ball toward me. I lunge and grab it, sliding it under my arm, and sprint for the finish line.

As soon as the white mark is behind me, I flatten the ball just between the posts, ensuring an easy kick to score the maximum possible point and give my team a good lead.

"Fuck yes!" I scream, throwing the ball to the ground.

"Yes, Miles!" everybody shouts as they rush to hug me. "Let's go!"

"Go, Bulldogs!" Riley screams from the stands. She's standing, her hands around her mouth, making as much noise as she can. I laugh. My personal cheerleader.

We play relentlessly for the rest of the afternoon. At halftime, we're dragging a bit behind, 18-15 but the second half tips in our favor. At the eighty-three-minute mark, with two tries and one penalty for our team that brings us to 28-32, the referee calls the end of the game. The Bulldogs cheer and scream, the celebration coming left and right of the field as we gather and give each other bear-hugs.

"We did it, boys, we did it!" I say, exhaustion dripping from my voice. But the excitement and happiness emanating from the other guys erases all signs of tiredness in my bones. And Riley in the distance, jogging toward me.

Riley

THINGS I NEVER THOUGHT I'D SAY: a testosterone-packed field of thirty men—each bigger than the other—sweating and grunting in tight uniforms for eighty minutes is the hottest thing I have ever witnessed in my life.

I also didn't factor in the effect watching Miles flex every single muscle in his body would have on me. Especially his thighs. The way his shorts rode higher with every sprint, the sharp definition of his muscles, the fabric stretching the curve of his backside…

Yeah, I didn't follow much of the game… All I know is that they won, and they looked pretty damn good doing it. I wasn't sure what to expect, but the sport is quite violent, and more times than not, I had to hold my breath. Especially when Miles tackled a guy headfirst, and they both crashed down but continued fighting for the ball.

I jog toward Miles, and as soon as he sees me approaching, he pats his friend Tyler on the back and heads in my direction.

I don't care if he's sweaty and dirty. Right now, all I want is to celebrate with him.

"What a game," I shout as I run to him, his face stretched into a grin, and deep inside, I want to believe it's because of me.

Miles reads me like a book and picks me up easily, engulfing me in the safety of his arms, his usual coffee scent mixed with sweat and grass working double-time to overpower my senses. I wrap my legs around his waist. He feels like home, and it is such a dangerous thought to entertain, but I can't get it out of my mind.

"I'm glad you came," Miles says, holding me tight against him. I revel in this minute of proximity I'm allowing myself. "Oh shit. I'm going to get you all dirty, and I probably stink." He puts me down but still stays close.

"I don't mind a bit of mud, don't worry." I look behind him as his teammates stretch on the grass. "So... This is rugby, uh?"

Miles chuckles. "Yeah, pretty intense to watch, I bet."

"I loved it. You're very good at it. It's nice to see the guys looking up to you. A true leader, even here."

Miles smiles softly. "Thanks, Ry."

The wind is blowing lightly in his damp hair, his shirt sticking to his chest. I wouldn't mind staying here with him for a little bit longer, maybe slide a hand under his shirt and tangle myself in his limbs.

"Tyler and I are going to grab a beer after. Do you want to come?"

I shake my head. "No, go ahead without me. I've got research to do on France tonight anyway. You know, so I can arrive on Monday and have a solid plan you won't be able to say no to."

He nods, a brief smile on his lips. "I can't wait to see what you come up with." He looks behind me. "I should go shower. Tyler's waiting for me, and I'll never hear the end of it if I drag my feet."

Unsure, he takes a step and wraps his arms around me. I hug him back a second too long before I let go and watch him disappear inside the stadium locker rooms.

THIRTEEN

Champagne Problems

Miles

$\mathscr{W}$e sit at our regular table at the Irish pub next door to the stadium, two brown ales in front of us.

"So, what's going on with you?" Tyler cocks an eyebrow, waiting.

I blink away the tears gathering at the corners of my eyes. "It's just… everything's piling up right now, there's no way out," I say, releasing a ragged breath.

Tyler frowns. "No way out of what?"

"No matter how I look at it, I always end up hitting a wall. With Ry, with my infertility. I'm trapped in my body, and it's fucking broken."

"Hey. You're not broken," Tyler says. "Why don't we take one step at a time, yeah? Are you still going to therapy?"

I snort. "Can you imagine the mess I'd be if I weren't?"

145 | FROM PARIS, IN Love

Tom, my therapist going on almost four years, isn't scared to call me on my bullshit. Like the time I almost punched Josh in the face at his sister's wedding for breaking Avery's heart. My sister would have never spoken to me if I had, so I kept it together. When I later told Tom about it, he took a deep breath and said with a chuckle, "Let's unpack how your reaction is a symptom of what we call 'toxic masculinity.'"

"Okay, good." He chuckles. "So, what's going on with the firm then? Isn't it going really well?"

"It is," I say, getting another sip in. "It's just more stress than I thought it'd be. We picked up a massive account, but now it looks like both Riley and I have to go to Paris and—"

"Wait—" Tyler puts his hands up. "You're going to Paris? When?"

"Supposedly in two weeks. Riley is putting a strategy plan together as we speak, and we'll see if it's feasible. Would you mind taking care of Happy if I go? I know it's a lot, but this is all last-minute, and all the boarding kennels are full. He knows you well, so it wouldn't be too much of a change for him."

"Of course, I'll take care of your pup, don't worry about it. I'm sure he loves me more than you, anyway. So, is this what's stressing you out? Paris?"

I sigh. "Yeah, I guess. I feel like we're putting the firm on the line already, you know? It's nerve-wracking. So many things could go wrong." Starting with the fact that we haven't gotten the full picture of the market in France yet. We don't have the contacts there. And once we're there, we have to keep in mind that there's a language barrier, a culture that we don't fully grasp, customs we don't know about. What if we don't get Peter his partnership with a French winery? What if the whole trip is just a big fat flop?

Do we really want to risk our firm's future to meet a goal—a very ambitious goal, no less—we set at the beginning?

"*Could* is the keyword here, friend. If I know you at all, you won't leave anything to chance."

He's infuriatingly right, 95 percent of the time. My days are meticulously planned, highly organized. It's part of the reason why Peter wants to hire us. Since I started in PR, I've slowly built myself a reputation as someone who gets shit done.

I rub my jaw, my beard coarse under my fingers. "I know, I know. I feel like I can't help it. It's like a gut feeling that something is going to go wrong. And on top of everything, there's Riley."

Tyler rolls his eyes. "Man, you have to stop fucking around with Riley. You two are grown-ass adults. Why did you start the firm with her if you knew this was going to be difficult? Tell her how you feel."

"Yeah, just tell her how I feel. Easy, right?" I can't help the sarcasm in my voice. "It's like you forgot the whole 'I don't want to jeopardize my company' thing, or that she just got out of an abusive marriage, and—oh! How I can't have kids."

I don't mean to sound harsh, but Tyler knows how hard it's been for me since learning that I can't have children.

Since Kristina. How badly I've always wanted to have kids of my own, how much it crushed me to be faced with the brutal reality that it would never happen for me. I took the time to heal and finally, *finally*, I'm at peace with it. I'm done blaming myself, done with the shame that consumed me for months. I have my low days, but I'm trying to move forward now.

I'm lucky to have a friend like Ty who can read me so well. He just about forced me to spill my guts when I got the news. I don't think I would have opened up to anybody if not for him.

Tyler takes a sip of his beer before putting it down and looking me straight in the eyes. "I need you to hear me when I tell you this, man. You are not a burden on anyone. So you can't have kids. You know there are other ways, right? I've said it to you before, and I'll say it again, and every time you need to hear it until it's ingrained in your head: none of this makes you less of a man. The ability to have kids biologically doesn't define a person, Miles. Stop punishing yourself for something you don't have any control over." He takes another swing at his drink. "Sucking at rugby though…"

I kick him under the table. "Way to ruin your love declaration," I tease, even though his words help glue the little pieces of my broken self back together. "But seriously. I'm not interested in 'other ways.'"

I've always dreamed about creating a mini-me and continuing our family tree. Although I know so many different options exist now, none are the right fit for me. Not to mention the emotional toll it would have on me. I've already done my fair share on that end. The years of waiting for those two lines, doubting if they'll ever appear. No, I'm not built for that.

For me, no kid is the bitter but better option.

"Maybe you'll find someone who already has children and doesn't want more any more," Tyler says. "Or maybe she'll be straight up about not wanting kids, who knows? There are a lot of women now who are honest about that. Maybe Riley is one of them."

"I'm not ready to bring it up with her to find out which side she stands on. I don't even know how to tell her," I say. "It's not really something I can bring up on a first date."

Or even second, or third, for that matter. Bringing it up too soon could mean risking any chance we might have. Bringing it up too late, and she feels blindsided. Lose-lose.

I'll never forget Kristina's face when I told her. She'd just come home from work, and I'd just hung up with the doctor.

"Miles, you home?" Kristina called from the entryway.

"In the kitchen," I murmured, turning the conversation with Dr. Pravesh over in my head.

Kristina came into the kitchen, Happy in tow. Her black hair was cut right above her shoulders back then, and she was wearing her usual navy suit and stilettos.

"Is everything okay?" she asked as soon as she saw my face, slumped in my chair at the kitchen table.

"I just got a call from Dr. Pravesh," I say. "You might want to take a seat."

"Okay…" She pulled a chair and sat in front of me. "What's up?"

Always so delicate, Kristina…

I ran my hand through my hair. How the fuck was I supposed to tell her?

"The results came back today. For our fertility test. Yours came back normal."

"Okay…?" she said again, studying me.

"Mine didn't."

"I see."

"I can't have children, Kristina." I didn't know why I felt the need to spell it out, maybe because I needed to hear myself say it, see how it would taste on the tip of my tongue. Sour, was the conclusion.

I watched her face go from passive to sad before she slipped a blank expression on again. But too late. I'd seen it.

We'd been together for four years at that point. We were engaged for three and had been trying since. The last year, our relationship took a turn for the worst—the questions, doubts, weight of never seeing two lines on those stupid sticks. Every month, she felt like a failure, and there was nothing I could have done to change that except keep trying and reassuring her the best I could. But the emotional rollercoaster of hope and disappointment started to put a strain on our relationship. We fought more than ever did in all our time together. We resented each other until we decided to finally get answers.

"I need time to process it," Kristina said.

"Me too," I whispered.

She got up, leaving me alone to pick up the pieces of my life. For most of the night, we sat in silence. We agreed to schedule another appointment with the doctor to get more information and figure out the next steps.

A week later, we met with Dr. Pravesh, who laid out the issue as well as the different options available to us.

"With your results placing you in the 'severe male infertility' category, regular IVF isn't a viable option for you," Dr. Pravesh said. "We could, however, do what we call an intracytoplasmic sperm injection, or ICSI. Success rates are higher for men in your position, but so are the risk factors. The likely outcome of pregnancy as a result of this procedure sits at around 30 percent."

"What would you recommend, Doctor?" Kristina asked.

"There are a lot of other possibilities you can explore as well, like donors, or if it's of interest to you, adoption."

Kristina tensed next to me. I didn't know what she expected from this meeting, maybe some kind of miracle. Perhaps she thought it wasn't as bad as I'd said.

"What do you think?" she asked when we returned home.

I sighed. "Honestly? I don't know. But right now, I don't think any of these options work for me."

We couldn't agree, it seemed. For weeks, she tried to get me to accept the ICSI plan and, if not, at least, a donor. Despite wanting more than anything to save our relationship and give her what she wanted, I couldn't make such a life-altering decision out of guilt. And deep down, I already knew that I didn't want to put myself through months of anxiety for only 30 percent chances of success and higher risks. I left my dream of being a dad on our doctor's doorstep that day.

One morning not long after, I woke up early and went running. I needed to get out of my head, get the frustration, my anger, sadness out of my pores.

When I came back, she was waiting for me by the door, two suitcases next to her.

"Where are you going? What's happening?" I asked, sweaty and out of breath.

"I can't do this, Miles. I want kids. I want a family. I love you, but it's no longer enough. You refuse to do your part when you're the problem. I'm done."

"What are you talking about?" It felt like a million cuts to the heart.

"I'm going to stay at my mom's. I'll come back in a few days to pick up the rest of my stuff." She moved closer and put her hand on my arm. "I'm sorry."

And then she left.

I never want to live through that ever again.

"I get that it's an awkward topic to bring up when you start dating someone," Ty concedes, bringing me back to the pub. "But you've known her for years. Maybe you can find a way to test the waters first."

I shrug and finish my beer. "We'll see. She has enough shit to deal with as it is."

"The ex-husband stuff? Come on, man," Ty groans. "Don't you think she deserves to make her own decision on that? How can she choose when she doesn't know you're an option? Stop being a controlling asshole. I'm sure she can tell you to fuck off if she feels like it."

"She has."

I'm lucky Ty hadn't taken a mouthful of beer because he would've spit it all over me. "What do you mean? What happened?"

Nothing. Everything. Not nearly enough. Is there really a right way to answer? "I almost kissed her the day we opened the firm. After work, at her place."

"No shit!" Tyler screams, and a few heads turn our way. "Sorry, sorry. No shit," he repeats, his voice a breathy whisper.

I roll my eyes. "Yeah, see? I tried already. She said her marriage almost destroyed her, and that she didn't want to risk losing the firm."

"She actually said those words?" Tyler raises one eyebrow.

"Pretty much, yeah. She panicked, mostly, and I didn't know what to do, so I told her I would never cross the line again. Then she told me her ex-husband threatened her with some bullshit about us having an affair while they were still married. She's terrified. If I'd have known, there's no way I would've taken it there."

"Hmmm…"

"What?"

"It just sounds to me like there's more to it. All she gave you as excuses are external factors. But she wanted to kiss you too, right? I'm assuming there were *signs*, if you catch my drift." He waggles his eyebrows, and I can't help grinning.

"What does it change anyway? The results are the same. I don't get the girl," I grumble.

Tyler shakes his head, a smirk on his face. "Miles, Miles, Miles. You really have to pay attention sometimes. It's exhausting having to explain everything to you. I'm telling you, she wants this. You have to give her time to find her footing with the job and the ex-husband. And you know what else you can do?"

"Is this what it feels like to be mansplained? Because it's annoying."

"Deal with it, you'll thank me later." He chuckles, before his tone turns serious, and he continues. "Be the opposite of her shitty ex-husband. Show her how a real man treats women. I'm telling you, you'll get the girl. Show her the Miles I know, but let her come to you first," he adds.

He's not wrong. It could work. I could test the waters like he said, try and find out what she wants in a partner before I lay it all on the line. It's terrifying, but for the first time in god knows how long, I feel hopeful.

FOURTEEN
I Can See You

Riley

"260 Carlaw Ave..."

I look up from my phone at the old industrial building before me. Am I at the right address? This place looks completely abandoned. And judging by the way the door doesn't seem to lock correctly...

I groan. Two days ago, Tyler pulled me aside at the rugby game after Miles went into the showers, waiting for him to get their beers. When he told me I shouldn't miss today's event, and under no circumstances should I tell Miles, I'd assumed it was to watch them practice.

But now I'm wondering if I was sent here to be murdered. And if Miles is even here.

"Why didn't I check before..."

I open the massive metal door, and the creaking sound makes my skin crawl. Is this how Charlee feels whenever she's called on a new adventure? Because no, thank you.

I open Instagram and message Tyler.

Riley: "Hey, I'm here. Not sure if I'm in the right place, though."

I send him a photo of the wooden stairs that look like they're about to give way. His reply comes immediately.

Tyler: "Right place! I can't come down right now, but we're on the second floor, the last door on the left. Just knock when you get there."

When I get to the second floor, booming laughter comes through the door at the end of the hallway. I was right about this being rugby related, but I'm still at a loss as to what the team is doing in the building. I knock on the door, smoothing out the wrinkles in my olive dress. I don't even know how I was supposed to dress this morning, but I opted for light and summery. The temperature is already getting unbearably hot.

The door opens just a crack, and Tyler squeezes his head between the door and the frame, blocking out everything else.

"Hey, Riley," he whispers with a grin. "I'm so glad you could make it."

"Hey?" I crane my neck to see what's happening in the room, but Tyler fills the space. Or rather, Tyler's floating head. "What are you guys doing?"

The flicker in his eyes screams trouble. Big trouble.

"Ty!" one of the guys yells in the background. "What's taking you so long? I'm freezing my ass off."

Wait, what? I raise an eyebrow. Tyler winks and flings the door wide open to reveal a photo studio bathed in spotlights and a bright white background.

But that's not what catches my eye, oh no. In front of me is Tyler, completely naked, covered only by a small white towel wrapped tightly around his waist, his chest gleaming under a smooth coat of what smells like almond oil.

"Um, Riley." Tyler clears his throat. "You're staring."

My eyes snap to his, my cheeks flaming hot. "Wh-what's happening here?"

"Riley?" a familiar voice echoes across the open room, sending a jolt of electricity through my nervous system. And that's when I notice Miles storming toward us, the rest of the team behind him, all wrapped in white towels except for two guys who are currently posing naked on the white background, a fan blowing air in their faces and a rugby ball in front of their –

"What are you doing here?"

Chest. Muscle. Sweat. Thick thighs. Hair. Tattoo.

So. Much. Skin.

Oh god, what is happening? The sight of Miles has fried my brain so much that my words are stuck in my dry throat.

"I think you broke her," Tyler snickers at Miles before clapping him on the shoulder and strutting back to the rest of the team.

"Ry?"

I startle when his fingers brush my elbow. "Hey! Yes, hi, how are you? Wow," I croak, fanning my burning face with my hand, "this room is really keeping the temperature in, uh? Is there maybe a water cooler around here somewhere?"

He swallows, his eyes fixed on me. "Yeah, um, over there."

He points to the other end of the room, beside Tyler, who just removed his towel, leaving me staring at his bare ass. Miles mumbles something before clearing his throat. "What are you doing here?" he repeats.

"I, um... After your game Friday, Tyler told me the team would be here. He suggested I come." For some reason, I still don't understand. "I didn't know what it was about," I add.

"Fucker," he groans, pinching the bridge of his nose. He whips his head in Tyler's direction with a glare that promises retribution.

But Miles is still standing in front of me, wearing only a very thin scrap of fabric, the tattoo wrapped around his arm on full display, and I'm still staring, unsure of what is happening to register or care about anything else he's saying.

"I'm sorry you got dragged into this," Miles sighs, scrubbing his beard. "Every year, the boys and I do this ridiculous photo shoot for our annual calendar, and all the sales profits go to a charity of our choice. We put them together ourselves, and they usually sell pretty well."

"Oh, I'm sure they do," I manage to get out.

"Yeah, well, what can I say?" he says and shrugs. "Half-naked rugby men look better than firemen."

I've never owned a firemen's calendar, but I won't deny that all the men in the room look damn good—especially the one in front of me.

"Who do you support this year?"

"An organization that helps children with learning disabilities. Do it for the kids, right?" My eyebrows shoot up, and his face turns crimson as he rushes to add. "*Selling* the calendars."

I chuckle. "Got it. I think it's a fun way to raise money." Some of the awkwardness between us dissipates. It's as if there's nothing more normal than being so close to each other with so little clothing on.

For the first time since I walked into this testosterone-charged studio, Miles is looking at me, really looking at me.

"You are beautiful today." I blush at the compliment, avoiding direct eye contact while I can still feel his eyes on me.

"Thank you."

"You look beautiful every day," he blurts as if his mouth is moving without permission. "But today... I... I love this color on you. Makes the honey speckles in your eyes pop."

"You're..." I gesture my hand up and down at his torso. Delicious? Mouth-watering? Hot as fuck? Eatable? "Shiny."

Miles laughs, his stomach rippling like shock waves from the impact, and I can barely tear my eyes away from the motion. Wait, did I just say *shiny*?

"Yes, I am," he says, chuckling. "We have a budget for oil, and believe me, with fifteen guys, we use a lot."

I try to laugh, but the sound gets caught in my throat and comes out strangled. I need water.

"You know," Miles adds since I can't utter a decent word with the two brain cells I have left, "you don't have to stay. I don't want you to feel uncomfortable."

"Oh, yeah, no, I'll, uh… I'll go," I babble.

"You can stay if you want," he hurries to say. "I don't mind having you here."

"You don't?"

Miles waves me off. "Might as well stay now that you're here. There are worse ways to spend a Sunday." He smiles broadly. Does this man not know that I'm already weak in the knees? Can't he have mercy?

I nod. Looks like I'm staying, then. Yep, it's fine. Totally fine.

"Let's find you a chair and some water, yeah? Give me a minute, and I'll get you settled."

He makes his way to his teammates, stopping right in front of Tyler, who turns to him when I hear Miles say, "You and I will talk later."

"Come on!" Tyler says loudly, smiling playfully. Miles walks up to the rest of the boys and points his finger at them.

"Behave," he warns. He picks up a glass, fills it, and pulls up a folding chair in the corner.

When he returns to me, the white towel still tied tightly around his waist, he unfolds the chair for me and hands me the glass. "If you need anything, just holler, and I'll be right over."

"Thanks," I say warmly.

"Miles, you're up!" The photographer calls.

He offers me a strained smile and nods at the white background. "Gotta go."

"What month are you?"

"December," he mumbles.

I hold back a laugh, my lips pressed tightly together because he already looks miserable enough for me to even joke about it.

I sit down, my eyes glued to the defined muscles of his back moving with grace as Miles stands in front of the camera. This is the second time I've seen Miles shirtless, and I don't think I'll ever get used to the fact that this man, grumpy and rough around the edges, who plays one of the most violent sports, is covered in tattooed flowers that weave in a delicate pattern around his arm all the way up to his shoulder. And I should thank him someday, for making me discover things about myself, like the fact that, apparently, I find flower tattoos on a man hot as fuck.

The photographer asks her assistant to apply a light touch of makeup to even out Miles' complexion before handing him a Santa hat and a rugby ball.

This time, I can't contain my giggles as he puts the hat on because he looks so adorable and awkward at the same time. He twists his head in my direction when the sound reaches him, and as if seeking payback, he tugs on his towel and drops it to the floor, leaving me gaping at what was hiding underneath. Satisfied, he grabs the ball and places it just below his navel, right between his legs, barely hiding *a thing*.

I am not strong enough. My willpower was already in a precarious condition when we were in my pool. What was Tyler thinking inviting me here today? Images of Miles' massive... nudity will be etched in my brain forever, and that's the last thing you want to think about when it comes to your business partner, isn't it?

But I don't take my eyes off him as he strikes several poses in front of the camera, playing with the stool, the ball and Santa's hat, flexing his muscular thighs and biceps as he stands like the ancient Greek statue Discobolus, one hand with the ball in the air, his left leg concealing the rest of his lower body. I don't look away either when his gaze meets mine, and he tracks the movement of my lips parting under the weight of his rapt attention, his eyes drifting down to my chest as it rises and falls harder with the quickening of my breath, those same eyes sliding even lower as I recklessly clench my legs, want pooling deep in my lower abdomen.

He grips the ball harder, his breath sharp. When his eyes find mine again, I read his urge to cross the small distance separating us and press me against the nearest wall, ripping off my clothes, never mind that thirteen other guys are in the room. And frankly, I wouldn't even stop him. I'd let him make a complete feast of my body right here, so much so that lust overpowers every cell of my being.

"I've got everything I need," the photographer says, startling me out of my contest with Miles of "who will give in first." "Thanks, Miles. Scott, your turn!"

It takes Miles a couple of seconds to tear his eyes away from me, and when he does, I catch my breath for the first time. He pulls on a robe and joins Tyler, who has a smirk on his face that immediately fades when Miles glares at him.

I'm not sure if I should be grateful to the photographer or secretly resent him for this interference, but either way, I'm royally fucked.

FIFTEEN
New

Riley

*W*hen I arrive at the office on Tuesday morning, Miles is already waiting for me in my office.

"Good morning!" I say, dropping my bag on the chair next to him. "You're early."

He checks his watch, shaking his head. "It's 9:12 a.m., Ry."

"Oops. I guess I'm late then."

He holds out a folder, placing it on my keyboard. "I went over your research for the French trip."

"And?"

I sidle up next to him, leaning on the edge of my desk. He straightens up, clearing his throat.

"And... you did an impressive job. I even deliberately looked for things I could have challenged you on, but I found nothing. I don't know how you managed to answer each and every one of my concerns, point by point, without me even mentioning them all to you. And you put this together so quickly. Especially considering that you weren't working on it yesterday afternoon..." he pauses, averting his eyes.

"Anyway," he says, clearing his throat. "I don't see how I could say no to your compelling proposal."

"Are you serious?" My heartbeat quickens. Are we really doing this?

"Let's go get our first million, Fletcher." He smiles, holding out his hand.

I grab it and use it to pull him up, bringing him in for a hug. He doesn't resist, his arms coming easily around me, his breath shallow in the crook of my neck. Yesterday's events flood my mind, and suddenly, it's as if our skin were touching and my body was aflame.

A colleague walks in front of my office at the same time, and I break our embrace abruptly. Shit.

I don't have time to think about it, though, because agitated voices from down the hall reach my office. Miles and I exchange a confused look. We move at the same time, hurrying toward the commotion.

Employees are poking their heads out of their offices as Sydney, our receptionist, tries to control the situation.

"Sir, if you could just sit down over there," Sydney says, visibly shaken up. "I'll go see if Miss Fletcher—"

"All I want is for you to point me toward her office, is that too much to ask? Or do I need to show you how to do your job?" The voice stops me dead in my tracks, causing Miles to slam into my back.

"What the—" He grips my waist to prevent me from face-planting into the hardwood floor, but I'm too petrified to even care.

Sean is here. Standing in my office lobby, looking very pissed.

"Sir, please—"

"It's fine, I'll just find her myself," Sean says, turning in our direction. Miles is still holding on to me. His hands flex against my hip, his fingers digging tighter into my skin when he finally registers that my ex-husband is standing a few feet away from us. Sean's gaze slowly moves down from my face to Miles's hand. Embarrassment takes over as I try to put some distance between us, but all it does is make him clutch harder.

"Let go, Miles," I whisper through my teeth.

His breath is rough against my neck. "Ry…"

"Let. Go."

He reluctantly loosens his hold on me. I take a step forward. Steady. Confident. I won't be intimidated by Sean. Not anymore. He lost his power over me a long time ago. I rectify my posture, straightening my spine and standing tall.

"Sean." My voice is firm, clear—the opposite of how I'm feeling inside, my blood frozen in my veins.

Sean doesn't bother with formalities, but who's surprised. Manners have never been his strong suit. "Can we talk in your office?"

"No."

The answer doesn't come from me. I turn to Miles, glaring at him.

"I'm sorry," Sean says, not sorry at all. "This is between Riley and me."

Miles takes a step forward, coming to stand next to me. I can't believe it.

"Actually, Sean," Miles continues. "You're in our building, so whatever you need to say to Riley, I should know too. Assuming it's business-related," he adds. "Otherwise, you can see yourself out."

"Miles," I seethe. I turn back to Sean. My mind is drowning in panic and anger, and it's like I'm functioning on autopilot, working really hard not to let my body shake in front of this arrogant asshole.

And what is it with men who can't let women fight their own battles? Why do we always have to push and force and struggle to make our voices heard? This is getting exhausting.

"Riley, get your boy toy in check, please," Sean says, a smirk on his face. I'm frozen, looking around at our employees as they catch every word of our exchange. "It's not enough that you cheated on me with him and humiliated me, you had to go into business together and steal my clients too? When are you gonna stop with your vendetta, Riley?"

"You have nothing to say?" he adds. I don't answer, paralyzed by his threats. "What about you, Matt? Is that your name, Matt? Have you been to Riley's house yet? I'm sure you've been enjoying the pool with how warm it's been lately."

"Shut the fuck up," Miles says. "Sydney, please call security. Riley, come on, let's go."

But I can't move. How does he know? How does he know that Miles and I have been in the pool? How can he know?

"Before I leave," Sean says. "I heard from Colin that Peter is switching firms. Didn't take me long to figure out the one he had in mind."

I snap out of my terror. Of course, he already knows Peter reached out to us. "What we do with our business doesn't concern you," I manage to get out, doing my best to ignore the weight of Miles's gaze on me. And the ones from our employees.

"Oh, Riley," Sean sneers, waving a finger at me. "Did you forget you signed contracts that specifically prohibit what you're doing?"

"Put your fucking finger down, and don't think for one moment to raise it back up at me." My voice is unwavering. Dangerously quiet. Sean's eyes widen before he regains his composure, but it's long enough for pride to poke a small hole in the storm of emotions blazing through me. Next to me, Miles hums in approval.

"Whatever you think you have on us, you don't," I add.

Sean scoffs. "We'll see. I hope you have great lawyers. If you sign Peter, you'll have a legal fight on your hands." Sean takes a step forward, but I don't budge. I don't even falter. "And trust me, Riley, you do not want to go up against me."

I take another step toward him. "I'll sign whomever I want, Sean. And you can throw as many legal tantrums as you want. You won't have any clients left by the time I'm done with you. Security can show you the way out."

I turn on my heels, not allowing him to even breathe in my direction, trying so damn hard not to shake with every step I take. He can threaten his way through life and yell as loud as he wants, I don't have to take it anymore.

Once in my office, I slam my door shut, collapsing against it, and burst into tears.

How does Sean know about Miles spending time in my pool? I don't understand. Should I invest in security cameras? Is he spying on me? I feel insane as these paranoid thoughts run rampant through my mind. He didn't need to spell the threat out for me to understand how dangerous he's willing to play.

And what will our employees think about what they just overheard? One of them just saw Miles and I hugging not even fifteen minutes ago.

Oh god, this is horrible. I don't know how to fix it. We're leaving for Paris next week. We can't afford any more slipups.

No hugging, no touching, no "friendly" gestures. This will be the most professional business trip in the history of business trips. I will make sure of it.

Miles

I PUNCH THE ELEVATOR BUTTON so hard I break the plastic seal.

"Come on, come on, come on."

As soon as the doors open, I leap inside, pressing the ground floor button with the same rage.

I hope for his sake that he's already long gone because the thoughts crossing my mind include multiple versions of me beating the shit out of him.

When I reach the lobby, I find Sean making his way to the building exit, his phone against his ear.

"Motherfucker."

The scene he just pulled could justify whatever sad fate awaits him at the end of my fists. But to question my credibility? My reputation? He's about to learn my name.

I'm behind him in three strides, grabbing his phone and throwing it on the ground. I don't give him time to realize what's happening. I turn him around like a rag doll and push him against the nearest wall, his back making a loud sound when it meets the brick. I register the fear in his eyes when I grip him on the sides of his collar.

"I'm not going to repeat myself twice, so listen to me very carefully," I say, my voice low. "Consider this the last time you disrespect me and my firm." I shake him once. "I will not have my reputation and credibility questioned by little shits like you. If my name—or whatever name you like to use when you pretend you don't know who I am—comes out of your mouth ever again…" I pause, tsking at him. "I won't be so kind as I am right now."

I drop him down and turn back toward the elevators, only breathing when the door closes behind me.

SIXTEEN
Invisible String

Riley

"*M*iss? I think you dropped this." The woman sitting next to me in the waiting area of Gate 36C is holding my book like it's a dirty tissue she's picked up off the floor. Which, to be fair, is an appropriate way to describe the state of what was a perfectly bound book. Let's just say that, after being read dozens of times and shoved in more bags and suitcases than I can count, my beloved first edition of The Notebook is looking more tattered than ever.

"Ah! Yes, thank you." I offer the lady a sheepish smile as I retrieve my book and check the time for the fiftieth time in the last ten minutes. Where is he?

Our flight to Paris leaves in an hour, and there's still no sign of Miles. I triple-check my phone, thinking he might have finally decided to text to let me know that his dog had last-minute diarrhea or his Uber took him to the wrong airport. No text. No call. No email. No DM.

I knew this trip wasn't going to be easy, especially after the scene Sean caused, but I've been doing my best to put those fires out before they got out of hand. I sent an email to our legal department yesterday, informing them we need to look over our previous contract carefully in case we missed anything when we signed Peter and his winery.

I probably should have gone to Miles's place to drag him to the airport myself, but I assumed he'd put his doubts aside.

We've covered all our bases; we have a solid game plan, studied the French market—everything is in order. I wouldn't have given the green light if I didn't think we could pull it off. We can, and we will.

"I'm going to strangle him," I mumble as I pace the busy floor of Toronto Pearson International Airport. Summer is in full swing, and people are frantically hurrying to their well-deserved vacations. "First, I'm going to give him a piece of my mind, and then I'm gonna take my time, wrapping my fingers slowly around that beautiful, strong neck and—"

"Who are you talking to?" The deep voice I know so well resonates behind me, and its vibrations shoot through me. I turn around, cheeks flaming hot.

"What? Nobody! What?" What are the chances he heard what I said? *Pretty great, Riley. Because that's just your luck.* And before he can say something else that would most certainly make me want to run onto the tarmac and throw myself in front of a plane, I quickly add, *"Where were you?"*

Okay, that was delivered at a slightly higher pitch than intended.

It's only when the cloud of embarrassment starts to dissipate that I take in how awful he looks. Miles Clark looks awful. Someone call CBC and make a news report out of it because never in the years I've known him have I seen him looking this pale and almost… ill.

His usually perfectly styled hair is disheveled, and not in a cute way. More in the "I want to pull it from my scalp" type of way. Even his beard looks like it wanted to start a revolution this morning, sticking out like pitchforks along his jaw.

When I finally meet his eyes, I notice that the usual spark that always shines mischievously has given way to a duller, dimmer light. And that's without even mentioning the bags bigger than my carry-on displayed under his eyes. Or the fact that he's wearing a weathered navy-and-yellow U of T sweatshirt and a pair of matching sweatpants that look almost more tired and worn than their counterpart. They're threadbare, clinging close to his thighs and his…

I clear my throat.

"Are you all right?"

Miles scrubs his jaw, staring off into the distance. "I'm fine. Sorry for the delay."

"You don't look fine."

His gaze cuts right through me. "I said I'm fine," he grumbles.

I raise my hands in surrender. "Easy there, tiger. Relax. They started boarding already, and business class has been called, so let's go."

I'm already moving toward our gate, but when I look next to me, all I see is empty space. Turning around, I spot Miles frozen where I left him. What is up with him today?

"You coming?" I call, impatience simmering beneath my skin.

"Yeah, yeah," he says, sighing.

We move to the priority boarding line, and I take my passport out, handing it to the woman.

"Have a safe flight," she says before turning her attention to Miles, her palm stretched out. But Miles doesn't move. He stares at her hand, face white as a sheet, the blood completely drained as he stands still.

What now? I stalk toward him when my steps falter, realization sinking in. I place my hand on his forearm, ensuring my next words come out as gently as possible. "Miles, are you scared of… flying?"

His pleading eyes find mine and he nods, his lips sealed shut. I apply more pressure to my hold, trying to focus his attention on this point of contact rather than what awaits him, but I quickly take my hand away. *We said no touching, Ry. Great start.*

"Listen to me," continuing in my soft tone, my hands glued to my sides. "We have an amazing two weeks planned in Paris, we're going to drink lots of wine and explore the city. It'll barely seem like work. But to do that, Miles, we need to board the plane. So, one step at a time, okay? Let's just give your passport to the nice lady so we can free the line."

I mouth a sorry to people behind us and am met with sympathetic smiles.

"Miles?" I ask when he doesn't budge.

Come on... I sigh, scanning our surroundings for anything that could make me think of Sean, but when everything seems safe, I hold out my hand for him, and without missing a beat, the rough pads of his fingers find mine and close around my skin, gripping tightly as if I'm his only anchor.

And I like that more than I care to admit.

I walk us down the loading bridge, dropping his hand as soon as we arrive at our seats.

I order us drinks when the beverage service commences—a wine for myself and a beer for Miles. With all travel expenses covered by the winery, we didn't hesitate to book our flights business-class. I'll be the first to admit that the comfort of these recliners will make the trip with an anxious Miles easier.

As soon as the plane starts moving, his whole body tenses next to me, and I can feel him trying to find ten ways to get out of here. The image of him yelling that he needs to get off the plane comes to mind, and a giggle escapes me.

"Are you laughing at me?" Miles says through gritted teeth, his gaze fixed on the seat in front of us.

"What? No! I was thinking about that episode of *Friends* where Phoebe tries to get Rachel off the plane, and she tells her there's something wrong with the left phalange, and everybody freaks out."

His eyes round like saucers, and I spy a bead of sweat running along his temple. "Something wrong with the *what?*"

I laugh. "Relax, I was just trying to make a joke. Here," I say, patting his knee, trying to distract his mind from the imminent takeoff. "Focus on me, Miles. Talk to me."

"About what?" he asks curtly.

"Anything. Something you like. Things you hate. An embarrassing story. Oh yes, let's do that one, tell me your most embarrassing story." I smirk mischievously, which manages to pull his lips upward an inch. Small victories.

"Is that your idea of distraction? Ridiculing me?"

"Aren't you entertained? Because I can guarantee you that I will be."

He scoffs. "Oh, I'm sure you're right. But I think for it to work as a distraction, it makes more sense if you're the one telling me an embarrassing story."

Well, he got me there.

"You know what? Challenge accepted, partner. And because I take my role very seriously, I will sacrifice my dignity for your entertainment pleasure."

Miles raises an eyebrow. I roll my eyes.

"You're such a guy."

He laughs. "Is that supposed to be an insult?"

"Whatever." I wave him off. His body has slumped further against the seat, his knuckles not looking like they're going to pull the leather off the armrests anymore. Good progress.

"So." I let out a big sigh. All my embarrassing stories somehow involve my carefree little sister. "When Charlee turned sixteen, Mom wanted to throw her the birthday of her dreams. I remember she worked double shifts for four months to put enough money aside for this wildlife convention in Vancouver where Char could meet her idol, Paul Nicklen. He's a pretty big deal in the milieu and a very renowned Canadian wildlife photographer. You know how teenage girls cover their bedroom walls with posters of the Backstreet Boys or Brad Pitt?"

Miles makes an unconvinced "uh-uh" face.

"Well, not my sister. She had Nicklen's work plastered everywhere. Anyway, we arrived at the convention, and I could feel my sister's excitement in this tangible way, you know? She was shaking, vibrating from within. When we spotted him a few tables away and made our way to him, he turned to us, opened his arms wide with a big smile on his face, and said: 'You came!'"

Nostalgia pulls at my chest as I take in Miles's attentive face. "You see, I was first in line. So you can imagine my confusion when a fifty-something famous photographer, who I didn't know anything about, was happy that 'I' came. But at the same time, he *was* looking at me. I started to think that maybe he and Char had exchanged a few emails when she was looking for an internship that summer and that she introduced the whole family, but wasn't it strange either way?"

Miles nods, his brows furrowed. "Very. Please tell me he wasn't a creepy bastard."

I snort. "Oh, I wish. It would have made what followed much more understandable."

"Uh-oh."

"Uh-oh is right," I say, enjoying how deeply immersed Miles is as he awaits the inevitable. "You have to understand that everything happened in a matter of seconds. I didn't have a lot of time to think, we were moving toward him anyway. I did the only logical thing the situation called for: I dove into his open arms and hugged him back."

Miles's mouth falls open. "You *what?*"

"Yes, sir. I thought, 'Why the heck not? Maybe he's just being friendly,' and part of me was still thinking he already knew Charlee, don't forget."

"What did you do next?" Miles whispers, flashes of horror passing through his eyes. "No, what did *he* do?"

"Well, he awkwardly patted my back. I hadn't realized yet at that point that I'd gotten it completely wrong. It was when I stepped back and saw the questioning look on his face that I started to ask questions. And then, I heard it, the throat clearing behind me. And when Nicklen's gaze traveled over my shoulder, he smiled apologetically at a petite woman with grey hair cut just below her ears. Definitely not my sister. In that moment, I knew I had just given a stranger a very friendly hug that wasn't meant for me. And so, instead of profusely apologizing and clearing the way, you know what I did?"

"What?" he asks right away, eyes riveted on me.

"I patted his arm and said: 'Good to see you again, Paul,' then turned around, walked calmly passed my mortified sister and mother whose jaws were hanging dangerously close to the floor, and I ran out of the building. I stayed outside the whole day with my sunglasses on just in case Nicklen might come out and recognize his hugger."

Miles is fighting a smile now, which I choose to proudly associate with my talented storytelling skills, and not the fact that he is most likely making fun of me. I don't think he's noticed we've taken off, and that is a victory in itself.

"What did your sister say when she found you after?" he asks.

"Well, I really thought she was going to yell at me and tell me I was insane, but apparently, just after I 'excused' myself, they laughed it off, and Charlee even got some time to talk with Nicklen about a possible internship. In the end, she just laughed at me."

This time, the smile he was trying so hard to hold back breaks free.

"For years, Miles," I add, knowing it'll make him smile wider. Even laugh, maybe. Because he doesn't do it often, or for anybody. He's more of the broody, grumbling type, which also has its charm.

But when Miles laughs, when he gives you that opening, you feel like the luckiest person alive. Because it's special, and it's for you. You hold on to the sound like it's the most precious thing you possess, but then it's gone, and all you're left with is its memory ringing in your ears and the hope you'll be lucky enough to hear it again. Be the one that pulls it from him. How many times have I tried to break this sound free, feel its deep vibration rumbling through me? And surprisingly, I can't say I've been unsuccessful, which makes me feel all kinds of ways I don't want to explore right now.

And so he does. He laughs at the fact that Charlee's tortured me with this story for years, and I couldn't care less about any of it right now, because Miles is laughing. Head thrown back against his seat, eyes closed, his stomach spasming under the intensity of it.

I want to capture him like this because, despite his beard, ridiculous height, and broad frame, he looks just like a boy, eyes crinkling from his cheeky grin.

I finally give up and join him in his outburst, marveling at the sound of our laughter intertwining and vanishing into thin air.

We must look like a couple of idiots, laughing at something that's not even that funny and doing so not very quietly either. I think for Miles, part of it is nerves and stress. But for me, it's the simple pleasure of sharing this moment with him.

A flight attendant catches my eye, and I nod apologetically, placing my hand on Miles's arm. His laughter dies, and he lets out one last long sigh before his eyes slide to my hand still wrapped around his forearm. His gaze returns to me, heavy and dangerous.

He lays his hand on top of mine and gives it a little squeeze, before pulling it back.

"Thank you," he says with a soft smile.

"For what?" I swallow.

"For making me forget that I'm facing my biggest fear right now."

"Oh, well, don't mention—"

"I'm not finished," he cuts me off, his gaze unwavering. "For being so formidably you, and not giving a damn what anyone else thinks. I admire that so much about you, Riley. Hell, I aspire to be like you."

Miles gives me another small smile that threatens to make me drop all my reservations. "If you don't mind, I think I might try to sleep now that I'm feeling more relaxed."

"Yes, of course, go ahead," I whisper.

"Good night, partner," he tells me with a wink before rolling over and adjusting his reclined seat.

And I sit there, heart thumping against the walls of my chest, unable to sleep after hearing what just blurted out of his mouth.

SEVENTEEN
Rien À Dire

Miles

*W*e're going to fucking crash, I knew it. This is how I'm going to die. In a fucking flying heap of metal.

We've been passing through a turbulence zone for the past half hour, although the flight attendant says it's "nothing out of the ordinary." Fucking bullshit. I grip my armrests as the plane shakes some more. There's everything out of the ordinary about putting blind faith into a box with wings that apparently does somersaults in the air, and where the only way out is through death. Because, let's face it, who has ever survived a plane crash?

I'm paralyzed in my seat, the heavy weight of my worries sitting on my chest and pushing me deeper in my spiral. All I can think about is death. I'm gonna die. The plane shakes again, and this time my heart plummets into my stomach.

I look at Riley, sound asleep with her noise-canceling headphones on. She doesn't even budge when the plane jolts again. For the millionth time. I blow out a slow breath, trying to minimize the panic threatening to overpower me.

I fucking hate this.

My breath is hot; sweat is rolling down my temples. The screen in front of me says we're scheduled to land in about fifteen minutes, but I know we won't even make it. It's only a matter of minutes before we all become casualties of yet another plane accident. They're common, right? I should have googled it before we left.

"Ladies and gentlemen, this is your captain speaking. We are currently flying at a low altitude to reduce the turbulence."

"Clearly failing," I mumble.

"We will be landing in Paris in approximately ten minutes, as soon as we are given clearance. In the meantime, please relax and keep your seat belts fastened."

Relax, sure. I check my seat belt, even if the only thing it'll do is make sure I die glued to my seat.

The plane coasts through another turbulence, and my stomach lurches.

"For fuck's sake," I shout, grabbing the first thing I can reach.

"Ow!" Riley cries, startling awake. She turns to me, panicked. "Are you okay?"

My palm is clutching her thigh. "I'm sorry, I-I got scared for a second, the plane... it went... and I—"

"Miles, hey, breathe." She lays a hand on my chest, right on my thorax, putting a slight pressure there. "One breath in." She inhales, and I mirror the action. "And out." We both exhale. "Okay, again." We repeat the same pattern a couple of times, the air coming in easier in my lungs.

I look down at my hand, slowly relaxing my fingers. Without thinking too much about it, I start stroking her inner thigh with my thumb, relishing the way the rough texture of her jeans feels.

Riley's gaze slides there too. "Miles…"

"A few minutes, Ry. Please."

She nods, placing her hand above mine. "Okay."

We stay like this for the rest of the flight, the heat of her body radiating against my palm.

It's like I've completely forgotten about the turbulence and my imminent fate. Right now, my senses are tuned to the beautiful woman seated next to me and how it feels so right to touch her, like my body knows she's made for me, and it responds with this humming approval vibrating through me.

I press my thumb into her skin, and I hear the hitch of her breath as a result. I look outside through the porthole, hiding my smile. I love that she reacts too; it burns me up from inside to know I'm getting her all fired up. It's not the first time I've caught her checking me out either. Her eyes lingering a few seconds too long in the office, the rosy blush on her cheeks when she follows my fingers stroking my beard.

"We're about to land," I say, spotting the ground coming closer. Relief washes over me. Well, okay, I was wrong. I might have overreacted a little.

"It's almost over," Ry says in that reassuring voice I love so much. "You sure you're feeling okay?"

I nod as the airplane touches the ground smoothly, braking hard and then easing back to cruise along the tarmac. I exhale deeply. I'm on the ground. I'm down on earth again, feet safely planted on French soil.

"Ladies and Gentlemen, Bienvenue to Paris. We have landed at Charles de Gaulle Airport. It is currently 6 a.m. local time, and the temperature outside is a beautiful 68 degrees."

"See? You did it!" Riley says. Gently, she pulls her hand off of mine and moves her leg slightly. I get the message and retrieve my own hand, already mourning the loss of her touch. I'm already looking forward to the next opportunity where I'll be lucky again to get a few justified minutes to hold her hand or feel the small of her back. Hug her.

She's magnetic, and I'm stuck in her orbit.

"Ready to practice your French, Clark?" Riley says, all smiles.

It's going to be two fucking long weeks.

"J'ÉTAIS LÀ AVANT!" A FRENCH woman yells at us, holding the old taxi door. She is very petite, sunglasses on, and looks to be in her fifties—rich, fancy, and pretentious, one hand on her popped hip.

I don't know what the fuck she's saying, but I'm exhausted from the flight and now jet lag, so not being able to understand a word is leading my patience to run thin. But from the way she's gripping the taxi door like she's holding on for dear life, my guess is that she doesn't want us to get the taxi we definitely saw first.

"I'm sorry, ma'am, je ne parle pas très bien français," Riley attempts, her accent strong.

"Américains, of course!" The woman rolls her eyes, and I don't see the correction that we are, in fact, Canadian, going over well. "Ils se croient toujours mieux que les autres." She huffs, walking away with her giant suitcase rolling behind her.

"Well, warmest welcome to us both," I grumble, less than excited at being reamed out by a middle-aged woman. Even more so at not understanding a word of what she said.

Riley claps my stomach. "Come on, Grumpy, let's get to our hotel."

"Me, grumpy?" I say, getting in the cab. "Says the one who almost knocked a guy out next to the baggage carousel because he didn't move out of your way fast enough."

"How stupid can people be, staying glued to the carousel to wait for their bags rather than waiting to actually see them before they go near it? It's basic common decency," she says, sliding beside me.

This is a very small cab. If I extend my arms on either side, I can touch the edges of the car. It also looks to be about a hundred years old and will probably give out any minute.

"I know, you're right. There, there," I tease her, and I'm rewarded with a glare.

She turns around to shut the door, but something gets stuck, and the door doesn't seem to want to cooperate.

"Um, okay, can you scoot over a bit more? The door isn't closing," Riley says, trying again.

"Uhh, I'm kind of against the door already, Ry."

"Maybe we should get another cab."

"Good luck with that," the driver interjects, eyes on us through his rearview mirror. "It's peak time at the airport right now. You'll be stuck waiting for an hour, at best." He gets out and comes around the car. "Here, monsieur, just put your arm around madame." He takes my arm and wraps it around Ry's shoulders.

What in the literal fuck?

"Madame, if you can please move closer to monsieur." Riley complies, and I get a full whiff of her hair in my nose. "Yes, like this, perfect. Okay now, attention, je vais fermer la porte. Careful…" He slams the door shut. "Parfait!"

Riley looks at me from under her lashes, her cheek flushed against my chest. For fuck's sake. "Sorry," she whispers.

I smile. "Don't be. It's not like we have much of a choice." Although, if I were given one, we'd be in a very similar position.

"Yeah…"

"Où c'est que je vous emmène?" the taxi driver interrupts. Riley and I look at each other, feeling utterly hopeless. Shit, we should've really done a crash course in French before leaving. I rack my brain, coming to the only possible conclusion. I take my phone out of my jacket and pull up the trip details Peter sent us before we boarded our flight. Fuck, how am I supposed to pronounce this?

"Hum… le hôtel est… Hôtel Mari…" What is "gnan" supposed to sound like? My mouth is definitely not made to speak this language. I show the driver my phone. "It's a hotel on the Champs-Élysées?"

"Oh, Hôtel Marignan, oui je connais. Very fancy hotel. We'll be there in forty-five minutes, if there's not too much traffic." He hands me my phone back. "But that would be something extraordinaire, no traffic in Paris!" He laughs to himself. "Never saw that in my life." The driver looks in his rearview mirror, straight at Ry. "What's your name, beautiful?"

I tense. Please let the stereotype of French men be just that—a stereotype. Riley doesn't seem bothered by it, though.

"Riley," she answers before hiking a thumb at my chest. "And this is Miles."

"Ahh, having a little romantic getaway in the city de l'amour. You are a lucky guy, sir."

"I am," I simply say, not looking at Riley.

"I'm Jean," he says, tipping his hat with a toothy grin. "Enchanté."

At least we have a friendly driver. After the chaos that was landing, finding our bags, and fighting for a cab, it's nice to be met with a little bit of kindness.

"AVANCE, CONNARD!" JEAN YELLS to the car in front of us. He honks several times, and the driver in question responds by honking too, then flipping him off. Okay, well, scratch any earlier thoughts of pleasantries from our new friend.

Forty-five minutes later, and we're not even halfway to the hotel. There are cars everywhere. Not. Moving. An. Inch. The heat is unbearable, and our driver is getting angrier by the minute.

"Putain! C'est quoi ce bordel, merde!" he groans, thumping on his steering wheel. I think it's safe to assume Duolingo wouldn't cover any of that in its beginner lessons.

"Is everything okay, Jean?" I ask.

"Yes, correct. Everything is fine. Welcome to Paris!" He laughs. This change in his mood is quite unsettling. I'm pretty sure he was shouting "fucking shit" two seconds ago. "You're living the real experience. Nothing more authentic than Parisian traffic."

I smile tightly and slide a glance at Riley. She's been silent for a while, her head buried in my chest. I don't know if she's sleeping, and I don't want to wake her up if she is, but she's radiating heat, and I'm sweating like I'm mid-game on the rugby pitch.

It's fucking hot in here. Tyler warned me about the lack of air conditioning in Europe, but damn, I didn't think it applied to cars. It's like I've traveled back to the 1800s.

"Jean, do you have air-conditioning in here?"

"Non, monsieur! But you can open the windows if you want. Aller, avance, merde," he shouts, honking again.

I wiggle my left arm, trying to reach the manual lever to roll down the window, but the heat outside is, if possible, even more stifling.

I don't know who said Paris was romantic, but they certainly never rode in a cramped hundred-year-old car with no A/C, running on a mix of jet lag and stale airport coffee, while their driver insulted half of the city. So far, my wonderful Paris experience has been filled with sweat, exhaust fumes, and French curse words. Truly heaven on earth.

In my arms, Riley shivers. I touch her forehead. She's burning hot. Gently, I move her closer to me, trying to make her more comfortable. She must be exhausted from our flight. My sister used to crash like this when we were younger after flights to Italy for our summer vacations.

Riley sighs, pushing harder against me. I rest my chin on the top of her head, her wild blond hair tingling my cheeks, holding her as close as I can. I wrap my other arm around her, testing the waters. I'm a greedy man, and I can't help wanting more at every turn. More of her touch, more of her laugh, more of her scent. What I would do for a shot at her taste.

"Mmm, Miles," Riley breathes out, stirring against me. She manages to drape her leg over my thigh while her arm lays heavy on my low stomach and fuck if I don't get hard on the spot.

"You gotta be kidding me," I groan, eyes on the fabric-lined ceiling.

I close my eyes, trying to get my breathing and my cock under control before she wakes up. Oh god, what if she wakes up and sees me like this?

"Comfortable, monsieur?" Jean asks, a knowing smile on his face.

"Mm-hmm, yep. How long till we're at the hotel, Jean?"

He checks his GPS. "Not too long. Maybe another fifteen minutes, tops. You and the lady will be alone soon, don't worry," he adds with a wink.

Oh god, is the taxi driver really making a sexual innuendo? At least it has the effect of putting my dick back to sleep. Nothing a Frenchman missing a few teeth in a car doubling as a sauna can't fix.

Fifteen minutes later, I'm shaking Riley awake. "Ry, we're here."

She yawns, snuggling closer. "I want to sleep."

I chuckle. I've never been around Riley first thing in the morning, but she definitely sounds like a little grump.

"Ry, we're in Paris, and we're at our hotel," I try again. "Let's get out of this car so we can go to bed." Separate rooms. Separate beds.

This seems to get her attention. She shifts and blinks her eyes open.

"Oh," is the only sound that comes out of her mouth when she notices she's half straddling me. Her cheeks are flushed red, either from the heat or her embarrassment, it's hard to tell.

She chuckles nervously. It's an adorable sound, partly because I've never seen her this frazzled. "Um, sorry 'bout that, I fell asleep. Obviously."

She maneuvers herself off and tucks her disheveled hair behind her ears. It doesn't do anything; it still looks like a lion's mane.

"It's okay, we're both tired. Let's start by getting out of this literal hellhole."

Outside, Jean waits for us next to our luggage. I tip him a ten-euro bill and hold out my hand. "Thank you, Jean."

"Oh, we don't shake hands here, monsieur," he says, grabbing my hand, pulling me into a hug, and slapping two wet kisses on each of my already sweaty cheeks. "Have a great romantic vacation, *les amoureux. Bienvenue à Paris!*"

I stand there, stunned, Riley silently laughing behind me. *Bienvenue à Paris*, indeed…

EIGHTEEN

She

Miles

"Wow, Peter spoiled us," Riley murmurs, looking around the magnificent hotel hall. The design is minimalist—crisp black-and-white lines and sharp edges complete the modern, high-end décor, with brightly colored rugs and furniture that accentuates the interior. The entire space is airy, and, blessedly frosty against our overheated skin.

"He really did."

We make our way to the massive oak front desk in the middle of the hall. It's almost 9 o'clock here, which means it's 3 a.m. in Toronto, and I barely slept on the plane. I need those room keys now, or I'm going to crash in the pear-shaped chairs to my right.

"Bonjour, good morning," the receptionist says. "Are you checking in?"

"Yes, we are. Two rooms, under the names Clark and Fletcher."

"One moment, please."

Riley's head falls against my arm. "I am so tired."

"We're almost there." I chuckle, ruffling her hair.

"Sir, it looks like I have a reservation for one king bedroom with a balcony for Miss Fletcher, but I'm afraid there is nothing here under your name."

This has to be some kind of fucking joke. "There must be a mistake. Can you look again, please?"

"Sir, I—"

"Please, look again."

I text Peter to the sound of furious clicking on a keyboard.

Miles: Hey, Pete! Riley and I just landed in Paris. Hope your flight went well. Just wanted to confirm that you made reservations for two rooms at the hotel for Riley and me?

"Don't worry, I'm sure we'll find a solution," Riley says, half asleep. "Worst-case scenario, we can sleep in the same bed. If it's a king, there'll be plenty of room." She yawns, not bothering to cover her mouth.

Wow.

She. Is. Out.

"Although"—she snorts and looks up at me through half-lidded eyes—"you're kind of a big guy, so you might take up all the space."

I laugh silently. Is it possible to be drunk from lack of sleep? Because I'm sure she doesn't know what she's saying, and she likely won't remember come tomorrow. I try my luck and bend down, whispering in her ear.

"Ry, if we share a bed, there won't be much sleeping happening."

Her mouth forms an "O" for a second, but then she's back to being sleepy against my arm.

Peter: Hey, Miles! Landed yesterday and ready to take over the festival on Monday. Yes, my assistant confirmed she made two bookings. One for Riley Fletcher and the other for Miles Clerk. Sorry about that!

Oh. I turn to the receptionist. "Hi, can you check if you have anything under Miles Clerk, please?"

"Miles Clerk... yes, here we go. One adjacent king bedroom with balcony for two weeks."

Oh, thank god. "The person who made the booking misspelled my name," I say, getting my passport out.

The receptionist checks my information before making the modifications. "You're all set, Mr. Clark and Miss Fletcher. Here are your room keys, with the Wi-Fi password underneath. The elevators are down the hall, on the right. Have a wonderful stay."

"Thank you," I say, relief washing over me. I shoot a quick reply to Peter to let him know everything is sorted, then head toward the elevators.

"Come on, sleepyhead," I say to a sleep-walking Riley.

I press the button for the seventh floor, one harm secured around her waist.

"You are very comfortable, Milesy," she mumbles. "Just like a cushy little Miles-shaped cupcake."

"You don't know what the hell you're saying," I say, amused. God, is it possible to like this woman any more? This side of her is brand-new to me, and it's so fucking cute it makes me want to shower her with hundreds of kisses and never let her go.

"No, I mean it," she says, snuggling closer and reaching for my other arm, squeezing my bicep. "You're such a big man. Strong but soft at the same time. Ugh, it's so not fair."

"Why is it unfair?" I ask, despite knowing the answer won't make any sense.

"Because!" Riley whines. "Every girl dreams of having a man like you."

My heart tightens. If only she knew how wrong she was.

"Let's get you into bed, come on," I say as the doors open. Riley takes a step forward and wobbles. "Whoa, there."

"I am tired, Milesy."

I exhale, pinching the bridge of my nose. She won't let this nickname go. Goddamned Tyler.

"Okay, hold on tight." I squat, one arm coming to snake around her waist and the other gripping behind her knees. Riley wraps both of hers around my neck, nestling her face in the sensitive spot by my ear. I'm sure she can feel the wild rhythm of my heart against her cheek, but I'm hoping she's exhausted enough not to put two and two together.

I lift her up with minimal effort and carry her in my arms until I find her bedroom door. Wriggling the card free of the little pocket, I swipe open the door. The bedroom is basking in the morning light, the design similar to the one in the hall—minimalistic, refined, but there's a cozier touch with the stacked pillows and the dim lighting.

I walk with Riley in my arms until I reach the bed. When I go to lay her down, she grips my neck. "No, not yet. I'm freezing."

I groan. She's really not making it easy on me today, but despite my body aching with fatigue, I sit down on the bed, Riley clutching me. I stay here for a few minutes because that's what she wants, and I have no way of saying no to her.

She's never needed me like this before, and the thought does a weird thing to my heart. It's nice, I realize, feeling needed for once. I don't think Kristina ever relied on me, not in little ways like this.

I've always been attracted to strong women with ambition and drive, but the women I've been with also lacked the vulnerability to let me in. No matter how hard I tried.

I hug Riley closer, enjoying the weight of her body against mine, her warmth. When her breathing starts to slow, and her hold on my neck loosens, I fold the sheets open and lay her down on the pillow. Once her shoes are off, I tuck her under the covers, close the curtain, and use the connecting door to go to my own bedroom. It's safe to say we'll both be out until tomorrow morning, with all the stress and adrenaline of the past twenty-four hours.

I drop my bags, heading straight for a desperately needed post-travel shower.

I turn the water on, waiting for it to turn scalding. Once the bathroom is filled with steam, I step inside, breathing a sigh of relief when the water hits the sore muscles in my shoulders. I lather my hair with coconut shampoo, my mind wandering freely to the woman in the other room.

Today will replay forever in my mind. When I lie in bed, I'll dream about her body against mine in the elevator. Or her leg draped over mine in the back of a too-small cab, making my skin feel tight against me, powerless to her hold on me.

My dreams are the closest I'll ever get to having her.

So I close my eyes and dream of her, the water keeping me warm and rinsing the soap down my body.

I imagine her here, with me, after a long day of strolling the streets of Paris, eating ice cream, and grazing my thumb along her bottom lip as I bend down to lick the chocolate staining her pink mouth and kiss her under the Arc de Triomphe like nobody's watching, her summer dress flowing widely in the breeze.

My hand travels down until I grip myself. I imagine her stepping in the shower with me, her nipples hard and peaked, rubbing against my wet body. With one hand on the shower wall and one wrapped around my length, I start moving slowly, the water rippling down the nape of my neck.

I shouldn't be doing this.

I shouldn't let myself think about her in this way, even more so with her asleep next door.

But I can't help myself. All day, I tried not to give in to my primal needs, and God knows she tested me. I can't resist any longer. I can't fight the urge flooding my brain, rushing down to my cock and making me so hard I'm having trouble breathing.

I need her out of my system.

In my mind, Riley's standing naked in front of me, a spectacular show of curves and femininity. I reach for her, pulling her flush against me, feeling every inch of her on every inch of me.

I fist myself harder, rougher, as I conjure up more images of my hands on her hips, spinning her around and pinning her to the tiles, her back against my chest. With my foot, I kick her legs open and grab her round ass with my hands, bending her so I can have the perfect view of her pussy.

"Fuck," I groan, increasing the speed of the motion.

I pant, feeling myself getting closer and closer to my climax, my chest heaving up and down. Riley's moans echo in my thoughts when I get on my knees from behind her and brush my nose against her center. I know if I taste her, it's game over. So instead, I dip one finger inside her, slowly, and watch it disappear deep into her pussy.

The thought sends my mind spiraling out of control, and my hand makes three more fast pumps before I come all over the shower floor in a loud, hoarse grunt, my dick still throbbing with the force of my release.

"Shit." I try to catch my breath.

I stand under the hot water for a while, letting the drops hit my shoulder blades and wash my pleasure down the drain.

There. Riley Fletcher is out of my system.

I dry my hair with another towel, put on some boxers, and slide beneath the covers.

When I close my eyes, it's golden hair and a pair of chocolate eyes that I see.

NINETEEN

Ceilings

Riley

At 3:30 in the morning, I wake up and rush to the bathroom with one hand over my mouth. I make it just in time to open the lid and empty my stomach. I hate throwing up. It's as if I'm a little girl again, needing her mother to tell her everything will be okay. Tears prickle my eyes, and I retch one more time.

I get up, catching a glimpse of my reflection in the dimly lit bathroom. Yikes. I look atrocious.

I splash water on my sweat-covered face, pushing the hair stuck on my forehead and cheeks away. I'm burning up, yet it feels like it's the dead of winter in here. *No.* I can't be sick. Not when we have the kickoff meeting with Peter in two days.

I search my bag in hopes I stocked my nausea pills in there. Bingo. I drag myself back to the bathroom, grabbing a glass, and filling it with water.

"Riley, get your shit together," I say, narrowing my eyes at my reflection in the mirror. "You cannot be sick, you hear me?"

Nothing a few more hours of sleep can't fix, right? The pills should kick in any minute, hopefully, knock me out too. I take a deep, calming breath. I've got this, I repeat myself, everything is going to be okay.

EVERYTHING IS NOT OKAY. If anything, I feel worse. I woke up two more times to meet the bathroom floor, before I gave up and spent the rest of the night curled up in a tight ball on the cold tiles.

A shiver rolls down my entire body. Sleeping on a cold, hard floor didn't help. I try to move, stretch my sore muscles from my night of puking my guts out.

What am I going to do? Who knows how long I'm going to be sick. Not even a full twenty-four hours in Paris, and something is already going wrong. I should've given Miles's doubts more credit, although I will never admit that to his face.

A soft knock sounds at the door. "Ry, are you ready?"

Speaking of the devil.

Shit, what time is it? I get up, stifling a yelp at the sharp pain rising from my feet to my waist. I grab my phone on the nightstand. How is it already 9 a.m.? Have I been lying on the floor for the past four hours?

"Ry? You awake?"

"Uhhh, yeah, give me a minute," I say, my voice so hoarse you would think I'd smoked a pack of cigarettes. *How very European of me.*

We had planned to go out to a café this morning, getting the full French breakfast experience—baguette, croissant, jam, and butter. My stomach churns at the thought. That all sounded much more appealing when I could envision keeping food down...

I stumble into the bathroom, rinsing my face and brushing my hair, pulling it up into a sad ponytail. Once my teeth are done, I get into some comfy leggings and an oversized shirt. Doesn't really scream hot Parisian girl summer, but it'll have to do.

"Coming!" I open the door, finding Miles leaning on the opposite wall, his large arms folded over his chest. My brain is foggy, my body is pleading with me to go back to sleep, but I can appreciate the sight of a handsome man when I see one.

"Someone decided to go full 'hipster mode a la française,' huh?" I say, doing my best to act unaffected. I hope it's convincing.

Miles is wearing brown boat shoes sans socks, paired with a deep green shirt tucked into his cream-colored chinos. His beard is neatly brushed, his wavy hair styled perfectly, and— oh gosh. He has a pair of black Wayfarers perched on his head. Sunglasses on men is my personal brand of sexy.

"Are you all right?" he asks, a concerned look on his face. He didn't even bother replying to my little teasing comment, too focused on taking me in from head to toe.

"I know I don't look my best today, but rude," I say, plastering a smile on my face. "Feeling a bit jet lagged still, I think."

Miles nods, but the frown between his brows deepens as he comes closer to me. He raises his hand and touches my forehead.

"Ry, what the fuck? You're burning up."

"What?" I scoff, swatting his arm away. "No, I'm not, I'm fine."

"Yeah, try telling me you're fine one more time, and we'll see if I believe you."

"I swear I—"

"Ry," he says, pointing to my bedroom. "Get your ass in there, and don't make me ask you twice."

I blush at his demanding tone but try to cover it with an eye roll. "Fine, Dad." I feel my face blanch and realize my mistake when he clears his throat behind me. This is going to be such a long trip…

I kick my shoes off, grumbling my way into bed. "I told you I'm fine," I say, dragging out the word in a last-ditch effort.

Miles sighs, coming from the bathroom with a wet cloth in hand. "Come on, you look horrible. You should rest up."

"Gee, thanks. Tell me what you really think."

"You know what I mean." Miles laughs. "How long have you been feeling like this? Here, put this on your forehead."

I do as I'm told, enjoying the cool relief on my head.

"I've been in and out of it all night. You shouldn't stay here with me. I might be contagious." I don't bother suppressing my groan when I roll on my side.

"What's the matter?" Miles promptly asks. "Why are you hurt?"

"For the millionth time, Miles, I'm okay." I wince. "I might have spent part of the night on the bathroom floor."

"What? Why?"

I give him a look. "Why do you think? Anyway, I don't know. I might have eaten something bad on the flight, or maybe the jet lag is messing me up a little bit."

"Okay, well, you need to rest today. Let's have a comfy day in. What do you say? I'll go to my room and change into something cozier, and we can watch a movie or something. We can even order something if you feel better later."

"If I say yes, will you stop freaking out?"

"Someone has to take care of you, Fletcher. And I don't mind it being me."

"Not very nice of you to throw that in when I'm already weak," I say, hiding my smile in my pillow, mentally snuggling myself in his words.

Miles winks at me. "Never said I was nice." He ruffles the covers, making sure I'm all tucked in. "I'm gonna run to a pharmacy and—tut-tut." He wags his finger in front of me just as I'm about to protest. "I don't care how much you complain right now, I'm going. Then I'll change and be right over, okay?"

"Fine," I grumble.

"Ohh, isn't Miss Grumpy making a comeback this morning," he teases.

"Go away."

Miles chuckles. "I'll be right back. Don't you dare move an inch."

"Yes, sir," I say, weakly saluting him.

He laughs awkwardly. Before he closes the door on his way out, he looks at me and winks. *Winks*. "Good girl."

And that is how I die.

TWENTY

La Déclaration d'Amour

Miles

*R*iley looked like shit, if I'm being honest. It tore my heart out. She was so weak when she opened the door, wobbling on her feet, dark circles under her beautiful eyes. I wish I could do something more to make her pain go away than buying out the pharmacy, which was an ordeal in itself. Between the language barrier and having no clue what brands of drugs they stock, it took me a solid fifteen minutes to try to explain her symptoms and what I needed.

On my way back to the hotel, I stop at a bakery on the corner and grab us both decadent hot chocolates in cardboard cups, just in case her appetite comes back and she needs a bit of sugar to power up.

I walk back into my bedroom, switch my chinos for my gray sweatpants and a more comfortable shirt. Spending the day in bed with Ry isn't a terrible way to kick off this Parisian adventure, although I'd prefer it if she were sweaty and dizzy because of me and not some stupid bug she caught.

Soft snoring travels up from under the sheets when I open her bedroom door. I don't know if it's because she's sick or if it's something she does when she sleeps, but I can't get enough of it. It's dangerously cute.

Gently, I lie down next to her so as not to wake her up. Her body is still warm, but the cold cloth on her forehead has helped bring the temperature down a bit. I snatch the remote from her nightstand, careful not to crush her in the process. She stirs a bit, moaning something I can't understand, and rolls on her side, her hand coming to rest on my chest. A little hum comes out of her mouth when she adjusts her head— right in the crook of my arm.

I watch a few episodes of *The Office*, Ry still tucked firmly against me. I want to capture this moment, so I take a mental picture, one that I store in my Riley memories folder. She always seems so worried about everything, has a million things on her mind. But at least now, she doesn't look like the world's fate is resting on her shoulders. She looks calm, relaxed. That she's letting me look after her right now feels like a much-needed reprieve, soothing something in me.

This basic instinct that I'm somehow responsible for ensuring that nothing bad happens to her.

When Riley's with me, I know she's in good hands, even if I'm aware that my hands won't be the ones to protect her forever. I don't want to think about that, though, the idea of her falling in love with someone. Of starting over again and having everything she deserves… Not when I know it can't be me. But as long as she'll allow me to stand by her, as her friend and business partner, no one will ever disrespect her again or make her feel worth less than she really is.

When she shifts thirty minutes later, opening her eyes slowly, I turn the TV off.

"Hey," Riley says, still sleepy. She notices her position in the hollow of my arm and plops herself back on her pillow.

"Sorry, I didn't mean to wake you." I nod to the TV.

She stretches, revealing a sliver of skin above her hip. I look away.

"Oh, you didn't. I shouldn't be sleeping all day, anyway."

"You need rest. I got you some pills to help with your stomach." I grab the bag. "And a hot chocolate, if you feel like it. It's probably cold by now, but it's delicious."

"I think my stomach settled a little bit," she says, sitting up. "Hot chocolate sounds nice, thank you."

She grabs her water and swallows the medicine with a grimace. "I think I need a shower. I stink."

"I didn't know how to tell you…"

"You can't even give me a rest when I'm sick, huh?"

I smirk. "Where would the fun be in that?"

She gets up before sitting back down. "Woah, too fast."

"Here, let me." I step around the bed and stand in front of her. "Let's go, Grandma," I say, holding both hands out to her. Riley chuckles and places her palms in mine, letting me lift her off the bed slowly.

She stops short, halfway to the bathroom. "Oh, no. Miles…" She doesn't finish her sentence, rushing to the toilet. I kneel behind her, gathering her hair in my hand.

"Miles, go away," she cries between two sobs.

"It's funny that you still think I'll listen when you push me away. You need me." I massage her back, making small circles while brushing the hair out of her face.

When she's done, I help her up, closing the toilet lid and settling her on it.

"Don't move, okay?"

She nods, her eyes red from tears and exhaustion.

I get the water running in the bath, making sure it's not too hot. Then I get another cloth and wash her face gently. She's not making any move to stop me. Either she's too sick for it, or she's accepted that I won't back down. Good. The quicker she gets that in her head, the less I'll have to push and repeat myself.

"Are you feeling good enough to get undressed and into the bath?" I ask once I turn off the taps. I add some lavender essential oil I found in her bedroom to help soothe her muscles.

A slight blush creeps in her cheeks. "Yeah, I think so. Thank you."

"Of course. I'll be right outside if you need me, okay?"

She nods once again. I take it as my cue to leave and close the door, going back to lie on the bed, focusing *very* hard on the TV screen and not at all on the knowledge that Riley's in the bath on the other side of the door.

ALMOST AN HOUR LATER, she emerges from the bathroom in a thick cloud of steam, only a white towel tightly wrapped around her figure, her wet hair all tangled up.

"I don't know what you put in that bath, Miles, but damn, I feel so much better," Riley says, fumbling into her suitcase. She's already making a mess, and my fingers are itching to fold her clothes properly. "Are we going out this afternoon?"

"You sure you feel up for it?" I quirk an eyebrow. "You should rest." But if she's set her mind on it, I'm not sure I'll be able to have my way for the second time in one day.

"I don't have anything left in me to puke. I think I need some fresh air." She holds a pink dress in one hand and a short and strappy linen top in the other. "Mr. Fashion, which one do you think?"

I choke on my water. "Mr. Fashion? Where is this coming from?"

She shrugs like she hasn't just called me something ridiculous. "You're always so well dressed at work."

"Oh, no. That's not me. It's all Ty."

I wouldn't know how to pick and pair an outfit that doesn't scream "five-year-old getting lost in the adult section of a store." Tyler, though, loves to shop and drags me with him every chance he gets. I don't complain, and in exchange, he picks out my clothes.

I look back at her, still pondering her options.

"The pink dress."

She smiles brightly at me. "Pink dress it is."

I get up from the bed, avoiding making eye contact with how little she has on right now. Clearing my throat, I say, "I'm going to head next door to change, I'll let you get ready. Meet you in the lobby in ten?"

"Maybe fifteen. I look like Rapunzel right now."

"Just don't let any guys climb up to your window, okay?"

"I'll have my pans ready if they do, don't worry."

I laugh. "Poor bastard."

TWENTY-ONE
Every Feeling

Miles

"You picked so fucking right, Miles, I tell myself as Riley comes through the revolving doors of the hotel. The pink dress is indecently sexy. Thin straps, tight fit, except for the dress hem that falls more loosely around her thighs. She looks like a modern Barbie with how she's styled her hair into a slicked-back ponytail.

I can't take my eyes off her as she comes closer and stops a few feet from me. Surely she knows how much she has me wrapped around her finger.

"Ready to go?"

She's still slightly pale compared to her usually rosy skin, but she looks better. Healthier than when I found her this morning.

"You look gorgeous," I say, and I like how my words deepen the color that brushes her cheeks. I offer her my arm.

It's late afternoon, the sun is still warm in the sky. The streets are busy with people rushing to make sundowners and tourists capturing the quaint cobblestone walkways, some playing host to street performers. I wonder if Paris is similar to Toronto in how people come alive in the summer as the days get longer. We walk around our arrondissement, stopping in front of the Palais de l'Elysée, housing the French President, and walking by the Petit Palais and the Alexander III bridge.

When the evening sets in, the lights that adorn the streets create that rom-com feel, the one that makes you want to brush your fingers against your crush while you stroll under a drizzling sky, finally mustering up the courage to slip your hand in theirs, your heart pumping at a hundred miles a minute as you lean in for a kiss, the Eiffel Tower sparkling a thousand lights in the corners of your eyes.

It's easy to picture it. I glance at Riley, seemingly as absorbed as I am by the beauty in front of us.

"I understand why they call Paris the 'City of Love,'" I say to Riley as we walk along the bridge. "It's easy to take it all in with rose-colored glasses, especially around iconic places you've grown up seeing in movies."

"I remember seeing it in *Midnight in Paris*," she says, her voice barely a whisper. "Owen Wilson was walking there"— she points to a spot in the distance—"with Lea Seydoux in the middle of the night. It looked almost magical. The quintessence of romance." She sighs deeply. "You don't need fancy frills or unnecessary props to make the scene romantic.

The atmosphere, the location, the architecture. The whole setting is enough to make it so sentimental."

"I can picture it," I murmur. We're standing side by side, our hands so close they're almost intertwined. I feel hers moving, barely, but enough to boost my confidence and lightly stroke her skin. Neither of us looks at each other, neither of us talk. But Riley moves her hand closer, and my heart picks up its pace.

A pigeon flaps its wings nearby her, landing on the edge of the bridge where we're standing. She startles, moving her hand away and rubbing her thumb over her knuckles.

"Oh my god, those birds are everywhere." She laughs, but it's stilted, like she's uncomfortable.

"Very annoying, yeah," I say absently.

On the corner of the street, a small crowd is gathered around a food truck. "Do you want to get something to eat?" I say, clearing my throat and pointing to the line forming.

"It says 'crêpes' on it." She's squinting at the sign. "That's like pancakes, right?"

I nod. "Yeah, kind of, but thinner. They usually eat them with salted butter, sugar, and lemon juice here." I guess my hobby is coming in handy now that we're in the country of patisserie and sweets. Crêpes are my go-to when we do brunch with the guys from rugby once a month. They usually disappear after ten minutes.

"I'm starving, actually," Ry says. "I could do crêpes."

"Right answer," I say, grabbing her hand and pulling her with me. "Come on." She doesn't protest. She doesn't take her hand away. Instead, she links her fingers with mine.

"There's a lot of people," she says as if she's justifying the gesture. The blush on her cheeks is endearing. "I wouldn't want to lose you in the crowd."

I shrug. "I figured. No problem."

We order our crêpes, a traditional one for me; Nutella for Riley. They come in cardboard cones, burning hot.

"Mmm," Riley moans after taking her first bite.

I exhale sharply. That little sound will be imprinted on my mind forever. "Shit, this is good."

She's talking about the crêpes, Miles. Get a fucking grip.

"Why don't we have these in Canada? So good!"

I force a laugh, trying to reverse the direction of my blood flow. Lucky for me, Riley takes another bite and melted Nutella runs down her chin. I laugh again, this time with full force.

"What?" she asks, following my gaze. "Do I have something on my face?"

"You do. Don't move, I'll get it." I bring my thumb to her chin, gently sweeping it across her skin, getting most of the Nutella off. I bring it to my mouth, licking my thumb clean. "Mm, I agree. Excellent filling choice, Ry."

She stares at me for a second. "Y-yeah, very—" She breaks off and clears her throat. "Very good."

We continue our exploration of the city, walking through the Jardins des Tuileries, posing in front of the Louvres, where Riley insists I take a photo of her while she pretends to be touching the top of the pyramid.

Our "little" walk turns into us sightseeing in Paris on foot for hours. Whatever stomach bug she had earlier, it looks like she puked it out. Even her lack of sleep isn't stopping her from marveling at the city.

We stop at a souvenir shop where Riley gets a few postcards to send to her sister. I get one for Ave and my mom too. I take a photo of Riley jumping in the air in the middle of the Champs-Élysées. We walk alongside the Seine, where dozens of people are hanging out on the banks, listening to live music from the streets, sharing cigarettes, bottles of wine, and memories that will last a lifetime. I breathe in the summer air, feeling a kind of carelessness about the world beyond this night.

"Can we make a stop at a few bookstores?" she asks, nodding toward the bouquinistes lining the shores of the Seine.

"I was going to ask the same thing. I've been wanting to find a book for my sister."

We stop in front of one. "Books always make for the best presents," she says, browsing through the display cart and picking up an old edition of *Madame Bovary*.

I browse for a few minutes before I find exactly the book I had in mind. "I think this will be great for Ave as a Christmas gift," I say, showing her the 50th-anniversary edition of *The Little Prince*.

We resume our tour, stopping only when we arrive at Place Pigalle, famous for its eccentric stores and the iconic Moulin Rouge on which the movie was based. Yeah, I might have geeked out in my research before getting on the flight here, what can I say? I like to be prepared.

"I've always wanted to see a cabaret," Riley says. "The ballet, the costumes, the feathers, the femininity of it. It's so beautiful and grandiose."

"Why don't we check if there's a show tonight?"

She swirls around. "You wouldn't mind?"

"Seeing half-dressed women displaying exceptional flexibility? Twist my arm," I say, bumping her shoulder.

We walk toward the entrance and get two tickets for the 9 o'clock show. We sit at our table, ordering two Shake Your Feather cocktails from the elaborate menu.

"Are you feeling ready for Monday?" I ask, sipping the very fruity drink. Is there even any alcohol in here?

She sighs. "A lot is riding on this, and we still need to agree on certain things. Pretty big ones actually."

I know what she's talking about. We've been discussing the strategy to best achieve Peter's vision for the festival, and surprisingly, we've had a major disagreement on how to implement it. So far, we've been able to table it for another day, choosing to take a breather rather than get upset. But now that we're a few days away, it's becoming glaringly apparent we're no closer to finding common ground.

"Let's go over what works first, if you want, yeah?" Riley nods. "We're both on the same wavelength with working with French brands and restaurants, right?

"Yes. Public Relations 101," she says. "Peter wants to get his wine out there, which means restaurants, hotel chains, and supermarkets should be involved. I meant to tell you that I scheduled a meeting on Thursday with the restaurant association."

"That's great," I say, taking notes on my phone. "And Peter'll be settled with Rachel during the first week with a booth in the 'Wineries to Watch' section."

"You managed to get him a spot there?" she exclaims. A few heads turn in our direction with disapproving looks. "Sorry," Riley whispers. "That's amazing," she adds at a lower level.

"I did, yeah. It's going to be perfect for showcasing his products."

"That's great. Then we have a wine-tasting event scheduled for the following week, and the Versailles Ball to close the festival on that Wednesday."

I massage the back of my neck. I know what's coming now. "Yup. I think our strategy will bring him a lot of new customers. Just need to decide on which ones."

She takes a big swig of her drink. "Remind me again why we're talking business in the middle of the Moulin Rouge?"

I smile, toying with the decorative umbrella in my glass. "Because it's a big deal for both of us? Because we love our jobs and are both committed to making this work?" I stab an orange with the end of the umbrella. "And because the show hasn't started yet. And we need to get over this issue."

"You're right," she says, slumping back against her chair. "Okay, hear me out." Oh, here comes that famous negotiation tone. I call it her "campaign speech" voice because she gets all serious and has a way of having whole roomfuls of professionals eating out of the palm of her hand.

"I think we need to appeal to millennials. I've seen the studies, and wine in France is way cheaper than in North

America. We shouldn't go the 'luxurious foreign brand' route. We should reach out to influencers instead, market it like a wine you drink at family reunions, dinners with friends, birthdays." She straightens, her hands flat on the table. "What we need is a big social media campaign that pushes the narrative that Winsome Wines is new and exciting but also familiar and approachable."

"But Peter has been clear that he wants to expand his brand in Europe, and in North America, it's a luxury. What will consumers think if they travel to Europe and see his product, but the quality doesn't match?"

"No, Miles. I'm not talking about having him lower the product quality, come on."

"So you want the consumer in North America to pay more for the same product?" I raise an eyebrow, not sure that I follow her logic.

"It's two different markets, you can't expect the same marketing strategies."

I finish my drink and flag the waiter down for another one. "My point is, I think we should target more refined consumers, higher class, people with more expensive taste. They should see Peter's wine as something you only take out of your cellar for special occasions. Michelin-star restaurants will be the only ones serving it. It'll create a buzz around it, make people wonder what about it is so special. And then we'll be able to tell them about its origins in Canada and how far it had to travel, giving it a unique selling point."

Riley doesn't seem convinced one bit. "I just don't see why people would pay that much for a wine when France has some of the finest on the market."

"Because it's that good. Everybody will want it. And you and I both know that when it comes to wine, France doesn't have the monopoly anymore."

"Peter's wine is good, but you can't tell me it's as good as a St-Emilion or a Côte du Rhone." She crosses her arms, not dropping my gaze.

"I get that. I do," I say. "But I still think French people are more sensitive to high-quality products. Our message should be targeted toward a clientele that has the means to consistently support the label and turn it into a household name among the more affluent."

Riley shakes her head. "I think you're wrong," she says, not budging. This woman is stubborn as hell, and she's testing my patience. I take a deep breath.

"You know what?" I say in an effort to appease her and shift the mood. "Let's discuss this with croissants, butter, and jam tomorrow, okay? The show's about to start."

But she doesn't reply. Her lips are pressed into a thin line, brows furrowed, lost in her thoughts. Did I say something wrong? We got a bit heated, but that's one of the things I love about our dynamic, it's full of passion. Plus, it's okay to not always agree.

"No," she says briskly, tapping the table with the tip of her finger. "You don't get to decide where we should discuss this or when we're done talking about it."

My jaw drops. What?

"I have a say in this as much as you do. You don't get to decide," Riley repeats, hammering out each word.

Wow, this conversation took a huge turn, and I have no clue how to bring it back. "Ry, listen," I try softly. "All I'm saying is maybe we can talk about it after a good night's sleep. And the show really *is* about to start."

Riley's shoulders drop, and she downs her glass. I wish I knew what was going on in her mind right now, how to soothe her worries.

She fixes her gaze on me, hard and confident. "I won't let my voice be silenced again, Miles."

The subtext hangs between us, heavy, imposing. It feels like a punch in the gut. I can't believe she's even considering comparing our situation with her ex-husband.

Comparing *me* to her ex-husband.

It disgusts me. I clench my fist on my knee, doing my best to regulate my breathing. All I've been trying to do this past year has been to uplift her as much as I could, empower her and make her feel valued.

What am I missing here? It's just further proof that she and I would be a terrible idea. She would always have this fear in the back of her mind, and I would end up resenting her for never fully trusting me.

The lights dim, and the music starts, making the chances of bringing this conversation to an acceptable end impossible. I see it on her face, that she feels terrible for what she's said. But her feelings don't make what I see in her eyes any less true.

I offer her a small smile, one that says, "It's okay. I understand. I'm sorry." But deep down, I don't really understand. And it hurts like hell.

Women come onto the stage, shaking their costumes, glittery and covered in feathers, and all I can think about is how I want to get the fuck out of here.

TWENTY-TWO

Conversations in the Dark

Riley

*O*ur fight last night might as well be labeled as the worst Miles and I have ever had. And dubbed the shittiest I've ever felt.

After the show, we returned to our hotel in silence. I felt my apology frozen on the tip of my tongue, unable to cross the finish line.

"Goodnight," he said when we arrived in front of my room, a small smile on his face that looked nothing like his real one. I know the way Miles looks when he smiles. His whole face lights up, dimples and all. That wasn't one of them. He didn't give me the time to reply, he just turned around and left.

For the rest of the night, even though he was literally on the other side of my bedroom wall, we favored emails and texts to iron out the last-minute details for the start of the festival.

And in the end, after a bit of back and forth—and looping Peter in on some minor aspects of our plan—we agreed to move forward with my strategy.

I dig myself deeper into the pillows now, pressing the heels of my hands against my eyelids.

I should come with a trigger warning or something. Hi, I'm Riley. Please don't make any constructive suggestions or I will blow up in your face. Make sure your totally reasonable ideas don't conflict with mine. Definitely don't calmly and rationally try to make a case for your opinions, either.

Yeah, I completely overreacted. It's just... It got to me.

It wasn't so much what Miles said, though it probably wasn't the right time or place. But the combination of the argument we were having and him cutting the conversation short made me see red, and before I knew it, Sean's face was flashing in my mind. It was like I was back there, with him, all over again.

I could feel my skin throbbing, my palms pressed against my pink dress getting sweaty, my heart pounding in my ribcage for the whole room to hear.

And so I just said the first thing that came to mind to make it stop. The sudden relief of not feeling trapped underwater anymore was short-lived, though, when I saw the effect my reaction had on him.

I wanted to take it back. Reach out and shove the words down my throat. But I didn't have the time. The show started, and with it went my apology. During the show, I snuck a few glances in his direction, but his expression stayed the same, his thoughts inscrutable. How I wished I could have taken his hand in mine, communicating my regret through this small touch. But I guess I choked.

I check my phone. It's only 7 a.m., so I grab a pen and the postcard I bought for my sister and open the French doors leading to the balcony. It's a bit chilly this time of day, even though we're in the dead of summer, but the view is totally making up for it: front-row seats to the gorgeous Iron Lady. I wrap myself in my throw blanket and sit down on the chair, flopping the Eiffel Tower postcard on the table.

Since Charlee is always traveling, we've made it a tradition to send each other at least one postcard from whatever country we're visiting. Granted, she's sent me way more over the years—I must have at least seventy at home— but it's something I've treasured since the first one she sent me almost six years ago during her first trip with *Wild Planet*.

Not being able to see her as much as I'd like is a weight I carry with me every day. But some days, when I come home from work exhausted and ready to hit the hay and see her sloppy handwriting on thick card paper in my mailbox, it makes me feel like a kid again coming home to a surprise. It's become our way to let each other know that even though we're miles away 90 percent of the time, our hearts are forever nearby.

Dear Char,

I've made it to Paris—the City of Lights, of Love. So far, the City of Love is still just a name because no Frenchman has swept me off my feet yet. I must be doing something wrong. All I've gotten is Miles looking like a bearded Greek god next to me, acting as a repellent and scaring all the men away *sad emoji*

Mentioning Miles gives my heart a little thump.

Speaking of, it's becoming harder and harder to ignore the effect this man has on me. You were right; I was wrong. I know. I'm starting to question the reasons I've been staying away, especially considering how much time I spend trying to resist him. It's getting exhausting.

I hope you're staying safe from the fires in Australia. Don't roll your eyes. And call me when you can. If you see a koala, send me photos. Don't bring any back.

From Paris, in annoyance,

Ry

I tuck the postcard in the envelope and write the address Charlee left for me. I'm not sure how long she'll be over there, but hopefully, it arrives before she jets off somewhere new. I lean back and shield my eyes from the sun creeping over the nearby trees, and it's then that I notice the time. No way am I going to be late today of all days. Miles won't have any choice but to see me this morning, and there won't be any option for me to avoid him either.

THE FESTIVAL IS LOCATED JUST a few blocks from our hotel. It's 8 a.m. when I meet Peter and Miles already waiting for me at the back entrance of the Grand Palais.

"Am I late?" I ask, avoiding making eye contact with the tall, bearded man on my left.

"Not at all, we're the ones early," Peter says, planting a kiss on each of my cheeks. "When in France."

I turn to Miles. "Hi."

"Hey," Miles says, clearly not doing any better than me despite how well put together he looks. I can't help but stifle a nervous laugh, and Miles smiles in return.

"So," Peter says, pulling me out of my thoughts. "What's our plan for today, superstars?"

Miles claps his hands together before he says, "Well, we're going to get you settled in your booth right now. The festival starts in an hour."

"There's going to be a lot of journalists and media today," I add. "But you're ready. Just don't forget the key points we've rehearsed."

Peter nods. "Yes, yes. We're young, fun, and trendy."

"Please don't say trendy," Miles grumbles.

He laughs, clapping his hand on Miles's shoulders. "Let's go then. Rachel's meeting us here in a few, she's coordinating the delivery of our products to the Grand Palais."

We find our table in the magnificent hall under the glass roof, the sun's rays glittering through it like a mirror ball and basking the room in natural light. Rachel arrives a few minutes later, arms piled with boxes and two men in a similar situation behind her.

"Hi," she says, breathing hard. "Sorry, I'm late. There was traffic."

Miles and I exchange a knowing look. "Congrats on surviving the experience," I say, grabbing a few bottles from the boxes.

At nine, the doors open, and people slowly trickle in. Journalists arrive first, cameras and mics in hand, ready to interview the wineries. Peter does great; he's a natural on camera. Charismatic and confident but not cocky, he delivers the well-crafted messages with ease and tact, earning him curious looks from several other newspapers. Miles and I smile at each other when Rachel answers a few questions in French, to the wonder of the crowd. When asked, she replies that even though she comes from an anglophone family, her grandma lived in Quebec all her life and instilled French in her at a young age.

But it's when Peter opens a bottle from his latest vat—a fresh, light white wine with fruity undertones—that he seals the deal. Connoisseurs swirl the wine in their glasses, getting a whiff of the aroma, before taking a sip and letting their taste buds become acquainted. People are captivated.

Around 4 p.m., Rachel and Peter sit down with the owner of a winery in Bordeaux who stopped by their booth earlier. Meanwhile, Miles and I are stuck managing the stand, plastering smiles on our faces, and doing our best to answer questions in our horrible French.

"I can't believe the turnaround, it's been phenomenal," he says when we have a minute to breathe, combing his fingers through his hair. "The French really do like their wine."

We're both sitting on swivel stools, a healthy distance between us.

I should say something... I'm gonna tell him how awful I feel. But Miles beats me to it. He drags my stool, spinning me toward him. I nearly yelp, gripping his thigh for balance. His gaze falls there before finding mine again, his throat bobbing. I jerk my hand away, following the movement of his Adam's apple, up and down, hypnotized by the way his muscles tic along his neck.

Not touching or hugging Miles has proven to be more difficult than I'd imagined. I don't know if it's something in the Parisian air or the incessant pull I feel around him, but I always end up leaning against him, resting a hand on his arm, always seeking his contact. It blurs my brain, and it's always when it's too late that I realize I'm touching him, getting closer, and acting everything but professional. Rules, Riley. You set rules.

"Ry, listen, about this weekend, I—"

"I completely overreacted, and I'm sorry," I cut in. His brows shoot up. "You didn't do anything wrong, I just got defensive. It woke up some old insecurities, you know... with Sean."

Miles's body stiffens. I'm a jerk for making him feel that way. "I'm really sorry. How can I make it up to you?"

"I shouldn't have shut you out," he says, exhaling. "In the moment, I just felt like…"

I want to reach out to him so badly, rest my hand on his thigh and show him that I'm here. But I don't. "Like what?"

"Like you were seeing me the way you saw him. And all I've been trying to do is make sure you feel comfortable and safe with me."

My heart squeezes. I've never wanted to undo something more. He does make me feel comfortable and safe. All the freaking time.

"It was a bit like a slap in the face, you know," he adds. He looks back at me, a little smile stretching his lips. "But it's fine, okay? I get it. I truly do. Let's forget about it, all right?"

I realize in that moment how much I know him, how well I can read his face and the hurt he tries to conceal, his body language, and his moods.

"How can I make it up to you?"

He pats my hand. "There's nothing to make up for, Ry, we're good."

"Please," I whisper.

Miles appears to be considering it for a second, but then he grabs my hand, my skin prickling like the heat of a million suns at the touch. "Okay, fine. I know how you can make it up to me."

The flicker in his eyes screams trouble, and my heart replies hell yes.

"Let's hear it, Clark."

"Riley, Miles." Peter beams from behind us, the woman from the Bordeaux winery standing next to him. Why? Why did Peter have to arrive now? I look at Miles and mouth, "We're not done here." He nods before winking at me, and I melt a little bit more inside.

"I'd like to introduce you to Myriam Hatem. She owns the Chateau Lautrec near Bordeaux," Peter continues when they reach the booth.

"Nice to meet you both," Myriam says, shaking our hands. She's an elegant woman, with olive skin and thick dark curls framing her face and highlighting her green eyes. I'd say she's about the same age as Peter, in her late forties.

"Our pleasure," replies Miles.

Peter rests his hand on Myriam's arm, and they both exchange a chuckle. Well. would you look at that...

"Myriam here has generously invited us to spend a few days on her domain next week after the festival concludes."

"I thought the two of you might like to visit the chateau and see how we make our wine," Myriam says, sliding one hand into her pocket. "It'd be a great way to talk more about business."

A few days in the French country, in wine paradise? Can this trip get any better? And in a chateau nonetheless. I can already picture us there, lounging on chairs in the middle of the estate, surrounded by tall oak trees that shade us from the sun, basking in the smell of flowers. Far from the city. Maybe even read a book? When was the last time I actually sat down and read more than a chapter? With a glass of rosé. Oh yes, that would be so lovely.

"That's very kind of you," I say. "I'm sure we can work something out." I reach for my purse and take out my business card. "Here, you can call me to discuss the details."

Myriam takes the card and thanks me before Peter pulls her away.

"Look at them already conspiring over there," Miles leans in to whisper in my ear. The hair on the nape of my neck rises as his breath hits my skin.

"This is incredible," I say, eyes fixed on Myriam and Peter laughing heartily together. "This is really, really good for us and the firm." I turn around, coming almost nose-to-nose with him.

One second.

Two.

Three seconds pass, and neither one of us makes a move to retreat back to our own space. I stare at him, standing so tall, so broad, so close to me, his maple and coffee scent overrunning my system and taking control of my body. And he's staring right back.

I want to kiss him, but I can't. I shouldn't.

Against my own volition, my body leans in slightly, but Miles squeezes my arm, holding me in place.

I straighten, clearing my throat to swallow the disappointment rising in me. He's rejecting me.

"So," I say, clapping my hands on my knees. Great diversion. Very effective. "What were you going to say before Peter interrupted us before?"

Miles holds my gaze for a second before saying, "Um, yeah. But it's okay, Ry, we don't have to—"

"No, no. Tell me." Please tell me my stupidity didn't ruin this.

"Okay, but it's probably not a good idea."

"I'll be the judge of that."

Miles grunts. "I might have seen in the hotel lobby that the hotel offers a French cooking class tonight. I thought it might be fun to try it out."

"A French cooking class with the one and only Milesy?" He rolls his eyes in a dramatic way. "Are you kidding? Yes!"

"Really, you want to do it?"

"Yes."

"All right, then. It's a d… delightful surprise."

I can't help but snort. "A delightful surprise? What is this, the year 1920?" I have to give it to him, though, it was a nice save.

"Yes, a delightful surprise," he mumbles. "Because I didn't think you'd say yes. So, that's why it was a surprise. And delightful, because it makes me happy. So, you know… delightful surprise."

I smile warmly at him. He's even cuter when he babbles.

"It's a delightful surprise, then."

TWENTY-THREE
Rub A Dub

Miles

*R*iley in a red-and-white striped apron might be the cutest thing I have ever seen. Or maybe it's the red scrunchie holding her blond hair up in a high ponytail and baring her shoulders that makes the whole thing adorable. Either way, she makes me want to spin her around, grab her face, and get a taste of those cherry-red lips.

And if I hadn't been a total idiot earlier today, she would have kissed me. Riley would have *actually* kissed me. And I turned her down.

I'm such an idiot. I can't continue to dance this miserable tango alone. Tempting myself one day, torturing myself the other.

"*Bonsoir, tout le monde*. Welcome to French Skills 101," the lady at the front says. "My name is Noémie, and I will be your chef tonight. I see some of you already have your aprons on. Perfect."

I smile and wink at Riley. She turns pink. Every time.

"Tonight, we will be preparing a three-course meal," Noémie continues. "First, we'll make a salmon and avocado amuse-bouche. For the main course, we'll prepare a traditional gratin dauphinois accompanied by a duck confit. And for the best part, mesdames et messieurs, le dessert. We'll try our hands at a delicious *tarte aux fraises*. Simple, but so refreshing during these hot summer days."

"Do you know what a *tarte aux fraises* is?" Riley whispers.

"Strawberry pie, I think." I nod toward the bowls of strawberries at the end of each table.

"Do you know how to make any of the things she just said? Because I only know how to boil pasta."

I laugh because she's not even really good at that. I've tried her pasta. Twice. I could have eaten it right out of the box, and it would've tasted the same. I'm all for "al dente," but she takes it to a whole other level. "Yes, I've made a gratin dauphinois before. It's basically potatoes and cream. And strawberry pie is my favorite dessert."

"I can't wait to see you in action, Milesy."

I ignore the way my cock stirs to attention and focus instead on the second part. "Ry, I swear, if you call me Milesy again, I—"

"You'll what, Miles, uh?" She raises one eyebrow because of fucking course she challenges me. She loves it and knows I can't turn it down either.

"I'll… I'll…"

I'll grab you by the strings of this ridiculously cute apron and pull you against me. I'll place one hand on your waist and the other on the nape of your neck, coaxing your mouth open and tasting you on my lips. I'll hold your body firmly against mine while I kiss you until you can no longer breathe, panting and gasping until we can't discern whose breath belongs to whom. I'll twirl you around until you're bent on the table, your beautiful, curvy ass on display for me. I'll order you not to move while I kneel behind you, trailing my fingers along the skin of your ankles, calves, thighs, kissing you there too. Licking. Biting. I'll hear you moan when I move my tongue higher, flat against your wet thong. I'll...

"Miles? I think you can let go of the counter."

"Huh?" I startle back to the room where my hand is grasping the counter so hard I'm pretty sure I'll leave a dent in the wood, and Riley is looking at me curiously. I abruptly let go of the table, some of the blood leaving my crotch and rushing back to my fingers.

Fuck, I'm half-hard in the middle of *cooking class*. She's driving me crazy. I'm having sex dreams about her in public now.

It's this fucking trip to Paris that makes things so damn unbearable when it comes to my craving for her. Being around her 24-7, knowing there's only one wall separating her bed from mine—it's all been playing in my head on a loop.

"All right, sous-chefs, let's get started," Noémie says, a big smile on her face. "One of you can mince the smoked and raw salmon in thin cubes first while your partner peels the avocados and mashes them."

"You do the avocados, Fletcher. I'll take care of the salmon," I say, pulling the chef's knife from the block.

"Oh, you're giving the orders now, huh?"

I lean behind her to grab the salmon on her right and drop my voice for only her to hear. "I always give the orders."

"Well, not with me, sir." She snatches the salmon from my hands. "You do the avocado. I'll take care of this." She grabs the knife from my other hand. "Thank you!"

Call me sir one more time and see what happens…

"I've been thinking," Riley says now. "Did you see the spark between Peter and Myriam earlier?"

"You mean the full-blown fire?"

"Oh, good, it wasn't just me then. I'd love to see Peter doing something else than work for once. She seems great. Imagine if he fell in love with a French woman who owns a winery."

"The perfect match." I glance at the way she's butchering the salmon and internally scream. This woman should never be allowed near a kitchen. But the way she focuses on the task, her tongue stuck between her teeth, all her attention on this simple act of cutting the fish right is too cute to fault.

"Okay, here," I say, dropping my avocado and moving in next to her. I pick up my knife and a piece of raw salmon and place my fingers on it, slicing a thick piece.

"You have to hold it here." I show her my position on the salmon. "It'll be easier for you to have more consistent slices. And keep you from hurting yourself."

Riley takes her own knife.

"No, not like that," I interrupt her. "You're going to cut yourself by holding the knife that way." I come behind her. "How have you managed to stay alive this long?" I say, shaking my head.

"Uber Eats, dining out, and you losing your bet last year and cooking me dinner basically every day for the last six months." She turns her head and grins.

"All right, let's see what we're working with here." I point to her hands. "May I?"

She nods. I gently hold her hands in mine and close them around the knife's handle, electricity zapping up my arms and causing my heart to short-circuit. I leave a little space between her body and mine, but I know she'd fit perfectly against me.

"Now, what you want to do is place your index finger here." I adjust us so she can see what I mean as I explain. "Your thumb should hold the knife on the side here. Yes, right here, perfect."

"This is some precise work, Clark," she jokes.

I take her other hand. "Place it right where I showed you earlier. Now put pressure with the tip of your finger. Yes, just like that. And then slice the salmon, starting with the tip of your knife and let the edge go through until the heel."

"We have a professional chef in the house tonight," Noémie coos from the end of our workspace. "Look at that knife technique." Some people raise their heads and look at us.

Great. All eyes on me, watching my every move.

There's a reason I love to cook. I can let my mind wander in every direction, no disturbance, no sound except for the kitchen utensils. It's just me and my creations. A solitary hobby.

"Great teamwork, chefs, keep going," Noémie says, walking over to the next table.

"You're gonna get a gold star at the end if you continue impressing the teacher like this." She bumps my shoulder with hers.

"Shut up," I mumble. "And focus on your salmon." I angry-mash my avocado while she snickers and cuts her salmon into little cubes.

"Ow!" Riley drops her knife.

I whip my head around to find her holding her finger between her lips. "Are you okay? Show me."

She winces when she lets go, blood collecting at the tip and forming a half-dome before dripping on the floor.

"I think I got my fingers too close to the blade," Riley hisses. "It fucking stings."

"Oh, you're cursing now?" I cock one eyebrow, amused. She's always so careful with her words. "Let me take care of it, I'll be right back."

I go to the front desk, ask for a first aid kit, grab the bandages and some antiseptic, and run back to the cooking class.

"Gimme your finger, Fletcher."

"Something I never thought you'd say to me," she says before reluctantly handing it over.

I pour a bit of antiseptic on her finger and press a small cotton overtop to absorb the excess blood. The wound cleaned, I wrap the Band-Aid, making sure it's not too tight.

"There you go." I kiss her fingertip. "Good as new."

She smiles, looking at me with something I can't quite discern. "Thank you, Miles." She looks at our entrée. "We should really get to cooking, though, or we won't get to the dessert. And you and I both know it's the best part."

We spend the next two hours juggling our time between potatoes, cheese, butter, duck, and strawberries. Everything we make tastes like heaven. I've never cooked with such high-quality ingredients. I always try, though, to get local produce from farmers' markets back home. But it's nothing compared to the taste of the butter here. Or the strawberries, juicy and sweet, without adding a pinch of sugar.

When we get to the dessert, I have to physically keep Riley away from the strawberries.

"Stop eating those, we won't have enough for the pie!" I scowl.

I make the mistake of booping her nose with my floured finger to annoy her. She replies by diving her hand into the flour bag, her eyes fixed on me, and clapping it to my cheek, spreading flour all over my beard.

"Riley…" I grunt, warning in my tone.

She looks at me with those big, innocent brown eyes, a sly smile stretching her lips. Oh, how I want to kiss it off her face. She wouldn't look so smug then.

I dip the tip of a strawberry in the custard cream we prepared and spread it on her full, red lips. I'm half mesmerized by the way it coats the plump skin, half tempted to run my tongue over them, licking them clean.

Her warm breath caresses my fingers where my thumb lingers on her bottom lip. She darts her tongue out, barely grazing me, but I feel it. It's there, and it is making me feral for more. I hold her gaze, and she holds mine right back as if she's daring me to take it one step further.

Suddenly, what started as a fun little game isn't all that fun anymore. Like every time I get too close to her, I lose sight of why I shouldn't. She gets under my skin like no woman ever has.

I drop my hand reluctantly, watching the disappointment on her face. Or maybe I'm projecting my own feelings.

"Do you want me to show you how to make the crust?" I ask, my voice hoarse.

"Sure," she says without much conviction, and I curse myself for making her feel like shit.

But it's for the best.

Right?

TWENTY-FOUR

Dandelions

Miles

"*R*iley, you ready?" I ask as I knock on her door.

"In a minute!" she yells.

I chuckle, shaking my head. *On-time* and *Riley* are not words that usually go well together. Although she surprised me early this week when she showed up at 8 a.m. sharp for the festival kick-off. We're a day away from closing this first work week, and so far, it looks like Riley finally got herself a watch. I'll need to think about how to get that habit to stick when we cross back the Atlantic.

I lean against the wall as I wait for her to come out, thinking about our night ahead and how I get to see my sister for the first time in over a year… in Paris. What are the odds, right?

Turns out that Josh has a premiere in Paris tomorrow for a movie he did the musical score for. And since Avery knew

Riley and I were in Paris with a client, she decided to join Josh for the trip. So tonight is pretty much a double date at a restaurant on a boat on the Seine, except Riley and I technically aren't a couple. But hey, details.

My phone buzzes in my pants.

Avery: We're leaving our hotel. See you soooooon :D

I smile, typing back to say I'm so excited to see my baby sister too, knowing she'll roll her eyes when she sees it, and put the phone back in my pocket just as Riley's door clicks.

And the woman of my dreams stands in front of me.

Lighting up the entire hallway. My whole heart.

Looking gorgeous in her olive-colored dress that falls just below her knee, a split on the side revealing long, tanned legs begging to have my mouth on them, and higher... fuck. The top of her dress is so fitted it looks like she's wearing a corset as it frames her chest, tempting me in the most delicious way. All I want to do right now is to rip the dress's poor excuse for straps and then trap her between my chest and the wall, where I can feel every inch of her body come alive under my fingers.

I hold my breath as my eyes find hers, molten chocolate staring right back at me, framed by her beautiful golden locks. I wonder if she chose that dress purposefully because she knows how much this color on her affects me, and the thought is enough to make me giddy.

And judging from the rosiness of her cheeks and the little breaths she draws as she takes me in, I don't leave her indifferent either.

I clear my throat, forcing myself to focus on her face. "You look incredible."

She smiles that confident smile of hers and slips her arm into mine. "I know. You've cleaned up nicely too."

"I know."

We exit the hotel and wait for our taxi to arrive. Once at the docks, two familiar silhouettes are waiting by the bow of the boat. I squeeze Ry's hand once before jogging toward them.

"Ave!"

My sister turns around, and it only takes her a second before she sprints my way.

"Miles," she calls as she throws herself into my arms. I catch her easily, hugging her close, her feet dangling in the air while her arms are wrapped around my neck.

"I missed you," I say, squeezing her just a little more.

Avery slips out of our embrace, puts both hands on my shoulders, and raises a single eyebrow. "Are you sick? Do you have a fever? Should I call a doctor?"

I roll my eyes. "Shut up," I mumble, but can't help smiling at her teasing.

I've missed her so much I can feel it deep in my bones. And even though she jokes that I'm not the type to show my emotions, my sister has always made it easy because she's been the constant throughout my life. There are certain bonds that distance can't break or alter. Invisible strings that are more powerful than anything.

I take her hands off my shoulders, place a quick kiss on her cheek, and say: "Come on, we're being weird."

She snorts. "I know, but it's so strange to see you here. And with company, no less," she adds, wiggling her eyebrows.

"Stop," I warn.

"Riley!" she says, patting my shoulder and heading toward Ry.

"Avery, for god's sake," I mutter under my breath, rubbing my jaw.

She turns around and mouths, "relax," and I hear muffled laughter behind me. I don't have time to see what Josh finds so fucking funny because my sister is currently kissing Riley on each cheek.

"A la française," she says in a terrible accent. "Nice to meet you, Riley."

"You look tense, man," a deep voice says from behind me, a hint of amusement in his tone.

I try to relax my shoulders and force myself to turn my attention away from my meddling sister to focus instead on my brother-in-law.

"Hey, J," I say, hugging him. Even though Josh is a tall guy, I tower over him by several inches. "It's been too long, brother."

A lot has changed in the last few years, the biggest being my relationship with Josh. Seeing how good he is with my sister and how happy he's made her, I've let go of the grudge

I held against him. When they got married back in Toronto last year, Josh officially became part of the family. And family is sacred to me.

Since then, we've developed a long-distance bromance, and frankly, I'm not mad about it. I like it. Especially when I introduced him to rugby and had him eating grass a bit the first few times.

"Don't worry, she told me she'd behave," Josh says while slipping his hands in his pockets. "She's just trying to get a reaction out of you, you know that."

"Yeah…" I trail off, shaking my head. "It's working."

"Always," he answers, his gaze trained on his wife, a knowing smile at the corner of his lips.

The girls wander back to us, and I don't miss the little glance that Riley shoots me, questioning, intrigued. What the fuck did Avery say to her?

"Are we ready to head in?" Josh asks, slipping his arm around Avery's waist.

Inside, the boat is barely lit, leaving instead the City of Lights to do a spectacular job of illuminating the night.

"So, tell me, J," I say after we order a few drinks. Champagne, to celebrate being in Europe together. "What's the movie premiering this week?"

"The new Pixar," Josh says. "Beautiful feature about a Vietnamese family that settles in Toronto and has to adjust to a new culture."

"That must've been a cool one to work on," Riley says. She's sitting right next to me, on the window side, and the city lights are dancing on her face. She's never looked more gorgeous than she does right now.

"It really was," Josh says. "I got to work with Vietnamese artists who taught me a lot about their culture history and how to best influence the music. It was very inspiring."

"He's been working so hard on this one," my sister adds. "There are even talks about a possible Oscar for the score category."

Josh snaps his head to his wife. "Baby, what did we say about awards talk before nominations are even out?"

Avery pretends to pout. "I'm sorry, but I'm just so excited for my incredibly talented husband."

They exchange heated glances as if the rest of the world doesn't exist.

"Get a room, you two," I mumble.

"Grow up," Avery shoots back. She looks from Josh to my business partner. "So, Riley, tell me. What's it like working with my super annoying brother?"

Ry chuckles. "He's not that bad. He's like a big bear. He has his moods, but once you figure out how to work around them, he's easy enough."

She drops her hand to my knee under the table, away from prying eyes. I glance at her, startled by such a rare gesture of affection. Riley returns a tiny smile as her thumb begins to trace little circles on my inner thigh.

I'm not quite sure I understand what's happening right now. Maybe it's the setting, maybe it's Paris. Maybe it's Avery and Josh's love filling the air, but I'm not about to draw my thigh away.

Although, she has some nerve to think she can get away with reducing my entire world to this one point of contact without thinking I'll reciprocate.

"Miles has been supportive these last few years," she continues. "At our old job, in my personal life, and recently with—" The last words come out of her mouth a bit strangled, probably because my foot is currently entangled between her bare calves, stroking her skin.

Riley practically chokes and breaks into a coughing fit.

"Everything okay?" Josh asks. "Should we get more water?"

"Yeah," I add, a smirk on my lips. "Is everything okay, Ry?"

Riley manages to regain her breath. "I'm fine," she croaks. "Just a piece of meat that went down the wrong tube." She chugs her glass of wine in one go before putting it back down a little too harshly. Avery and Josh gape at her. My sister turns her attention to me, squinting her eyes. I shrug.

Before she has time to say anything, Josh—thank fuck—directs the conversation onto another subject. "How's rugby going?"

"Great! We have a solid team this year, it's been fun to play more competitively than we're used to."

"Have you been kicking ass?"

With Riley's hand still stroking my thigh, my focus is everywhere but on Josh's question.

"Hm?"

She faintly brushes her fingertips on my inner thigh, and yet the sensation feels like she's staking a possessive claim on me.

"Uh, yeah, the team is doing great…." She draws small circles, my heart threatening to stop as blood rushes down. I clear my throat. "… very, very good guys."

I jerk my arm to catch her wrist and stop her before she makes me come in my boxers and bump the table in the process.

"Sorry." I smile tightly. "I dropped my napkin." I lean down, pretending to pick it off the floor as the cruise continues its gentle glide down the Seine. Paris is slipping by gracefully as the sun vanishes beneath the horizon, revealing the lights of the most romantic city in the world twinkling on the shimmering water.

During dinner, we pass under the iconic bridges of Paris, the Pont des Arts, the Pont Neuf, and the most breathtaking of all, the Pont Alexandre III. In the twilight, we catch a glimpse of the Notre-Dame Cathedral and the Orsay Museum, their architecture so typical of Paris.

We laugh, we eat till our heart's content, we drink the finest champagne and wine. It all feels so natural, the four of us together.

But when the sun rises over the tiled rooftops of Paris tomorrow morning, this evening will only remain alive in my memories, and I'll be left to hold on to that feeling of happiness for as long as I can.

"Attention, mesdames et messieurs," a French voice says through a speaker, interrupting my thoughts. "We'll soon be arriving in front of the Tour Eiffel, where we will witness a spectacular show."

We all look out the window as the boat approaches the Iron Lady softly lit. And at 8 p.m. sharp, the Eiffel Tower sparkles with a thousand lights, glittering like a diamond in the night. Covered in a golden hue, the entire city of Paris is dazzling under this extraordinary sight right before our eyes.

It is magical.

"I've never seen anything like this," Riley whispers, her face turned toward the show. From my spot beside her, I can see the lights reflecting off her skin, turning her cheekbones into a golden disco ball, and my breath catches in my throat. I take back what I said earlier. Riley has never looked more beautiful at *this* moment.

"Me neither," I reply simply, my gaze still glued to her as I slip my arm around her shoulders, bringing her against me. She lets herself go without any kind of resistance, soft and warm on my chest. I tuck her head under my chin, bringing her closer to me.

We remain like that for a while, quietly taking it all in. When I look at Josh and Avery mimicking our position, my insides scream and roil with envy that on the outside, we look like two couples enjoying a romantic evening when I know the truth.

As the boat resumes its motion, the servers clear the tables and serve the desserts.

Josh grabs the bottle of champagne. "Last round with dessert?"

"With pleasure," I say, holding out my glass. He fills both mine and Riley's as well as his own and sets the bottle down.

It's only then that I realize he doesn't pour my sister a glass. I've been so preoccupied with trying to make sure Riley has a good time that I missed the fact that I don't think Avery's had a drink all night.

My throat tightens. "No champagne, Ave?"

She shakes her head. "Nope, I'm good, thanks."

I raise an eyebrow. "Sure? You didn't have any wine either."

My hands get clammy as my wheels turn a hundred miles a second. Is she—

"No, *thanks*," my sister says, holding my gaze.

Avery exchanges a look with her husband, who gives her hand a squeeze and a nod.

She lets out a sigh.

My heart races.

"Well, I guess now is as good a time as any. We're pregnant!" Avery exclaims.

Emotion grips me, crawling into every corner of my body and pushing the words out of my lips. "I… I'm going to be an uncle?" I say, my throat thickening.

Avery's eyes blur under the onslaught of tears. "Yes."

I let my tears roll down my face because fuck it, my sister is going to be a mother and she's going to be incredible and I'm going to be an uncle, for god's sake. I'll never be a father, but I'll always have this.

I get up, walk around the table, and take my sister in my arms, holding her tight.

"I'm so happy for you, Ave," I whisper so only she can hear.

She clutches me a little tighter in response.

I turn to Josh. "Congrats, man," I say as I pull him into a hug.

"Thanks, brother," he says, clapping my back.

"Congratulations to you both," Riley says, and I notice the wetness in her eyes. "This is amazing news."

"Thank you," Avery says. "Josh has already made plans for the nursery. He's unstoppable."

"Come on." Josh flushes red. "I'm just trying to help, you're the one doing all the work." He softly places his hand on his wife's stomach. "It's the least I can do."

"I'm so happy for you," Riley says. "Children seem like a huge adjustment, but the most wonderful thing to have in our lives."

And those last words make me freeze in my chair, knocking the wind out of me. Like a knockout punch to the gut. The answer I've been dreading. I feel Avery's gaze on me. She knows what Riley's words are doing to me. She knows it stirs my demons, my fears, my anxieties.

I scramble to draw a breath, sliding a placid mask over my face.

I can never be with Riley.

Because I can't give her the most wonderful thing that can happen to her.

TWENTY-FIVE
Wildest Dreams

Riley

*T*he air leaves my lungs. "Ow, easy!"

"Sorry, ma'am," says the woman at the rental store. "It's supposed to be a little tight."

"I understand, but this isn't the eighteenth century. Women should be allowed to breathe," I say, a strained smile plastered on my face.

The saleswoman pulls the string tight on another row of the corset. "Almost done."

I can't believe a whole week has gone by since we landed on French soil. Tonight's gala will close out the international wine festival, celebrating a very intense week of work. One last epic evening, a chance for us all to let our hair down, so to speak. A ball at the prestigious Palace of Versailles, dressed as if we were guests of the court of King Louis XV. After several attempts, I eventually found this rental store in the

254 | ELODIE COLLIARD

6th arrondissement filled to the brim with period dresses and dug out this beautiful red dress covered with white lace on the bodice. Like the 18th-century gowns, the corset makes my waist appear narrow, accentuating my lace-contoured chest and showcasing the generous curves of my hips. The tight, dark red sleeves halt just above my elbows and finish with a frill of delicate white lace. At my waist, the dress spools out in a puffy princess cut, a twirl of red velvet and lace falling graciously at my feet.

With my blond hair spun in a sophisticated high bun, big curls falling on both sides of my face, I look like a sexy Marie-Antoinette.

Maybe now Miles will get out of his head and finally make a move on me. After a week of pent-up sexual tension between us that could have lit the whole city on fire, it isn't just that I want him to kiss me. I *need* him to kiss me. Otherwise, I'm going to lose my freaking mind, and who knows what I'll do when that happens. Probably something like rip his clothes off and rake my teeth on his chest.

I've tried to stay away, but I no longer have the strength. It's too consuming, taking away my focus from my work. And all of this, for what? Fear that Sean could find out that we held hands in Paris?

I smooth the creases in the skirt of my dress, twirling in front of the mirror, feeling the velvety texture slip between my fingertips. I wonder what Miles will think when he sees me, if he'll clench his jaw and clear his throat like he usually does when I catch him checking me out. He thinks he's so sneaky, but there's nothing more obvious to me than the feel of his stare gliding the length of my body, as if he's taking off one piece of clothing after the other with each second his eyes linger.

"Don't go soft on him, Riley," Avery whispered when she hugged me goodbye last night.

Last night had been... actually, I'm not quite sure I can put words to how last night felt. Freedom seemed so pale compared to the strange sense of calm my body was plunged into, as if it were the first time I'd allowed myself to relax my shoulders and dared to be more myself than I'd ever been. To speak freely without fear of judgment or repercussions. Without feeling paranoid that my shitty ex-husband would be there, misinterpreting my actions, spinning them around until they hardly made any sense.

And Miles... Miles was a snack last night, and I was hungry. Hungry to feel like a woman wanting a man and not letting fear, shame, or doubt take the wheel. The trip has been going great for the firm so far, we're exceeding Peter's expectations and cashing in a substantial amount of profit each day we're hitting and surpassing our goals. I haven't heard anything from Sean or gotten any whiff from home regarding his threats. So it was only fair I finally cut myself some slack, dipping my toe in the pool of Miles's magnetism.

The night was gorgeous, Miles exquisite. Everything happened like I was dreaming with my eyes open, up until Josh and Avery's announcement.

I felt the change in Miles's demeanor instantly, the way his breath caught, his shoulders becoming stiff. Even the smile he'd had on his face all day disappeared.

I can't help but wonder what about his sister being pregnant got him so turned upside down. My first thought was that he would have been over the moon happy to be an uncle. And if I didn't know him better, his words would have probably convinced me.

Kids have never really been at the top of my list when it comes to how I envision my future. A successful career, making sure that my sister is provided for and safe, a life where I want for nothing—those are the things that keep me up at night. Maybe finding love down the line when everything else is secure. Definitely not being trapped in an abusive marriage. But little munchkins running all around the house? Never really on my mind.

Maybe that's the reason why he was so out of it. He's thirty-five, has a stable job, and is still single, god knows why. And he's great with kids. I've seen him at Christmas work parties with other colleagues' children. He'd be a fantastic father one day. So perhaps the top of his list includes children, and Avery announcing she and Josh are expecting awoke some feelings of envy rooted too deep for him to feign pure excitement. Whatever it was, he was rattled. And I plan on finding out why.

"You're all set!"

I startle at the employee's chirpy voice, not realizing I've been staring at my reflection in the mirror all this time. I pick up my purse, pay a deposit for the dress and the heels, and head toward the door, waiting for my cab to take me straight to Versailles.

We've been booking meetings left and right since the start of the festival, signing partnerships with influencers and supermarket chains. This week has been busy *as hell*. One of the campaigns we've been negotiating will debut in the fall at Monoprix, one of France's major grocery store chains, and we couldn't be more ecstatic. We're on track to meet our ambitious goals without too many bumps in the road so far.

And tonight, it's all about scoring the final goal.

TWENTY-SIX
Love Me Like You Do

Riley

I feel like a scene from *Bridgerton* has burst out of my TV when my cab pulls up in front of the venue.

It's a show of ribbons, tall curly wigs, lace, and ruffles in every flamboyant color parading in front of me toward the palace entrance. Men distinguish themselves with sober tones of beige, black, and maroon, some wearing hats, others with white wigs and walking canes.

That's when I notice him, hands in the pockets of his purple breeches. I haven't spent too much time thinking about what Miles would look like as a scruffier and taller version of Jonathan Bailey, and I can see now that it was a good thing for my sanity.

He's wearing a luxurious tailored purple coat draped over a cream waistcoat that accentuates his already broad shoulders. The cotton shirt he wears below is adorned with a white jabot and a gold neckerchief.

I swallow hard when my eyes linger lower, on the *very* tight breeches tucked into white stockings and polished black shoes, molding everything to perfection, from his muscular thighs to the curve of his ass, and… my cheeks burn hot as I flick my eyes up to his face. Above the waist at all times tonight, got it.

I slowly make my way to him, every nerve in my body quaking with excitement and anticipation to finally have his eyes on me.

He stands in the Marble Courtyard, black-and-white tiles lining the floor beneath our feet, the palace softly and tastefully illuminated with warm lights, showcasing the fine and detailed work on the façade, the majestic gold decorations glimmering from every side. Truly a work of art.

"Good evening, my lord," I say, holding my skirt and curtsying before him. I smile when I straighten and see the dazzled expression on his face as he roams my body with his eyes, warming my blood in a matter of seconds.

Miles takes my satin-gloved hand in his, delicately slipping the garment off my arm.

Up close, I notice the more intricate pattern of his waistcoat, embroidered with golden and purple threads woven into the fabric.

I hold my breath when he slowly bends, his eyes fixated on mine. I can't ignore the usual spark missing from his gaze, and I wonder if he's feeling the pressure tonight for our firm. It almost feels like he's wearing an impenetrable armor that even I can't manage to break through. I push the thought away when he brings my hand to his lips, brushing a soft kiss on it, sending a ripple of tingles up my arm.

"Good evening, Lady…"

"Fletcher," I whisper, out of breath.

"Lady Fletcher." He smirks and adjusts the lapel of his coat. "What a beautiful sight." His voice is low and scrapes at my skin. He offers me his arm. "Shall we?"

I nod because I wouldn't manage to get a single syllable out even if I wanted to, and slide my arm in his. I'm too consumed by the weight of his arm against mine, my chest pushing against his bicep. I don't know if he notices how close we are, how there is zero to no distance between us, but I'm not complaining. I like it.

With an assured step, he leads us inside.

INSIDE, I AM BREATHLESS AT the beauty of the place. The Lower Gallery opens right onto the Gardens of Versailles. The iconic tiles continue into the room before morphing into sand-colored stones also covering the walls, vaulted arch ceilings, and antique statues in the same hue.

"I don't know if there are words in the English dictionary that describe how beautiful this place is," I say, turning on myself, trying to brand every corner to memory.

"Truly extraordinary," Miles murmurs next to me.

We head toward the stone stairs, where a bar has been set up with an abundance of wines of all sorts. We each grab a glass of white, blending into the crowd of puffy skirts and top hats.

"Rachel just texted me that they'll be here in ten minutes," I tell Miles. He appears to be light-years away.

"Perfect," he says and smiles tightly. "Just enough time for us to do some recon."

"Do you have the one-pagers we prepared for the winery?"

He pats his chest. "Right here, folded and neatly placed in envelopes. Don't worry."

"I'm not worrying," I say, defensively. "I just wanted to make sure you hadn't forgotten them at the hotel."

"I'm the organized one between the two of us, remember?" he says, winking at me.

"Right…"

Miles frowns, his gaze sliding to me with a bit more intent. "Did I say something I shouldn't have?" He looks like he's about to take a step closer but hesitates, deciding to stay where he is. "I was teasing you, you know that, right?"

I lay my gloved hand on his arm. "I know, don't worry about it, it's nothing."

"Tell me."

I sigh. "We're about to go meet with the client, Miles, it's not the time."

"I don't want us going in with anything weighing on us. Tell me. Please?"

"Okay." I smile softly. "I *did* worry you'd forgotten the one-pagers. Tonight is a big deal for Peter and Rachel, and I completely forgot to double-check with you before leaving."

"It's okay," he says. "I can remember stuff too, you know."

"I know, it's just… it gets to me that I panicked for a second, just because of how disorganized I am sometimes. I should have remembered and taken care of it earlier today."

Miles frowns, confused. "Have I given you any reason to doubt me?"

"No, not at all." I sigh. "Before Sean, I didn't mind letting fate decide things for me, pointing me in the right direction, nudging me toward the right people. I felt in control that way too, you know, kind of a choice I was deliberately making."

Miles listens attentively, his focus on me like nothing else exists outside of us.

"And then I met my ex-husband, and each day I spent with him, he took that choice away from me. The change wasn't noticeable because it happened so slowly over the years. It started with a few suggestions on things he expected of me or clothes he liked me wearing. I didn't question it at first because I was so in love with him, and if it meant he would look at me like he wanted to undress me, I would wear whatever he wished."

Miles waits patiently for me to continue, not trusting himself to speak, I'm guessing, by how his lips are pressed into a thin line.

I take a big inhale. Explaining this part of my story to others has always been challenging. *Why didn't you do something? Why didn't you put your foot down? Stand up for yourself?* Questions I didn't have and still don't have the answers to. "Love" seems too simple, but then again, I *was* in love. I thought Sean was my lobster.

"Riley?"

"Yes, sorry," I say, shaking my head. "Lost myself for a second."

"It's okay," he murmurs and then presses me gently. "Go on."

"After a few years, it became more manipulative, insidious. It was making me cancel plans with friends, with my sister, because we had more 'important' things to do or attend. It was looking at me in disgust because I wasn't wearing a specific dress or my hair didn't look the way he liked. And so I would change, in the hopes that I could erase that look on the face of the man I loved. To make him happy. It was doing everything he wanted and none of what I chose.

"He ripped the power to choose out of my hands," I say, my voice trembling as my mind flips through the memories I've been working so hard to be at peace with. "He took control of my life until I was unable to decide for myself, until I began deferring to him every time a situation requiring a decision. When I filed for divorce, I didn't know who I was anymore. What I wanted. What I needed. I got this wild rush of freedom smacking me in the face, and all the possibilities that used to be closed to me were suddenly wide open." I smile softly. "I ran like hell toward them. But sometimes, I forget people depend on me to have my shit together. My mess works for me because it's what my freedom looks like."

I didn't plan on having this conversation in the most beautiful palace in the world, wearing a dress that squeezes my bones so tight it's almost impossible to breathe. But here we are.

I study Miles, waiting for his reaction, but nothing comes out. After several seconds, I ask, "You okay?"

Miles runs a hand through his perfectly combed hair and slides his fingers to his jaw. "You're worrying about me?" he says, disbelief in his tone. "Of course I'm okay. But… fuck! I can't believe he put you through that shit. I can't believe any man would put his wife, the love of his life, through that shit."

I take a step forward, but Miles closes the gap before I can reach him. I sink into his arms and let him hold me, support me. Miles buries his head in the crook of my neck, dropping small kisses at the base of my shoulders. He keeps murmuring "I'm sorry" against my skin, and I don't know what he's apologizing for, but it doesn't matter. I hold on to him tighter. For once, I don't think about work decorum, the firm, or even my fear of trusting another man, and I just let myself feel.

Feel the warmth of his body against mine, his breath below my ear, his fresh coffee scent invading my senses, the strength of his arms around me, making me feel safe and protected.

"We should go meet Peter and Rachel outside," Miles says, setting me back down, but still holding me close. "Not that I especially want to right now, but they're probably waiting for us."

I chuckle, hiding my smile in his chest and getting one last sniff of him before pulling away. "You're right, let's go. Wait, before we do…" I stand on my tiptoes and brush my hand in his hair, trying to tame the mess he made a few minutes ago. His eyes don't leave me, the weight of his stare causing my heart to beat faster.

"There, better," I say with a smile. "The one time you had your hair styled properly."

"Okay, okay, I get it," he says. "Message received. And, Ry?"

"Yeah?"

"You'll never have to worry about losing your voice with me."

Miles extends his arm to me again, unaware of the wreckage he just left on my heart.

TWENTY-SEVEN
If I Ain't Got You

Miles

*W*e've been drinking, talking, and dancing for the past three hours. There is no shortage of food or alcohol. Peter's worked the room impressively, getting meetings with two new wineries—one from the Rhône and one from the Jura—both looking forward to hearing more about Ontario wine.

I blow out a breath, rolling my shoulders to loosen up all the accumulated tension of the night. Peter is delighted, over the moon—and all the other superlatives my brain is too fried to think of. The fact that we managed to score him a night in Versailles was already a win in itself.

And so here I am, spending my evening in the fucking Palace of Versailles, drinking and eating the finest wine and food in the country, dancing with the most beautiful woman I've ever seen. And, of course, my mind is elsewhere.

I'm still stuck on yesterday's boat, my sister's voice ringing in my ears. How could I be so stupid to let myself forget? How could I let myself envision something more with Riley? This trip has messed with my head.

And I tried, okay? I tried to keep my distance after the night of the cooking class when we shared a few passionate moments, lingering looks sending jolts of awareness through me. But how can I when she's pouring her heart out to me like she did downstairs? How else can I react but to pull her close?

Or when she's looking at me like she is right now, pleading eyes and all, leaving me no choice but to say, "Lady Fletcher, would you do me the honor of allowing me this dance?" I bow, holding out my hand to her. I can do this. I can make her happy and still hold my ground.

I lead her to the dance floor in the Hall of Mirrors, where the main event is being held, overlooking the beautiful Versailles Gardens. More than 300 mirrors decorate the long hall, according to the evening's presenter. French opulence at its best, where kings and queens have stood and held royal balls and weddings. You can feel the weight of history in the walls, on the grounds where the greatest monarchies in the world walked.

In here, the music from the orchestra is louder, violins resonating in this beautiful room and playing a rendition of "State of Grace" by Taylor Swift, Regency-era style.

Riley curtsies before saying, "I'm flattered, my lord, but my stamp card is already full for the night."

"I think it'll be okay, just this once," I say, pulling her gently against me, making sure her breasts don't press against my chest.

"I'll allow it." She grabs my arms to steady herself, and I don't miss the slight tint that now colors her cheeks.

I take her hand in mine while she rests her head on my shoulder, and I lead us to the rhythm of the music.

I bend and brush my lips against her ear. "Are you having a good time tonight?"

She raises her eyes to meet mine. "Now I am."

I chuckle, trying to hide the way those three words make me feel, allowing them to be mine for a second before pushing them out of my mind. "Peter is going to be delighted when we meet up tomorrow."

"If he ever wakes up," she says, her gaze traveling to the other side of the room. I spin us around and find Peter in a vivacious conversation, throwing his head back as he laughs loud enough for the sound to make its way to us.

"I don't mind sleeping in a bit."

"After the past week we've had? Me neither," she says.

We dance and twirl for a while, the music carrying us through the hall. Riley is breathtaking tonight. I can hardly take my eyes off her, and feeling her so close to me, in my arms, makes my head spin faster than our waltz. I rest my chin on top of her head, her breath in the crook of my neck tickling my skin. Instinctively, I tighten my embrace around her waist, almost as if we were one. Riley doesn't seem to mind as she digs her fingers a little deeper into the fabric of my coat.

When the song ends, I don't let her go right away. Electricity crackles all around us, charged with everything that could be said and done. Or at least that's what it feels like. Like we're in the eye of a hurricane, the world spinning around us with us frozen in place. And so, we stay here, like this, against each other, neither of us wanting to settle back to reality and let this moment go.

But we have to.

I can read the disappointment in her eyes when I break our bodies apart. The song came to an end, and there's no reason for us to still hold on to each other.

I clear my throat, wanting to dissipate the awkwardness, but if anything, I just made it worse. "Would you excuse me for a moment?"

Riley nods, brows furrowed like she's trying to read words between the ones I spoke.

I bolt toward the bathrooms, frilly skirts and canes getting in the way of my anxious pace. I throw the door open when I finally reach the bathroom, struggling to get out of this fucking coat that weighs heavy on my shoulders, reducing my breathing to small puffs of air. I hurl it on the floor and rush to the sink, my knuckles white as I grip the edges like it's the only thing tethering me to the earth.

"You're losing it, Miles," I mutter to myself. "Get your shit together right the fuck now." I raise my eyes to the mirror. All I see is a desperate man staring back at me. Desperate to get his girl, wishing like hell she hadn't lit up like the motherfucking Eiffel Tower when Avery announced her pregnancy last night.

I let out a sigh from deep in my stomach. I can't control the things she wants in her life. And last night was concrete proof that Riley wants what I can't provide. I had feared to find out, I delayed it. But now I know, and now I can move on. Even if it's without her.

Shaking my head, I splash cold water on my face, droplets falling from my beard.

When I exit the bathroom, my coat back on and a smile perfectly in place, I spot Riley in full conversation with a tall, lanky man, wearing an awful curly white wig. I stop short, out of her sight, watching her throw her head back and laugh, pressing her hand on his forearm. What in the…

He guides Riley onto the dance floor, and they begin to twirl and spin and laugh and smile at each other in a way I know isn't innocent at all. My fists clench tight at my sides, and I grab a glass of champagne when a tray full of them appears in front of me.

I down my glass a bit too fast, probably, when the arrogant ass dips her in an exaggerated bend, his gaze fixed on the way her chest threatens to spill out of her dress.

"For fuck's sake," I mumble.

Twenty fucking minutes later, Ry is still flirting openly with the same man. I try to cool down, get some air, a glass of water, smile politely and converse with other guests, but inside, I'm paralyzed with envy.

Hasn't she seen me? Wondered where I've been this whole time? Has the thought of me crossed her mind at all?

She's over there on the couches, laying her hand on his shoulder as she laughs at something he says. I want to take a step closer, my whole body vibrating with the need to put an end to whatever this is.

But I don't. I keep my feet rooted to the ground.

If Riley is interested in flirting with this pompous French asshole, it's none of my business, now, is it?

She isn't mine.

She isn't mine.

Damn it.

Riley

WHY IN THE HEAVENLY FUCK isn't Miles doing anything? I've been dancing and flirting with Jacques, a wine specialist critic for a French magazine I can't remember the name of, for longer than I would care for.

And although the man is gorgeous, chiseled jaw and sharp features, Jacques isn't the man I want holding me in his arms. I know Miles has been watching us from the bar. Did I use the handsome French man to get a rise out of him? I would be stupid not to.

What I didn't factor in, though, is the thrill it would provoke. I've never been the kind of woman to flirt my way through men, being openly seductive.

I've never allowed myself to stoke desire from a man to make another jealous. Poor Jacques is practically drooling over my dress, and weirdly, I'm kind of... flattered?

It's as intoxicating as drinking a whole bottle of champagne, that feeling of being wanted. Of having a man look at you like he'd make an entire meal out of you if you'd let him. Like tasting freedom on the tip of your tongue, seeing a whole world that's been hidden for years, and not once fearing the consequences of your independence.

I lean closer to Jacques, glancing discreetly at Miles.

"Why aren't you moving that perfect ass?" I mutter in Jacques's chest, too low for him to hear me.

What does a woman have to do? Do I need to drag him to a dark corner in the gardens to get a reaction out of him?

Well... now, that's a thought. If Miles won't make the first move, I need to take matters into my own hands. I've given him ample time to come and grab me, but if it's still not enough...

I raise my eyes to Jacques, still twirling us on the dance floor, my feet aching from waltzing so long.

"I think I need a little break," I smile coyly, pressing my hand to his chest.

Jacques takes my hand and bows, pressing his lips against it. "Of course, my lady. Will I ever see you again before the night is over?" His English accent is thick, giving him yet another facet of charm I didn't know I could be sensitive to before tonight.

A pang of shame zips through me. In other circumstances, maybe. But...

I force an apologetic smile onto my face. "I'm here on business. I won't be around much longer."

Jacques nods. "Ah, I understand. I envy the men in whatever city you live in. They are very lucky, sharing it with a beautiful woman like you."

"Thank you, Jacques," I say, feeling the heat spread on my cheeks.

We part ways, and without waiting another second, I storm in Miles's direction.

His eyes round like saucers when he sees me approaching with a resolute look on my face. "What is wrong with you?" I seethe.

I don't wait for Miles to answer before dragging him out of sight, his hand firmly tucked in mine.

"What's going on?" he demands from behind me. I don't answer. Instead, I pull him toward the stairs that lead to the gardens. Outside, the night is pitch black with the exception of the dim light of the moon crescent casting a white glow on the beautiful French gardens.

"Ry!" he says, impatience seeping into his tone. "Where are you taking me? What the fuck is happening?"

I continue farther into the gardens in silence until it's just us, and the party is but a faint sound in the background. Miles stays quiet, switching from growling at me to huffing in anger. I know him so well I can practically see the smoke coming out of his ears. Well, too freaking bad. If he hadn't forced my hand, I wouldn't need to resort to such extreme measures.

There, just what I was looking for.

"For fuck's sake, Riley, what ar—"

I turn around and push him into the small alcove cut like an arch in the back hedges. He grunts when his back hits it, stuck between the rose garden and my body, but my mouth is on his before he can get another word in.

TWENTY-EIGHT
Bad Guy

Miles

I'm not sure in which parallel universe I just landed, but whatever is happening right now, I'm savoring every millisecond of it.

Riley is kissing me like she's going to die tonight, and I'm her only source of oxygen, and I will gladly give her every last molecule if it means I can keep my mouth on her.

She's kissing me with all the ferocity I know she's capable of. It's years of pent-up tension being released as we clutch to each other in some desperate attempt to get even closer. She tastes just like I imagined, like passion and power. I raise my hand to her throat, my thumb under her chin. She's ready to be feasted on. My new favorite meal.

When she breaks our kiss, her hands grab the collar of my coat, not letting me move an inch. I use the moment to swap places, her soft and curvy figure pinned under me and the hedge.

"Don't you know that it's forbidden for a lady such as myself to be out and about with a gentleman without her chaperone?" she says, her hot breath brushing my skin.

"I'm no gentleman, Ry." I bend down and nip at her lower lip, and she rewards me with another one of her whimpers. "I'm the rakest of rakes."

I rip off her bodice that was squeezing her breasts so tightly. Riley gasps.

"Fucking finally," I say, my gaze landing on her exposed chest, heaving with every sharp breath she takes.

"Miles…"

"Tell me to stop, and I won't set another finger on you again."

Riley stares at me, silent, her nipples hard beneath the summer breeze blowing through the Gardens of Versailles.

"Tell me. To stop." We're standing so close, her tits rub against the fabric of my coat.

"I can't," she whispers.

Her words are my undoing. I grab her breast, feeling her smooth skin under my fingers as my mouth dives to capture her other nipple between my lips, flicking it against the roughness of my tongue. Fuck, it feels so good. So fucking good. I don't want to stop. I can't stop. Not when her body is malleable like this under my hands, her fingers gripping the base of my skull with a force that sends my eyes rolling into the back of my head from pure pleasure.

"Miles," she pants. "Miles."

I tear myself away from her reluctantly, my hand on her waist still holding her firmly against me. "What?"

"What if someone sees us?"

I arch an eyebrow. "Would that turn you on?"

"Wh-what?"

I brush aside a strand of her hair that fell loose from her bun, and her skin prickles at the mere graze of my finger.

"Would it turn you on if someone walked by as I slipped a finger between your legs, my face buried in your breasts? If they spotted us in the darkness?"

Even in the twilight, I can see her skin warming up. "I don't know. I…"

"Imagine it. Close your eyes and imagine my hand slowly moving down your belly, down between your thighs, venturing right where you need me the most," I say, kissing her bare shoulder. "Imagine a group of people strolling through the gardens and hearing you moan my name. Picture them pausing for a moment, their breathing ragged as they realize what they're witnessing." My mouth moves up to her ear, sucking on her lobe. I whisper, "Now tell me how that makes you feel."

Riley closes her eyes, exactly as I asked. I place my hand over her left breast and feel her heart quicken. First, a steady rhythm, then as it thumps harder under my palm. Ah, I have my answer.

I inch up her collarbone until my fingers curl around her neck and squeeze a little, just enough for her to part her lips and moan.

"You're such a good girl, Riley," I whisper against her skin as I nibble her jaw. "Are you turned on?"

Riley opens her big brown eyes to look at me, and damn it, my cock stiffens.

"You know I am," she says.

She puts her hand on the one I have around her neck, and one finger at a time, she undoes my hold on her and spins me around, pinning me up against the thickets, my arm locked overhead in her grip.

I try to free myself, but her hold is too strong, and I'm too fucking stunned to try harder.

She smirks. "You didn't expect that, did you?"

"I learned a long time ago to always expect the unexpected with you," I pant, rock hard.

"Does it turn you on?" Riley says, flipping my question on me, "to not be in control?"

I don't hesitate. "Yes, but only because it's you."

I catch the surprise on her face before it vanishes a second later.

"Where the fuck did you learn to be so strong?"

"What? Surprised that women can be powerful too?"

"Fuck no," I breathe. "You're fucking turning me on, that's what's happening right now."

"What are you going to do about it?" One of her hands lets go of my wrist and cups the bulge in my pants.

I growl. "If you don't stop, I'll—"

The sound of a phone ringing startles us. Riley moves aside and fumbles with the pockets in her skirt.

"Fuck."

"What?"

"Peter wants to leave in twenty to debrief at the hotel tonight instead of tomorrow."

Of course. Of course, Peter is cockblocking me tonight, right after something finally happens between us. Fucking luck.

I sigh. "Okay, let's go."

I glance at Riley, her bare chest.

"Here," I say as I take off my coat and wrap it around her shoulders. I chuckle. "If you button it up, you should go unnoticed. I'll order a taxi."

"Thanks," she says softly, picking up her discarded corset.

I want to kiss her again, but I can't work out whether the moment has passed or not. Instead, I just stand there dumbly, staring at her and hoping tonight won't remain a memory from another era.

TWENTY-NINE

Grapejuice

Miles

*I*t's been an excruciating sixty-five hours and thirty minutes since Riley and I have crossed the line. Sixty-five long, interminable, agonizing hours where not only did I pace my room in every possible direction, but I've also been racking my brain as if this was just a fluke or if she meant it like I did.

I've been replaying everything; it's all I've been able to think about. One particular moment is stuck in my mind, though. Because of my stature, I'm used to being the biggest guy in the room, always the one in charge. But three days ago, in the Versailles Gardens, when she held my arm in the grip of her hand above my head, I felt something I've never felt before.

Safe.

Vulnerable, but safe. Like I could relinquish all my control to her—something I've never done—and she would take care of me, cherish me, show me what it's like to be loved and cared for unconditionally.

So, I'll finally be vulnerable and tell her everything.

That there is no other woman on this earth for me. That she's fucking *it*. That my heart belongs in the palm of her hands. Truth is, she's been holding it all along. It's not that I didn't know it, more that I refused to admit that this fiery slip of a woman had me wrapped around her finger since she first laid her eyes on me. That she wrecked any chance I had of finding love if it isn't her.

There's no hiding from it anymore. Not when our kiss last night made everything so crystal clear. I love her.

And I'll tell her what I've never been able to.

And everything will be fine because Riley makes me feel safe. Whatever happens will happen, right? But at least the overwhelming weight I've been carrying around for years won't have power over me anymore.

"Sir, your coffee," the barista says.

"Thank you." I take it from his hand and check the departure board hanging in the middle of Montparnasse Train Station. We're meant to be boarding in fifteen minutes, and there's still no sign of Riley, Peter, or Rachel. I gave up waiting for Riley this morning when, at 10 a.m. – our agreed time to leave for the train station – I knocked on her door, and she opened in nothing but a white towel and matching hotel slippers, her wet hair dripping on her bare shoulders. I left the hotel, my cheeks red, failing to get annoyed with her for being late. Again. Not when she was smiling so apologetically and babbling nervously about what to bring for the weekend. Not when all I was thinking about was how to get the fuck out of there as fast as I could before I slowed us down anymore.

I sit down on one of the station benches, my leg jiggling.

Ten minutes later, I spot them at the entrance. I whistle to get their attention in the middle of the crowded hall and wave when Rachel sees me. They rush to where I stand, suitcases in tow.

"Cutting it close, guys," I say as they reach me.

"Sorry, we got held back by an accident on our way here."

"Let's go then, we don't want to miss our train. Platform C," I yell to Peter as he and Rachel hurry to the tracks.

"Hey," Riley says softly next to me.

I turn around. "Hi."

There's definitely something different in the air. Charged and heavy, but the good kind. Like, for once, we're both wanting to leave our worries piled together in a closet and shut the door. That unspoken understanding of just being content like this, knowing there's a possibility, a maybe, waiting for us if only we just dared.

"You feeling okay?" I brush my hand down her arm.

"I'm feeling perfect." She smiles, stopping the back and forth of my hand and threading her fingers with mine.

I look at our joined hands, the soothing feeling it brings me.

"We should get going," I say quietly. She nods, and I grab our suitcases as we head off to find Peter and Rachel.

Riley looks radiant today, younger, almost. I'm glad her nerves ended up settling down since this morning, as if just the idea of escaping to a quiet place for a few days is enough to recharge her batteries before she even set foot on the property.

Or maybe it's because she feels it too—the pull between us.

We all sit together in the TGV train going at full speed through the country. In less than two hours, we'll be in Bordeaux, near the Atlantic Ocean.

"I can't wait to see Myriam again," Peter says. Riley and I exchange a knowing look. Oh, I bet he can't.

"She texted me that she scheduled a tour of her estate this afternoon," Riley says, looking up from her book. "And a wine tasting to follow before dinner tonight."

"So remember, Pete, what we're going for is a collaboration with Myriam's winery," I add. "Ideally, we're aiming for mutual product exclusivity, but we're open to discussing the possibility of a limited-edition wine too."

"I like that idea, actually," Rachel chimes in. The four of us are sitting in this face-to-face duo booth, making the last-minute planning so much easier. "Maybe Myriam could come to Ontario later in the year."

Peter nods. "That's an excellent idea."

I can't help but smile when Ry holds her snort back, cowering behind her book.

"*Mesdames et messieurs, nous arrivons en gare de Bordeaux dans dix minutes. Gare de Bordeaux dans dix minutes.*"

The heavy, dry heat engulfs us as soon as we step outside the train in Bordeaux. Every puff of air feels like drinking three shots of pure vodka.

"Did anybody see a warning for a heat wave?" Riley says, fanning her face with her large straw hat. She's the perfect picture of vacationing in the south of France, with her cat-like leopard sunglasses, a prune-colored linen jumpsuit, and wedge heels, highlighting the dip of her waist and the generous curve of her hips.

"Myriam said she'd be here in a minute," Rachel says, already wiping her forehead. "Let's move to the train station hall, I'm sure they have A/C running."

Spoiler alert, they don't. It's France, after all, I shouldn't be surprised. But luckily, Myriam is already here, waving at us, her black curls bunched up in a big bun on her head.

"I'm so happy you made it," Myriam says, slapping two sticky kisses on each of our cheeks.

"I bet you love having strangers kiss you on the cheek every time they say hi," Riley whispers as Myriam moves to greet Rachel, a smirk on her lips.

"Shut up," I groan, still feeling the dampness from Myriam's sweat.

Peter moves forward and places his hands on Myriam's arms. "Thank you so much for having us, Myriam. I'm sorry we're all sweaty and stinky from our travels."

She waves him off. "We're all in the same boat here." Myriam picks up one of our suitcases. "Supposed to be like this until Wednesday. But don't worry, nights are usually cooler."

We gather our suitcases and head for her car, a small Renault Clio.

"Are we supposed to fit in this?" Riley whispers nervously.

I grunt. "Looks like it."

We get in the car, Peter in the passenger seat, Rachel, Riley, and I crammed in the back, my knee digging into Myriam's seat and almost coming up to my chest.

"Sorry about that, Myriam," I say while fighting with the seatbelt.

"I need to buy a new car. This old lady has had her time," Myriam says, tapping the dashboard.

We ride for forty-five minutes in the stifling heat, traveling further into the countryside of the Aquitaine region. Concrete and the city turmoil give way to quiet pasture fields and vineyards stretching as far as the eye can see, a beautiful blend of greens and purples filling the postcard-like landscape. This must be paradise for Peter, and from the marveled look he wears on his face, I'd say he's having the time of his life right now.

I taste the sweat on my tongue, dripping down from my upper lip. It's so fucking hot in there. I glance at Ry, squished in the middle seat, her golden hair sticking to her face. Rachel is looking out the window, seemingly lost in her thoughts, while Myriam and Peter are exchanging winery stories. Unable to wait another minute, I slide my hand from my thigh to hers, linking our fingers together. Riley smiles, returning the pressure on my hand. We hold hands like we're in high school for the rest of the ride.

Twenty long and barely breathable minutes later, Myriam drives the car through black gates, a row of cedar and olive trees on each side of the white gravel driveway leading to the chateau. And chateau it is...

"Is that... Myriam, is that your house?"

Myriam laughs. "Part of it, yes. Some sections are actually used as a B&B that my father and I worked on for years before he passed away. The winery is a great place for romantic getaways." She looks in her rear-view mirror. "This is where you will stay."

I stare at the massive propriety, the pristine stonework accentuating its presence among the greenery.

"The chateau of Lussac is one of the oldest wineries in Bordeaux," Myriam continues. "We celebrated its seven hundredth anniversary last year. The estate has been in my family for generations, but what makes it unique in the region and attracts a lot of tourists is the history behind it, and you'll see why pretty soon."

"Intriguing," Peter muses from the passenger seat. "Where's the vineyard?"

"A little farther down over there," Myriam says, pointing to her left, where the outline of the vines appears. "The vineyard was actually one of the first in France to plant vines in rows," Myriam adds. "As opposed to the plots being scattered around the estates in a disorganized mess."

"Sounds like you and me," I whisper to Riley, who softly laughs in return.

Peter and Myriam engage in a lively discussion on plot distribution while we get out of the car, Riley's hand no longer in mine. I stretch my legs and arms, hearing some joints crack after being held in this awful position for so long.

I look around, taking in the idyllic sceneries straight out of a French countryside storybook, freshly cut grass where you can lay down a blanket and bask in the afternoon warmth, olive trees offering a bit of respite from the sun, iron benches to rest and enjoy the view.

Riley walks next to me. "I feel like a movie star on the set of a glamorous '50s French film. You know, like Brigitte Bardot with her scarf tied around her hair and sunglasses perched on her nose."

I take a step closer to her, our arms brushing. "You'd look very cute with a scarf in your hair, Ry."

She tucks a lock of hair behind her ear. "Can we talk? Tonight?"

I nod. "Tonight."

And just like that, I bought myself a few more hours to face what I've been avoiding for so long.

THIRTY

Onde Sensuelle

Riley

"You'd love it here, Mom," I whisper, the words getting lost in the warm breeze. I walk near a pond, a bench draped under a weeping willow that must be several hundred years old. I sit down, the ripples of the water lulling me to my thoughts.

While Miles has been checking in with Adam back in Toronto and sitting in on our weekly staff meeting, I've been enjoying the stillness of the grounds, walking through the beautiful gardens behind the chateau, listening to the sounds of nature in tune to the beating of my heart.

My heart, which for the past three days has been betraying me, pounding against my chest every time Miles has come close to me.

"What are you doing, Riley…" I whisper.

Why am I letting another man get in the way of the future I imagined for myself? Getting in the way of my success. I don't need anyone to hold my hand. I just need me, myself, and I.

I'm an intelligent woman, most of the time. But when it comes to Miles Clark, it seems like my brain cells abandon my body and all my energy goes toward snuffing out the light that only grows brighter the more time we spend together, the more he shows me what it's like to be taken care of.

And to be honest, I'm tired of fighting it.

"Riley!" Rachel calls from the terrasse, pulling me out of my cocoon of tangled thoughts and gesturing for me to come over. Peter and Miles are chatting next to her, a glass of wine in their hands.

When I join them, Miles hands me a wineglass—a rosé from one of the bottles we picked out earlier today.

"Thank you for today, Myriam," Peter says, raising his glass. "I can't believe our luck to be able to spend a few days on your beautiful property."

"We're truly grateful," Rachel adds. "The winery tour was especially fascinating. I took a lot of notes."

"We are spoiled," Peter adds. "Cheers, everybody."

During dinner, I catch Miles's eye several times. Knowing that neither of us can seem to tear our attention away makes me smile.

We haven't had a moment to ourselves since we arrived. It terrifies me, the knowledge that a conversation is inevitable, but at the same time, a small part of me wants to find out what else can happen if I let myself be in the present moment.

So when the table is done being cleared, when late-night cigarettes have been smoked, and the goodnights have been said, we each retreat to our rooms, my heart beating a hundred miles an hour.

As soon as I close my door, my phone vibrates in the pocket of my dress.

Miles: Can I meet you in your room in 10 minutes?

Riley: 10 minutes sounds good

Ten minutes doesn't sound good at all.

I throw my phone on my bed and rush to the bathroom, jumping in for a two-minute shower. Once out, I pull my hair out of my hot pink scrunchie and brush my waves smooth. I slip on my comfortable pajamas—cream satin shorts and a black cotton tank top. Bra or no bra? Shit, should I put on a bra? Are my boobs too "on display" like this? I check the mirror. I mean, they are, but at the same time... No bra it is.

I settle on my bed, waiting out the last minutes before Miles walks through that door. Weirdly, I'm not scared. No matter what happens tonight or the conclusion we come to, Miles and I will always make it through unscathed. That much I know with plain certainty.

I don't even know what I want out of this conversation. Status quo? Something more? The selfish part of me wants to tell him to let his guard down and be spontaneous for once.

But I know it's not how Miles works, and I wouldn't want to change him for anything in the world. I love—like. I *like* him just like that.

Ten minutes on the dot later, Miles knocks on my door. Three slow, torturous knocks.

"Hey," I say when I open the door. His gaze falls straight to my chest, and I hide my smile. He's casual too, with his black shirt and my favorite grey sweatpants of his that mold his legs perfectly, and... other places too.

"Hi." He looks at me, amused. Clearly, I wasn't subtle. But again, there's nothing subtle about his pants either.

"Come in." I move aside to let him in, closing the door gently behind him. "Do you want anything to drink?" I open the mini-fridge. "Your choices are wine, wine, or... wine."

Miles laughs softly. "I think I've had enough wine these past few weeks to last the next ten years of my life."

"Yeah, I never thought I'd say this, but I could need some water."

"Water's good for me too." I nod and turn to fill two glasses, settling them on the low table in the suite's living room. We sit on the couch, each on opposite sides, even though Miles's frame takes up two-thirds of it. I cross my legs and wonder who will break this awkward silence first.

Eventually, he does.

"I haven't been able to stop thinking about Versailles."

"The costumes really made an impression on you, huh?"

He chuckles. "Yeah, that's what's kept me awake for the past three nights. The costumes."

"You couldn't sleep?"

"Could you?"

"Not really."

I see the effect my words have on him. His shoulders loosen a bit, he lets out a shaky sigh.

"I want to kiss you again," he says, his eyes fixed on me.

I don't hesitate. "I want you to kiss me again." I already feel need coursing through me, warming up every inch of my body and pulling me to him.

"But..." he hesitates, and the effect on my desire is immediate.

"Ah..."

"No, no," he says, sprawling his hand on my thigh as he scoots closer. I look down at my skin, imagining it evaporating under his touch. "There's just something I've been meaning to tell you."

"You can tell me anything, you know that."

I take his hand in mine, and Miles turns it over, brushing my palm with his fingertips. Goose bumps erupt on my skin.

"You remember a few years ago when I was going through a rough patch? I told you I broke off my engagement." He struggles to find the words, his focus on the movements of his hand on mine.

"It was hard for me to talk about it at the time, even to Tyler. I was having a hard time accepting it myself. Kristina and I had been trying to get pregnant for a long time, but we weren't getting anywhere. We got some tests done, and that's how I found out I can't have kids."

"Oh... I'm sorry, Miles," I say. My heart plummets. It must have been so hard for him when he got the news. And what about the dinner with his sister…? Oh god… I wish I'd known then. I would have held his hand firm and supported him through the bittersweetness of the moment.

"Kristina and I disagreed on our options and what to do. We fought about it for weeks until I found her one morning with her suitcases packed, ready to leave."

"I can't imagine the pain you must have felt, handling that on top of everything else," I murmur.

He shrugs. "I turned to therapy, and after a while, I came to terms with it. I still struggle sometimes with being okay with the fact that I won't be able to have kids. When I got my infertility diagnosis and told Kristina… well, I didn't expect any of it. I thought we'd come out stronger. After she left, I had to rebuild myself as not just a single man, but a single man who couldn't have kids. I don't know if you know, but dating is fucking hard."

"So I've been told," I say.

Miles scrubs his beard. "Well, add that to the discussion. I'm in my thirties, you know? I don't want to waste my time with small talk, so it was something I always brought up pretty quickly, as soon as it felt right. After a while, I just stopped dating altogether. It was too hard."

"I'm sorry," I whisper, even though some part of me firmly believes it brought him to me.

"You have nothing to apologize for," he says, a gentle look on his face. He clears his throat and raises his eyes to me. "But there's nothing I can do to change this reality. I know this is heavy to talk about after all we've done is kiss… I don't even know what you want or what's going to happen between us. But I need to be transparent from the start because I care about you. And I would never want to put you in a position where you feel trapped or don't have a say. This is me giving you an out in case this changes anything on your end."

Miles falls silent. My heart is breaking for this man who had his dreams crushed, endured so much loss in a short amount of time, and was made to believe his worth was reduced to his ability to father children. And on top of that, instead of letting me comfort him, he's still making sure I'm the one with the choice.

"I don't want an out," I say, making sure my voice carries each word with meaning.

He looks at me, confused. "But I thought... when we were out to dinner with my sister, didn't you say that having kids was the best thing that could happen in our lives?"

I dig into the hazy memories of the evening, but I can't recall having said anything like that.

"I think what I was trying to say," I say, carefully choosing my words, "is that having children is a wonderful thing if you're someone who wants them. And I wanted to congratulate your sister because she was so excited about it. I didn't want to be like, 'kids, meh.'" Miles chuckles, his shoulders loosening up a fraction.

"I don't care that you can't have kids, Miles. It's never been something I've wanted for myself. I love kids, but my life is complicated and busy enough as it is. It's never been in the cards for me, and I'm perfectly content being the fun aunt if Char ever wants kids down the line."

He looks at me as if I just told him I played rugby at a professional level.

"Ry…" Miles starts in a measured tone, gathering my hands in his. "Can you repeat that for me, please?"

"Miles…" I watch as his eyes dart from my eyes to my lips to my collarbone, and I make sure I enunciate every word that comes out next. "I don't want kids."

Miles reaches for me and grips my waist, lifting me from my end of the couch and settling me on his lap so that I straddle him, my thighs on either side of his.

"Can I have you?" he asks in the slope of my neck as his nose trails up my throat.

My only answer is a whimper when his teeth sink into my skin, biting me gently. His beard scrapes against my collarbone as he moves lower, planting small kisses over the curve of my left breast, right above my heart. He hovers there for a second, his breath hot over the fabric of my shirt, my chest rising and falling hard, the ache spreading hotter between my legs.

"Riley," he rasps.

"Yes."

It's a single syllable. One word. And yet, it pulls the trigger on any restraint Miles had. His teeth and hands tear my shirt away before he closes his lips around my nipple and sucks greedily.

"Fuck, Ry," he groans, his teeth applying just the right amount of pressure.

"*Yes.*"

I throw my head back, pleasure invading every nook and cranny of my body, leaving no part unturned by the strength of his want, while he continues to latch on my hard peak like a man starved. He flicks his tongue over it once, twice. The third time, he pulls a drawn-out moan from my mouth as blood rushes through my veins, a direct line between my nipples and my center.

"That's it, Ry, don't hold back on me."

My hands fly to his hair, taking a fistful of his dark curls for balance as he holds me firmly against him, his fingers digging in my waist like he's worried I'm going to wake up from this dream and realize what's happening. I'm not going anywhere. I'm right where I want to be, rocking my hips back and forth on the thick bulge growing in his sweatpants under me, the friction just enough to make me see stars.

Miles inhales his way to my other nipple, his hand coming up to clasp it from beneath and bring it to his mouth, humming when his tongue makes contact with me, the sounds reverberating against my skin and sending shockwaves straight to my core.

I marvel at the hundreds of sensitive nerves coming alive under his tongue, something I've never experienced before. I've always been indifferent to getting my tits sucked, never sought it out for pleasure.

Enter Miles.

The way he works my sensitive beads in his mouth, rolling them tight between his lips, grazing his teeth against my skin, and adding just the right amount of torturous pleasure to the mix almost makes me climax on the spot.

And through the daze swirling around my brain and overpowering my senses, I hear him murmur my name in an almost reverent way.

I wriggle, positioning myself at a better angle, and feel just how turned on he is too.

"Hold on to my neck," he breathes, yanking my hips flush against him, but all I hear is my heart thundering in my chest, right under his thirsty lips.

"Riley," Miles says more forcefully. I snap to his eyes, watching me, dancing with a bright, feverish hunger I've never seen before. "My neck."

I wrap my arms around his neck, and before I can process what's happening, this hunk of a man pulls me against his chest and stands. He carries me, my legs tight around his waist, his cock pressed firmly to my crotch, until his legs bump the edge of the bed, dropping me on it without any finesse.

My head hits the pillows with a thud, sinking in the softness of the duvet, my nipples bare and now cold from the absence of his warm mouth.

I don't have time to take a breath before Miles is hovering over me, his hands braced on each side of my arms, holding his weight up.

"My god, Ry," he whispers, his gaze on my chest. "I'm going to be very blunt and not smooth at all right now, but fuck... This is the most beautiful pair of tits I've ever seen in my life."

I burst out laughing, my knees coming up and bumping his ass, taking Miles by surprise and propelling him to me, cutting off my air supply.

"Told you it wasn't smooth," he says, chuckling as he brushes my hair out of my face.

"Still not a bad thing to hear," I say, cupping his face in my hands. I bring him down to my lips, kissing him for the first time since Versailles. It's soft, tender, slow—the tip of our tongues brushing against each other a few times, tentatively, hesitantly, before Miles loses patience and dives for my mouth.

My *god*, can this man kiss. I draw him in, opening my mouth for him to slide his tongue between my lips, our breath mingling until we're both gasping for air. His chest pressed against my bare one, I sling my legs around his waist, pulling him even closer. Judging by the deep sound that erupts from his throat, I must have done something right.

As if on autopilot, his hips start moving, rolling against my open legs, trying desperately to get what we both want through multiple layers of clothes.

"You don't think we're going too fast?" I ask in between kisses. Not that I'm complaining, really, but I'm also realizing how monumental this is. I don't want to mess it up.

"We can take it slow, I've got all night, Fletcher," he says, his voice hoarse, his hips pressing me into the mattress. I know Miles is saying something right now, but all I'm hearing is the sound of my gasps as he trails kisses down my neck, licking my skin—a promise of what's to come.

"I am in no hurry. Actually, I have every intention in the world on taking my time tonight. Especially when it comes to you."

My heart thumps in my chest. "What does that mean?"

Miles takes my wrists in his hand, ignoring my question, and pins them above my head. "Don't move these."

"Or what?" I ask, cocking one eyebrow and acting braver than I am.

The way he looks at me when he says his next words has me choking on air. "Every time you don't do as I say, Ry, I will stop." He slowly moves lower, his hands splayed on my skin, the dip on my waist, my hip bones. "Every time you listen, though," he adds, a wicked smile on his face. "You'll be rewarded."

"Dear god," I breathe out as he kisses my navel. How he knows precisely how to push the right buttons, I don't know.

He hooks his fingers in my silky shorts, raising his eyes to mine for permission. I nod, because, let's be realistic here, there's no way I can utter a single word at the image of him tugging my shorts and panties down my legs.

He kneels back, still in his black shirt and gray sweatpants, his erection setting up camp with the fabric while I lie here in nothing but my tank top pulled down. He puts his hands on my knees, his throat working long and hard.

"Open up for me, Ry."

I do as he asks, not dropping his gaze. I want to see his face when he lays his eyes on the most intimate part of me for the first time.

He sucks in a breath. "Jesus fucking Christ." He grips my thighs, my skin turning white under his tight hold. I squirm, trying to lift my hips, meet his crotch, get a little bit of friction to ease the ache building, *anything*, but he holds me in place and tsks me. "Do not. Move."

Slowly, *oh so slowly*, he lowers himself, kissing his way up my thigh, nibbling where the skin is most sensitive.

"Miles, please…" Is this what it's come to? Begging?

"All night, love. We got all night."

The combination of his face between my legs and what he's just called me makes me lose all reason. I've only ever been Ry to him, and the word *love* in his mouth when he refers to me triggers a shift in my brain chemistry that I'm not ready to delve into just yet. All I know is that it sets me off even more.

He inhales deeply, as if bracing himself for what's to come, and finally closes his mouth on me, groaning loudly as he tastes my arousal on his tongue. I arch my back and close my eyes at the sensations rippling through me.

But Miles is having none of it. His forearm comes down on my hips, holding me in place. I look down to find him watching me. "Can't follow simple instructions, Fletcher?"

"You know it won't be enough for me to come, right?" I tease, but I regret it the minute his eyes darken, settling on me with an insatiable appetite.

"Oh, love, trust me, you won't remember your name or what country we're in by the time I'm finished with you."

Oh god… I'm done, aren't I? It's game over before it even begins.

"Now, look at me while I make you come all over my tongue."

This man is confident, I'll give him that. It's not that I don't trust his abilities, but you can't blame me for questioning any man's knowledge of the female anatomy and the ways to draw out our pleasure. Sean barely went down on me, let alone knew where to find my clit.

But when Miles places his tongue flat and hard against me, giving me a single long lick, his beard scraping the sides of my center and creating this delicious, torturous feeling, I quickly understand that I've vastly underestimated him. No, this is no ordinary man. This is a man who knows his way around a woman's orgasm. And I can already feel it building in my lower belly, this warm need twirling inside me.

My eyes locked on Miles, I watch as his broad shoulders fill the space between my legs, his wavy hair moving as his lips and tongue explores the most intimate part of me, humming filthy words I never thought I'd hear come out of his mouth. From time to time, I spot him raising his eyes to me, making sure I'm still watching him slowly make a mess of me. And if I take my eyes away and he catches me, or if I release my arms from above my head, he stops. Sits back. Takes away the pleasure he's granting me.

"Miles!" I cry out after I closed my eyes for five seconds, making him retreat.

I fix my stare on him again.

"Good girl," he purrs and gets back to work. "See what happens when you listen, Ry?"

The sensations are multiplied, as if his withdrawal enlightens every touch of his tongue, his lips, his fingers holding my thighs open.

"I can't get enough of this," he grunts, right before taking my already swollen clit between his teeth, closing his lips around it, and sucking at a pace that makes my head spin, my heartbeat pick up and race.

"Oh god, Miles, don't stop, I'm right there, I'm right—" My legs clamp around his head, trapping him between my thighs. I don't care that I wasn't supposed to move. I don't care that my legs shake uncontrollably as Miles adds a finger, pushing it slowly inside me, twisting it so the tip can hit my G-spot, doubling his tongue's pace.

All I care about are the stars I've never seen before when I climax hard on his tongue, my body shuddering from the intensity of the pleasure ripping through me.

Did I shout his name? I don't know. I don't know anything anymore. All I know are the tangible things surrounding me—the pillows, the sheets, my exposed breasts. And Miles between my legs, looking at me with a satisfied grin on his face.

THIRTY-ONE

I Wanna Be Yours

Miles

I watch as Riley comes down from her high, the thin layer of sweat on her upper lip glistening in the soft light, her lips parted in an "O." Her chest rises and falls hard, catching the breath I worked up.

Fuck, I'm still coming down from *my* high, her scent and her taste all over me, in my beard, my lips, my nose. I inhale deeply, not wanting to leave this moment just yet. My mind is reeling from what just happened. Riley, her voluptuous, naked body under my palms. Perfect, feminine, sexy.

I've imagined this moment more times than I care to admit, but nothing could have done justice to the woman lying in front of me right now, giving me her trust, surrendering her control, letting me boss her around just so she could get off even harder. I took a bet, allowing my filthiest side to come out and play, but the way she responded, her eyes obediently trained on me, her body pliant and ready for me? God, I wasn't expecting it. It fueled the primal beast inside me, roaring for dominance, wanting to make her mine, be at my mercy. And fuck, she was. Hooded eyes and want all over that beautiful face, almost making me explode in my pants without even touching me.

But if she thought I was done...

I bend down, kissing the curve of her hip, her jasmine and sweet orange scent lulling me to this state of semi-consciousness, lost between the friction of her skin on mine.

I run my hand up her thigh, kneading the soft and plump flesh with my fingers, until I reach the round curves of her perfect ass that is just begging to have my face buried in it.

"If I knew this was what you were hiding under your pantsuits all this time, I would have gotten you naked way sooner," I growl, taking a bite, soaking in Riley's whimpers. My cock pushes painfully against my pants, banging on the door to be set free. I want to hear that sound again. I need to hear her whimpering again.

"If I knew you were an ass guy, I would have flaunted it in front of you way sooner," she retorts.

"Not an ass guy, Ry. This one, though..." I exhale sharply and roll her onto her stomach, enjoying the view from where I'm standing. "It's hard to decide what kind of guy I am with you, love." I put my hands on each of her cheeks, gripping them tightly until her skin goes white under my fingertips. I'm rewarded with another moan. "But this ass... goddamn, if you knew the dirty thoughts crossing my mind right now."

I release her flesh, my imprints red on her skin. I grit my teeth at the sight. Fuck, I can't drag this out any longer.

I get rid of my shirt, pull off my socks, sweats, and boxers, and throw them on the other side of the room. Riley twists under me, peering at me from the corner of her eye. I grin when her gaze slowly trails down my chest, fixating on the muscles hidden beneath my dusting of hair before her eyes round like saucers when they reach my rock-hard cock.

"Liking what you see?" I say with a smirk.

Riley blushes hard. She clears her throat, schooling her features. But then she runs her tongue across her bottom lip, her eyes—filled with promises—locked on my length.

I swallow. Hard. How did she do that? How did she go from being flustered to making me sweat with a single gesture?

"Very much," she replies softly.

My cock twitches, and I grip myself at the base, squeezing tightly.

"Can I take you like this, Ry? On your knees?"

"Yes," she breathes, almost moaning in a desperate plea.

I slide my arms around her waist and bring her to her knees, feeling her naked body against mine. I hold my breath, savoring her warmth, her softness, how right it feels to hold her close like this.

"Comfortable?"

She wriggles her ass in response. My hands come down fast to halt her movements.

"Give me a chance, would you, love?" I position myself behind her, caressing her arched back, enjoying the goose bumps appearing in the wake of my touch. I bring my hand down between her thighs.

"Is your pussy ready for me?" I run a finger along her center, my question answered when I feel her wetness coating it. Just for good measure, I slide one, then two fingers inside, shuddering when she grips me with her inner walls.

"Don't move," I warn. I take a step back, getting condoms out of my bag, but Riley's hand grabs my calf and stops me in my tracks.

"I haven't been with anyone else since my ex-husband, Miles."

She hasn't... she hasn't had sex in over a year? I choke on my saliva, a blend of nervousness and lust boiling through me. No pressure, no big deal, play it cool, dude.

"I got a full physical before our trip," I reply, trying to keep my voice steady.

Riley arches an eyebrow. "Do I have to beg, then?"

"That could be an idea."

"Please," she purrs in that sultry voice of hers, and my balls tighten.

I bring my cock to her entrance, the head brushing against her center, and I suck in a breath. You're about to fuck the woman of your dreams for the first time. Bare. But you're gonna make it good for her. You're not gonna come prematurely like you're sixteen, Miles, come on.

I ease into her, inch by inch, bit by bit, watching as her pussy struggles to work around me, sinking deeper into her delicious warmth. I exhale through my nose, narrowing my focus on the thread by which my control is hanging.

"You're doing so well," I whisper, stroking her lower back as I give it another inch in.

"Miles…"

"I got you." I withdraw entirely before sliding back inside. "That's it, love, see?" I say, bracing myself because—fuck. She's squeezing me so tightly. I can already feel my orgasm building at the base of my spine, and I can still easily fit another inch inside her.

"Shit…" Riley pants, her head in the pillows, her fists clutching the sheets.

I grab her cheeks in my palms, steadying myself as I pick up my pace.

"Fuck, you feel so good. If you could see how good you take me, Riley," I say, moving faster, my eyes riveted on where our bodies meet. "So fucking good."

I don't think I can control myself much longer. Not when her tight pussy is sliding so perfectly over my cock, keeping me warm and wet.

"Oh god, Miles."

Fuck, not when she moans my name like that.

"Harder," she whimpers, almost sobbing the word as I continue to pump at a gradual rhythm.

"Fuck, you can't say shit like that," I grit through my teeth, willing my orgasm to back down. "And you're not the one giving out orders, Ry."

I take hold of her hips and sit her firmly on me, my cock deep in her heat, her ass against my thighs. I angle myself so I can reach that heavenly spot in her, and then I start. With one hand holding her hip, I thrust forward, not holding back anymore.

She gasps loudly, and I maintain my punitive pace, my other hand flying to her hair. I grab a handful of blond strands and wrap it around my fist, causing Riley to arch her back even more while I pump harder and deeper from behind. My abs constrict with the effort, sweat beading on my chest hair.

"Oh my god, Miles, that's it, y-yes!"

"Do you like being at my mercy like this?" Her moans tell me everything I need to know. "Do you trust me?"

"Yes."

If I do this, it'll be the end for me. It'll be giving up the last shred of control I still possess. But I also know that Riley will come like she never has before. And just the thought of her exploding all over my c—No. No, Miles. Now is not the time to think about that.

I let go of her hair and rest my palm at the base of her neck, letting her understand where I'm going. When she doesn't budge, I move my hand up and wrap my fingers around her throat, bringing her back flush against my chest, my cock still working inside her. I hold her just like this, her tiny gasps of air echoing at the base of my spine where every nerve ending burns with the need for release.

"D-don't s-stop, Miles, please, don't s—"

"I won't ever stop, Ry."

"I think I'm g-gonna… oh my g—"

I don't let her finish that sentence. I can't hold it in anymore, and I need her to come before I fill her with my release.

"Come for me, love," I whisper in the slope of her neck before sucking her skin there, my free hand flat on her stomach, holding her firmly against me.

"Oh fuck." She comes crashing all around me, squeezing me so tight I don't stand a chance.

My lips leave her skin as my orgasm coils deep in my lower belly and shatters through me with impressive speed. My arms tighten around her waist as my climax rolls in waves through my body, moaning her name in her ear, over and over again.

"Holy shit." I exhale, still wrapped in and around Riley.

She laughs softly, pushing me out of my new favorite place.

"Holy shit is right," she says, crashing face down in the sheets. "You've got some moves."

I lie next to her, unable to keep myself at a distance now that I know how good it feels to hold her close to me. "I wish I could come up with a witty reply, but my brain is pretty useless right now."

She turns her head toward me. "Miles Clark, speechless?" She pretends to be shocked. I slap her ass, and she yelps, "Hey!"

She giggles as I bring her back to my front, draping my arm over her waist and dropping kisses on her shoulder. She tastes like long sweaty summer nights and passionate sex on rainy days.

I close my eyes, allowing myself to enjoy this simple moment between us, willing my mind not to think about the consequences of our actions, or the possibilities of tomorrow. The questions will come, I know they will, but now is not the time. Whatever conclusion we might come to later is not for me to think about right now.

Riley takes a deep breath, snuggling closer to me, exhaling with a contented sigh, and my heart nearly bursts in my chest in response. Just like that, she becomes my everything.

THIRTY-TWO

Late Night Talking

Miles

*W*hen I wake up, the room is basked in the faint light of the moon, darkness engulfing everything else.

Shit. How long have I been asleep? I might have dozed off when Riley snuggled closer, her ass perched on my lap and my face in her hair.

I turn my head, finding her snoring softly on my right, one leg under the sheets, one leg out, the better part of her body uncovered and free to be explored.

Gently, I move and check my phone in my sweatpants lying on the floor. 2:30 a.m. Fuck. What am I supposed to do? Was I supposed to stay in the first place? I'm not about to sneak out of the room like a teenager…

…Should I?

Not gonna lie, I'm scared she's going to wake up to find me next to her and freak out. Or, she'll wake up, find me gone, and still freak out. No perfect options here…

All right, I'll go… it's probably the wisest ch—

"Are you done overthinking?" Riley mumbles from her pillow.

"What?"

She lifts her head. "You keep stirring."

"Oh. Sorry, I…" I run my hand through my hair. "I didn't know if I should leave or stay."

"Easy. Stay."

My heart misses a beat. "Okay."

I lie back down, one hand coming to rest behind my head. Riley scoots closer and drops her head in the crook of my armpit, one arm slung on my stomach.

"What time is it?" she asks sleepily.

"2:30." I drop a kiss on her hair. "Go back to sleep."

She nuzzles closer. "Can't. I'm wide awake now."

"You're not." I chuckle. "You've yawned three times in the past twenty seconds."

"Okay then, if you insist," she says, her eyes already closed.

Two minutes later, she's back to snoring.

THE. FUCKING. ROOSTER. The morning light is just filtering through the blinds, but that bastard is already singing—nay, screaming—at the top of his lungs.

"Make it stop," Riley whines, pulling her pillow over her ears.

"I can't, it won't shut up," I groan.

It's only five o'clock. I'm exhausted. But it's impossible to fall asleep with the cacophony of animal sounds outside. So instead, I roll over and take Ry in my arms, making sure I don't press my morning wood against her.

"Morning," I mumble in her hair.

"Morning."

"Freaking out?"

She makes a show of thinking about it. "Only twenty percent. You?"

"About the same," I say. "But the good kind of freaking out." She turns around to look at me. "You know, the 'never thought we'd ever cross that line' kind. Makes me appreciate it even more."

Her body tenses slightly in my arms. I guess the 20 percent is in full force right now. I brush a strand of her blond hair out of her face. She closes her eyes. "Are you okay?"

"Do you think we should've done that?"

I still my hand in her hair. "This is more than a 20 percent freak out, Ry," I say, trying to lighten the sudden change in the mood.

She wiggles herself out of my arms, putting some distance between our warm bodies, sitting cross-legged on the bed. "I'm serious, Miles. What if Sean gets wind of this?"

"Are you seriously telling me you believe Sean would go through all this trouble just to get his revenge? Come on, Ry. He's an asshole, but he's not that stupid."

"I think you're the one not thinking it through and not taking it seriously enough," she replies.

It's funny how things can switch from heavenly to bad to worse in a matter of minutes.

I straighten up. "I think you're scared and making it more of a big deal than it should be and finding an excuse to back out."

She gathers the sheets around her, fumbling to find her clothes. "I need some air," is all she says. She slips a dress on, and before I can stop her, she's out of the bedroom, the door slamming shut behind her.

"Fuck!"

I inhale a deep breath. It's okay, I get it. It's a lot to take in. She's just scared, but she'll come around. Eventually. Maybe. I hope... Shit.

Grabbing my phone, I slip on my boxers and a shirt before calling my Tyler.

"Pick up, pick up, pick up."

At the last tone, his deep voice comes through. "Hey! Almost missed you. Happy and I were playing tug of war."

"I told Riley about my infertility and then we kissed and had sex and now she's freaking out and she left and I don't know how to salvage this," I say in a single breath.

"Okay," he says, dragging the word.

"I don't know how to right now."

"Switch over to video, please."

I do, and Ty's face appears on the screen.

"Why do you have a mustache?"

He smooths the end at the corner of his lips. "Trying something out. You like it?"

"It's annoying how good it looks on you," I say, even grumpier now.

"What happened, man?"

"She freaked out this morning when we woke up. She's terrified of what her ex-husband will do if he finds out."

Tyler grimaces. "The guy did a real number on her, uh?"

I sigh. "I just don't know how to turn it around now."

"Be patient, I'm sure she'll come around." Before I can cut in, he adds, "I know, I know. Not your strong suit. But there's nothing you can do right now. Respect her space. Let her deal with her feelings about what happened and handle it like she needs to."

"And then what?"

"Damn, I can't believe *I'm* the one giving you relationship advice," he chuckles. "When she's ready to talk, listen to her, her fears, whatever she has to say. Do not interrupt her. Be the man she needs you to be."

Isn't that what I've been trying to do this whole time?

I sigh. "You're right. Thanks, Ty."

"Thank me when you get the girl."

Before we hang up, Tyler moves the camera to Happy, allowing me to steal a few seconds with him before I'm left in an empty bedroom filled with last night's memories.

THIRTY-THREE

Flowers

Riley

"So, to sum up, Myriam," I say in a voice as steady as I can manage, "we think this could be a great opportunity for you to expand your market in Canada. And we would be more than happy to help you understand how the market works so we can maximize your sales. But the idea is to forge a strong partnership with Peter and go from there."

"Seeing the popularity for Peter's product during the festival," Miles cuts in, "and the number of contracts we've managed to secure amongst small restaurants and grocery stores—"

"Don't forget the influencers too," I add, maybe a bit too sharply.

"Yes, those too," Miles grumbles, glancing my way. "We truly believe this can benefit your brand here in France. You'd be the only winery promoting Peter's wine in the country. That brings pretty damn good visibility, if you ask me."

"Advantage in France, expertise in Canada, what more could you want?" I conclude.

Did I try to get the last word in? Maybe.

Myriam looks carefully over the documentation we prepared, nodding as Miles and I continue to offer details on our plans for strategy and communication in France and Canada, our schedule for her potential visit, and how she could make the best of her time overseas.

At the opposite end of the table, Miles is hunched over the paperwork. If his body could speak, it'd be screaming, "get me the hell out of here!" and I get it. I'm not the person he wants to be in the same room with right now. But this isn't the time to let last night hinder our hard work. It's not the time to consider what it might mean for us or the future of our firm. Not to mention how I'm feeling about it all.

Because even I don't know the answer to that.

When we're done, Myriam exchanges a look with Peter, who offers her a smile in return.

"Well, Miles, Riley. Rachel, Peter," Myriam says. "I need to consult with my brand collaborators, and while I don't want to get ahead of myself, I am very interested in this proposition. I've been looking to break into the North American market for some time, but I lack the necessary knowledge. I think this partnership would suit our interests well."

I let out an internal sigh of relief. It looks like we pulled it off. We fucking pulled it off. We took all the risks coming here, and one by one, we ticked them off the list and pulled the whole thing off.

I dare glance at Miles and regret it immediately. The thought of last night crosses my mind before I brush it off immediately. Focus, Riley.

We wrap the meeting up thirty minutes and half a bottle of wine later. Miles, Peter, and Myriam slip away to the local village market for the rest of the day while Rachel and I stay behind to start on our operations report.

"What do you say we grab our sunglasses and laptops and work on this outside?" I ask. "I want to soak up every last ray of the Aquitaine sun before we leave tonight."

Rachel lets out a big sigh. "Yes, please."

We move our stuff out on the terracotta terrasse, settling in the shade of the olive trees.

"So…" Rachel says coyly, putting her laptop down. "I see there have been some interesting developments since our last chat over margaritas."

I raise an eyebrow and play the ignorance card. "What do you mean?"

"Riley. Come on. The tension between you and Miles during our meeting had me in a chokehold."

Fuck. "Was it that obvious?" I laugh nervously.

Rachel smiles. "Just a smidge. Sorry."

"It's okay," I say, dropping my head in my hands. "Ughh… I don't know what to do with him. He's just so… Miles."

"What does that mean?" She laughs.

I take a deep breath. "What would you do if you were me? Knowing how I lost everything once already, working with my ex-husband. Would you risk it, all over again?"

Last night pops in my mind, and this time, I allow myself to sit in the feeling for a while. How right it was, being held by his strong arms, flush against his sweaty chest, kissing his surprisingly soft mouth hiding under all that beard. Having him inside me, in all his manly glory... My lower belly tingles. Okay, that's enough.

Rachel tucks her black hair behind her ear. "Well, do you think Miles is capable of doing something like Sean?"

I take a moment to think about it, and it becomes clear as day to me.

"No," I reply. "I've known Miles for a while now, and I believe that I know who he is deep down. Sean and I got together pretty quickly after we met. It wasn't something where we were friends first and then became more. We didn't have that solid foundation."

Even though my instincts tricked me the first time, I think I've come a long way. I need to learn how to trust them again, and there's no better time than the present, right?

"It's impossible to be a hundred percent sure, and anyway... who knows what could happen in his life and the impact it can have on him," I add. "But I can't imagine Miles doing anything even remotely resembling what Sean did. Everything he's done for me has been out of kindness. He's a selfless guy with a huge heart... He's my biggest cheerleader, always has been."

Rachel nods. "From what I know of him, I have to agree. I get it, though, your fear. It's normal and valid. You've put it all on the line after taking probably the biggest risk of your life. I'd be terrified too."

"Thank you," I whisper, offering her a small smile. "It feels good to talk about it with someone who understands."

"I agree," Rachel says. "It can be lonely and alienating for women like us who've been through this. I still have a hard time saying the word."

"Domestic abuse?"

"Yeah… I don't want to be seen as the poor victim, you know?" she says, fidgeting with the spiral spine of her notebook. "I don't want pity from strangers. Nor from my friends, for that matter. I spent too long being invisible. I want them to see me for who I am: Rachel, an independent and empowered woman, working hard on her career and being her best self. So I usually keep it to myself. It felt good when I opened up to you in Toronto."

Don't cry, don't cry, don't cry.

When I look at her, I try to convey all my gratitude in my next words. "For as long as I can remember, it was almost impossible for me to say those words too." Shit, my voice is quivering. "Trust me when I say I went through a lot of therapy just to be able to articulate it. The first time I was able to say I'd been a victim of domestic abuse, I wanted to rip the skin off my bones. I was screaming on the inside because it made me feel so weak and reduced me and my whole world to this insignificant term. I felt stripped away from my identity."

Rachel bobs her head in approval. Of course, she knows what it's like. It makes me fucking sick that a beautiful soul like her lived through such heartache.

"But after a while, I found another meaning to it, one that gave me strength. I recognized that being a victim of domestic violence didn't make me weak or less than. It made me realize and accept the reality of what I'd been through. And you know what? Knowing that I could get through it and that, through everything, I managed to find myself again? It made me feel fucking invincible. I realized that if the tables had been turned, Sean could never have endured the things he put me through.. Yet I did," I say, tapping my index finger on my chest. "I did. And more than that, I survived it. I came back on the other end stronger than ever. That makes me a goddamn hero in my book."

"A *she*ro, you mean."

"Damn right." We clink our iced tea glasses together. "To sheroes everywhere," I say. "May we continue to slay the toxic men of the world."

"Amen," Rachel says, taking a sip. "Wow, are we starting a revolution?"

I laugh. "Not quite, but I promised myself to never stay silent or docile ever again."

"You should give a TED Talk, just saying. I would listen to the shit out of it. And I'm sure many other women would too."

I chuckle lightly. "I don't think I'm quite there yet, but thank you, that means a lot to me."

The conversation dies down, and we remain silent for a while. We bask in the peacefulness and the last rays of sunshine, working on our own reports and the next steps once we're back in Toronto. I can't believe how fast the afternoon went. Our last hours in paradise.

"I'm going to miss it here," I say, looking out at the vastness of the estate. "It's so quiet."

"Would you quit everything and live out of the city?" Rachel asks, her gaze fixed on the horizon too. "Live that small-town romance Hallmark movies sell us every Christmas?"

I scoff. "Absolutely not. I love how calm it is here, but only for a vacation or a country home." I sink deeper in my seat. "I would grow restless with nothing to do. I'm a city girl through and through."

"Me too," Rachel laughs. "Toronto is pretty chill for a city of two and a half million people."

She's right. Even through the noise and adrenaline buzzing all around the city, Toronto doesn't feel like one of the busiest cities in North America. Even Paris feels like Toronto on steroids.

"I wonder where the rest of the gang is," I say. "They've been out for a long time, and our train leaves soon."

"I'm sure Peter is stopping at every cheese, bread, and wine stand." Rachel chuckles. "And Myriam must also be trying to make every minute she has left with him count."

I gasp. "You think that too, huh?"

"Can they be any more obvious?" Rachel rolls her eyes. "She's all Pete has been able to talk to me about since we met

Myriam at the festival. And you know something is up when Peter doesn't annoy you to death with wine talk," she says wryly.

I snort in my glass. "Damn. Ouch for Peter."

Rachel waves me off. "Oh, you know it's true."

"You're right. He can get pretty fired up. All right, I think I'm done with work for the day," I say, gathering my stuff. "I'm going to go pack my bags. I'll meet you at six, okay?"

"Perfect!"

I start to walk away, but Rachel calls my name. "You know, I didn't really answer you earlier. When you asked me what I'd do if I were in your situation with Miles."

"Yeah?"

"He is a great guy, Riley, and if it were me, I would go for it. A thousand percent."

I look at her, her eyes displaying only sincerity and fondness. "Thank you, Rach."

"You're welcome, Ry."

As soon as I get back to my room, I collapse on the bed, exhausted. How long am I going to deny myself a future I want based on my past? Let Sean terrify me and dictate how I should live and who I should be with? If I can't even take that step with Miles, then I'm just fucked, aren't I? Might as well pledge to be single forever and forget about having a man to share my life with.

And yet... I can't get him out of my mind.

Since day one in the City of Love, everything Miles has said and done has proved to me that I've been wrong in trying to keep my distance from him in the name of not jeopardizing our firm. As if he would ever let that happen. As if I would.

He's not the one I've been afraid of.

I realize that as long as he's beside me, we can face anything. Together. The firm, the demons of our past, our lives. We can figure it out, but most importantly, we can succeed.

Truth is, I've been lying to myself, purposefully blocking out any possibility of seeing him as something more. But Rachel is right.

No more.

THIRTY-FOUR
Rose-Colored Lenses

Miles

I'm deep into organizing my bag when someone knocks on my door.

"Yes?"

"It's me," Riley says.

Oh. My heart stumbles and falls in my ribcage.

I inhale slowly, roll my shoulders, and open the door to a sun-kissed, gorgeous Riley. In my fantasies, I drop to my knees and bury my face in the crease of her skirt, begging her to give me a chance.

In reality, I'm standing still, staring at her like a creep.

The sound of Riley clearing her throat breaks the awkward silence. "Hey, um… can I come in?"

I move out of the way. "Of course, of course. Sorry, come in."

She comes inside, and I divert my attention back to folding my clothes and packing my suitcase.

"How was your afternoon? Did you get a lot of work done?" I say because if she's not going to talk, I'm gonna go insane.

"It was fine. Rach and I wrapped up the report, then we had some time to relax."

"Nice."

"Yeah."

Oh god, this is excruciating.

I look over at Riley, still standing near the door, clearly wanting to be anywhere but here.

"Are you going to stand over there until I'm done?" I ask, raising one eyebrow.

She looks around the room. "Where can I sit?"

"Just come over here and sit on the bed, Fletcher. Don't be all weird around me now."

"I'm not weird," she says defensively but moves and sits on the edge of my bed. "How was the market?"

"It was good. We stopped and said hi to every single person there. Also, Peter and Myriam definitely have a thing. I caught them holding hands."

"Shut up!" Riley slaps my sheets. "I knew it! Rachel and I were talking about it this afternoon. Apparently, she had her suspicions too."

I don't know how long this pretend dance will go on, but Tyler is right. I can't force her to talk to me, she needs to want it too.

After a few minutes that feels like days, she says softly, "I also did a bit of thinking…"

I whip my head up. "About?"

She gets ups and circles the bed, standing in front of me. "Us."

I suck a breath in. Us. It sounds so right, so beautiful on her lips. "And?"

"And…" She takes a step forward, forcing me to sit down, and comes to stand in between my legs, resting her fingers on my shoulders, slightly digging in the skin of my tensed muscles.

My hands move to cup the back of her knees. When she continues, it's with all the intention in her voice that I know her to have. "I'm done hiding behind my fears and looking the other way when I feel so much for you."

I frown. "What does that mean?"

"It means that I feel safe and right with you."

"I'm glad, love," I say, still a bit confused but not mad at the direction the conversation is taking. "That's all I want you to feel when you're with me." I move my hands up, pulling her to sit on my lap.

"I don't want to talk right now," she whispers.

I quirk an eyebrow, surprised. "You don't?"

"No."

"Can I kiss you then?"

"Yes."

I cup the nape of her neck and bring her down to my mouth. Our lips meet, sweet and gentle, full of future promises of days spent loving each other and nights panting in one another's arms. But then, I softly pull her lower lip between mine, and a gasp escapes her throat. The sound sets me aflame. I groan, opening my mouth and demanding her to do the same. And she does, and my hands shake under the aching devotion in every sweep of her tongue against mine, every breath she exhales when I leave kisses on the column of her neck, every desperate touch of my hands on her body.

When we break apart, we both laugh softly.

Riley rests her head against mine, closing her eyes as she says, "This doesn't scare me anymore."

Have there ever been more beautiful words spoken in the English language?

"Good. Because you're all I've been able to think about." I'm definitely pushing my luck.

But to my surprise, Riley says, "I've been thinking about us too, you know. Since we've landed in Paris."

"Yeah?"

"What it would be like…"

I cock an eyebrow. "…And?"

She smiles. "Doesn't even come close to this."

I wrap my arms around her waist and roll us on the bed, her chest against mine. "I'm sure I can make it even better."

"Cocky."

"Confident."

I grip her thighs, wrapping them around me.

"I'm gonna need to test your theory to be able to confirm or deny."

I check the time on my phone. "I have thirty minutes to live up to your expectations before we need to catch our train."

"Better make it the best thirty minutes of my life then, Clark," she says, all nonchalant. She doesn't know what she's getting herself into.

I smirk, rolling and pinning her under me. "Challenge accepted, Fletcher."

TWENTY MINUTES LATER, we lie naked and sweaty in each other's arms, as if this morning didn't happen, my craving for her stronger than ever.

I know I shouldn't question the situation right now.

But I can't make that little voice inside me shut up.

The one screaming that this morning wasn't a fluke and that it's still bothering her. That if we don't talk about it, she'll never be able to move past it and give me her all if that's what she wants to do. That I need to listen.

Fuck.

I bring her closer to me, finding relief in the softness of her body against mine before I break the peaceful silence. "Do you want to talk about this morning?"

I wait for her to answer, but I'm met with the soft late-afternoon breeze flowing through the curtains. After a few moments, she clears her throat. "When you said you didn't think we would cross the line, I got a harsh reality check about what we'd done. Especially after being so cautious the whole trip to avoid any kind of situation that could cause us and the firm complications.

"My life is so complicated, Miles," she says, sitting up straight. "We work together. Not only that, but we own a business together. I know what it's like working with your life partner. And look how that turned out. I had to start all over again. Don't you think it's a huge risk to take?"

"I don't," I reply honestly. "Not anymore. I've thought about it so many times during this trip, Ry. There is not a single thing in this world that would make me compromise what we're building professionally."

"You sound so sure," she murmurs.

"It's because I am."

She raises her eyes to me. I can see she's conflicted, pulled between what she wants and what she thinks she should do. One thing is becoming evident to me, though; she wants me too.

"When I divorced Sean, I told myself I would never rely on a man again. Never lose myself in a relationship. I would build something that's mine and not his and show him just how little I need him to succeed." She put her hand on her chest, right above her heart. "I need to do this on my own. To prove to him that I can. To prove to myself that I can be strong alone."

Oh, Ry. I pull her by the waist until she's back down, her head resting on my chest.

"You don't need a man to hold your hand, but sometimes, it's okay to need help. To want help. You don't need a man to be fulfilled and be the strong woman you already are, but sharing the highs and lows with someone you can count on is what a real partnership is all about." I run my fingers through her hair, gently stroking her scalp. "You don't need me. You want me. And I want you. Just as you are. Wholesome, strong, beautiful, and stubborn. I want the woman who decided enough was enough and left an unhealthy relationship to start her life over. Who was fearful but full of determination. You can do it all by yourself, I have no doubt about it. You're the fiercest woman I know. I just want to be by your side, holding your hand while you conquer the world. Just because I want to."

If I can give her back even a dash of the confidence she gives me every day, I'm sure as hell going to try. And I know with the way she's looking at me right now that she's working really hard not to tear up in front of me.

But I want her to.

I want to see her cry and be vulnerable and be the one to pick her up when she doesn't feel like being so strong all the time.

I want to be her person, the one she turns to for comfort, to rant about her day. I'll pretend to be shocked, outraged— even though I'll likely have been right there beside her. All of that, just so she can feel supported and heard.

I want to finish work early to cook her a homemade dinner after a long day, so she can come home, exhausted, to the smell of my homemade lasagna. So I can greet her at the door, help her take her coat off, get Happy out of the way, simply because I need my hands on her even after spending the whole day in her orb.

I want to be the one undressing her before she gets to bed and be the one loving her every night.

I could go on for hours. I've got it all mapped out.

It'd be a happy life.

She nuzzles her face deeper into my chest, putting my worries to rest with it. "These past few weeks, it's like I forgot why wanting more was a bad idea. What you said this morning brought it all back, and I panicked."

I wait, sensing she's not done yet. But I let her know that I'm here, I'm listening, still stroking her hair gently, my fingers dipping in the softness of her waves.

"But then I gave myself space to think about it, and gosh, I don't want to live my life like that! If I'm waiting in fear that Sean will use my happiness and my moving forward against me, I'm back in that miserable house that was never a home. How is that being free of his hold?"

She stretches her neck and looks at me from under her eyelashes. "I'm sorry."

I hold her closer. "Don't be, I understand. I'm just glad you're here now."

"Why didn't you freak out this morning?"

I laugh. "Oh, trust me, I did that plenty when you left."

Riley laughs too. "I mean, when I had mine."

I shrug. "Because I'd done all the panicking I could do already." My gaze wanders to the curves of her naked back disappearing under the crumpled sheets. "All this time, I've been scared to have you like this with me because I didn't want you to be out of my reach. So it was better for me to live in the unknown. Plus, we had so many roadblocks in our way. The firm, your ex-husband… I didn't want to put you in an impossible position. And the fear of losing you… shit. It was too powerful to overcome. It was paralyzing. I couldn't handle you turning me down for something I don't have any control over."

Riley grabs my chin between her thumb and index, and forces me to look down at her.

"I don't know many things for certain in my life, but one thing I am sure of is the kind of man you are. And that's the only thing that matters to me. The rest is irrelevant."

Her words wash over my wounds like waves erasing footsteps in the sand. Bit by bit, she's picking up the pieces of my heart splattered on the floor and putting them back together, working hard to find the careful, gentle words to repair it.

Riley moves her fingers on my arm, tracing the peony tattooed on my skin. "When did you get this?"

"A few months after I got the news I couldn't have children," I say, linking her fingers with mine. "My therapist suggested it to help me heal. One peony for the one thing I lost. And little blooming peonies all around as a reminder that joy and happiness are always around the corner, even if it seems out of reach."

"I love that you chose flowers. Tattoos are sexy, but a man who can wear flowers proudly on his skin like that? Oof…"

My hand idles along her hip, resting on her ass. "Glad to know I'm not the only one affected, love."

"You're not…" Riley sighs. "Okay," she murmurs.

"Okay, what?"

"Okay, let's do this." Her eyes damp, Riley stretches and drops her lips on mine, softly.

I cup her face in my hands, tenderly stroking her cheeks, saying everything I haven't said yet through the tiny gesture. We kiss like two people who've had their fair share of heartache in life, two people who've lived through the pain that shaped who they are today. But through those layers of past hurt, I can feel a flicker of hope in the soft brush of our tongues melting together. It's hesitant and fragile, but it's there.

Hopefulness that we might just have found a way out of our burdens.

THIRTY-FIVE
Dangerous Woman

Miles

I got the girl. I got the fucking girl. I pace my hotel room back in Paris, running my hands in my hair, breathing hard. Ever since our conversation last night in Bordeaux, I've been relentless. All I've been able to think about is her taste, her scent, her laugh.

Her, her, her.

The sound of my heart beating to the rhythm of her name. And the four little words she uttered yesterday. *Okay, let's do this.*

When she said that, my world imploded, and I saw stars. The future I'd worked so hard to barricade from my mind became crystal clear. One where I spend every day with the love of my life until I draw my last breath, the two of us being just enough as a family of two.

I pick my phone up and dial my sister's number. It's pretty early in Los Angeles right now. Two rings in, she answers.

"Hey! What's going on?"

"Do I need a reason to call my sweet little sister?"

Avery snorts. "Uh, yeah? I'm always the one calling you."

"How are you feeling? You're up early."

"Eh," she sighs. "I have been having trouble sleeping past five these days, but to be fair, I also go to bed at like eight o'clock."

"Grandma," I say, teasingly. "I can't wait to be an uncle. I'm going to spoil that kid crazy."

"Please don't." She chuckles. "Josh is already way ahead of you on that, and I can't believe I'm gonna say this… but if I receive another Amazon package this week, I'm gonna lose it."

"Well, too bad. I'll do it anyway. Listen, I have something to tell you…"

"Ha!" Avery exclaims. "I knew something was going on."

I roll my eyes.

"I finally talked to Riley. She wants to give us a shot, Ave."

I hold my phone away from my ear while Avery shrieks out an impossible number of incoherent sounds. It goes on for two solid minutes. I should have known she'd have no chill about it.

When the line goes silent, I bring it back to my ear. "You done?"

"What do you mean, am I done?" she shrieks again. "Stop acting like it's not a life-changing, I've-been-waiting-forever-for-this moment!"

"I know it is. Why do you think I called you," I say. "I'm out of my depth, Ave. I'm so scared I'm going to fuck this up. I was counting on you to calm me down, not spike my anxiety."

She sighs. "Relax. You won't fuck this up. Just be yourself, just like you've been up until now. Riley is an amazing woman. I'm so happy for you. You got the girl, bro."

I look at my phone, surprised. "Bro?"

"Yeah, was trying something out."

"It's weird."

"Didn't work, I agree."

"Okay." I chuckle. "Thanks for the pep talk. I gotta go. We only have a few days left in Paris before we board the plane on Saturday, and I want to make the most of it."

Avery coos. "Ohh, look at you, getting all mushy and romantic. What happened to my grumpy brother?"

"He'll be back before you know it if you continue annoying him."

She laughs, and my heart squeezes. "I'm so happy for you, Miles," she says. "Call me when you're back in Toronto, yeah? Love you!"

"Love you too, Ave."

I hang up. As soon as I'm back in Toronto, I'm booking tickets to California. Maybe Ry will want to come with me. We could go walk on the beach, and spend time with Ave and Josh, see my sister's little bump, and… One thing at a time, Miles. I open our text thread and send her a quick message.

Miles: Dinner tonight?

A few minutes later, my phone chimes with her name.

Riley: Actually, I have a surprise for you. Two surprises. One that requires you to come to my room asap.

Miles: Are you okay?

Riley: Come and find out.

How can she both turn me on and make me nervous through text? I sneak a look in the mirror and school my features before knocking on her door.

"Come in," she chimes.

Nothing could've prepared me for what my eyes land on when I open the door. Riley. In fucking black lingerie. And high heels. And... she's... her thighs, and...I-I...

Fuck.

I scrape my beard, mouth probably hanging open, dick already painfully hard. What is she doing? Why is she dressed like fucking temptation incarnated?

"W-what are you doing?" I groan, teeth and fists clenched as I remain firmly planted in the doorframe.

She walks toward me, slowly, swaying her hips in a tantalizing rhythm, and of course, I follow her every curve, hypnotized by her skin. Goddamn, she looks so fucking sexy. I'm already heaving, panting little puffs of air.

She's let her honey hair down where it's now falling over her shoulders, her lips painted a red I could only describe as sinful, her eyes smoky and looking dangerously mischievous.

I can't take my eyes off the cupped, strappy design of her bra that dives into a neckline between her breasts. She wears a matching lace, black thong contouring the dip of her hip in the most sensual way possible. Just above, a suspender belt is attached to matching pantyhose, finishing in very high black heels.

Riley stands close, and I'm towering over her, even though right now, it feels more like a physical detail than how I'm actually feeling. She cups my pants over my cock in her hand and gives me a hard squeeze. Air deserts my lungs.

"Miles, honey, I'll be the one doing the talking." She turns around, leaving me utterly dumbfounded and on the verge of coming in my pants. Fuck that's hot. The way she looks at me, confident, authoritative—a kitten playing with its prey.

I watch as her black thong traces the silhouette of her ass in a way that makes me want to rip it apart with my teeth. My heart thumps so hard against my ribcage, echoing in my ears, pulsing in my cock as I grip myself, trying to contain the hot sensation coiling through me.

"Riley…" I rasp. I need to put my hands on her, be inside her, or there won't be anything left to work with in a second.

She looks at me over her shoulder, smirking flirtatiously, but she doesn't say anything. Instead, she leans forward, one leg straight, one slightly bent, popping her hips and bringing her ass out for me on a silver platter while she works on unclasping her heels.

I lurch forward. Enough is enough. I can't take this any longer. It takes me only two strides to reach her and grab her round booty in my palms, my crotch coming flush with her thong.

"Tsk-tsk," Riley says, shaking her head as if she wasn't even affected by the feel of my cock pressing against her ass. "What did I say?"

She turns around, putting some distance between us, and if I had an ounce less of self-control, I would've screamed in frustration.

"Take off your clothes and go sit in the chair," she orders, and fuck, I do as she says. I peel my shirt off, sliding my pants and boxers down, my cock springing free, thick, and swollen. All the while, I keep my eyes on Riley, and she keeps hers on me, not leaving my gaze, even as I stand completely naked before her.

I sit down, legs wide open for her to slide in between. And she does. She braces her hands on my knees, and slowly, provocatively, she squats down until her knees bump the floor and her face is level with my dick.

"Now, it's my turn to play" she purrs, wetting her lips, and I follow the path of her tongue with deadly precision. She takes my wrists in her hands, resting them on each arm of the chair. "Do not move them until I say so. Or…" She turns my wrist and places a soft kiss on the thin skin there. "I'll stop whatever I'm doing. Understood?"

"Yes," I almost whimper, aroused like never before. Images from the night in the Versailles Gardens flicker through my mind, Riley holding my arm above my hand in an iron grip, the ferocity with which she held my gaze. It surprised me and inexplicably turned me on to be in the passenger seat. It was a new feeling, and it felt *right*.

And right now, we're a whole notch above. Not only is she at the wheel, but she also owns my fucking world.

Right here, right now, I know that she's it.

She is it for me.

She's the woman I'm going to marry and grow old with. She owns me in all the ways I'm willingly giving myself to her. She's the woman I'm going to fuck every night, edging her to the point of insanity till she begs me to let her come. She's mine, and I'm entirely hers, in ways I can't even make sense of.

Riley brings me back to the room by brushing her fingertips along the length of my cock, her shallow breath blowing warmly against it.

"Love, please..." I clench my stomach, my fingers gripping the armchair and bucking my hips as my dick twitches under her touch. The way she's sitting on the floor with her legs folded underneath her, I'm getting one hell of a view of her peach-shaped ass.

"Patience, Miles," she says, running her hand up the hair on my chest. "We'll get there, but only if you're a good boy."

Fuck me sideways and bury me alive.

"What's gotten into you?" I say, panting.

She gazes up at me and winks. "Nothing yet, but hopefully soon, you."

I swallow hard.

Riley draws her attention back to my length, but this time, she grips me firmly between her fingers, moving her hand to the base and back up till she squeezes the head of my cock. A groan slips free from my mouth, pleasure scattering in every nerve ending of my body, a blazing fire spreading at the speed of light.

What I wasn't ready for, though, was her leaning forward and putting her lips around me, surrounding me in the wet heat of her mouth.

"Fuuuuck." I grit my teeth, willing everything I have in me to stay put while Riley continues to suck me so well.

She hums and takes another inch of my cock. And when I thought she couldn't be any sexier, she goes and looks at me behind her long lashes while flicking her tongue over my swollen head where I know she can already taste the liquid gathering at the tip.

She's going slow, *so slow*, like she's savoring every inch of me, working me deeper in her mouth. I throw my head back and close my eyes. Some part of me wants to continue watching her suck me off, but I know if I do, I'll blow in five seconds.

Riley still has her hand on my chest, tangling my hair between her fingers, scraping her nails gently on my skin.

"Ry, slow down," I manage to get out when she picks up the pace and tightens her lips around me. My chest rises and falls hard, the muscles in my thighs getting more tense as my orgasm builds in my lower back.

"Miles?"

"Yes, love?"

"You can touch me now."

As if her words were the keys to the shackles around my wrists, my hands fly to her hair and grab a fistful. I start to move my hips, holding her head gently over me, sinking deeper until she can't take an inch more. When I know one more move would make me come in her mouth, I pull her back, taking a shuddering breath as I see the pleasure painted all over her face.

"Come here." I stoop down to pick her up, both hands comfortably resting on her butt cheeks so she can sit on my lap, my cock pressed between her soaked pussy and my stomach. "Lift up," I grunt.

"Are you coming inside me?"

My chest rumbles with the low sound I make. "Yes, Ry. Is that okay?"

"Yes."

"Good." I angle myself below her, and when I feel her entrance pushing down on me, I grip her hips and sink myself deep inside her. Fuck, she's snug around me. "God, you feel so good, love."

I drop my head against her breasts, the beating of her heart under my ear echoing mine, while she bounces on me effortlessly, using my shoulders to balance herself.

"Miles," she moans. The walls of her pussy tighten around me, gripping me so hard it almost hurts. The delicious kind of pain, the kind I want to feel every fucking hour I spend with her around my cock...

I wish I could capture her face right now, with her lips parted, and her eyes closed, head slightly tilted back, and remember her like this forever. She'll probably haunt my dreams every night, invade my psyche as soon as I close my eyes. She must see the adoration on my face because she beams when our gazes meet, looking so perfectly content and making me fall even harder in love with her.

My fingerprints mark her waist as I hold her firmly above me, pumping hard and moving my hips up in fast punches.

"Are you close?" I pant, sweat beading on my brows.

"Y-yes," she hiccups.

I need to speed the process up because another minute and I'll explode. My hand flies to her clit, circling my finger for about two seconds before I feel her legs convulse on my thighs, and her pussy ripple all around me, the aftershocks lasting longer, harder than anything I've felt before, and pulling me down my own precipice. Every muscle in my body tenses under the strength of my release, burning through me hotter than a thousand suns.

Riley cups my beard while I try to catch my breath. "Are you okay?"

I link my fingers with hers, bringing her hand to my lips and dropping a kiss in the crease of her palm. "Am I okay?" I chuckle lightly. "Let me think... I have the sexiest, most confident, smartest, and fucking hottest woman in the entire world currently sitting on my lap with my dick still inside her after she just gave me an orgasm I'll replay in my mind for years to come. I'd say I'm doing great. How are you doing?"

"Eh." She shrugs, but I can see the crack of a smile at the corner of her lips.

"Oh, yeah, huh?" I jab my fingers in her ribs, poking her playfully as she starts to laugh and wiggle and squirm on me. We slip from the chair slowly until we're two idiots cracking up on the floor, her from my tickling, me from hearing her laugh hysterically, knowing I'm the one causing her to be this happy. In this moment, everything is perfect.

THIRTY-SIX

Paris

Riley

I think Miles has ruined all men for me.

It's actually brilliant when you think about it. This is all part of his evil plan to make me fall in love with him. Step one, be the kindest man to ever walk this earth. Step two, give her the best sex of her life. Several times. Step three, make sure the sex is so good she'll only have two options: become a nun or stay forever.

"Where are you taking me?" Miles grunts behind me.

"I wish I could say this attitude surprises me, Clark, but alas, there's no definition of Miles without the word grumping not too far away."

He would fit perfectly here in France with everybody constantly complaining about every possible thing. Yesterday, an older woman got angry at a server for how hot the summer was this year, and the poor guy had to stand there and wait for her to finish complaining about something he had no control over. "I'm not 'grumping,' I am simply inquiring about my whereabouts."

"Careful, if you ask me this one more time, I might confuse you with a three-year-old."

He's already asked so many questions since I told him I would be the one picking out his outfit for the evening, and then again when he saw me in my black jumpsuit, wearing the high heels I had on this afternoon. When Miles stood there, dressed in a simple black suit and crisp white shirt, the first two buttons open, his eyes immediately dropped to my heels and zipped right back to mine, fire in his stare capable of melting steel. I had to pull myself together if I didn't want to end up locked in his room all night and ruin my plans.

We stop at a traditional Parisian bistro for a quick bite, clearly overdressed if I'm to judge the curious glances grungy locals throw our way.

"Is this the surprise?" Miles asks.

He still looks confused, and I'm enjoying this way too much.

I put a solemn face on. "Yes. Yes, this is the surprise. How are your fries?" I steal one from his plate. "Mmm, crunchy and salty, perfect."

"You're not funny, you know that?" Miles says, raising his wine to his lips. "And for the record, if it truly had been the surprise, I would have loved every minute of it."

I roll my eyes, but inside, I'm all mush. "Corny should be your new nickname."

He bumps my leg with his foot under the table in response, a smile at the corner of his lips.

We finish our meals, and as the minutes tick by, my heart races faster.

He is going to freak. Out.

The plan formed in my head in Bordeaux. I reached out to Pauline, a woman I met during the festival who's a pastry chef for none other than Miles's idol, Cyril Lignac. When I say I begged for her to arrange a little something for us tonight, I mean I *groveled*. And trust me, nobody wants to hear me butcher the name Cyril Lignac fourteen times in my "American" accent. I might also have promised some pro-bono work if they were ever looking to open a bakery in Canada.

We stroll down the Avenue des Champs-Élysées, streetlamps brightening the night, tourists busying themselves among the most famous stores in the world.

Miles walks next to me, holding my hand in his, pressing small circles between my thumb and index finger. Since we left the hotel, he hasn't let go. Even at the restaurant, he kept brushing the back of my hand on the table. I love it, his constant need to reach for me.

Down the Champs, we pass in front of the Arc de Triomphe until we reach the 17e arrondissement. It's almost ten now, stores are closed, which raises Miles's suspicions even more.

"Are you planning on having me murdered? Kidnapped? Sold?"

I glare at him. "Yes, to all the above."

I stop when we reach Le Poncelet, a rustic patisserie store. The place is quiet, no lights revealing signs of life. Curtains are even drawn closed.

Miles turns on himself, confusion written all over his face. "What are we doing here? Ry? Why are we in front of Cyril Lignac's bakery?"

Of course, he knows. "What happened to your patience?" I smack my head. "Oh, right! You don't have any."

"And your jokes are still not funny."

"Tell that to your smile, Milesy."

Miles rolls his eyes. "You know, the more you use it, the less effect it has on me."

"Let's wait a minute or two, shall we? We're a bit early."

I send a quick text to Pauline to let her know we're here, and a minute later, the soft click of a door echoes in the night.

A head full of red hair coiffed under a chef hat appears. "Riley?"

"Hi, Pauline." I smile, walking up to her. I kiss her on the cheeks. "Thank you so much for this, you don't understand how big of a deal it is," I whisper.

"My pleasure," Pauline says. "Cyril loves to meet fellow patisserie nerds."

I turn to Miles, still standing where I left him, his gaze riveted on the bakery's name. "Are you going to stand there all night?"

He looks at me then, stars shining in his eyes. "What's going on, Ry?" he asks, voice low and deep.

"Why don't you find out for yourself?"

Calmly, he closes the distance between us, holding his hand out to Pauline while his other comes resting on the small of my back. "Hi, Miles Clark. Nice to meet you."

"This way, please," Pauline says, gesturing for us to walk inside.

We pass the red velvet curtain, finding the whole bakery dipped in the soft light of dozens and dozens of candles arranged around the room, our shadows slow-dancing on the walls.

Miles's grip on my waist tightens when he realizes we have the whole place to ourselves, that this is for him.

Pauline pulls a chair from a table settled in the middle of the room. "If you would please sit down, I'll be right back."

"Thank you," I whisper in her direction. "You're quiet," I say to Miles as we sit down.

He crosses his hands on the table, holding his eyes to mine. "I'm trying to understand how on earth I am standing in Cyril Lignac's bakery right now, and more importantly, how did you know about it?"

"I have my secrets, you know, Milesy." I pat his hand. "Can't reveal them all."

Before I can retrieve my hand, he lays his on top of mine, flipping it over and bringing it to his lips, dropping a soft kiss at the center. "How did you get the whole bakery to ourselves?"

The place where he kissed my skin is still imprinted with the lingering burn that he prompted. "You're full of questions tonight." I smile.

"I can't believe you did all of this for me."

"I would do so much more for you, Miles."

Just as I say the words, Cyril Lignac comes out of the kitchen, two small plates in each hand. And I swear, Miles's jaw hits the floor. Literally. I have to say, I don't know how I feel about this chef having more effect on him than me in lingerie, but I guess I'll let it slide. Just this once.

"Bonsoir!" Cyril says, shaking the hand of a captivated Miles. "It's a real pleasure having you both in my bakery."

Cyril sets the two plates in front of us, combing his brown hair back. "I hope you'll enjoy the selection of desserts I put together for you. To start us off, we have a Paris-Brest, composed of puff pastry and hazelnut cream."

"Thank you," I say.

Cyril smiles before directing his attention on Miles. "Pauline tells me you're quite the patisserie chef yourself?"

Still starstruck, Miles manages to close his hanging mouth and says, "I don't know if I would consider myself a patisserie chef, but I like to bake, yes." He bows his head, almost reverent.

"Any questions for me?" Cyril asks, clasping his hand on Miles's back.

"Qu-questions? Yeah, of course. I just don't know where to start!"

Cyril chuckles. "Why don't you start with one, and then…" he trails off as he fumbles into his chef's jacket, pulling out a card and handing it to Miles. "You can get in touch with Pauline and schedule a Zoom call with me."

"Seriously?"

I try to contain a snort. It's so sweet to see him like this. I can't remember a time when Miles was so in awe of someone else he was at a loss for words. He's almost shy, which isn't a word I would ever have used to describe him. But I like that side of him too. Makes him seem a little bit more mortal.

"Seriously." Cyril nods. "So, how about that question?"

Miles leans back and crosses his arms. "Okay, okay," he says after a few seconds. "I guess what I've always asked myself is how do you do to always make the perfect macarons?"

"Ah, the macarons." Cyril sighs. "The mystery of French patisserie. It took me years to master the technique, and even now, it's a delicate balance. Always make sure your kitchen and oven aren't too humid, it'll affect how the shells rise. And most important of all"—he leans in, lowering his voice—"do not overfold the batter. Everything rests on the way you turn the spatula and your wrist movement."

Miles takes mental notes of everything Cyril says as if he's just solved the most complex equation on earth.

"All right," Cyril says in his melodious south of France accent, clasping his hands together. "I will leave you to enjoy your evening. Miles, it was very nice to meet you." He turns to me, holding out his hand. "Riley, let's keep in touch, yes?"

"Absolutely," I smile.

Cyril walks out, and suddenly, it's just Miles and me in the room, silence stretching between us as candles warm the place up.

"Why?" Miles murmurs, breaking the soft quietness.

"Why what?"

"Why did you do this, Riley?"

I hold his gaze, my foot grazing his under the table. "Why did you take care of me when I was sick? Why did you bring me sushi on opening day? Why did you stay beside me when I was sobbing in the bathroom at work? Why did you agree to start a business with me? Why are you always doing everything with my interest in mind and putting me first?"

I get up and round the table, wrapping my arms around his neck, and find some room to sit halfway on his lap. Almost immediately, Miles's hands close around my waist, bringing me against him.

I comb my fingers through the strands of his hair. "You have done so much to show me what it means to be heard and cared for. Now it's my turn."

"You already do that every day, love," he says, brushing his nose up the column of my neck, inhaling deeply when he reaches the place just below my ear. His fingers tighten on my skin. "You've been an electroshock to my system that I didn't know I needed, and since you came into my life, I've never felt more alive."

I lean in and kiss him with all my being, my lips, my hands, my heart. I kiss him like he's been the greatest love of my life all along, and I've just realized it. But in that moment, I know.

I know I've been falling in love with him since that day when he found me broken on the bathroom floor, and my life was falling apart. There was a worry in his voice, in his eyes, that was lost on me at the time. Why was Miles concerned about *me*? But that very same day, he became my shelter.

This love is not a kind that happens suddenly, and your whole world is turned upside down in the blink of an eye. It's a slow love that you don't notice right away. It's the kind of love that takes its time, shaping and revealing itself as trust and affection grow, relishing in all the quiet and tender ways that only true love will ever know. It's every touch, word, and gentle whisper.

So I kiss him like I might die if I don't, like I'm the air and he's my lungs.

And he kisses me right back, making me so intrinsically his with every press of his lips on mine.

And as the night grows longer, we stuff our faces with dessert, each more delicious than the last, in a symphony of moans and clattering spoons.

I take the last bite on my plate before putting my spoon down. "I'm so full."

"You're such a lightweight." Miles smirks.

"I'm not a giant like you." I throw my napkin on the table. "Get up, come on."

Miles looks at me, surprised. "What?"

I wave my hand. "Up, come on!"

I connect my phone to the speaker Pauline left on the counter and play "Paris" by New West. The guitar strings echo in the small bakery as I make my way to Miles.

"Dance with me?"

His answering smile warms every corner of my being. He places his hand in mine, softly molding his body against mine, his other hand coming to rest on my hip. And like that, we sway slowly to the lazy rhythm of the song. I rest my head on his chest, his heart fluttering as my fingers drag up and down his arm.

And because Miles is Miles, he leans in, brushes his lips against my ear lobe, his breath cooling my skin, and whispers. "What are you doing to me, Ry?"

I turn my head, bumping my nose against his. "Just wanted to do something special for you. Is it too much?"

He looks at me as if the mere fact that I'm standing in front of him overwhelms him with happiness like he's about to burst from joy. "I love it, Ry. I love everything about this."

The tenderness in the creases at the corner of his eyes, the warmth in the browns of his pupils, how much he manages to express with so little. I understand it all, I think, hoping that maybe, some translate in the way I hold his stare. *I love you too*. And I do. So why does it feel like such a big thing to say out loud? Why does my heart make cartwheels all over my chest at that big, giant breakthrough, and yet, my throat refuses to let the words go through?

I'm not ready to share it with him yet.

"What's going on?" He frowns. Shit, did I actually sigh?

I pat his chest. "Nothing. I was just lost in my thoughts."

He bends and kisses me softly. Oh, the tingly feeling scouring my body.

I should have known Miles would go for the home run. Or the touchdown? I don't know anything about rugby. Whichever, he scores it as the song comes to an end, and he twirls me around, almost in slow motion, my hand in his raised above my head while his other rests softly on the dip of my waist. When I complete my spin, his hands slide down my sides before one moves up my back, holding me there while he leans me backward, looking so elegant in his black suit.

He doesn't hesitate and, in this position, him hovering protectively over me, his frame filling my sight line, Miles brings his lips to mine and makes me forget anything around us exists. When we part, I can't tell if the stars I see in his eyes are a reflection of mine, or merely from the dampness I notice in them, shining in the dimness of the room.

Miles brings me back up, cupping my face.

"One day, love, I'll tell you how long I've been waiting for this to become more than a dream," he says, resting his forehead on mine. "And I'll explain everything that I've felt all these years, how excruciating it's been not to hold you close to me just like I am right now, how my hands knew what you felt like without having even touched you. How my body knew how well you'd fit against it without haven't held you." He inhales deeply, blowing a shaky breath. "And you'll see then and understand that I was made for you, and you were made for me. And I have never known anything to be more true."

THIRTY-SEVEN
The Night We Met

Miles

*O*ur final forty-eight hours in Paris arrive fast. Since coming back from Bordeaux, we got busy with some last-minute meetings with French vendors, but if I'm being honest, most of our time was spent in a daze of tangled bodies and crumpled sheets.

There's an undeniable charge in the air between us, as if Riley's last barriers have come crumbling down. Or maybe it's me. Maybe knowing she feels the same toward me has healed something in me I didn't know was broken. Like a jasmine-scented balm on my heart.

The only problem is that now that I can touch her, and kiss her, and cuddle her, and love her out in the open, I can't bring myself to stop. I crave her contact like I haven't had it in months. And it looks like she's in the same boat as me. I caught her nibbling her bottom lip yesterday when I was going through my drawer to find clean boxers after coming out of the shower. I had my white towel wrapped around my waist, and she was in bed, her eyes still heavy with sleep from our late-morning snuggles.

I knew what I was doing, *please*, of course I knew. I learned fast that Riley had a weakness for my backside. So it wasn't totally innocent on my part to come out like that and flaunt it in front of her. A man's gotta do what a man's gotta do.

"Are you coming back to bed?" Riley mumbles from the bedroom. The rest of the trip is just ours, just a few days to enjoy Paris on our own, even though we might have set a new record last night for how horny two people can be. We stayed up all night and only fell asleep around five in my bed.

We set up camp in my bedroom after the night at Le Poncelet, and it immediately looked like someone had robbed the place. How much mess can one person make? I'm going to need to work on something clever to have her clean up after herself without her figuring out what I'm doing, or I'm sure she'll make it worse just to spite me.

I finish trimming my beard and mustache and order us something for breakfast on my phone—a little morning surprise for her, full of carbs and butter. I'll have to do some serious running when we get back. French people sure know how to put good food on the table.

I find Riley lying on her stomach like a starfish in the late-morning light as I come out of the bathroom, one ass cheek peeking out and one leg bent at the knee, her face lost in the pillows.

She's a fucking sight.

A sight of sensuous curves and voluptuous lines drawing me in the coziness of their nooks like sirens out at sea.

I crawl above her, dropping my lips on her calves, her thighs. I'm already hard as my hands grab her ass and lift her cheeks, opening the way to her glistening center. I growl when my tongue dips into her flesh and takes in the delicious taste that makes her so addictive.

Riley hums in pleasure but doesn't move from her comfortable position. I part her lips with my tongue, finding that little bud that makes her go off every time. I give it a little flick, and Riley stirs.

"What are you doing?" she moan-whines. "It's too early for that, I'm not awake yet."

I chuckle against her skin. "I'm waking you up." I press my tongue flat against her. "Very gently, and slowly." I move up, making my way to her backside, stopping briefly to give her a little bit of pleasure there too. And I calculated right because she lifts her hips as I do. Smart girl.

"Okay, now I'm awake," she says, breathing a little bit harder.

I continue my exploration, licking and kissing her spine, seeing the chills spread over her body. Her neck is the spot that gets me every time. It's where it smells the most like her, where I find myself losing track of space and time.

"Are you awake enough for me?" I say as I nudge myself at her entrance.

"Hmm, you'll have to find out for yourself."

I brace myself for the warmth that will engulf me when a phone rings somewhere in the room.

"Is it mine or yours?"

"Mine." She sighs. "Let it go to voicemail."

"With pleasure," I say. I push myself in slowly, but I'm not even two inches in when her phone rings again.

Jesus Christ. "Okay, don't move. I'll go get it for you." Reluctantly, I withdraw. This better be important, otherwise, it's going out the window. I move aside, my cock still stiff and wet from her arousal.

"Where is it?" I ask, lifting her shirt off the floor.

"Somewhere over there." She waves toward the desk. Luckily, the phone rings again, and I follow the sound, bringing me to the opposite side of where Riley directed me.

I pick up her phone. "Why is Adam calling you…" The call goes dead, and her screen lights up with several missed phone calls. Shit. "… Five times?"

There are a few email chains too, from Adam and Sydney, our office administrator. All dating back from yesterday.

Riley straightens up in bed. "What?"

I don't snoop, but I catch the word urgent in one of the email subjects.

What the fuck is g—

Her phone rings again. Adam. Again. "Here," I say, bringing it to her.

She picks up. "Adam? What's going on?" Riley listens attentively, her expression unreadable. "Slow down, slow down." An interminable pause. "What? When?"

Her unreadable face suddenly becomes very readable, and I don't like what I'm seeing. I find my own phone, hoping for any clues as to what's going on, while Riley becomes frantic.

I curse when I see that Adam tried to call me too, and left several messages. I have the same emails as Riley, but my phone must have been on silent.

I open the thread messages. Fuck. Fuck! Sean just had the firm served for illegal business competition practices and contract violations based on our non-compete. I glance at Riley. The color has left her face. She struggles to get out from beneath the sheets, running to her laptop sitting on the desk.

My chest tightens hard around my heart. I can see it playing out in front of me. But the difference is, this time, I won't let her freak out on me. She can fucking try.

"Okay, let us go through the document, and we'll call you right back." Riley hangs up and looks at me, expression blank. I wish I could see the emotions on her face to give me an idea of how to handle the storm coming. But no. She almost looks like she's… resigned? "Sean is suing the firm."

"I know."

"Says we've breached the terms of our non-compete clause because we're working with Peter."

"I know."

"He warned us before we left…"

"I know…" I reach her, kneeling in front of her so she can see my eyes when I say, "Ry, I'm sure Sean has no legal ground. He's only doing this to scare you because he can. He knows you'll react to any threat, even unsubstantiated ones."

"Exactly." Her voice is stern. Determined. Not showing weakness when I know how scared shitless she is, wondering how to get out of this mess. "I don't know how I could have gotten so distracted."

Here we go. I beg my heart to stop hammering in my ears so I can set my focus entirely on convincing her that we can work through this together.

I squeeze her thighs, but her response throws me off. She tenses at my touch.

"Ry, listen to me. We worked our asses off for the past two weeks. We didn't get distracted. Our focus was here. We knew it was a possibility that we'd miss things happening in Toronto while we were in Paris. Remember? Remember how stressed I was about leaving the firm?"

She nods, but still, she doesn't loosen her shoulders.

"Sean would've done this with or without us there. You wouldn't have been able to prevent it," I say hoarsely, and I curse myself for not staying strong for her.

Her eyes return to her laptop, roaming over the opened legal document. "That's not the point. I got distracted with you. Today, I let the calls go to voicemail. I never do that. I never miss a phone call."

She continues to deliver blow after blow without even looking at me, and all I can do is listen to her. I can't even move. "I took my focus off my goal for one second, and look what happened."

"Love, come on, there's no correlation between this a—"

"Of course there is."

"No, there's not!" I burst out, getting up. "Us getting together has no impact on the firm, Riley! Or on your focus. This is a load of bullshit." I shake my head, pacing. "If you want to back out because you're fucking scared, then do it. But don't pin this on Sean, please."

"I'm not backing out of anything, Miles, because the only thing I'm in—*we're* in—is in making sure our business succeeds."

I scoff. "Oh, is that so? That's it, huh? That's the only thing going on between us? Are you fucking kidding me?"

I can't stop the sour taste of anger filling my mouth as Riley keeps her eyes trained on the screen and pretends so hard that we haven't just had the most magical week of our lives.

She finally looks at me, but honestly, I wish she didn't, because I can't stand the coldness in her stare. Where is the woman who couldn't get enough of my touch these past few days?

"Miles," she says slowly. I hate it. "You can't be surprised that I'm putting the firm before you."

"I'm not asking you to put me before the firm, Riley, I'm not stupid," I retort. "All I'm asking is that you think rationally about the situation. You know this whole thing is to scare you off, and it's working! Come on, Ry," I plead. "Let's be smart about this."

"You're wrong, you know. If I had focused on work the whole trip, I would have seen it coming. I'm sure if I look, I'll find emails telling me what Sean's been up to." She pinches the bridge of her nose, closing her eyes and muttering, "I received those documents yesterday, and I didn't see them. Fuck!" She exhales and says louder, sharper, "I've barely checked my emails in the past three days. And why, Miles? Because I was too busy fucking you."

I recoil at her words. "That's not fair. That's not fucking fair, and you know it."

She's trying to make what we have into less of what it is, reduce it to a fling or an itch we needed to scratch. But we've shared so much more. She knows it. She's just lashing out. And I get it, she's scared. Confused, hurt. But I'm on her side here, and she's aiming at the wrong target.

Her phone chimes again, and she practically lunges for it. Her face crumbles as she reads the text.

She looks up at me, dead in the eyes. "And you said you wouldn't jeopardize the firm."

"Jesus Christ," I mumble. "How is this my fault?"

She turns her phone to me without saying a word.

Sean: Seems like you finally got my present. I hope your boy toy will think twice now before threatening me.

"What did you do, Miles?"

"Fuck."

"What did you do?"

The fucking bastard. I should have knocked his face out when I had the chance. There's no hiding from this, so I fess up.

"After he made a scene at the office, I followed him into the lobby before he left." I sigh, shaking my head. Riley waits

365 | FROM PARIS, IN *Love*

in front of me, arms crossed, betrayal written on her face. "I gave him my two cents. And I might have been a bit... forceful while doing it."

"I can't believe this," she says, exasperated. "Why did you have to do this? Why couldn't you let me handle it myself, just like I asked?"

"Because!" I shout but regret it immediately when I see her wince. "It's as much my firm as it is yours, Ry, and when someone is spreading lies and threatening my work, my reputation, I don't give a fuck if that person is your ex-husband or your cousin or the fucking king of England. I'm allowed to have my say and defend myself."

She stares at me, unfazed. "Well. Looks like your say got us here now, so... well done."

She turns around and sits at the desk, typing something on her laptop I can't read.

I walk over to her, kneading her shoulders, a white flag waved. "I'm sorry. I didn't mean for this to happen. Or to raise my voice. I don't want to be fighting, love. Can we talk it out and come up with a plan to handle this? Together? We're a team, remember?" I look at her computer screen. What the f— "What are you doing?"

"Booking my ticket. I need to be back in Toronto tonight. I'll be able to handle it better once I'm there."

"Hang on, Ry," I say urgently. The situation is slipping out of my control, and I don't know how to bring it back. "You're walking straight into his mind game, don't you see? He has you right where he wants you. You think he's really *that* shaken by our exchange a month ago?" I scoff. "He doesn't give a fuck about it. He wants you to react. And you're doing exactly that. Let's take a breather. Let's go outside and get some air. We don't have to make a decision right now."

"Actually, we do, and it's done. I need to go back so I can handle and fix this. Can you please meet with Peter and Rachel tomorrow to fill them in? Tell them I'm sorry I had to leave so quickly but that we have the situation under control, and we'll keep them updated once we know more. Ease their worries. We can't lose them."

She gets up and pulls her suitcase out from the closet, throwing her clothes in it. For a hot second, flashes of Kristina with her bags in our entryway go through my mind. Same determination in her eyes, same sharpness in her words.

My mind is going in every direction, trying to find a solution that will put a seal on Riley's anxieties for a second. But I come up short. Because in her mind, Riley is already on the plane, and there's nothing I can do to stop her. I don't know what to do, and I should know what to do, right? Shouldn't I be able to comfort and stop her from spiraling like that?

I sigh, defeated. "All right. I'll text Peter and meet them first thing tomorrow," I say, running a hand through my hair. I swallow past the lump growing in my throat, blinking the stinging in my eyes away.

It takes Riley about thirty minutes to pack her bags and confirm her new plane tickets, and then she's standing by the door while I sit quietly and watch her from the bed.

"My taxi will be here any minute," she says, her voice softer than earlier.

I walk over to her, stopping before I get too close. Again. "Have a safe trip back," I say, offering her what I'm sure is a less-than-convincing smile.

"Thank you."

She rises to her tiptoes, balancing herself with her hand on my forearm, and softly kisses my cheek. Before I can pull her into my arms, tell her how much I love her and that everything will be okay, that we'll be okay, she lets go of her hold on me. And just like that, she's gone.

THIRTY-EIGHT
You Should See Me in A Crown

Riley

*I*f that fucker thought he could take me down that easily, he has another thing coming. He hasn't met the new and improved Riley yet, and he's about to have a pretty brutal introduction.

I had Adam arrange a meeting with Sean today, the two of us. Sean agreed to it. And even though I'm jet lagged and exhausted, the fire that's raging inside me right now could burn down an entire city.

There is, however, a corner in my body that is safe from the flames of my anger, and it's moping for the man I left alone in our hotel room in Paris.

I landed two days ago, but today was our scheduled return trip. By now, Miles must be back in Toronto. I haven't heard from him except to let me know that Peter and Rachel have been informed of the situation and that they're waiting for us to update them.

Do I regret how things went down in Paris? Yes, of course. There are many things I would do differently, many things I wish I hadn't done or said. Would I still leave the same night to handle this? Absolutely, I would.

I just wish Miles and I hadn't fought like we did. But at the same time, he shouldn't have kept what he did from me. He shouldn't have done it in the first place either. He should have kept his ego in check and trusted me to handle Sean how I saw fit. Because if there's one thing Sean hates more than competition, it's humiliation. And I'm sure Miles landed that in the bull's eye when they had their run-in. And if Miles had bothered to consult me first, to tell me he was thinking about doing something like that, I could have told him how bad of an idea it was.

But there's no point in rehashing what's been done. I can't sulk about this, not when the rest of my life holds in the balance, even if my fingers are aching to pull my phone out and call him. I don't want to repeat the mistakes of my past and get lost in a relationship, not prioritizing what I worked so hard to build. Miles knows that about me, and hopefully, he'll understand where I'm coming from.

I get to our offices, ready to mop the floor with the asshole who's fucked with me for the last time. When the elevator doors open, Adam is waiting for me, file in hand. His shoulders drop as soon as he sees me.

"Morning, Riley. It's good to have you back."

I give him a quick hug. "Thanks, it's good to be back too. Wish it wasn't because of all this drama, but it's fine, just another roadblock on our way. Nothing to worry about."

We walk together to the conference room while Adam briefs me in. "As discussed, I've had our lawyers review every detail in your and Miles's contract. There is a non-compete clause, but there's a way to get around it."

I nod. "The whole 'who approached whom first,' right?"

"Precisely," Adam says. "You can't poach clients from Sean's firm, but nothing prevents them from coming to you on their own. As long as you're not the one initiating the conversation first, you don't have anything to worry about. Do you have proof that Peter contacted you first?"

"I think so?" We settle in the conference room. "I'd need to double-check with Miles, because I can't remember whether it was me or him who Peter first contacted. Can you please ask Sydney to get us some coffee and water in here?"

"Sure, I'll do that right now. Do you need help with anything?"

"No, I'm good. Thanks, Adam."

"Oh, I know that look," he says, grinning wide. "That's the 'I have a plan' look."

"That's right. He better back down, or he's in for a rude awakening."

I thought about everything on the plane ride home, and looked at the problem from every angle. What do I do if he doesn't back down? Do I have any leverage? And that's when it clicked. I do have leverage. Something on him, something that would hurt him so badly he'd have no other choice but to back down. *Except.* Except, I won't let him in on my little secret. He'll have to back down on his own to make the choice to stop the lawsuit himself, without any convincing on my end, apart from the fact that he doesn't have valid ground to stand on.

Or else… Well, let's just say there won't be much left of him or his firm if it goes the other way.

Adam whistles. "Damn, I'm so glad you're here right now. Get him, Riley."

He starts to walk away, but I call him back. "Can you ask Sydney to get some muffins from the coffee shop downstairs too, please? I want him to see what it's like to get beat at his own game. Respectfully."

"Sure thing." Adam chuckles.

Next up, Sean Myers.

OF COURSE, HE'S LATE. That's the number-one power move in the playbook of insecure men. But it's one that certainly won't work on me. Nice try, though.

I sip my coffee, going over the different scenarios in my head. In every one of them, the firm and I come out on top.

"Riley?" Sydney stands in the doorframe of the conference room.

"Yes?"

"Mr. Myers is here."

I nod. "Send him in, please."

I stand up, straightening my forest-green leather pencil skirt that goes down to my knees, and arrange the matching fitted silk shirt to be carefully tucked inside, the sleeves rolled to my elbow. When I picked this outfit this morning, I decided to channel my inner Meghan Markle and styled my hair in a tight bun, one loose strand tucked behind my ear: honestly, it's a vibe. I'm feeling all kinds of powerful right now.

"Right this way," I hear Sydney say. A minute later, Sean appears, still handsome as ever in his navy-blue suit over a white crisp fitted shirt, his dark blond hair cropped very neatly to the sides. And all I can see is the despicable man he is. His power over me is nonexistent, and I mentally give myself a high-five.

He grins. Big. Like he believes he's already won. I don't let him think otherwise, and keep my face neutral.

"Good afternoon, Riley." He extends his hand. His eyes drift to my skirt. "A touch provocative for work, no?"

"Good afternoon, Sean." I ignore his hand and remark, and gesture toward the chairs instead. "Please, have a sit."

He drops his hand and slides it into his pants pocket before he walks to a chair and sits down.

Sean crosses his hands on the table right after he opens the button of his suit jacket. "So, you—"

"Thank you for taking the time to meet with me on such short notice," I cut in. I pour water in a glass and put it in front of him. "I can't say I was surprised you're suing us. Quite predictable, Sean." He makes a face like he knows but doesn't really care. "What I didn't expect was for you to feel so threatened by us that you'd stoop so low."

He laughs scornfully, and it takes all I have not to smack the contempt out of his face. He brings his hands up like he's going to mansplain something to me. "Riley, please. I'm everything but threatened. You think my firm rests on Peter's account?" I raise an eyebrow because, frankly, we've had more than just Peter's account coming our way. And he knows that.

"What I'm doing," he continues, "is simply reminding you of the consequences of your actions. Of your little boy's actions. You can't afford to humiliate me like you did, serving me divorce papers in front of my employees, taking my clients away from me. And now you have the audacity to parade around with the man you left me for in front of my clients, my network, on my territory. Who do you think you are?" As he continues to deliver his well-rehearsed speech, his temper rises. "You can't simply do whatever you like in business, Riley. Actions have consequences. But again, you wouldn't know that. You can't just become a CEO overnight. It was a good try, though, I have to admit. But you don't have what it takes. The sooner you realize it, the sooner I can get back to work."

I inhale deeply, his words sliding over me like water.

When I speak, I look him in the eyes, my voice steady and calm. "I have spent the past ten years being walked all over by you. There's nothing you can say or do that you haven't said or done already. If you think your little act will affect me like it did when we were married, think again."

Sean lies back in his chair, chuckling. "See? You can't even talk business with me. You're getting personal, attacking me on things that have nothing to do with the matter at hand." He leans in on the table like he's about to let me in on a secret. "Give up, Riley. Let the grownups do their jobs and go back to whatever you're qualified to do. I have an open position for a secretary, if you're interested."

"That's very mature, Sean. God, what a favor you did me the day you locked me out of my own house."

His face hardens, his lips pressed in a thin line. "You disrespected me and needed to be taught a lesson," he says sharply.

I play coy. "Oh, I disrespected you? Did I also disrespect you with my weight or how I styled my hair? Did I disrespect you when I went out to see my friends, my family? How about the time you humiliated me in front of everybody at work? Was that me disrespecting you?"

"Everything I did, Riley, I did for you, our marriage, our future. You can't blame me for wanting what was best for us."

I scoff. "Right. Well, let me cut straight to the point, then. I can save us both some time, and we can go on with our lives and be finally done. This"—I tap my finger on the file in front of me—"has no foundation, and you know it. Miles and I didn't break our non-compete clause by working for Peter. We didn't reach out to him first; he reached out to us."

"That's not what I've heard," he says. "And how are you planning on proving that Peter contacted you first? He's not even the only client of mine who left, coincidentally right after you started your firm. How do you think it'll look to a judge? Come on. Be smart."

"I can prove that we didn't contact Peter first."

Sean leans back, putting his hands up. "Then you have nothing to worry about."

"Here's the thing, though, Sean," I say, getting up. "Going to court with you isn't an option. It's a waste of my time, my clients' time, and *my* money. Either drop it, or risk everything you've worked your whole life to build."

Sean cocks an eyebrow, his smirk still plastered on his face. "Is that a threat, Riley?"

I shake my head. "Oh, sorry. Did that sound like a threat? No, no. It's a promise, Sean."

"Okay, okay." He snickers, gathering his stuff and getting up. He walks to me, stopping a foot too close, forcing me to lift my gaze. Bastard. "I guess I'll see you in court, then?"

I put the fakest smile I can muster on my face. "I wish I could say it was a pleasure to see you again, but I fear I would be lying through my teeth. I would wish you well, but again—" I grimace, shrugging. "Lying. So, instead, I'll say this, and know that I mean it from the bottom of my heart: I wish for this to be the last time I see your face in my life. Goodbye, Sean. Sydney will walk you out."

I don't give him the time to answer before I close the door in his face. I slump in my chair, my legs giving out under me. I fucking did it. I held my ground, didn't shake or show weakness, didn't reply to any of his attacks.

With a victorious sigh, I take my phone out of my bag and hit stop on the recording app.

THIRTY-NINE
The Man

Miles

*T*he past two weeks have passed in a blur. I've thrown myself into work since being back in Toronto, working on the next steps of Peter and Rachel's PR plan, that now includes coordinating Myriam's upcoming visit.

I haven't heard back from Riley. I've been working from home mostly, avoiding stepping foot in the office and bumping into her. I know she's still handling the lawsuit, although Adam told me everything was under control. That's good, I guess. But I should be involved. It's as much my firm as it is hers, and I should know what's going on.

We've exchanged a few work-related emails here and there, but not a word has been said about us. Or the lawsuit.

I hate that she's acting like nothing is happening, keeping me out of the loop as if she's punishing me for putting the firm in this situation in the first place. I'm mad at myself for losing my temper, sure, but I'm fucking mad at her for falling for Sean's threat and refusing my help.

When she should have stuck with me, when we should have turned to each other and faced the storm as a unit, she bailed on me. She left me. And here we are, two weeks later, with nothing but radio silence.

Maybe I should come to terms with it. That she won't come back to me. That we'll go back to being partners and nothing more. But is that even what we are if she's shutting me out?

I don't know if I could even do it, go back to pretending to be indifferent to her body and soul.

That our little blip in Paris was just that.

A blip.

A stroke of luck that reached its end.

Today, the feeling is more overwhelming than usual. Avery called me again, and for the hundredth time, I sent her to voicemail, texting her I'd call her later and that everything was fine. That I've just been busy with work and catching up with training with the team for our upcoming game.

Running helps when my thoughts become too loud and wear too heavily on my heart, just like today. So I pick up my pace, the rain pouring hard on my face now, Happy strapped to my waist, not minding one bit that he's drenched too. He's coming with me to today's game, he loves to be on the bench watching a bunch of idiots running back and forth with a ball in their hands.

I don't know what I'd do without him. He hasn't left my side since I stepped through the door from the airport.

We reach the stadium, and I slow my pace, my shirt sticking to my chest. I stop in front of the doors, heaving hard as I brace my hands on my knees, trying to catch my breath.

"You okay, buddy?" I ask, and Happy shakes the water off his fur and barks, his tongue hanging out. "Of course you are. Okay, let's get inside."

Tyler is already there when we get to the locker room, pulling his socks on. "Happy, my man!" he shouts, and Happy barrels down toward him, stopping just when his nose makes contact with Ty's crotch.

"Oof, easy."

I laugh. "Happy, come here." I snap my fingers, and my dog strolls back to me and sits at my feet. "Hey, Ty."

"Hey, man." He takes my soaked clothes in, my messy hair, my red face. "The rugby game wasn't enough for you, huh? I take it there's no news on the Riley front?"

I sit on the bench beside him, my back slumping against the wall. "Nope. Not a peep."

"Give it time," Tyler says, giving me a soft smile. "I'm sure she'll come around. It was a tough blow for her."

"I know," I say with a sigh. "I know."

He clasps his hand on my shoulder. "I'm sorry, bud. You know what? Why don't we head to my cabin next weekend? Get out of the city for a bit, crack open a few beers, smoke a few joints. Let our manhood run free in the wilderness for two days."

I chuckle. "Sounds like a good idea if you're seriously offering."

Tyler faux gasps. "When have you known me to be anything but serious, Milesy?"

I wince. I know the nickname is something Tyler came up with, but in the last couple of months, it's not him who's been using it the most. And now, I realize how much I miss her calling me that.

"All right, head in the game," I say, fumbling through my bag to get my phone out. I freeze when I see the text on the screen.

"What?" Tyler asks. I don't answer. I can barely swallow my own saliva. "Miles. What's going on?"

When I still don't answer, Tyler grabs the phone from my hands and reads the text out loud.

Riley: Are you free tomorrow night? I'd love to see you. 6 p.m., my place?

"Damn, dude." He hands the phone back to me. "It's good news, no? What do you think she wants?"

"How the fuck would I know? Probably to clear the air and give me an update on the lawsuit. I have a meeting with our clients next week. I should know what's going on."

A very small, hopeful part is hanging to the fact that she wants to see me, period.

Tyler scoffs. "Damn right, you should. That's a little fucked up that she's not involving you."

"I know…" I sigh. "I think the whole thing turned a bit personal for her, and she wants to prove to herself that she can handle it on her own."

"I get it, but it's still shitty."

"I agree. Hopefully, she found a way to deal, and we can all move on."

We get ready, the guys slowly starting to trickle in. I put on my shorts, high socks, jersey, and crampons and dry my still-damp hair with my towel. Happy is going back and forth between the guys, just thrilled to say hi to everybody and get his fair share of petting.

We're playing Edmonton today. The rain is going to make the game interesting. The grass will be slippery, and with our crampons, things will get muddy. It's going to be a tough one, but my guys are tough. I missed the last one, being in Paris, but the team won by a landslide against Halifax. A little rain won't scare us away, especially because we've trained in these conditions already.

When the guys are all here, I get up and stand in the center of the room.

"Boys, I'm thrilled to be back with you on the field today," I say. "The conditions are not ideal but remember: we're doing this to blow off steam, not to win trophies." The guys nod in agreement. "That being said, I want us to give the best of ourselves today and play the game like we always do: with everything we got. Okay?"

The guys grunt a mix of yeah and *Go, Bulldogs!* and I look at Tyler, not paying attention, his eyes glued on his phone. He catches my annoyed expression and motions for me to come over.

I sit and nod toward his phone. "What's more important than being a team player, Ty?"

"Oh, fuck off. You're going to want to see this. You're welcome."

He hands me his phone to an open article from the *Globe and Mail*.

THE UGLY AND MISOGYNISTIC FACE OF BUSINESS

By Melany Lawrence
August 17, 2022

We all thought the #metoo movement that began in 2017 would end the culture of abuse toward women in our predominantly male-dominated society. In particular, the business world has been a long-time stage for rampant discrimination, misogyny, and sexual misconduct. Yet, more than six years later, the question begs to be asked: How much has really changed?

That's the first question I ask Riley Fletcher, co-president of the public relations firm Fletcher & Clark, and by the look she gives me, it's not hard to deduce her thoughts on the matter.

I contacted Fletcher back when she launched her new firm with her business partner Miles Clark. At the time, I had reached out to her for a "Canadian businesswomen to look out for in 2022" feature, and my thoughts after sitting for an hour with her were: this woman is going to shake the business world.

When I ask her why she wanted to sit down with me again, she doesn't hesitate. "I owe it to myself and all the women struggling to find their place in business to speak up about my own experience," she says. "I want to set the record straight."

It's no secret that her departure from Sean Myers's firm last year amid their divorce has sparked a few conversations in the rumor mill. Yet, Riley Fletcher never paid much attention to it and preferred focusing on building her legacy.

However, some challenges remain, and Fletcher is well aware of issues surrounding women in male-dominated industries. "I have to make my voice louder, my presence bigger, never hesitate or show any signs of weakness," she says.

The topic awakens something in her, and she becomes very passionate about ensuring women don't give up when confronted with "insecure, entitled old men." Which brings me, naturally, to the lawsuit her firm is currently facing.

Her ex-husband and ex-employer, Sean Myers, is suing her for breach of her non-compete clause in her previous contract. "I can't go into too many details as it is an ongoing legal issue," she says. I probe a little more, and Fletcher confesses very bluntly that she believes Myers decided to get personal by suing her.

It became apparent to Fletcher then that Myers was out to get her, no matter what. She reached out to several ex-employees to corroborate the story she's about to share with me. "I needed cold hard proof and people I could trust," she says. "Luckily, many came through for me."

Before I sat down with Fletcher, I met with four ex-employees of Myers's who all confirmed that Myers is instilling an abuse culture toward women inside his firm, where he is known to be demeaning, verbally abusive, and controlling.

"I think it's about damn time I speak up about what I've been through," Fletcher says. "I was in an abusive marriage where Sean continuously belittled me. Unfortunately for me, that abuse also extended to the workplace, where he displayed the same behavior in front of my colleagues."

Fletcher shares with me that she was so terrified for the future of her firm and the lengths Myers would go to, she took all the necessary precautions to ensure she'd be believed. "When you're a woman, nobody believes you if you don't have proof. That's the sad truth," she says. "I met with Sean last week and recorded our conversation as security for my firm and myself."

Fletcher shared the recording with me. When I ask her how she found the strength to sit through it, she shrugs. "I knew that I needed to do this for my firm, my future, my relationships. And for myself."

Extracts of the recording are available at the end of this article, but some might be triggering. Go into it cautiously.

Her biggest takeaway, she tells me, is that, unfortunately, women are still a long way from equal treatment in business, and intimidation tactics are still commonplace. "If you are a woman, you better have robust shoulders to endure what will come at you."

Closing the interview, I ask for Fletcher's thoughts on the future of women in business. After a beat, she tells me: "I hope women continue to speak up when unacceptable behaviors like these are present. I hope to see more women in leadership roles and not be afraid to take their rightful place. The future looks bright to me because if it didn't, why would I continue to fight this?"

The Globe & Mail *reached out to Sean Myers for comments, but his lawyers declined any comment.*

I lock Tyler's phone, my mind reeling, trying to piece together what happened during those two weeks of silence, understanding her train of thought, all the things that weren't explained in this article but I know she thought of, anticipating the ramifications and aftermath of this bomb she just dropped...

I worry. Of course, I worry.

This is massive. Not just with regards to Sean but because of our clients too. Has she thought this through? Why didn't she ask me about it? Or at least told me she was going to do this? Did she think I would have dissuaded her? Because I wouldn't have.

Because above all the noise and chaos in my head, one emotion dominates everything else. I'm fucking proud of her.

FORTY

I Guess I'm in Love

Miles

*T*he moment of truth is here. No turning back now. I park my car in Riley's driveway and grab the bouquet I picked up on my way over. My heart is beating like it's getting ready to take off, and I'm one step away from shaking. This is ridiculous.

I rap on her door. Riley opens it a few seconds later, and it's hard to remember why I'm angry with her, sad and hurt, when she stands like this in front of me, looking like a goddamn vision. Seeing her in her black bodysuit tucked inside some washed-out jeans, barefoot, the only thought that comes to mind is how much I've missed her.

My body is reminded of the effect she has on me, stirring awake when she roams her eyes on my frame too, stopping at the rolled sleeves of my grey shirt exposing my tattoo, before her eyes meet mine and she smiles that shy smile of hers, one I've only seen her use around me.

"Thank you for coming," she says, moving out of the way so I can step inside.

"Thank you for inviting me," I say, my voice hoarse. I clear my throat. "Here." I hand her the flowers.

"Oh, Miles…" she whispers. "Thank you. Please come on in."

She sways her hips as she walks toward her living room and makes some room between the dozens of pillows decorating her couch for me to sit down.

"Do you want anything to drink?"

"Water is fine," I say tightly.

She sets the glass of water in front of me when she comes back and sits on the opposite side of the couch.

I don't know where to start. *I missed you. How could you have kept me in the dark about this? Never do that to me ever again. Do you still want this? Us?*

But Riley takes the lead. "I'm sure you've seen the *Globe and Mail* article…"

I nod, not leaving her gaze. "I did."

"Okay." She sighs deeply. "There's so much I want to tell you; I don't know where to start."

"We're not in any rush," I say. "Start at the beginning."

"Okay," she repeats. "I want you to know that I wasn't planning on doing the interview when I left Paris. The whole thing came about just before I met with Sean."

The sincerity in her eyes makes it hard not to believe her. I don't think she'd ever lie to me anyway.

"I know I should have reached out to you sooner and involved you in my decision-making process. You have a say as much as I do. But Sean made it so personal, Miles, I felt it like an attack against my person, not our firm. I didn't need you to fight my battles. I needed to do this myself."

"I know, Ry," I say. "And I get it, I truly do. But it doesn't make the way you left less hurtful. Or what you said. Or how you made me think it was my fault."

She drops her head between her hands. "I'm sorry, Miles, I truly am. I have been replaying this night in my mind again and again, wishing I could change everything. What I said to you." She shakes her head. "God, I hate myself for the words that came out of my mouth that day," she continues. "Believe me when I say I regret it. But all I could think about then was how to get out of this mess. It's no excuse, I know, but the anger and fear were so all-consuming that I let it empower me and trample over my feelings for you without a second thought."

I study her face, the pink of her cheeks, the roundness of her nose, the plump of her lips. She looks at me as if she's trying to read every thought in my mind—sweet chocolate melting into mine. So I give her a little glimpse.

"Back in Paris, the last few days were hell. I thought I'd screwed everything up. I racked my brain trying to figure out how to fix this. Us." I close my eyes and breathe slowly through my nose. "Trying to figure out how you could have slammed the door on me like that without an ounce of hesitation."

When I open my eyes again, I see the effect my words have on her. It hurts, but I needed to say them. She needed to hear them.

"I don't expect you to forgive me tonight," she says almost in a whisper. "But I'm gonna try my darndest to earn your trust back every day, even if it takes me months."

I can't help but chuckle, for I have no doubt that this stubborn woman sitting next to me would go to the ends of the earth to get what she wants if she had to. I bask in the feeling that I'm the one she'd put all that effort into. But let's be real. I have no way of staying mad at her for another second.

"I'm curious to see how you're going to make it up to me then," I still say, because I enjoy seeing her squirm way too much. "But at the end of the day..." I move closer, gathering her hands in mine and putting everything I have into my next words. "I'm really proud of you, Ry. It takes guts and courage to do what you did."

Her brows shoot up. "You are?"

I frown. "Why wouldn't I be?"

"I thought your frustration with me would have taken over. That you were going to be mad for treating you like I didn't care for you. For not telling you sooner that I love you."

My eyes snap to hers. "What?"

"I thought you'd be mad I didn't include you in my plans."

I grunt. "Riley..."

"I love you, Miles. I love you."

I don't know when or how my body decides to move, but it does, and I throw myself at her feet, clutching her thighs against my chest. This woman. The woman I would go to the end of the earth for. Is that what it feels like? To feel perfectly complete? Like every part of your soul is exactly where it should be? Like the world could come crashing down, it wouldn't matter because you're finally whole?

Riley slides her hands into my hair and bends down, holding me to her body. We stay like this for a minute, an hour, a day—I don't know. I don't care. Neither of us says a word. There's no need. We know how much this moment means to both of us, how significant and rare it is to find love again after what she and I went through.

We had our hearts broken, and we picked the pieces on our own, fitting them together as best as we could. We duct-taped the whole thing, crossing our fingers we did a good enough job to have them beat again. But then, Riley came into my life, beautiful, confident, sexy-as-hell Riley. She filled me with love, even if she didn't know it. She added her trust, kindness, lust, laughter—all the ingredients for the perfect healing recipe. And just like that, she healed a heart she didn't break in the first place. How could I be anything but entirely hers? I was hers from the moment she laid her eyes on me.

Riley sinks to the floor beside me and cups my face in her soft fingers, brushing gently on my beard. "I love you. My beautiful, strong, stubborn man. For so long, I thought I knew how being loved felt, what it should be like. But then you came along and proved me wrong every chance you got.

You showed me what it was like to be listened to, to be heard without shouting, to be looked at like I was the most gorgeous woman you had ever seen."

"You are," I say, my throat tight.

Riley chuckles, trailing her fingers on my face, tangling them in my hair. "You showed me that I could trust a man again without losing myself in the process. I missed you so much these past two weeks, Miles."

I can't speak, I can't move. The words exist somewhere, I feel them, I know they're there. And yet, I'm mute, hanging on her every word instead.

"I cursed myself for not letting you know this while we were in Paris, for letting you believe that you had gotten in the way of our business, that our relationship could ever be the downfall of our success. For doubting you." Riley comes even closer, skimming her lips along my jaw. I shiver. "But I know now that I couldn't be standing—or rather sitting on the floor with you right now if I hadn't gone through this all and realized what I lost. The only man to show me what it's like to be truly loved. To be cherished beyond anything I could have ever imagined."

Her gaze is fixed on me when she whispers those last words, her mouth so close to mine. A breath away. Riley leans in, capturing my lips between hers, kissing me urgently, murmuring how much she missed me between gasps of air, how much she loves me. I feel every word like a warm blanket wrapping me in the safety of her arms. Fuck, I missed the feel of her against me so much.

I groan when her breasts come flush against my chest, parting my lips and giving her full access to what we're both craving. My arm comes around her waist, pulling her as close as humanly possible, needing every inch of her in contact with every inch of me. I'm drunk on her touch, the way she keeps asking my forgiveness against my lips as if I haven't forgiven her ten times already. As if she isn't forgiven for everything she hasn't done yet.

I lay my palm above her heart, feeling the little guy thrumming like a woodpecker on cocaine.

When we come up for air, I slide my fingers in the silk of her hair, pulling gently so she raises her eyes to mine.

"Every atom in my body belongs to you. I never stood a chance, don't you understand? You stole my heart with those big brown eyes and that beautiful smile the first day we met, and you never gave it back." I graze my nose on her cheek, inhaling her jasmine scent.

"I've loved you since the moment I met you, and you told me you'd make my life a living hell if I ever got in the way of your work." Riley chuckles and slips her hand in my hair, resting it at the base of my neck.

"I've loved you since you cooked me your awful pasta, and I had to pretend it was the best I've ever had. I've loved you since you called me Milesy, and I acted like I hated it. I've loved you since I got to know what it's like to have you naked in my arms. I've loved you even when you didn't love yourself. I love you. Always have and always will."

I grab her waist and pull her onto my lap, straddling me. There. Way better. "What do you say, love? Are you ready to spend your future with me?"

Riley tilts her hips, angling herself perfectly on me, the promise of the rest of the night hanging between our heated bodies. "Hell, yes." She grabs the collar of my shirt, tugging on it and bringing me closer. "Now kiss me again before I lose my mind."

I chuckle, low and dark, as I dip my gaze to her lips. "I'll give you anything you want, Fletcher."

"Maybe I should up my demands then," she says, pressing herself to me. I groan, feeling the warmth of her body through our clothes.

"Maybe you should."

"Is that a challenge?" she asks as I spin her and lay her down on the rug.

"It's an order."

I don't give her time to answer, ripping the clothes off our bodies, eager to start our future right now.

EPILOGUE
Paris

Riley

"*R*y, where did you put the camera?" Miles shouts from the bedroom.

"In the red-and-black bag!"

He joins me on the balcony in nothing but his sweatpants and the camera in hand. He looks so yummy like this, the warm summer breeze brushing his chest hair, his tattoo shining in the sunlight. I wouldn't mind getting a bite of those arms either if it weren't for the exasperated look on his face. Well, maybe later. I'm sure I can get him to forgive me for whatever he seems pissed off about now.

"We've been here for four days, and the room is already a mess, love."

I get up on my toes and plant a quick kiss on his lips, his beard tickling my mouth. "It's not, see? You found it!"

I peek behind him. Yeah… okay, clothes and souvenirs are strewn everywhere, but like I've been reminding him for the past year, this is an *organized* mess. Everything is in its rightful, chaotic place.

"Any ideas where we're going tonight?" I ask, changing the subject. No need to spend more time over this, or he'll get grumpier. And god knows what I'll need to do to get him out of his mood.

"Hmm, a few."

"Want to take a guess?"

Miles raises an eyebrow. "What happens if I win?"

I put my index finger on his chest, slowly moving it down until I reach his sweat's waistband. "A very nice and long reward." I watch as his throat works overtime. I snort internally. This is too easy.

"Okay, let me think," he says, running his hands up and down my arms. His gaze is fixed on me like he's trying to read the answer in my eyes. Shit, that's probably what he's doing, actually. "I think I've got it."

"Oh, yeah? Please, enlighten me, Sherlock."

"I know how much you've been wanting to go back. Since we started planning our one-year anniversary six months ago, you've said that we need to make things right, and it should be high on our to-redo list."

Ugh, shit. He got it.

"So, if my calculations are correct, Watson, we're going to the Moulin Rouge tonight."

I slap his chest playfully, a little bit disappointed I couldn't keep it from him. Especially after the surprise he pulled off last night. "You're not funny."

Miles grips my waist, pulling me flush to him. "Am I getting my reward now?"

"Nope," I say, freeing myself from his hold. "After the show. Maybe. If you're good."

I sit back down at the table, a croissant in front of me, and the Eiffel Tower in the distance.

I can't believe we're back in Paris a year later, where it all began for us. Miles even managed to book the same hotel, same room.

It's an odd feeling, like everything is the same and the world stood still while we were away. The croissants taste the same, the Eiffel Tower is still sparkling every hour of the night, Paris is still the most romantic city on earth. But at the same time, everything is different. We're different. We finally removed the tight lid on our feelings, and it's like we're experiencing the city all over again through a different set of eyes. Rose-colored glasses. Probably obnoxiously in love and the perfect North American cliché. But we don't care because all that matters is that it's Miles and me, me and Miles, and the perfectly imperfect *us* we created together.

Miles comes up behind me, bending to rest his head on my shoulder. "You should know by now I'm always good, love." He moves to my ear and whispers, "Especially when it comes to you."

The way he always manages to turn my switch on so quickly leaves me impressed. Sometimes, I wish I would have seen it sooner, or, more accurately, admitted it to myself faster. Looking back now, I can say without a doubt that we were both two idiots in love who couldn't face their fears. We wasted so much time…

Miles would correct me if he heard me say that out loud. He hates it when I do. He prefers to see it as part of our journey, our necessary hurdle to finding each other that led us to where we are today.

I turn my head and kiss him softly. "Stop distracting me."

"All right, I'm going to clean your mess before we head out." I watch as he strolls back inside, his shoulders filling the door frame when he walks in.

I return to my emails, scrolling through my never-ending inbox. Doesn't matter that I'm supposed to be on vacation, clients always need us in emergencies. The firm has grown so fast over the past year, we had to hire additional employees and refuse new clients because we were already at full capacity. I've never thought we'd be where we are today in so little time. Our success at the International Wine Festival propelled us in the spotlight, and suddenly, everybody and their mother wanted to work with us. Which is good, you know, but it also means that Miles and I are always busy. Even on vacations.

The festival isn't the only reason for our success. The feature in the *Globe and Mail* attracted its fair share of work. I got invited to talk at every women's empowerment conference in the country. For two months, Rachel and I traveled from east to west, meeting one inspiring woman after the other, sharing our experiences, and listening to their struggles.

After the publication of the article, Sean dropped the lawsuit, and the authorities became interested in his case, following several other employees coming forward. He didn't get convicted, no, we're still very much living in a world that doesn't hold powerful men accountable for their actions. But he lost everything, and that in itself was my small consolation prize.

"What time are we leaving?" Miles asks from our bedroom.

"Just finishing a few things over here, and then we can get ready."

"I hope you're going out in this outfit," he says, peeping through the door.

I look down at my white bathrobe split open down to my navel, revealing part of my breasts.

I cock an eyebrow. "Do you really want me to go out in this?" That would surprise me. That other men might get a peek at what's his? No way.

"Maybe not..." he grumbles and goes back inside.

I shake my head. *That's what I thought.* Emails done, I just have one more thing I need to do. I hold the post card I chose two days ago and the little blue, white, and red pen I found in the hotel lobby.

Dear Char,

We made it to Paris... again!

The city is even more beautiful this time around, and I can't help but think that a certain big grumpy guy has something to do with it. I hope we get to experience it together one day. It's become a special place for me, and I'd love to share it with you.

A little something happened while we were here...

Miles proposed last night!

I gaze at the sparkling diamond perched on my finger. I still can't believe the man of my dreams got down on one knee last night, in the cheesiest place he could pick—the top of the Eiffel Tower—and asked me, in as many words, to become "my wife, my soulmate, the missing piece of my heart, and the mother of Happy."

Cheesy or not, it was the best night of my life, with the most romantic view of Paris. Spoiler alert: I said (okay, yelled) yes.

I know, I know. What happened to "I'll never get married again"? Well, I guess I didn't think I could have a man like Miles fall in love with me.

So I guess you now have a brother-in-law! I can't wait to celebrate it with you when you're back from Indonesia (or is it Japan—where are you now?) In the meantime, I'm going to enjoy Paris as a newly engaged woman!

I love you. Please stay safe and don't do anything stupid.

From Paris, in love.

Ry.

I slide the postcard in the envelope, close it, and walk back in the bedroom to find Miles dusting the dresser.

"You're such a Monica Geller," I say, laughing.

"You put your hairbrush there, and there was blond hair everywhere, Ry."

I come behind him and wrap my arms around his stomach, but he turns to me before I can properly hug him.

"Are we getting ready to go?"

"Our first night out as an engaged couple," I say with a sigh.

I see the swell of pride in his eyes at the words. He takes my jaw in his hold and raises my eyes to his. "Can I do something else with my fiancée before we head out?" His other hand tugs on the belt of my bathrobe. "I might have several ideas in mind that don't involve much clothing, but definitely a lot of fiancée-friendly activities."

He smirks, and I might have found a clever retort to unravel him if it weren't for his fingers sliding between my legs and doing the exact same thing to me.

"I think we might find a few minutes to spare," I say, already losing all sense of my surroundings.

Miles backs us up until we hit the bed, holding me tightly against him as he falls in the pillows. I straddle him, my bathrobe half-opened, enjoying the now familiar feeling of his hardness against me.

"Miles," I say as I lean in and brush my nose against his, my hair falling around us and trapping us in our own sanctuary.

"Yes, love?"

"I don't want to wait. I want to get married here. Tomorrow. I want to be your wife yesterday. I don't want to wait," I repeat.

Miles grunts, his hands gripping my thighs. "What about Charlee?"

"It'll be impossible to plan a wedding around where my sister might be." I plant a kiss on the tip of his nose. "I want to get married, just us."

His arms circle my waist, bringing me against his chest. "Let's do it then. Let's get married tomorrow," he whispers. "You and me."

I kiss him, for a few seconds or a few hours, I can't really tell. I lose all sense of time and meaning when he's invading my mind and body like this. We spend hours celebrating our love, this new chapter of our lives that began way later than either of us would have thought, but that's life, and sometimes shit happens.

I don't think Miles and I would've found each other without the pain we went through in our past. It shaped us, and made us realize how little time we have on this earth.

By the time we emerge from the bed, exhausted, sweaty, satisfied, the night has already set in. We missed the show at the Moulin Rouge, but neither of us care. Because that's exactly us: a perfectly organized, chaotic mess.

ACKNOWLEDGMENTS

Writing a romance novel while separating after a long relationship isn't the easiest thing to do. How do you make two people fall in love when your own life isn't going that way?

I wanted to do justice to Miles and Riley's love story, and it took longer than I expected, but in the end, I'm proud of the book you're holding in your hands. It's the fruit of a long journey of doubts, sleepless nights and questioning, which led me to grow as an author and as an individual.

Which is why, first and foremost, I'd like to thank you, my readers, for being so patient through it all, and continuing to support me all along. You are the very reason this book exists. Many times I wanted to give up, but remembering that you were eagerly awaiting it drove me to persevere. Thank you will never be enough.

Thank you to the book community on Instagram, TikTok and Twitter. Seeing your enthusiasm for Miles and Riley is something I treasure every day. Most especially, thank you to Emily @librarybyemily, Emily @emilysbookshelf_, Heather @booksbyheath, Carol @shelfie.queen, Jules and Breanne @readwithjulesandbre, Kelly @readingwithbeans, and Rachel @rachelturnsthepage.

I would never be where I am today without my best friend, Katie. You have supported me every minute of every day for the past year, listening to me complain that my book wasn't going anywhere, crying, getting upset and celebrated the little victories with me. I don't know what I'd do without you. I love you so much.

A gigantic thank you to my beta readers, Stephanie @stephonashelf, Kristin @kfals_consciousreads, Jocelyne @readwithjocelyne, Shannon @smalltownbookmom, Stephanie @wearecompletelybooked and Serena @coffeeandgoodreads for your invaluable feedback and advices.

To Ashley Winstead, my role model. You inspire me to be a better writer, to push myself, to write stories that matter and empower women.

To Leni, my illustrator extraordinaire. Not only am I extremely lucky to have my book covers illustrated by you, but the most beautiful development is the friendship that has grown between you and me.

To Pierre, for always supporting me. Thank you for being in my life.

A big thank you to my editors, Kate, Britt and Jennifer, for bringing this story to where it is today.

Finally, to David. You made me rediscover what it is to be loved. I'd lost that a long time ago, and I'm certain that your love for me shines through in every line of this novel.

The third and final book in the *It's Always Been You series* is coming to you next year!

ARE YOU READY FOR CHARLEE'S STORY?

We're headed to British Columbia and the Great Bear Rainforest!

Expect lots a camping, small town shenanigans, found family, adventures and second chance romance.

ABOUT THE AUTHOR

Originally from France, Elodie moved to Montreal, Canada in 2014 to pursue her studies in politics.An avid reader since her childhood, it wasn't until 2021 that she rediscovered her love for books, especially romance novels.

Because she never does anything half hearted, Elodie has shared her love for reading with other book lovers on her Bookstagram (@elosreadingcorner) where she has found an incredibly supportive and inspiring community.

When she's not immersed in reading or analyzing public policies during her workdays, you can find Elodie baking sweets for the whole neighborhood, cuddling with her cats or behind her keyboard, trying to create a world and love stories that everyone can dream of.

FOLLOW HER ON

Instagram/Threads @elosreadingcorner
Tiktok @elodiecolliard
Twitter/X @elocolliard